LADIES OF THE MOUNTAIN

LADIES OF THE MOUNTAIN

Victoria Pearle Hart

Library of Congress Control Number:		2021909629
ISBN:	Hardcover	978-1-6641-7402-3
	Softcover	978-1-6641-7401-6
	eBook	978-1-6641-7400-9

Print information available on the last page.

Rev. date: 05/20/2021

To order additional copies of this book, contact:
Xlibris
844-714-8691
www.Xlibris.com
Orders@Xlibris.com
827946

With great thanks to my Husband and my family for their encouragement and faith in me. For allowing me the time to write my stories.

For my sister-in-law, she worked beside me through the process of this book, reading, discussing, and mostly laughing at me.

Thank you

INTRODUCTION

BERTHA BECAME THE head lady of the house. She shows her family how a true Scot works. Her ability to be a gentlewoman and a tough Scot lends to her story. She has always been a protector of Liz. She was glad to relinquish that job to Liz's new husband, Mitchell. Liz teaches her hubby how smart she is and her ability to organize and run her part of the family. Her son needs a rude awakening, and she gives it to him by allowing Charlie to do what needs to be done. His wife Denise, called Denny by the family, appreciates the help she gets from Liz with her shyness and from May-Ling, Louise, Lois, and June to improve her life and ability to stand up for herself. Liz met Carol when she was working for Tony. Carol learns through Liz that she doesn't have to be the mouse her best friend Caitlin calls her. Carol discovers that being part of this family has given her the backbone to move forward. The strong women include May-Ling, a therapist who is always in the background until she is needed. Her sister-in-law, Louise, is there for the family as well. Charlie loves his wife May-Ling with all his heart, but his respect for her is strong. His daughter June and niece Lois work on the compound with him, his son Peter, and the rescue crew.

These ladies all work hard to act like they are in the background while their men do their thing. Each man has a lady behind him to hold him up. Erica does well to hold up her husband George, their adopted son Michael, and Tommy.

LIST OF CHARACTERS

Bertha	Gentle lady, Tommy's wife Strong-willed, from Scotland
Liz	Stronger than her husband thinks Worries about what her family thinks about her upcoming surprise.
Denny	A shy, timid woman who learns her value Puts her husband in his place.
Carol	Adopted by Liz and Mitchell An architect, good at her job, shows the strength that her best friend thought she would never have, meets her man.
Caitlin	Officer, nosey, wants to know everything. Finds love in an odd way.
May-Ling	Charlie's wife, a trained therapist, works with children, but if necessary, she will work with adults. She is also one of the ones.
June	Charlie and May-Ling's daughter, vital, intelligent but young, works with her Dad and Tommy.
Louise	Sister-in-law and therapist

Lois Niece who works with family

Erica Ex-soldier who works for Tommy
Knew Michael before he knew she worked for Tommy.

Tommy Looks older than his years
Is extremely affluent.
Loves Bertha to no end. One of One.

Charlie A chef, Tommy's right-hand man, head of the rescue crew
Is one of one.

Mitchell Liz's husband, who hides what he knows from Liz
Is a lawyer, owns many businesses.

George Works for Tommy and Charlie.

Jon Franc FBI agent

Michael Adopted son of Bertha and Tommy

Marcus Tommy's twin (not like his brother), one of one

Bertha's Language Dictionary

Bertha came from Scotland at the age of fourteen. She worked for two families in the same town and she never lost her Scottish Brogue

Aboot	About
Ache	Oh
Agin	Again
An	And
Aye	Yes
Banshe	Wild Beast
Barin	Male Child
Boyo	Boy
Buyen	Buying
Canna	Can You
Commen	Coming
Daft	Crazy, Nuts
Deef	Deaf
Denna	Do Not
Doon	Down
Feared	Fearing
Fer	For
Fortnight	Half a week
Gahauffen	Belly laugh
Gawd	Awful
Git	Get
Gitten	Getting
Gonna	Going

Growed	Grown
Helpen	Helping
Hered	Heard
Hert	Hurt
Holleren	Hollering
Hoose	House
Ifa	If I, If you
Inta	Into
Jest	Just
Lass	Lady
Lassie	Girl
Leaven	Leaving
Lovey	Sweetheart
Meself	Myself
Na	Not
Neigh	Almost
Ner	Never
Nery	Not a thing
Nothen	Nothing
No ting	Empty
Oot	Out
Roond	Round
Rumblen	Hungery

Runne	Running
Ta	To
Teley	Television
Tink	Think
Tither	Thing
Toon	Town
Thrice	Three
This'n	This one
Treasuren	Treasuring
Wanten	Wanting

Wedden	Wedding
Wee	Tiny, small
Werd	Word
Werk	Work
Wit	With
Ya	You
Ya'll	You will
Ya've	You have
Yerself	Yourself
Yers	Yours

Chapter One

LIZ WAS GETTING excited, five weeks before the wedding. Bertha had her gown cleaned and pressed. Erica looked gorgeous in and out; it was her turn to shine down the aisle. The ladies of the family were going shopping for dresses for the wedding. Bertha wanted to come, so Liz told her she would wait for her. "Liz, have ya any idea ah what yer looken fer the lassies ta wear?"

"No, Mom, just that it complements my gown." They met the girls at the shop. They were standing outside. "Why are you not inside, trying on the dresses? We want you to get an idea of what would look good."

"We were told we could not go in until the bride showed up." The shop owner opened the door and asked Liz why her daughter was not with them.

"My daughter is here, and what has that got to do with it? I am the bride."

The lady looked at Liz. "I am sorry, madam. We do not carry dresses that will suit you or your ladies. We carry gowns for young brides." Carol started to snicker, so she turned her back to the woman. Caitlin hit her on the arm and told her to stop, but she was doing the same.

"We will be going to the bridal shop at the mall, ladies. I heard they carry gowns for everyone and every size. By the way, you will not be getting a recommendation for your shop from our families, the Maxwells and McClouds. I assume you know who that is." The woman stopped there, with her mouth as well as the door open.

Carol told Liz, "Mom, I can take Erica, Caitlin, and Denny if you can take Christene with you and Grams." Liz agreed, and they were off.

They were wandering around this new bridal shop and were amazed at the size and selection this new shop had. The girls showed some dresses to Liz, and she shook her head no to them. Bertha called her over. "Liz, can ya come ta me, love, see this fer yerself?"

Liz walked over and was shocked; it was perfect, pale mint green, backless, with a swallowtail. "Carol sweetie, would you try this on for me, please?"

Carol took the dress from Bertha. "Grams, this is special. I love the lace and the colour, and wow! No back." She went into the changing room. Caitlin asked Gram if she could find her size, and then they all wanted to try it. Bertha found the sizes for them that they needed. One by one, they came out of the changing room, each looking better than the one before. Liz found one gown identical, just a few shades darker. She handed it to Carol and asked if she would try this. When she came out, it was perfect, exactly what Liz wanted. Her maid of honour was the same but different.

A timid little girl approached Grams. "I know you don't work here, but do you think you could help me? I don't want a snow-white gown. My skin is so pale the white would wash me out." Bertha looked, then went to the young woman that ran the shop and asked her if she had a slightly full-skirted sweetheart neckline with a slightly low backline. The girl took her to the half-price rack, and there it was.

Bertha called the shy little thing over. “No look at it, jest put it on an’ come oot ta me.”

Within a few minutes, they heard a squeal, and a smiling teary-eyed young lady came out to Bertha. It was perfect for her; her skin shone a soft pink, and her eyes were of the same shade of blue as the gown. “It’s what I wanted. Oh, thank you, and it is perfect, thank you.” She gave Bertha hugs and kisses and shed her tears on Bertha’s cheek. She was so happy.

The young owner gave her the gown at cost because she liked her so much and she had just made her biggest sale all week. “Wait until I tell my uppity sister the sale I made, and her shop would not want to wait on you because of your age.”

“The store on Beal Street was unfriendly to older brides and their ladies. I told the owner she would not be getting a good review from our families, the Maxwells and McClouds.” The girl in the powder-blue gown fainted.

They rushed to her side, and Bertha gathered her up in her arms. Are ya unwell, child?” she asked her.

“I-I don’t know what to say. I have been looking for a Mr. Marcus McCloud for the last four years. He is my father. I was hoping to get to know him. I just wanted to have him walk me down the aisle as I will be walking it alone otherwise.”

“Yawl no be doin’ that, lassie. I’m yer Auntie Bertha, an Marcus is me brother-in-law. Can ya come hame with me an meet yer Uncle Tommy? He will git in touch with yer da fer ya.”

The girl said she walked to the mall, hoping to find a gown that was cheap and looked good on her.

Liz told her she had done that; she had already paid for it and told the clerk not to tell her who had. Liz told her they would take her, and then one of them would take her home. "Do you have family here, or are you alone, and what's your name, sweetie?"

"My mother just passed away about three months ago from a car accident. It's just me and my sister Faye, and I'm Joan. We are twins. My mother used to say the only way she could tell us apart was I always had a smile for her. Faye had to be tickled to smile."

Caitlin said she was walking over to the station from here with Christene. They had some things they needed to clear up from the hacienda but would be out for the barbecue later that afternoon. Carol suggested Joan ride with her and Erica. They met at Liz's house, with Bertha calling Tommy before she took her shoes off. "Tommy, ya git over here. I've jest met yer niece. Marcus has twin daughters, an one of 'em is here."

"Hold on. What are you talking about, Bertha, my love? Marcus has never married, so who is the mother, do you know?"

"No, I don't. Git over here and call Marcus. Has he left St. Helen yet, do ya know?"

"I'm on my way while I call me brother. Oh, am I am going to give it to him." He started to laugh.

"No, yer not. This little thing is so shy she will start ta cry if ya scare her with yer loud gahauffen."

Tommy came through the sunroom door, off the back of the house. He called to Bertha to go to him, please. "Bertha, does she look like Margaret Jean or no?"

"In a way, yes, but she's older than Margaret Jean."

Tommy walked into the living room to meet his niece. She was standing by the window. His knees went weak. She stood just like his girl, but her hair was darker. Joan was older-looking, but she was similar. It was when she turned to face him, he thought he would die. Her smile was that of his wee lass, and she was very similar in looks. "Hello." He walked slowly up to her. "My name is Thomas McCloud, your Uncle Tommy." Smiling, Joan put her hand out to him, and they shook briefly. "Your dad will be here shortly. May I ask who your mother might be?"

An unfortunate-faced girl told her story. "My mother was Margaret McKellen. She worked for a textile company for years. When it failed, we moved here. She worked as a waitress until she died in a car crash." She took a picture of herself, her sister, and her mother out of her purse.

Tommy sat down quickly and looked at Bertha, then handed her the picture. The woman was beautiful with the palest skin ever. He knew who she was. She worked for his mother, doing odd jobs when the textile company gave half shifts to the female workers. Marcus cared for her, but her dad did not like that they were lowlife Scots that ran a pub.

Marcus knocked on the door but walked straight in. "Liz," he called, then waited for her to come.

It was Bertha. "Marcus, are ya afeared ta see the wee lass?"

"Yes, Bertha, she probably hates me and wants to kill me."

"Ache, no such thing, she's wanten ya ta walk her doon the aisle fer her weddin'. Now git in there."

Marcus walked in, and one look at her said she was her mother's daughter; his knees were weak, and his heart was bursting. Tommy stood and led him over to the wee lass at the window. "Joan, this is your dad Marcus McCloud."

They all left the room but not so far that they could not hear what was being said. She told him of her mother's fate and that her sister was working as a receptionist for the architectural company that was closed right now. She had just started there when they had to close because of structural problems, but they would soon return to work. Her boss was still paying her wage while they were waiting. Carol choked on her coffee when she heard that. "Liz, that would be Faye. She is a whiz at anything I ask of her to do. She's the one I want to send to school full-time."

Marcus asked, "Joan, what do you do for a living, if you don't mind me asking?"

"No, it's okay. I do dog walking and teach piano. There is no need in St. Helen for a concert pianist. I plan on going back to school and learning a trade or profession."

Tommy asked her if she would like a cup of coffee or tea. Marcus wanted one, but it had better be more than coffee. "Your mom told you I was your dad, so why did she not tell me? I would have been there for all of you."

"Granddad would not allow it because of your family business being a pub. He thought it sinful. I wanted so much to contact you when I played Carnegie Hall, but they wouldn't let Mom or me. I have pictures of it, though."

"When are you getting married, Joan? I would like very much to walk you down the aisle."

"We have to wait until next spring because there are no available halls until then. That's okay. It gives me time to save for the reception. Jason works in an import-export company. He works for a man named Giles."

Liz turned to Grams. "Poor kid, Giles is a real piece of work to work for."

Marcus asked Joan if her grandfather was still alive.

"Nobody passed away before Mom's accident. He left her owing lots of money. I guess he liked to play cards and bet on the ponies. Mom paid every cent he owed to the loan company."

Marcus told her he would like to meet her sister. "What does she look like?"

Tommy said it for the girl. "If you are looking at Joan, you are looking at Faye. They are twins like we are."

"Tommy, why did she not come to me? I never married because I loved her so much. I could never be with anyone else." He was crying and shaking at the same time.

Joan went to him. "Dad, don't blame yourself. Mom felt the same about you. It was her dad that stopped her when she tried to contact you when we were born. She left us a letter about you and who you were and the town where you lived. Faye and I started up north, then worked our way down to Washington from there. We went to Canada and returned to Baltimore, where we heard that you were here, from a man who works for Uncle Tommy. Please let us get to know you. Mom said you were a good person." She held him and cried with him.

Tommy asked Carol to find out where Faye lived. Someone would get her. Bertha swatted him. "Are ya daft? If she's as shy as wee Joan, she won't be commen to the door."

Caitlin came in, asked who they were talking about, and saw Joan in the living room. She told Liz she checked up on the girls; they were legitimate. They were about to be put on the street though, because they were a month behind on the rent and the guy they rented from was a real shit. "Sorry, Grams, but he is. If they won't come across, well then, out they go."

"What do they have ta come across with, Cat? I'll help them oot." Carol spit her coffee in the sink. Liz burst out laughing. She whispered to Bertha what that meant; she was still laughing even though she got a good whack from Bertha.

When she got herself under control, she motioned to Tommy and told him where the girls lived and what the situation was. "Joan, can you call your sister for me? I want to invite her out for the family barbecue. Would you do that for me, dear?"

"Sure, but she won't be able to come because she has no car and no money for a cab."

"Call her, and I will pay for the cab."

Joan called Faye to see if she wanted to come to meet her dad and her family. Faye asked if she had to dress up. Joan told her they were having a barbecue, so jeans would be great. Marcus, who finally could speak, excused himself to visit the washroom. Tommy stopped him. "They live in the worst end of town, and their landlord is going to throw them out because they owe a month's rent. They will not give what he wants for payment."

Marcus hit the wall, putting a hole in Bertha's old bedroom. "Tommy, they have to be at least twenty-five. I missed it all."

"Get a grip. We will work it out. It's not like we can't do something."

It was Liz that asked Joan what her last name was. "We go by my mother's maiden name, McKellen."

"Faye works for my daughter Carol. She is the lady that drove you out here, so she is your cousin." Robert and Mitch came into a house full of people. Liz and Denny took them outside with Bessie and told them the whole of what they already knew. Robert looked at Mitch. "Shit, Dad, this family grows every time someone sneezes." This warranted him a clap behind the head from his mother. Mitch asked if anyone checked them out to make sure they were legitimate. Liz told him that Caitlin had. They went back in just in time to see the cab pull up on the land. Faye got out; she was identical to her sister. Marcus stood there, watching her walk up the lane to the front door. He was going to answer it, but Bertha stopped him. "Yawl scare the wee lass. Let her in first." She opened the door and bade her come in. Faye wasn't too sure what to expect; she looked around for her sister. Joan walked her over to Marcus and told her who he was.

"Hello, Faye, you can call me Marcus, or whatever you want."

"Is it all right if I call you Dad? I used to say good night to your picture every night when I said my prayers. I got the picture from Mom, and she hid it from Granddad. So is Dad okay?"

"It's great with me. I would love it. I want you to know that I loved your mother so much, and I know she loved me. You and your sister came from that love. Faye, I want very much to get to know you and Joan and start being the father you two deserve."

Faye started to cry and put her arms around him and said, "I would love that too. Joan and I are more than overjoyed to find you, and once we get some money under our belts, we would love to visit you wherever you live."

"How about you and Joan move into the house I bought to stay in while I'm in St. Helen? I only use it when I am here, so it sits empty. You would be doing me a favour if you did."

Joan looked at Faye and said, "Dad, we are about to be thrown out of our apartment, so having somewhere to go would be a godsend. Thank you, Dad."

Tommy asked them if they had furniture or anything special they wanted to keep because their landlord just threw all their belongings on the street. "I have someone picking up all your things. If you want to go check it out, your dad and I will go with you." Both girls wanted to get their things before somebody ruined them. Tommy got the truck out of the garage, picked them up in front of Liz and Mitch's house with Marcus.

When they got there, the landlord tried to sell their things before realizing the police and the girls were there watching him. Officer Dugan arrested him for vandalism, theft, and destruction. The girls began picking up their things. Faye started to cry; she was screaming, "Where is it, damn it? What did you do with it, Brian, where is it?"

Joan tried to console her. "We'll find it."

Tommy put Brian up against the wall even though Dugan tried to stop him. "Give it to me, or I will personally put you through that window."

Brian reached into his pocket and pulled out a locket on a gold chain and gave it to him. Tommy let him go. Brian slid down the wall.

Tommy said to Dugan, "He's all yours, boyo." The girls didn't have much, barely filled half the truck, but what they had was theirs, not other people's. Two boys came up and told Marcus that Brian had put some of their things in his shed behind the apartment house. The other officer, Pete, went with Marcus and the girls to look in the shed. They found their jewelry boxes, a photo album, blankets, pillows, and pictures of their mother as a young woman. Behind this, Pete found other people's things and a good stash of prescribed medications. "This boy is going to face more charges than he thought. Are either of the girls on medications? If so, check and see if the meds are here."

Both girls said no, they were not. "Let's take your things to the house."

They were so upset. Faye thanked her Uncle Tommy and her dad for helping them. They would not have had a place to go. "I know that my boss is giving us our pay, but with Joan dog watching and house cleaning, it's hard to make ends meet. We will pay you,

Dad, for letting us stay at your house. Mom taught us to pay our own way so no one can make us do their bidding."

Marcus looked at her. "She taught you that because she did not want you dependent on anyone but yourselves. I never had to pay my dad or mom to live in their home, nor will you pay to live in our home because from now on, it is your home as well as mine."

Marcus walked up to the house and pushed the bell. A man dressed in livery opened the door, stepped aside, and allowed them entry. "Pablo, this is my daughter Faye and her sister Joan. They live here now. They are to be cared for as you would care for me."

"Yes, sir."

"There are a chef and a housekeeper as well as Pablo. All you have to do is take care of yourselves. Joan, you said you wanted to go to school. I will help you with that. Decide what you want to do."

"Dad, I will be getting married in the spring, so what can I study before that?"

"You can study something that not only helps us now, but with your life after marriage, sis, a profession in something, an accountant, a medical technician, legal secretary. See what I mean? Just like Mom told us, life gives you what you give it." Faye thought to herself, *Sometimes I think her brain is out in space, looking for a new place to live. This guy she wants to marry is an odd duck, and that is putting it mildly.* Maybe finding their father would help her Joan the light and not get married to this guy. Should she mention to her dad that he acts strange when other people are around and won't take her to a public place, only shows at night, or walks in the park when it's dusk? Maybe Uncle Tommy could help. He knew we were getting thrown out before we did. I must find out if he will be bad for her or hurt her, or worse, if he is a killer.

The house was huge, decorated expensively, and felt empty. "Dad, will you ever be here to live with us, or will we be here with your servants only?"

Tom got the message loud and clear. "He lives with here all the time, Faye. He told you that because your dad did not want you to say no to staying here. He would have been staying with me, which by the way, I do not want because I just got married to that lovely lady that speaks with a funny accent."

"Faye, did you meet her?"

"I didn't."

"She is a blessing to know, Faye, and she is so sweet."

"After the barbecue, we will all be coming home here, Dad?"

"Yes, if that is what you both want, I will not invade your privacy."

"We want to get to know you. How else will we get to know you if we don't stay together, even if it's a short time?"

"From here on in, I will be here for you in every way possible."

The girls changed clothes and went back to the barbecue with their dad and uncle.

"Do we call your wife Aunt Bertha, Auntie, or what everyone seems to call her—Grams?"

"They call her Grams because she is their grandmother. She is Robert's and Carol's grandmother. The others call her that because they have known her since they were kids. You can call her whatever makes you happy. She is that kind of person, okay?"

"Auntie Bertha—I like that. It is special to us." Faye agreed.

"Faye, can I ask a personal question? How old are the two of you? Don't answer if it is too personal."

"We are twenty-six this month on the thirtieth. I am fourteen minutes older than Joan. She took her time being born." Marcus looked at Joan, then started to snicker. She had stuck her tongue out at her sister.

Liz asked them if they wanted shrimp salad or veggie salad with their steaks and baked potatoes at the barbecue. She was surprised they were different. Faye wanted the shrimp, and Joan wanted the vegetable salad. They were different; they looked alike.

"Auntie Bertha, can you teach me to cook? Jason and I will have to rely on our cooking, and he cannot cook for his life."

Bertha smiled; no one had ever asked her to teach them anything. "I can teach ya, darlin', whenever ya wants ta learn. Ya canna make tea an' coffee?"

"Auntie Bertha, I use tea bags and instant coffee. Does that count?"

"No, sweetheart, we start there. So ya think ya can shorten the name ta Auntie B?"

"Yep, we can."

Marcus thought if Maggie were still alive, they both would be good cooks, then he thought she would have started that when they were young. "Hey, Joan, didn't your mom try to teach you to cook?"

"Granddad wouldn't let her, told her she didn't know what she was doing in the kitchen, to begin with. She couldn't show us."

"Yes, but when he wasn't there and his cook was out, she could do a damn good job, Joan, and you know it."

"Yes, I do, and I miss everything she did for us. I know it's wrong, but I hated that man. He used our mother, just like he used our grandmother until she died working for him."

"What does that mean, Faye, worked her to death?"

"She did everything—cooking, cleaning, washing, even fed him when he insisted his hands hurt too much. She had to bathe him and dress him because he wouldn't have a nurse or a helper come in. She fell, and he kicked her. I watched it. He told me if I ever told, I would be his next wiping post. He was an evil man. Grandmother told us to stay out of his view."

Marcus wanted to throw up and beat something at the same time. That bastard used his daughter as he did his wife. He probably had sex with her as well. "Did he leave anything to you girls when he died?"

"No, he left it to his girlfriend, all of it. She threw us out right after the funeral. Not his, Mom's. He died two weeks later. His girlfriend lived with us, and Mom had to wait on Zelda as well. She would knock over ashtrays and flower vases so that Mom would have to clean them up. When Mom got sick, he told us we would have to take care of her because she wasn't worth the money it would take to care for her. We did until it got so bad she went into the hospital and died there." Marcus intended to have his men check this out. This was just not right. Tommy thought the man was crazy, or were the girls telling them a bucket of crap? He didn't think they were.

"Tommy, put Paul on this for me. I don't buy this. He had to have left them something, even if it was a memento from their mother."

Liz asked Bertha to find out what the girls had to wear at the wedding. "Tommy said Marcus was taken them shoppen fer some fancy dresses. They'll no be standees, so they can sit with Marcus jest so he'll no be alone. Tommy asked me ta ask ya if he an' the lassies could sit behind him an' me."

"They can sit next to you and Tommy, okay."

The guys were taking Mitch out for his bachelor party two nights before the wedding. Liz was concerned that he would get to drunk and be sick for the wedding. He might do something foolish like Tommy was hoping for, like when he didn't bother telling the boys the girls were back from shopping. She only wished she had taken pictures of her two men standing there, red from head to toe with only Mother Nature between them and us. Cat and Carol had made a reservation for dinner and a live show for Liz.

Tommy had reserved a room in the best hotel just outside St. Helen because he was tired of the chirpy people of the town picking on this family. Gossip was their favourite hobby. Marcus hired a DJ's equipment, no DJ, to play the music. His reason was the same as his brother's; no one could talk about what they couldn't see or hear. Robert wanted to hire a stripper, but the brothers vetoed that. "If Mitch were your age, Robert, maybe, but he is not, so no strippers" was Marcus's remark, and the rest of the men of their age laughed at Robert. Tommy took him aside. "What would your mother think if she found out we had strippers and you were the one who hired them?" Robert looked at Tommy and nodded; he said not a word.

Charlie came in with the food, and soon and the meal was cooked and ready for them to eat. He had special cookware with which he could prepare hot food, from a raw status to fully cooked in no time. Charlie seemed to know Mitch from somewhere. Robert wasn't sure where. They played tricks on Mitch, like having Liz record her voice on a doll saying, "Mitch, what are you doing with that babe?" She did not know the doll's voice box belonged to a full-size, fully functional adult doll. Mitch was blindfolded and the doll dressed in sexy see-through lingerie. Mitch was already red, but when he heard Liz's voice telling him off for doing something with this doll, he dropped it on the floor. Allen laughed the hardest. "Remember what you did to me when Shantelle and I got married—payback, my friend. We have pictures of this for blackmail later."

"Allen, I have more on you than you will ever have on me." He received many gifts he would never show Liz: a year's supply of prophylactics, eatable underwear, and a CD that played music to have unforgettable sex. The T-shirts that said, 'single because I'm old' and 'old but sexy' were okay for her to see. The others need not be mentioned or shown to anybody. Robert got loaded, and of course, Allen took pictures of him and the dolly in promiscuous positions. Tommy did not drink; they could not get him. They had Mitch dress in a kilt and try to do the Highland fling, during which (after four mixed drinks) he landed on his ass. Tommy was taping all this. It would be shown to the ladies, especially Bertha, and she would love watching Mitch do her favourite dance. The whole night was full of good fun; Robert was not alone in being drunk.

Liz had a tiny white veil on, with a plastic tiara to hold it there. They made her wear a sweater that said 'bride.' Just before they were to leave, Bertha blindfolded her. "Ya be glad I did, darlin', jest know I canna help ya oot a this." She started to giggle, then it turned into a laugh.

"Mom, what do you know that you are not telling me? We planned a dinner out, with something extra for the bride-to-be. Then to a live show with all of you. Is this not what we planned?" No one answered Liz.

The bridesmaids were taking her to a particular unique restaurant outside St. Helen, a reasonable distance from the central area of the city. It was in a classy place; this was when they took her blindfold off. "Why, this is beautiful, but, girls, this is expensive. I have never been here before. What town or city is this?"

Carol smiled and said, "Oh, it is still just outside St. Helen, but in the upper part where the snobby people eat."

"Are you girls going to cause trouble for the damn town to gossip about?" She was getting nervous, angry, and ready to call it all off.

Bertha told her, "Liz, 'tis all in fun, an' no one from the toon will ever know we was here, so enjoy yer night." They entered.

A young, strong, tall man came up to them, holding a tray, and had nothing on except the tray. "Ladies, have you a reservation?" Carol spoke up and told him they did and gave him the letter she was to present. He handed the tray to Liz, and she did not know where she could look. Look up, and he was smiling at her. Down—well, down only made her turn sixteen shades of red. He told her and the ladies to follow him to their designated room. Liz had to follow that gorgeous backside to the room he was going to. All she could think of was "Please don't turn around, please don't turn and stand right there and look at me." When they got to the door, he turned, bowed to her, and left.

The doors opened by two young men dressed the same as the doorman, they took Liz by each hand, guiding her to a throne in the front of the room. She was speechless. The girls, including Bertha, laughed at her. They told her this was her last chance at freedom so enjoy the view. The dinner was served for the ladies on a beautiful table covered in a gold cloth with white tableware. Her table, however, was not covered in a gold cloth; it was a young man on hands and knees with a tray on his back. Her dinner was served by another male dressed the same, carrying it on a gold plate with gold tableware. He placed them on the table-tray on the other guy's back, laid a gold napkin in her lap, and asked if her highness would need anything else. Liz could hardly speak. "No, thank you, I will be fine."

He placed his hand on her shoulder and told her, "We're only too happy to serve and obey you, so if you want or need any service, we are only too happy to comply." With that, he kissed her hand and her cheek and left.

Liz looked at the girls and started to laugh. "How do I explain this to Mitch?" Carol got up and showed her. The man at the entry with only a tray held her hand to show her where to go. The picture was of Liz and him, fully dressed. Her table was a small white table with a gold cover and white tableware. The waiter was in a tux; he only held her hand, not her shoulder, and did not kiss her on the cheek. Liz liked this a whole bunch more. By the look on Bertha's face, so did she. They had a great dinner, drank champagne, and some of the girls danced with the waitstaff. Around midnight, a gigantic cake that looked like a wedding cake was wheeled in. Her waiter came, took her hand, asked her to follow him, please. "We are going to cut the cake and share it with your friends now." Liz smiled and went with him. "Liz, may I call you Liz?" She nodded yes. "We have to climb up some steep stairs. I will assist you, all right?"

"Sure, I guess so." When she saw the stairs, she knew she was in trouble; he would literally have to lift her or pick her up to get to the next step, and there were four of them.

Now the girls were rooting for her. "Go, Liz, get to the top. We want cake, we want cake. Go, Liz, go!"

Liz said to the young man, "What is your name? If you are picking me up, at least let me know who is doing the lifting."

He smiled then laughed. "My name is Larry, I own this restaurant, and it was my idea to do special occasions only. So if you enjoy your experience, let other brides or divorcées know." He lifted her up into his arms like she was weightless and climbed the stairs one at a time, each time turning to the girls, who were taking pictures with the cameras given them at the table. Each picture showed Liz being carried to the top step by step by a young man in a tuxedo. At the top, he told her, she would have to stand on his back or climb on his shoulders to cut the actual cake; the rest was wood and steel covered in white decoration. Liz opted to climb on his shoulders, and she told him why. He looked at her and said, "When was your accident?" and he had a grave face. She told him, and he said to her, "Can we talk after cutting the cake, please?"

Liz was curious; she said, "Sure."

He turned around and squatted down, which brought screams of joy from the ladies on the floor. Liz put her legs one at a time over his shoulders and gave him her hands. "Ready, here we go." He took the last step with her on his shoulders, and she cut the cake. As Liz did, a young blonde came out of the top and handed her plates to put the cake on. All the ladies were snapping pictures of this. It was too good to miss. Larry waved at the girls and put Liz down. Larry jumped down each step, lifting Liz after him. His timing was perfect, and they were on the main floor as the waiters served the cake to the ladies. "Thank you, ladies, and your highness, for allowing us to serve you. Enjoy your cake, and have a good evening." He walked Liz to the head of the table and said, "While they eat their cake, can we talk?"

"Sure, Larry, what is it that seems to be bothering you?"

"Was it a drunk at a shopping mall just off the main highway out of town that hurt you?" She nodded yes. "My father was the drunk that hit you. He paid for it, but you never knew that he was not an alcoholic. He was so drunk that day because he had just lost my mom to cancer, and he had to raise us boys by himself. He didn't know what to do, so he gave us all up to different people. We finally found each other. Tadd, the oldest, and I finally found him, a drunk with a new wife who was a drunk raising three little girls. We took the girls, and we are raising them. I want to tell you we are so sorry for what he put you through. I am glad that you got your legs back. I went to the same school Robert went to. I was two years ahead of him."

"Thank you, Larry, but there is no need. You did not hit me, nor did you pour the alcohol down his throat. People make their own decisions. He could have gone and talked to someone, or gone to the family and grieved with them—you lost your mother, just as he lost his wife. I give you credit for taking on your little sisters to raise."

"Do you know of someone who can send us to a lawyer that deals with legal guardianship? Those drunks want them back so they can collect city welfare. They buy their booze with that."

"Yes, I do. She is sitting right next to Carol. Her name is Shantelle Lamb. She is the top family lawyer in the city. Shantelle, can you speak to Larry Monday at your office? He has a case I want you to handle personally."

Shantelle came over to them. "What's up, Liz?"

"Larry needs help getting guardianship of his three little sisters. They are being raised by the drunk that hit me. Can you help him and his brothers?"

Caitlin came up and said, "I will testify for you, Larry. I pick up your dad and his wife weekly for DUI."

"I will take the case, Larry, bring everything you have on the girls and the parents. We will get the guardianship you want. By the way, do you work here or own it?"

"I own it. Will it matter to the case?"

"Not if more than one brother is raising these girls."

"There are four of us. Jack is a plumber, and his wife is a hairstylist. Bill is an accountant, and his wife is one also. Pete—well, you met Pete. Liz, his wife, works in social services. Me, unmarried—I am gay."

Shantelle shook his hand and told him she would see him on Monday. Larry walked away. Shantelle said, "Too bad, he is one hunk of a man." Liz just laughed at her. Larry stopped by Cat and said, "Thanks, Cat, how you doing now?"

"I'm doing better, Larry. Each day gets better." The ladies were done with their cake and asked if they could take a group picture with Larry and the other waitstaff. "You can with me but not the others. They have other jobs, and well, let's face it, this could cause them some trouble. Two of them work for the Forberts, and they are hard to work for."

They all turned to Denny.

"Hey, they don't work for me, and soon my name will not be the same as theirs. If they are having a hard time, tell them to speak to Richard. He will go after them. He is in the process of buying all their holdings now."

They left, knowing they gave Liz a great send-off. The girls knew Mitch should be having fun at his party.

Chapter Two

MITCH'S HEAD FELT like it was six times its size. He was bloody glad the wedding wasn't until tomorrow. Both the guys and the gals decided that they would do the parties, so they had a day to get back to normal.

"Mitch, did you have a good time last night, dear?" Liz already knew he got loaded even though he thought he had not.

"Liz, to be honest, I don't remember most of it. How was your party, my lady?"

"It went well. We had dinner, a live show of dancers, and then I got to cut a cake, and we came home."

"I wish I were there. I wouldn't have the head I have right now."

Liz smiled. *Glad you weren't, dear, glad you weren't.* "Let's go have breakfast. I'm hungry."

"Sure, Liz, but I think coffee will be it for me, just a cup of black coffee."

She was laughing out loud at him. "Did you not have enough sense to watch what you were drinking, or what they were giving you to drink? You know what Tommy is like."

"Yes, Liz, I do."

Bertha and Tommy were waiting for them. "You feeling okay, Mitch? You need a hangover remedy, do ya?"

"Tommy, I swear I only had two, maybe three mixed drinks, and I don't remember half of the evening. I don't remember coming home."

"Neither will Robert, but me lovely has the remedy already made for you and your son. It tastes of the devil himself, but it works within ten or fifteen minutes." Mitch just shook his head.

"Mitchell, do as I tell ya, doon it like one big chug, else ya ner git it doon."

He looked at Bertha, tried for a smile but did not succeed. "Can I have a tea first?" he pleaded. Both Tommy and Bertha shook their heads no. Mitch picked up the glass, holding the vile-looking stuff. One sniff, and he thought he would throw up; not stopping, he downed the whole glassful. He wanted to say a few explicit words but knew better. "What is in that? It tastes like the devil urinated in that glass!"

"I know, Mitch, but I promise it will work. But I have never tasted it. Others have, and they say it works quick." Tommy was having a hard time keeping a straight face, watching Mitch was as good as last night.

Liz had just finished her first cup of coffee when Mitch started to smile and said, "Well, I'll be damned. It does work. I feel better, and my headache is gone as well. Is it safe to eat breakfast now?"

"Ya can have what'er ya want, Mitchell. I made fresh scones and jam, eggs if ya think ya canna eat them, with bacon and toast."

Liz piped up, "Oh, Mom, can I have a scone and eggs and bacon, and another coffee? I am as hungry as a horse."

"Comin' up, love." Tommy and Bertha made the breakfast for all of them.

Denny came in with Robert in tow, looking like the walking dead; Tommy told Robert to drink and not stop. Robert did and held it down. "Dad, they do this to you too?"

"Yep, and it works. Just be good and sit there for ten or fifteen minutes real quiet, okay?" Robert nodded, wanting very much to go empty his stomach.

Denny told Liz she called her brother about the two waiters that needed help at their full-time job; he said he would look into it. "He hopes you had a great time. He owns part of that exclusive restaurant we took you to." Liz went to get herself another coffee to hide her red face. Denny joined her at the counter. "I didn't know that until this morning. I was as red as you. I was grateful Robert was still snoring." They both started to laugh and returned to the sun porch.

Robert was smiling when they returned to the small round table on the sun porch. "Grams, that crap really worked. I do feel better. Is there any breakfast left?" Before he could ask her to get it, he was told to get his own, just as the rest did. He kissed Grams and brought her another cup of tea as he put his breakfast on the table: eggs, bacon, toast, scone, jam, and sausage.

"Ya puts that back. 'Tis fer Bessie, she likes hers a wee bit cool. Now ya no eats her breakfast, ya thief." He knew the sausages were for Bessie, but he had to get a rise out of Grams. Tommy was learning the family traits slowly, but he had Robert figured out; he had a nickname for him: "trickster."

There was to be a rehearsal dinner after they finished at the church. Everyone who had a spouse or beau was to bring them along to the feast. Carol asked Liz if she would stay at home as she was alone and the rest had mates. Before she could answer Carol, Mitch told her that one of the male attendees felt the same way. "Would you mind sitting next to him? His name is Douglas Robbins."

"Oh, sure, Dad, if he doesn't mind. Mind, I want to run and hide, I don't know him, and what if he wants to dance? Damn it, Dad, you know me better than that."

Mitch hugged her and whispered in her ear, "He is as shy and timid about the opposite sex as you are. You have no reason to worry, Carol."

After rehearsal, the dinner would be at seven as the minister could not do the walkthrough until six that evening. Mitch heard Liz's tummy growl. "My lady is hungry, yes?"

"Your lady is starving. Got anything in your pocket to stave off the growling?"

He handed her a chocolate bar. "We share because, my love, I am as hungry as a bear." They both smiled and ate the chocolate bar.

Pastor Boyd met them at the back of the church. "Where are the flower girls and the ring bearer?"

A small but strong voice came from behind him. "Where we are supposed to be, Pastor, in the church where Mom told us to sit until the bride came."

"Well, all right, shall we begin? Liz, arrange your ladies. Mitch, go up front with the fellows, and I'll be right there." Mitch gave Liz a chocolate-flavoured kiss and went with the guys. Denny was to go first, then Erica, followed by Caitlin, then Carol; behind her came the flower girls and then his highness, the ring bearer, as he told Liz he had the most important job here. After all, without him, there would be no rings—no rings, no wedding. She told him he was right; he was essential, the Vip of the wedding. He held his head high, nodding to the pews as he slowly walked up the aisle.

Liz took Robert's arm, and they started up the aisle, only to hear the church door slam behind them. "Sorry, am I late?" It was Richard, Denny's brother.

The little ring bearer turned and said, "If you are not in the wedding party, sit down and shut up." Richard slunk into the seat next to the bride and tried not to laugh, as did everyone else, including his parents. They finally made it up the aisle; Robert slid in beside Tommy in the second row. Boyd explained the service to them. Mitch did not want to do the untraditional wedding. He wanted to stare at her while the pastor did all the talking; he was good at that.

"You will both turn to the congregation, and I will announce you as Mr. and Mrs. Maxwell. You can either lead the attendees out or follow them, but decide now." Mitch nodded at Carol and Douglas, who paired off and went down the aisle; when all were gone, he told the ring bearer to take the arm of both his sisters and escort them down the aisle just as he had Liz. The ring bearer did as he was asked, slowly nodding to the pews and walking arm in arm with his sisters. Mitch and Liz gave them a good head start, then they walked arm in arm back down the aisle.

Robert asked Richard, "Do you feel told, my friend? Because between you and that kid, you stole the show. Even the pastor tried not to laugh out loud."

Mr. and Mrs. Parsons told them they would not be going to the dinner, as the kids would need to sleep to be at their best; Jack said to her that they needed at least nine hours of sleep to be at their best. He was, after all, the Vip of this wedding, and there were to be no mistakes by his sisters or him tomorrow. Liz hugged them both and whispered to Jack's mom, "He is a darling boy."

Mom whispered back, “You mean, a real piece of work.” They both laughed.

Everyone gathered at a long table for dinner. Carol sat down last, as she was hoping this Douglas was not going to be at the dinner. There he was. Mitch ushered her over to him; he rose from his chair. “Doug, this is my daughter Carol. Carol, this is Doug, a friend and a worker. I hope you both get to know a little bit about each other tonight—you will sort of be stuck with each other tomorrow.” He left them to join Liz.

Doug pulled her chair out for her, and she sat down. He sat next to her and said, “I’m not much of a conversationalist, so if you don’t mind, I’ll ask a question, then you ask one, and everyone will think we are chatting up a storm.”

Carol smiled at him; he was trying to be friendly at the same time enough that his face was already red. “Okay, I work as an architect, and I run my own company. What do you do for a living, Doug?”

“I work for a charitable organization up north. Have you owned your own company long?”

“No, thanks to my dad, he helped me get the company started by giving me space in his complex. I had the whole of the second floor. The contractors work out of their own yards and offices. Denny and I do the interiors from our home. We also do the printing of blueprints and first drafts. Do you work just for the charity, or do you do other work?”

“As a matter of fact, I do. I love to cook and bake, so I run a restaurant where you can come and eat and pay if you can or give what you can to help feed others in need.”

“Wow, that must keep you busy.”

"Yes, in a way, there are people learning the art of being a chef in my restaurant. They learn from volunteer chefs and then go to the college to write their exams. If they pass, we do our best to help them find a start in some restaurant. As you know, you start at the bottom and work your way to the top. We have one that has made it to the top, but he is embarrassed as to where he works, although he loves it."

"Where would that be?"

"It's an exclusive restaurant that only handles reservations."

"Oh, like bachelorette parties and divorcées' parties."

"Yes, how did you know? It has only been open for a short while."

"Can you keep a secret from your friend at the top of the table? I mean, keep it forever?"

"Yes, I can. I'm very good at keeping information to myself."

"We took Liz there last night. It was great—she had a ball. She ended up helping the owner out with a lawyer for his girls."

"Larry—that's great. He and his brothers were so worried the childcare people would take them back to those drunks."

"You know the people?"

"Yes, she hit my car two months ago. All they did was take her license away. She did not have insurance. She can't drive until she gets some and pays for the damage to my car, good luck with that."

"Wow, can you tell me where, so I can see the building?"

"It's a house, and it is right next door to Mitch and Liz's house. It is for my grandparents. They want to be close to the family, because as Grams says, 'Er time I turns aroond, there's a new bairn in the hoose.'" They were both laughing at her poor imitation of Bertha's accent.

Mitch nudged Liz in the knee, and she looked in the direction he was and saw something extraordinary. Carol was smiling and laughing with this young man. "Mitch, have you known him long?" she asked quietly.

"I knew his parents for about as long as I've known you, Liz. They were great people. They died of malaria two years ago. Both contracted it over in Cambodia. They were missionaries. He does some of their work also." He told her of Doug's unique restaurant and learning centre. Liz was pleased her daughter was with a good man.

After dinner, the band came in, and there was dancing and karaoke for anyone brave enough to try. Mitch and Liz danced; they were practicing the steps to a dance they had learned from Allen and Shantelle, who had done a version of it at their wedding. Denny and Robert loved to dance; they were up dancing and the rest of the table, except Carol and Douglas. He finally asked her if she would dance with him, as they would have to dance tomorrow night. Carol rose and offered him her hand, something she had never done. She was one to wait to be asked, praying she would not. They got up, and Carol was surprised to find he was an excellent dancer. She followed him so quickly. When he tried a few intricate steps, she went with them. Soon they had command of the floor. Even they did not notice they were the only ones on the floor. When the music stopped, Carol looked around and realized they were the centre of attention and were being applauded for their efforts. She was so embarrassed, she turned to Doug and said, "Did you know we were alone on the floor?"

"No, I had my eyes closed, pretending we were dancing outside on the patio by ourselves."

"So was I. Oh, shit, let's just sit down, please." He took her back to the table. "Where did you learn to dance like that, Doug?"

"My mother insisted I take dance lessons, as I would never win a lady with my wonderful way of conversation. So I took classical dancing for five years, then modern waltz for another four. Did I impress you, Carol? God, I hope so."

"You more than impressed me. Let's wow them tomorrow night, okay? I'll tell you why my nickname is Mouse. I have had it since I was at least eleven." She pointed to Caitlin. "We call her Cat. She gave it to me. She is my best friend. We were known as the Cat and her Mouse of the neighborhood. Mind you, I was made fun of because I could not run from the boys when they chased us. My knee would give out, and down I would go. Cat would always come back for me and stop the boys from picking on me. Thus, Cat and her Mouse."

"They are playing a tango. Do you have any idea how to do it?"

"If what you learn in school works, yep, got the basics. Why?" He grabbed her hand, and they were back on the floor; he took her through an elegant, sexual dance that again cleared the floor. She didn't know why she trusted him, but she did. She was so happy, she had tears in her eyes and she didn't care who saw them. "Thank you for being my partner, Doug. For the first time in my life, I'm not the Mouse."

He pulled her close and did a slow slide waltz back to the table. "You are welcome, thank you for letting me be me for the first time in my life."

Cat came up and plopped herself down beside Carol. "Well, Mouse, when did you take dance lessons, and can I have the teacher's name?"

"Caitlin, this is Douglas Park, dancing teacher extraordinaire."

"Well, Mouse, will you share him for at least one dance, please?"

"Maybe tomorrow, not tonight, I am having the time of my life."

"I can see that. I am so happy for you." She left them.

Doug thought, *She came over to get a good look at me so she can check me out. So be it, officer. You won't find anything we do not want you to.*

Mitch asked Caitlin what she was up to when she talked to Carol. "I want to make damn sure, Mitch, that Mr. Nice Guy is exactly that. I haven't seen Carol that happy, well, ever."

"Not to worry, he's a missionary and a restaurant owner that caters to the poor who can't afford a meal—they clean to pay. Those with money pay what they can."

"I am still going to run his name, Mitch, just in case."

Mitch thought the same as Douglas had: *Go ahead and check. You won't find anything we don't want you to.*

Tommy watched his young protégée dance with Carol. They looked great; they were getting the attention he was supposed to be getting. *See, I am here with a lady, dancing my ass off, not anywhere else.*

Marcus danced with both his girls and enjoyed the company, for a change from being alone. *How many times did we have to change places to get a specific job done? I was always the last one on the pole to clean up the mess. We are getting too old for this shit, and I know it if Tommy doesn't.* But he loved what he did, loved what the results brought for the people he worked for. The girls would think nothing of Dad going on a business trip. Travel was part of his business.

He had taken them to a hip dress shop for young women. He told them, "Pick out the best dresses you can find, girls. This is a special wedding, and I want you to be happy."

"We can be happy, Dad, as long as we are with you. Mom told us to find you: 'Look high and low until you find your dad, and he will take care of you.' She was right." They chose different styles of dresses, and in different colours. You knew by what they decided who was outspoken and brave and who was shy and quiet. They looked beautiful, just like their mother, except he noticed they had his eyes. He had Liz make hair appointments for them, and while they were getting their hair done, he stopped in at a jeweller's. Marcus bought earrings and a matching necklace for them, in the tones of their dresses. When they were ready to go, he gave them the jewelry to wear.

"Oh, Dad, they are beautiful." Each had to have him do the clasp on the necklace, and each did the other's earrings.

He wanted to hug and kiss them so much. He was surprised they did the hugging and kissing, one on each side of him. "Pedro, come take a picture for me. I want to have it done for the wall in my study." Pedro set up his superior photo equipment. He had the three of them pose for him. The girls asked if they could please have a copy. Pedro was taken aback by their gratitude. He decided to make three copies of the picture, with wallet size as a surprise for all of them.

The car arrived, and they were off to the church. Faye asked him if they would be able to see the bride and groom.

"We are sitting with Uncle Tommy and Auntie B, and you will see it all."

"This is the first wedding I have ever attended, you too, Faye."

"Yes, and it will be such a thrill to see the bride. I look in those magazines at the bridal gowns and think, *Who can afford such dresses?*"

Mental note to Dad, these girls have had nothing but poverty all their lives. "What ya think, girls? 'Tis a beautiful thing, this is."

"You bet, Auntie B. Look at how the men are dressed in long suit coats and funny ties."

Tommy said to Joan, "They are called bolo ties, to go with the old western-style dress coat and boots."

"Mitch looks a wee nervous, dear. Is he no gonna make it?"

"He'll do fine, love, just fine." The music began.

Chapter Three

THE CHURCH WAS full of all their friends and family, with the exception of Denny's parents, as they did not want to be there. They were so against this wedding. They did not approve of this family at all. The ushers were moving up and down the aisle so much that some of the male guests helped them. The bridal party in the anteroom was getting anxious, as were the little girls, until the Vip decided to take over. "I will go see what the holdup is. We need to get this show on the road. We are fifteen minutes late as it is."

One of the girls, Susan, said, "There he goes. Jack thinks he's so big because he has a title. Wow, Vip—what can that mean? Gosh." The group snickered among themselves.

Vip returned. "Showtime, ladies, it is time to get in line and prepare to walk down the aisle."

Everyone was put in the proper order and waited for the music. Vip leaned his head out, and the music started. "Alice," Susan's sister whispered, "he is the Vip."

The ladies started down the aisle; as Carol started out, she whispered, "Congrats, Mom, you are beautiful, and I love you, thank you for being you."

The flower girls waited until their brother told them to go and not to forget to drop the flowers on the way. He turned to Liz. "Are you ready to do your part, lady?" She nodded to him, and Robert held back a laugh. Jack started down the aisle, nodding to the people in the pews, to snickers all the way.

Robert waited until Jack was at least thirty feet in front of them. "Here we go, Mom. We are going to get me a dad." They walked down the aisle slowly to hushed voices. They had stood, and every eye was on her; she was gorgeous in her secondhand-store gown, which looked like a million bucks. Her veil covered the back of her train completely, with some on the floor itself. She walked like a princess and looked like one.

Robert took her hand and was about to give it to Mitch. "She was all mine for so many years. Now she is yours. I only ask that you share her with me on occasion."

Mitch stepped down and hugged him to his chest. "I will, my son, I will."

Robert gave her hand to Mitch and went to sit next to Grams. She handed him a handkerchief. "I know, Robbie. Blow quietly, please." The service was beautiful. The wedding procession back down the aisle was perfect. Vip had the time of his life. He would hold on to that title at least until school on Monday.

Mitch had asked that no confetti be thrown, as the church caretaker was ill and it wasn't fair to leave it to the ladies of the church committee to clean up. As they exited the church, they were showered in bubbles blown by the congregation. The bubbles hung over them as pictures were taken. They stood for what seemed like forever for the photographer to be done. Andrew finally said it was time to do the usual drive around town if they wished. The newlyweds decided to go to the reception hall. There would be guests to greet before dinner.

Carol stood up at the head table and announced that unless you were prepared to sing for your supper, there was to be no clinking of glasses or singing of silly songs until the dessert came out. Robert leaned over and said, "Like that is going to happen."

His words were barely out when the first clinking started. "I have known this man for eons, so I want to see his lips on hers."

Mitch stood, lifted Liz out of her chair, and kissed her long and deep. The room burst into applause. Mitch and Liz were not bothered for the rest of the meal.

Tommy gave his speech about how great a man Mitch was and how lucky he found a woman who would put up with him. "We all like our lawyers. Even Mitch is lovable. Here's to the couple."

Carol was a little longer. "As you all know, Liz and Mitch made it legal, so I am truly a Maxwell, and I am proud of it. They have given me strength, love, and the bravery to start my own company with their help. They are the perfect people to me, except they gave me a bratty brother to pick on me. Thanks, Mom and Dad. Congratulations, with all my love. Hear, hear." She raised her glass of champagne.

Everyone gathered around the cake as Mitch and Liz prepared to cut the cake. She took a small piece in her hand, and Mitch said, "What are you doing with that, babe?" and she schmucked it into his mouth. He did the same right back. "No holds barred, my lady." Cameras were snapping as fast as it happened.

As they were doing their dance to oohs and aahs, he told her how beautiful she was and how she took his breath away when he watched her walk up the aisle to him. "You looked like a million-dollar bride to me."

The disc jockey announced that each of the wedding party couples would come up and do a dance separately; as each part of the song they had was done, they would leave the floor, and the next couple would come up. The Vip had something to say about that: "Does that mean I have to dance twice because there are two flower girls?" His dad said he would dance with one of them while the Vip danced with the other.

The disc jockey called Carol over. "You and your partner are to go last, okay? That is what the bride and groom have requested." She okayed it and walked back to Doug and told him. He was all right with it, but he could see she was a little scared.

"Carol, can you envision a sandy beach, no lights, just the music and us?"

She looked at him and got what he was doing. "Okay, I will close my eyes and let you take me to that beach with just you." It was their turn, and the music was "Love Me Tender." They started to dance at the edge of the floor and worked their way into the centre. He was doing the Vienna waltz, so precise and so sensual there were no words heard; she followed him like she was his partner in a dance contest. The music changed, and he switched to a tango even more sexual than the waltz.

He told her, "You make me look like a professional. Want to enter a contest? We could win some money on this." She smiled and laughed.

Everyone applauded them as they left the floor. Everyone started to dance; even Bertha and Tommy danced. Tommy thought to himself, *Way to go, me boyo, there is no way they can say you were not here. Douglas's lookalike left the hall right after the dinner. Doug could do his own dancing. Poor shit had no dinner. I only hope he got the job done. I would hate to hear what the brothers would say if he didn't.*

Caitlin thought, *Did he gain weight at the table then lose it on the dance floor?* Her nose was twitching; something was not kosher, and she wanted to know what it was.

Doug saw it on her face; he knew what it was. “Caitlin, does it still show on my face?” he asked her when Carol excused herself to go to the ladies’ room.

“Does what show?”

“I had a tooth removed early this morning, because I couldn’t stand the pain. They took it out at the hospital. They said the swelling would be gone by this evening, but I didn’t think it did. I had a hell of a time trying to eat.”

“You looked like you gained a few pounds, but you’re all right now. I thought I saw another man sitting next to Carol. It looked like Doug, but not. Now I know why—sorry about your mouth. Did you get enough to eat?”

“Not really, Cat, but I will fill up on the dessert table.” Carol came back and teased Cat about trying to steal her dancing partner. The song “I Could Have Danced All Night” started, and he and Carol were dancing once again.

Marcus noticed a young man looking for someone from the edge of the ballroom. He was just about to go over to him, when his daughter Joan went to him and gave him a hug, took his hand, and led him over to Marcus. “Dad, this is Jason, my fiancé. Jason, this is my dad, Mr. Marcus McCloud.”

Marcus was leery; something was not quite right. The kid’s face changed; he was white with fear, and he was reaching for something. Tommy saw it and was moving like lightning toward them. Jason pulled a plastic gun out of his jacket pocket, pushed Joan out of the way, and aimed at Marcus. He never got the shot off. Tommy had him on the floor, and two of Tommy’s men had the kid out of the room faster than he came in.

“Care to explain that to me, Joan? I don’t like to be shot at with any kind of gun.”

Faye was holding her. Joan was crying; she looked up at her dad. "I didn't know he was going to do that. He asked me if he came here just to meet you, would it be all right? I told him sure. I didn't think it would be any harm, dinner was over, and everyone was dancing. So I told him to come but dress nice."

"Faye, take her into the lounge so she can calm down, unless you know something she doesn't."

"No, but I wish I did." She took her sister to the lounge.

Tommy asked Marcus if he wanted to speak to the kid or he wanted him to do it. "I'll do it, but you had better stay close. Go talk to Bertha, tell her the truth, no need to hide this one."

"I'll be right back," Tommy said. "Bertha dear, Marcus was shot at by our Joan's fiancé. We are going to have a talk with him before we hand him over to the police. Would you mind being by yourself for a few minutes?"

"I can look after meself."

Doug came up with Carol and said, "We can sit with Mrs. McCloud if you like, sir."

"I would, very much, thank you, Doug, is it? And you, Carol." He walked back toward Marcus. Marcus gave one of the servers a hundred-dollar bill to get an empty room far enough away not to be heard by the guests.

"Care to tell me what the hell you thought you were doing, Jason? If that is your name."

The kid sat there and looked at the floor, said nothing. Tommy slowly walked around him till he got to the front of his chair. He was holding a cotton bag filled with beans. This could cause significant pain but leave hardly a mark. The bag scared him enough to squirm in his chair. Marcus put his hand on the kid's shoulder and applied enough pressure to cause him discomfort. "Now you don't want my brother to use that toy of his on you, do you?"

Easy—that was all it took; the kid whined then said he would tell them everything. "I was paid by their grandfather to get rid of you and then the girls. He would pay me when I got to Florida."

"Just exactly why would he need me and my girls dead? Think before you answer, kid, because I am six inches away from doing you a favour and taking you out right now."

Jason spoke. "All I know is that he hated the fact that he owed you and your brother so much money, and he wasn't about to pay you, tramps, for knocking up his daughter, who by the way was not his daughter. His wife had an affair with some English dude, then left her in the family way. She died trying to prove that it was a lie, that Margaret was his daughter, but he said she couldn't be. He killed his wife and then he killed his daughter. His girlfriend Zelda did it for him. She set it up so it looked like he died two weeks after his daughter. He lives in Florida with Zelda, on your money."

"What made him think he owed us money, great or small?"

Jason told him, "He borrowed from your father hundreds of thousands of dollars when he was drunk and forgot he did. Your mother found out and went after it. She knew something was wrong when your dad asked her to sign the deed for the pub over to him."

"I am not sure how all this goes," Marcus said. "I never paid attention to my dad when he told me all this shit."

Jason whispered, "I was to do what my dad didn't do twenty years ago, to make sure it was done. He has my mother in Florida. I want her back. I don't give a rat's ass for Joan, never did. She is a bit slow, if you get me." Tommy, infuriated by this remark, knocked him out with one swing of his magic beans.

"Now what? The son of a bitch is alive and kicking, and my Margaret is six feet under."

"We will get him, Marcus, and take this little twerp with us. He wants his mommy. Jason will have to earn her back. He will show us where the bastard is. We will teach him some proper manners. What say you?"

"I say yes, Tommy, I will make the arrangements, but you have to talk to Bertha before anyone makes a move."

"Aye, lads, what did this little bugger do ta upset ya?"

Tommy told the truth, all of it, just not the part that they ran a rescue operation.

"Best be tellen the wee girls a tall tale, they no needs ta know this. Tommy, I'll go wit' ya 'cause I knows ya an' ya will git yerself in the shit."

"Yes, love, that will be fine."

Faye and Joan were told Jason was a hired gun to kill their dad for a price. He had no intention of marrying anyone; he was gay. Faye looked at Joan, hoping she would be all right, but knew she wouldn't be. "Joan, he wasn't right for you and now you have a chance to meet a good man, one that wants you for you."

Joan just nodded her head and started to cry. Marcus held her while the rest left the room. He crooned to her like he used to do to her mother when her father was mean to her. "Joanie, it hurts like the blazes now, but it will get better. Think of all the odd things he did, and you soon will see he did not care for your feelings at all."

"He was the one that didn't want me to go to school or get a real job. He wanted Faye to stay at home, but he couldn't afford to pay the rent, and we had to have a place to live. So here we are." She cried some more.

It was time for the wedding couple to go; they were leaving on the train to Canada—British Columbia. They were going to tour the province for a month then return home, hopefully back to work and a new family life, with everyone close but not too close.

Chapter Four

CAROL AND DENNY were happy that Grams and Gramps were pleased with the house. Grams loved her kitchen and her master bedroom. "I ner had a room so big an' fancy, Carol, and Denny, 'tis a wonder, that bathroom. Did ya see the shower? Like a rainfall it is, I jest love it, so does his mister, stands there like a statue, he does."

"The only thing left is for the two of you to pick out your living and flex space. So when do you want to go shopping?"

"Tommy won't be comen wit me, girls. He's away with Marcus, an' I ner know when he's ta be back, so 'tis me doin' the picken, all right?" Sure was, they told her. Denny would bring her into the store in the morning. "I'm bringing Liz with me, okay?"

Denny told her they wouldn't have it any other way. Liz asked her if she had a style in mind, or did Tommy say what he would like?

"His highness told me ta git what I want an ner mind the cost. We can afford it. Liz, is me man that rich?"

"Yes, Mom, he is, and more than you can imagine, so when he says the sky is the limit, he means it." They met the girls and went into the store. The owner spotted Carol, Liz, and Denny, thought maybe that the little old lady was one of the ladies' mother or grandmother out for the day while the others shopped for a client. He did not relish having to put up with an older woman thinking she knew it all.

"Greetings, ladies, what can I do for you this bright, sunny day?"

Carol told him, "We are here to shop for a large living room and a spacious flex room."

"Does your client have time to come in, or are you picking these items for them?"

"I'm here to pick me own, sir." Liz turned her back slightly to him as she laughed. So he thought she was just an old lady, did he?

"Mrs. McCloud has carte blanche, Mr. Blueit, so can we start with the living room?" Carol spoke sternly as he had just insulted an essential client whom they had.

As they walked toward the more expensive items in the store, he asked Denny, "Is she wealthy, or is Carol trying to pull my leg?"

"No, Mr. Blueit, she is the richest lady in this town, in the state." He moved up and offered Bertha a coffee or a tea while they shopped, or perhaps a light dessert to go with the tea or coffee.

"No, thanks, had me breakfast before we came. Can ya show me some reader chairs fer in front of me fireplace, in me bedroom."

Liz smiled. *Good for you, Mom, you got his number.* They shopped for nearly two hours, and Bertha picked two lovely chairs for her fireplace, a large comfy sofa for the flex room, for Tommy to lounge on when watching his sports games. She liked the high-back chairs for the living room, but they did not have the colour she wanted. He would have to special order those. He wanted her to take the ones he had. "I ner liked that colour. It canna go with the colour of me room. Ya no can order them, I can go somewheres else."

"I can and will order them, Mrs. McCloud."

They went to another furniture store. Bertha found what she was looking for in the living room, a lovely square table with matching side tables. Bertha wanted three of them and a large bookcase for her books in the flex space.

Carol said it was lunchtime, so they headed for Liz's favourite restaurant. Bertha was getting tired but hungry. "Liz, after lunch, canna we go hame? I'm a wee bit tired."

"Sure, Mom, right after lunch, we don't need to shop anymore today." Bertha looked more than just tired; she looked weak. "Mom, are you all right? Are you feeling ill?"

"I can use a lie-down, Liz. I feel like me legs are noodles."

Liz told the girls, "No lunch—the hospital, now." She had a feeling Bertha was having a stroke or heart attack. They were two blocks from the hospital. Liz called ahead; they were ready for her.

"Mrs. McCloud, just let us take care of you and don't fight us this time." Bertha did as she was told, got on the gurney, and lay down; she didn't like the straps, but she put up with it. They took her to the cardiac department right away. They did an ultrasound and then X-rays; on the way back to her room, she passed out, her heart rate went up, and her blood pressure did the same. Dr. Braggo came rushing in, she made everyone leave, and a team of nurses and interns rushed in. She was making every effort to get Bertha's heart rate and pressure down. A nurse came out and asked Liz to call her husband. Things did not look too good.

"Carol, call Mitch. Denny, call Robert, and I will call Tommy." Liz had to try three times to get ahold of Tommy. His phone kept going to message.

Finally, he answered. "Thomas McCloud here."

"Tommy, it's Liz. Bertha is in the hospital. They are not sure if it is a heart attack or a stroke, but they want you here like now!"

"I'm on my way. I'll be there in less than three hours. Tell her I love her and wait for me, love, wait." He turned to Marcus. "Tie the bastard up. We are going home, so is he. Bertha is in the hospital. I want to get to the bottom of this, but she comes first, Marcus."

"You can't take me back to St. Helen. I am not going there."

"Oh, but you are, you son of a bitch. You are going to face those girls and tell them the truth as well as me. You used those women like slaves, and now you pay, so get in the plane—it is ready. Let's go!"

They arrived in St. Helen in less than three hours and had a police escort, compliments of Caitlin, to the hospital. Tommy was at her side as soon as he could be. "Sweetheart, what happened?"

She looked up at Tommy and said, "I'm glad yer here, me love. I no canna feel right. Me ticker wants ta bang and me head hurts awful. Am I gonna die, Tommy? I wants ta live, and I'm so happy to be wit ya." She passed out again.

Dr. Braggo made him leave. "Marcus, I'm afraid she doesn't look good at all." Tommy was crying. Marcus had an idea that maybe the cause was not a heart attack or stroke. He went to the nurse and asked to speak to the head of the hospital.

Dr. Kline came down to the department because he knew the family. "Mr. McCloud, what can I do for you?"

"I need you to bring in a forensic specialist, as I think Mrs. McCloud has been poisoned, and it will take someone of that caliber to find it before she dies."

"Are you sure? I know we are all worried about her—she is an icon in our town, but poison, where, when? I don't understand your thinking."

"Do it, Dr. Kline. I will personally cover all costs to the hospital and the specialist that are needed to save her life. Now get on it." Dr. Kline knew he had better. They owned the damned hospital. He also knew he had better get the best of the best.

Dr. Beth Flower told him she could not be there, but if they could send her blood samples or fly her to Baltimore, she could help. She was involved in a homicide that made it difficult to leave. Tommy had the plane prepped for flight; he would take his wife there himself. He was told she would be helicoptered out to John Hopkins; they would have her there faster than Tommy's plane could. He could fly with her, but the rest of the family would have to find their own transportation.

"Mitch, you and Liz come on my plane. If you think Robbie has to be there, bring him." He grabbed Marcus. "Call Caitlin, tell her we need her to keep that SOB in lockup with no one around him. Do you think she will do this for us?"

Marcus punched in her cell phone number. She answered on the second ring. "Yes, Caitlin here."

"Cat, Marcus—we need your help. Bertha is in hospital—we think poison, but we must airlift her to John Hopkins. I have a man in handcuffs and leg cuffs. Can you hold him in a cell without visitation? Because he will request a lawyer and his girlfriend. No one, Cat. He is a killer. He paid to have my daughters and me killed. Tommy and I want to get to the bottom of this, but Bertha comes first."

"Where is he, and how long do you want me and Dugan to hold him?"

"Until we get back, please." He told her where to get him and the combination to the locks on his wrist and ankles.

Liz thought it best that Robert and Denise stayed at home; Carol told them she would stay with them to finish her home and it would be ready when she was. They left right after Marcus gave Cat the info she needed for something. Liz asked Mitch about it. "What has Marcus got to do with Cat, and what information does she need from him?"

Mitch told her, "It has to do with his business, and she knows what he wants. Let's leave it to them." Mitch would have loved to help Marcus and Tommy out. Bertha's illness had nothing to do with their business.

Dr. Beth Flower met them at the helipad and directed them to the quarantine department. She looked into Bertha's eyes and saw something that said it was not a stroke. Tommy introduced himself and shook her hand. "Please help my lady. She does not deserve this—she is such a good woman."

He was crying. He had not cried when his first wife died, nor did he when his mother died.

Bertha was placed on oxygen; the lab tech came in to take her blood, but the doctor stopped her. "I will be drawing her blood and doing all the tests myself. No one is to touch Mrs. McCloud unless I personally say so. No written orders are to be accepted. You got that? Not only lab techs, but nurses as well—no one touches this lady without my authorization."

At first, Liz didn't get it. "Why would she stop people from helping Mom?"

Tommy explained it to her, and he could see she wasn't happy about this. "Liz, Marcus was the one that spotted it. Not even the doctors at our hospital at home saw it. I, for one, I am grateful he did."

"What did Marcus see that we didn't?"

"You told us she started to show extreme tiredness, loss of hunger, then numbness, all typical signs of heart failure or stroke, correct?"

"Yes, that's why I took her straight to the hospital and called you."

"What you, the girls, even the interns at the hospital and the heart specialist did not see was the colour change in Bertha's eyes. None of us noticed that the beautiful blue of her eyes had turned green, Liz, green like an unripe lemon. Marcus did. He acted on it right away. God, I am so glad he did. She would be dead right now if he had not spotted it. The doctors at our hospital gave her a fighting chance with an intravenous antibiotic. I can only hope Dr. Flower can help her."

"What could possibly cause her eye colour to change? She didn't eat out—she had breakfast at home. What could have given her that poison, Tommy? I am as frightened as you, so talk to me."

"We figure she was given the poison at your wedding, slow-acting non-detectable until too late. Thanks to you, it might be her saving grace that you did what you did, Liz."

Dr. Flower came to them and said, "We have ruled out ricin, from the castor bean. We are working hard, Mr. McCloud. I will not give up trying to save her. This is just one of the poisons we will be testing for. Each one from here on in will be harder to detect. Some have no symptoms, others have very few, but none of them will be undetectable like they say on television and in suspense novels, Mr. McCloud."

"Please call me Tommy. I'm not used to being called by my surname."

"Okay, Tommy, I'm back to work, and you can stay with your wife when she's lucid. She is a chatterbox. The times are short, so don't worry too much until I tell you it's time to get things in order." With that, Dr. Flower moved like she was on fire.

Tommy sat with her, held her hand, and talked to her. Even Tommy could get a few things done, as he said to Mitch. He was never gone long. The nurse came in and said she was to take a blood sample for the doctor and would everyone leave. They stood, but Tommy had her by the arms before Liz saw him move.

Mitch was checking her pockets and found a full syringe. Liz did as Tommy told her, ringing Bertha's buzzer continuously. Dr. Flower came in first, then two huge guards. They took the nurse out, not gently.

Liz was more frightened than ever. "Mitch, what in the hell is going on? I feel like I'm in a horror movie. Tommy moves like a man half his age, and you knew what to do. How did you know?"

Tommy took Liz out of the room. "Liz, you are showing signs of hysterics. Deep breath, and listen to me. Bertha needs you to stay calm. When she wakes, you show her a smile like everything is okay, she is going to get better, and she is still in St. Helen, so nothing scares her and makes her blood pressure change or her heartbeat harder, because if it is a poison, those things will cause it to work that much faster."

Liz started to cry and then straightened up and said, "Okay, Dad, I will do as I am told," and gave him a big kiss and hug. He held her until she was breathing normally again.

Dr. Flower came in and motioned to them to join her at the back of the room. Talking in whispers, she told them, "They found no strychnine or arsenic so far, nothing, but she is holding her own and not dropping her blood pressure; the drug in the syringe was an overdose of arsenic. The police have her, and your brother is with them. He told me to tell you he would see you very soon."

Again, the waiting game: Liz walking the floor outside Bertha's room, Tommy talking to Bertha, who was sometimes awake, making no sense at all. Bertha would wake and chatter incoherently. Tom knew whatever poison was used, it was doing the job. She was making less and less sense each time she woke. Mitch brought them tea, and coffee for Liz. Dr. Flower came in and gave them sandwiches. She knew they would not take anything from anyone now. Tommy looked at her, and she shook her head and left.

Marcus came back. "Where is the doctor, Tommy? I know what the poison is." They both ran down the hall to her lab.

"My brother has the name of the poison. He got it from that nurse or whatever she was."

"It is ricin mixed with abrin, similar to ricin."

"Yes, it is, only a lower dose can be used for the same effect."

"I'm on it. We now have a chance. An hour from now, I would have told you to make your arrangements." The lab people worked at breakneck speed to perfect a serum to counteract the abrin—not easy, but they did it.

Four days later, Bertha was finally told where she was and why. Tommy stood back from the bed; the lady was shooting fire and brimstone from those now-blue eyes. "Ya put me in a plane agin. Ya left me wit men I didn't know, Tommy. Yer daft if ya think I'm no mad at ya."

"You can be mad, darlin', but we have been through hell, waiting for you to wake up and talk to us. You were an hour away from the pearly gates, my love, and we asked you to mention our names to the big guy up there." For that remark, he got the water pitcher thrown at him.

Mitch ducked and Liz laughed. "That's my mom."

Dr. Flower came in just in time to see the action. "I know you don't know me, Mrs. McCloud, but I feel I know you. We have had a few odd conversations. If you feel strong enough, you can fly home today, if not tomorrow, whatever is good for you."

"I thank ya, Dr. Flower, fer all yer help. I'll be goin' hame this day if that man ah mine behaves." She was still angry with her husband for not keeping her in St. Helen.

"Bertha, if Tommy hadn't brought you here to Dr. Flower, you would have died in St. Helen. We saw the colour of your eyes change, from blue to a yellow-green, and we knew you had been poisoned. He only tried to save his beloved wife."

"Tis hard fer me ta believe. I canna see why me. I ner hert anyone."

The flight home was uneventful; Bertha had no trouble on the small plane. Marcus was very quiet. Marcus knew something he would not be sharing with anyone, and that included Tommy. He would explain to them after he talked to Pablo.

They were met at the airport by Robert, who was glad to see his grandmother was all right and happy. "Grams, so, so excited to see you up and healthy." He gave her a hug and opened the car door for her. Tommy got in beside her. They drove home, listening to Robert talk about what happened at the hospital after they left: "Four of the nurses were found dead, and an intern in the lab too. Dr. Kline has retired. He wants nothing to do with that kind of business. He said that our town was a quiet place to stay, not anymore."

When they arrived at the house, Marcus was already there. He had driven himself. "Tommy, I need some help with the boxes in my car. Can you give me a hand, please?" They went outside; Marcus opened the trunk of the car and told him, "The threat on Bertha's life was to make sure we leave the old man alone. His girlfriend, if that is what you want to call the witch, did it to Bertha at the wedding. The old man is supposed to be returned to his lady friend by midnight, or she will kill or try to kill one of us."

"Not while there is breath in me, Marcus. The woman must be mad to think she can take us on. Where is the old man now? The girls must know what is going on. They can't possibly be that stupid."

"I thought the same. We will bring the old man to the girls. Let's hope we can settle this. Get McKellen, and we go."

"What do we tell Bertha and the family?"

"Ya tells me the truth. Ner lies ta me, Tommy. Please do what you must, but ya tells me or ya go yer own way."

They arrived at the house; Pablo let them in. "The girls are upstairs. Shall I get them, sir?" Marcus nodded.

Tommy pushed the old man into a chair. "Had you left the family alone, we would have left you alone, but you want some kind of vengeance, and for what I have no idea." When Faye and Joan arrived downstairs, they both stood there and stared, not believing who they saw sitting there.

"What the hell are you two trollops looking at? No better than the rest of the women of your blood." For that, he got a shot right in the face from Marcus.

"They are my girls, not trollops like that bitch you live with."

"Dad, is it really him? He didn't die. We lost our home, our mother for him. Mom told us he was not to be trusted. He stole from Dad's family before we were born and tried to kill our mother, so that her father would stop threatening him to pay back a large amount of money he owed him. Mom said that he paid someone to drown Barbara and her daughter Margaret Jean so the boys would not know about the money."

"Shut your traps. You don't know what you're talking about. I never owed anyone anything."

Faye opened her jewelry box and gave her dad the paper that her mother gave her when she became so ill. "She said this would tell you everything you needed to know."

Joan gave him the papers out of hers. "These are the adoption papers that belong to my mother. She was adopted when they went to Scotland for vacation so people would think she was theirs. He can't have kids. When he decided he wanted to disgrace his wife, he told everyone Mom was your father's daughter—that he had an affair with his wife. McKellen had your father killed. He said your dad was a useless piece of work. If your dad were gone, the money problem would be solved. Your mother knew more than he thought. He started working on her. She was smarter and had people take care of his problem for him. Leave the north or die, end of story. Here is the proof."

"I don't need to see the proof, Joan, but I believe you," Tommy told her.

"You have hidden this from the world since your mother died?" Marcus asked them.

"That and more, Dad, he sold Grandmother to men to be beaten or for sex, whatever they wanted. Master would watch it all. When she died, he started doing it to our mother. She fought back, and the men didn't like that, so they stopped coming. Only the ones that wanted to beat her came. He would kick her and make her do awful things. His girlfriend did the same. I vowed if I ever got the chance, I would hurt him and her. But he died, and we were thrown out." Joan started to cry, and then she ran at McKellen, kicking and slapping him, screaming, "Feel good, you old bastard? How's this feel?" She jammed her foot into his crotch and jumped up and down.

Faye held her down and let her cry. "He killed Mom, and we both know it. She was poisoned with the same stuff he gave Grandmother when he deemed her useless."

Marcus asked her, "Was it abrin, Faye?"

"Yes, I still have the rest of the vial in my case upstairs. I wanted evidence to prove he is a murderer and a thief."

"Say goodbye to your grandchildren because where he is going, you will never see again." He stood and spat on Faye. She turned, and sucker shot him in the gut then in the groin.

Pablo came in. "Shall I take the garbage out, sir?"

"Yes, Pablo, make sure it is taken care of."

Faye asked, "Will he ever see a courtroom, Dad, or will he get away with this?"

Tommy answered her, "Darlin', he won't see a courtroom, but he will see the devil's office sooner than he would like. Would that be okay?"

Both girls moved over to them and nodded yes. "Can we see Auntie B? Is she better? Please tell us it wasn't Moana that hurt her."

"Tomorrow, you can go see her. She is probably in bed if I know your aunt Liz, so tomorrow. Right now, I must get back and help with the unpacking, so I'll see you tomorrow too. Marcus, I'll call you later, or I'll see you." He knew what his brother meant by that: she loves me, or she'll throw me out on my ear.

He went back to their house; she was waiting for him in the bedroom, the only room with furniture besides the kitchen stools. He looked at her, got down on his knees, and said, "I love you with all my heart, and I know you abhor violence, so I was afraid to tell you of the other business that my brother and I run. We save people, rescue them from harm or bad parents, slavery, whatever the situation is, and we see to it that it's legitimate. The people or kids are in dire straits. We go in and get them out. You were hurt not because of that, but because Marcus took in his daughters. The grandfather was still alive and wanted us dead, Marcus and me. You were supposed to make us stop looking into the mess for the girls. It only made me as well as your brother-in-law angrier.

We found him and his girlfriend. Neither one will be bothering us again. The law will take care of that. The girls both want to see you. They feel it is their fault you were hurt.

"Bertha, my mother started this years ago when a man upon the mountain was beating his daughters, not his sons. She found out he was selling them to whoever wanted them. Mom bought them for three thousand dollars. She sent them to England, where they had medical treatment and got healthy. Mom had people come to her with different problems and did what was needed to help them. That was when she started charging for rescuing rich people's kids. This, she said, was to offset the cost of the other rescues we did. Bertha, you have no idea how many rich people's kids are stolen from their parents every day. We rescue them. Some are easy, some are not. The people up at our chalet work for me as rescuers. Charlie runs things for me when Marcus or I am not there. At our wedding, Marcus could not be there because he was in Australia, getting a baby that a nurse from Canada took to be her own. The baby was two months old. The mother nearly died from the loss of the baby boy when he was taken. Her father paid the price to get him back. That baby is in his mom's arms because of Marcus and the company we run. So if you want to toss me out on me ear, I'll go. The house is yours, love, and anything you want in it."

"Ache, yer daft, Tommy. I loves ya. I jest needed to know the truth. If there's ta be violence, ner tell me, jest come hame ta me."

"That I will, lassie, that I will."

Chapter Five

"DOES MITCH KNOW of yer business? And Liz?"

"No, darling, they do not." He had his fingers crossed behind him for that whopper. He knew if she thought Mitch was in on this and Liz did not know, she would before the end of the day.

Robert was still wet behind the ears, and young; he needed to stay that way. Raise a family, which Robert does not know that his wife is expecting. He saw the doctor's report when he went snooping to find out who or what did this to his Bertha. "Love, we don't advertise. The clients come to us because we are discreet. No one knows we were there, and then we are gone. So please don't ask Marcus about it unless he is here or he is alone, because I know you are going to want to know more, are ya not?"

"Yes, an yer gonna tell me someday." She kissed him and told him it was bedtime, call his brother and tell him he was staying home. He laughed and did just that.

Everyone was glad Bertha was okay. Liz told them over coffee that now she was okay. They were going to leave for Canada, seeing that they didn't make the train the first time. "We will be leaving in the morning, so if you two need anything, make Robert do it."

The ladies chatted on about the trip until the furniture truck pulled up in front. "Are we supposed to be getting furniture, Liz?"

She had called the store and asked Carl, the floor manager, to send the furniture out today. “Okay, thank you.”

“Yes, you are getting some you picked and some Carol and Denny picked. They said if you didn’t like it, you could tell the men to take it back today.” In came the two chairs for the fireplace, then the sofa for Tommy to watch his sports on, which Mitch said he was stealing the next vacation they went on. Then came a love seat, matching chair, and long couch. They placed it where she wanted it. The living room looked fabulous. The sports coach went into the flex room where the TV was. Her tables went well with the furniture.

Carol came running over. She had parked in Liz’s lane. “Grams, what do you think? Do you like what we picked?”

“I loves it all, lassie.”

Tommy piped up, “Wait a minute. Don’t I get a say what goes in my space? I get a fat sofa and one table. I feel neglected.”

“Oh, Gramps, you and I will go pick out your flat screen and, of course, the game table you wanted. I saw one yesterday.” She winked so Grams wouldn’t see; it was bright red with white legs, and black pockets on the sides and the poker table has got a purple card cloth on it.

“You ner gonna git that stuff in me hame, Carol. I will box yer ears, lassie, sure as the sun rises.” Bertha stamped her foot.

Tommy hugged her to him. “No, sweetheart, they match both and are purple.” She swatted him on the backside hard. Carol had ordered an antique billiard table with a matching poker table in dark oak. They would be delivered to their house later today.

Liz missed her best friend living with her, here every day, talking, cooking together. They came every day for tea, and she brought a batch of scones with her. It just wasn't the same. They were all packed and ready to go tomorrow morning.

Liz had a daily planner full of things that she and Mitch wanted to see. Liz had a list of the things she wanted to see and another for Mitch.

Liz was so excited about going whale watching; to see them jump and splash down into the ocean would be fantastic. Her next place to visit was Hope, where they made the Rambo movies. The Empress Hotel was next; the concierge booked them to have high tea, and they could even buy the china pattern that the queen had been served. Then to tour Victoria and see the old buildings and stores—Liz loved old, antique buildings and articles.

Mitch wanted to see where they built log homes in Williams Lake. He thought of how it would be unique to have a log home. She told him she liked the house they had. He wanted to go to Whistler Mountain. There was a bridge he wanted to see in North Vancouver, the Capilano Suspension Bridge. He said it would be an excellent experience for both of them. He also wanted to visit this tram thing at Grouse Mountain. Mitch wanted to have fish and chips at Stanley Park. It was supposed to have totems and flowers and exhibits of all kinds.

The one place she told him she would not be going was Wreck Beach, a nudist beach. Liz told him, "Not in your lifetime, buddy."

Robert and Denny drove them to the airport. Bertha and Tommy said their goodbyes at the house. Bertha felt slightly sick to her stomach; planes, or the thought of them, made her ill. She was okay with Tommy's wee plane, but not the big ones.

Tommy wanted to be sure of what the girls were telling him. He knew to say that to Marcus would end in an argument. "I want some time with the old man, then with the girls, Marcus. First,

McKellen—let the girls know, then send one of them in, either one." He could see Marcus did not like this at all.

"Look, Marcus, I'm not saying there is something not right. I'm saying I see a problem. I just want all my ducks in a row. What was it Mother used to say? 'There's your side and there's my side and then there is the truth in the middle.' She was usually right."

McKellen was a few years older than their mother, and she knew this man. She had no kind words for him. "You and your brother mean nothing, unpolished hoodlums. I fully intend to destroy you, and all attached to you."

"You are having pipe dreams, McKellen. Who has who right now? Oh, your lady friend—she is now in a cell in my chalet. A good friend of mine has her. You know how that works, don't you?"

Marcus did not know if Tom was lying or telling the truth, and what was so damned important about her? *Okay, Tommy, I will play along with your game, but only until it is hurting my children. Please, God, don't let them be part of this like Tom thinks.*

Joan came in and jumped back when she saw her grandfather in the room. "He can't hurt me, Uncle Tommy, can he? I mean, he's not untied?"

"He's not tied up if that's what you mean, Joan, but he knows his manners, so to speak. He tries to touch you, and he's the one hurting."

She stayed as far away from him as she could. "What is it you want, Uncle Tommy? I don't want to be near him. My skin crawls with fear."

Marcus was just about to interrupt, when McKellen said, "Your skin should crawl. I'll put you back in that vat of cockroaches again if you open your mouth!"

So, Tommy thought, *there is more they know about this bastard and they are too afraid to speak.*

"Hey, Joanie, how about we put him in a tub of those critters? I can get them out from his storage if you'd like."

She changed; her eyes grew wild. "Lie to him and tell him they are scorpions. If you move, they bite and sting and kill you, right, Master Walt? And you have just one hour to agree to extra duty. Shall we get you ready, have your men take your clothes off?"

Tommy picked her up in his arms; she was whimpering. "No, darling, he will never do that to you again. Can you tell us what duty you didn't want to do, to be punished like that?"

Tommy put her on the sofa next to her father. Marcus covered Joan with a blanket and held her close to his side.

"We were to show off our breasts and act like we wanted to have sex with whatever man or woman he wanted to butcher for whatever crime Master Walt said they did."

"No, you mean to kill that person, right?" Marcus said to her as he rubbed her back and prayed he was right.

"No, Dad, the person was butchered, part by part, until all the information was gotten, sometimes not—in that case, they bled to death. They would take the parts they wanted to eat, and we would have to clean up the rest just like Mom and Grandmother had to."

Marcus thought for sure he was going to be sick. "One more thing, sweetie, do you or Faye know the people or their names?"

"We knew all. The last was a man called Johanson Drifus. His crime was he worked for the FBI and some other organization that he would not give up. We felt terrible for him and his wife, the pain he suffered as they slowly butchered his body, and his wife—well, she was forced to watch. Master thought she knew and would give it up to save her husband. He killed her too, shot her in the end, then said, 'Lunch, boys, it's on them.'" Tommy and Marcus knew exactly what that meant. She was crying and shaking when Faye burst into the room.

"You made her tell you what he did. Look at her. You should have asked me. She was forced to watch as they ate our mother, her head sitting in the centre of the table." Marcus was losing it; his control was all but gone.

"Marcus, take them out of here."

"Oh no, you don't. He can take Joanie, but I want to see this. I need it to see this." Her eyes were large and full of rage. She walked up to McKellen and spat in his face, then reached into his mouth.

Tommy stopped her. "Not before he talks to me, Faye, unless you can tell me what I want to know."

She released McKellen's tongue. "Let me help you. I know his fears. I found Grandmother's special notebook. She wrote down every time he showed the slightest suspicion of something, anything. Like the fear of spiders or snakes. And oh yes, huge men wanting to do to him what he had done to them."

Marcus returned to the room with Pablo, who pulled off a latex mask, like a second skin. Pablo turned to McKellen as he removed the mask. "Remember me, Walt?" He walked over to him. "You butchered the woman you thought was my wife before the FBI broke in. You got out through the help of your men, or I would have done you in myself. I am sorry you and your sister had to watch that. If you want to talk to your dad and your uncle about him and his dealings, I will only be so happy to dispose of this garbage for you. If not, I will leave the room. Like Joan, my skin crawls from the sight of him. To me, he is nothing but vermin."

Faye walked over to him. She smiled. "Jackson, you are okay. I begged that agent to tell me if you were all right." She hugged him.

"Faye, that woman was a Washington cop, and she didn't deserve what he did to her or her body. I couldn't tell them, I—"

She knew why. "It's called a date-rape drug on the street, sin equal or nortriptyline. Sometimes he used duloxetine, whatever he could get to deaden the nerves. They also could have given you a drug—not one muscle works. He used it on me a couple of times." She didn't bother to explain why; she figured they were intelligent enough to know. She turned to her father and uncle. "You are the rescue organization for hire he wanted stopped. He hated that he lost money to you every time you rescued his ordered kills. He wanted a man named McFadden the most for taking a million-dollar prize kill right out from under his nose. That cost him large. He had to have his face changed, move into the south, and work his way back up. During one of those moves, a team of men got the twin boys they were to get out and us. That was nearly ten years ago."

Tommy looked at her. "That was the Mandela twins. All we knew was they were twins, not the sex of the twins and that they were young kids. You were never brought to us. Why?"

"They spoke Spanish to the boys first, on the plane. The older man asked Joan who she was, and she lied, said we were captives to do his cleanup jobs. It was almost the truth."

Marcus said in a voice barely audible, "We could have had you back then. Oh God, Faye."

She put her hands on his shoulders. "It's best we didn't meet then. I'm almost sane, and the nightmares are less, but Joan, not so much. Her fantasy to be married and live happily ever after was being filled by that so-called idiot Jason. She needs more help than you know but won't leave my side."

She took her phone out of her pocket. "Joan honey, can you and Pablo bring that big blue box down to the room for us, please? If you don't want to come in, just leave it at the door. Thanks, honey. There is every case I could record, names where Master Walt wanted them taken, what he wanted from them, who he hurt to get them to talk, who they ate. He preferred women, said they were not as tough. Now I need to go and rock my sister to sleep and stay with her through her nightmare. It will be a doozy."

Marcus got up with her and said, "I can help with that. No, not a drug. I can hypnotize her and give her a beautiful suggestion to sleep. Shall we try, Faye?"

"You go, Dad. I need to stay with Uncle Tom, okay?" Marcus knew he would not change her mind.

Breakfast was a simple affair but great to Joan and Faye. They were used to toast and coffee when they could afford it. The girls thought it was something: scones, jam, eggs, bacon, sausage, and orange juice with tea or coffee.

"Now yer all here, we're haven a chat, an' no one ya tell me a lie. Marcus, sit yerself doon. Yer no getten away, ya canna lie fer yer life." Bertha cleared the table, and Joan and Faye helped; they enjoyed the time they spent with her. "Faye, can ya tell me how much ya know of Tommy's and yer dad's business?"

"Auntie B, Uncle Tommy and Dad save people and children that were stolen from their homes."

"I thank ya, Faye, but I know ya know more'n yer tellen me." Bertha left the kitchen just as Carol came in.

"Grams, I need to know what you want for your two guest rooms, you know, colour, furniture style, wallpaper, no wallpaper, wall colour . . ." She was laughing. "You know what I mean, don't you?"

"Sweetie, come in. I've pictures ta show ya." She motioned to Faye and Joan to follow her also. Bertha had taken pictures of different styles of furniture and bedding as well as colours out of magazines. One was a French provincial style in white wood, with mint-green bedding and green walls. Another was a Norwegian style in blonde wood, with blue bedding and grey walls. She told Carol she preferred the French provincial style, but could they do each room in different woods, one dark, one light. They all agreed that would suit the house and her taste.

"Auntie, on the white wood, could you do extremely dark blue coverings and maybe some wallpaper for accent?" said Joan.

"I love this idea. Grams, what do you think?"

"Carol, ya no think it too dark fer that room?"

"No, Grams, it would be perfect. I'll pass it on to Denny. She will get a colour wheel over to you so you can see the different blues and some paper samples." She said her goodbyes to everyone and left.

Faye hoped this would make Auntie B think of other stuff, not the damned jobs her dad and uncle were doing. Bertha patted her arm and said, "Carol's away, we have ta talk, an' I'm counten on ya ta git the boys ta own up an' tell me the truth."

"Do you need to know the bad things, Auntie B? Do you need to know the pain they go through to save people? Just know, yes, it's dangerous. Yes, they know how to do what they do. It is not a small thing. The FBI wishes could do what Dad and Uncle Tom do, and catch the bad people like they do. They are the heads, but there are so many people that work for them. I would love to be one of them, but I know my dad and uncle will never allow it."

Bertha leaned on the wall and turned white.

"Uncle Tom, Dad, anyone, Auntie is fainting in the hall!" Faye yelled as she held Bertha against herself and the wall. Tommy was the fastest; he had Bertha in his arms and laid her on the sofa.

"What the hell happened, Faye? What did you tell her." He was so upset. Faye was scared she did wrong.

Marcus told her, "There is nothing to fear, Faye. He is worried about Bertha."

"I told her some of the truth, not the bad things, just that you save people and capture bad ones. I told her she didn't need to know the awful things that happened. Was I wrong, Dad? I love Auntie B even though we just met her this month. She is like the grandmother we never had."

Tommy carried Bertha into their bedroom. "Carol, could you make her some of her favourite tea, please?"

"Sure thing, Gramps. Faye, you and Joan want to help?" She hoped to find out what the hell was Faye talking about—bad things, bad people. Joan went with her, but Faye sat quietly with her dad.

"Dad, I'm not a small child even though at times I act it. I didn't think Auntie was either. Is she too delicate to be told what trouble and pain are and what the men and women that work for you go through?"

"Believe me, Faye, she knows all too well. Do you know of the story that hit the papers about a year ago, big splash on how the FBI worked with the US Army to capture Stewart King?"

"Yes, Walt had it on his wall, said he was his hero. Why?"

"That man was Bertha's illegitimate son. He tried to kill her and her whole family. He was Liz's first husband. Auntie didn't know about that until she met with Liz's dad, who wanted her to work until Liz's baby was born and maybe after.

"Oh, Dad, I'm so sorry for her and Uncle Tommy. It must have been terrible."

Bertha answered for him. "'Twas terrible, an' I no want ta live wit that kinda fear an' pain er agin. So here's ta ya all, ya do as ya do. Tommy telled me 'tis a good thing. That's why we caught Stewart. Ya keep the bad and the why ya do oot me hoose, an I can live wit it. Now where's me tea? Carol, are ya haven one wit me?"

Tommy looked at Marcus. Carol heard everything, well, almost. And sure as the stars shine above, Bertha was about to tell her all about it. They walked into the kitchen in time to hear Bertha tell Carol that the new construction company that Marcus started was dangerous because it was high, tall buildings, and he was up on the top of them with Marcus, scared her half to death it did. Tommy thought that for someone who did not tell lies, she was getting damn good at it.

A call from Marcus's men told them that Zelda and the brother had been captured. The brother was not as backward as they thought; he spilled the whole bag of beans on his keeper, as he called her. He would be glad to have a new worker. Zelda went for the same ride as the other two. No more human dinners for her.

Chapter Six

CAROL HAD A date with Doug tonight; they were going to a light opera in Baltimore, so she was in a hurry to dress for the occasion. Denny told her to wear an after-five dress, no floor length; they didn't do that anymore. Carol knew she was falling for Doug. Her heart was filling up with thoughts of him. She very rarely thought of Tony anymore, and that too surprised her. These two weeks had been marvelous, and she did not want them to stop. She hoped he felt the same.

They went to dinner after the opera. Carol thought the opera meant Italian singing and weird costumes. She enjoyed it so much. "I loved it all. I must say I was surprised that it was in English and modern dress. The word *opera* to me means that old-style dress and loud singing."

Doug laughed. "Yes, I thought so too, but my stepmom took me to my first, it was about teenage boys and getting into trouble." They chatted about the trip home, and he asked her if she would like to go out again on Sunday afternoon; there was an art show at the high school he would like to visit. She agreed to go even though she knew the art would be the same as it had been for the last five or six years.

Caitlin called her and asked what was up, how the opera was. "Hey, Cat, it was pretty good. It was all in English, and they wore modern clothes."

"Are you behind the times, girl? He did say light opera, didn't he?"

"Yes, so what has that got to do with it?"

"Oh, Mouse, light opera is singing but not long-hair kind of crap. Go on your computer and look it up. You didn't say anything dumb to him, did you?"

"Well, yes, I told him I was surprised they didn't have funny costumes and loud voices."

Cat started to laugh. "That's my Mouse for you, sweetie. Are you seeing him again anytime soon? I hope."

"Yes, we are going to the art show at the high school."

"Do me a favour, wear something sexy and look like you want him."

"Not on your life, you are so bad, Cat. I think I could easily care for this man. Doug makes me feel good about myself."

Cat sure hoped so; Carol had such a raw deal with Tony, and she was still shy. She sure didn't look shy on the dance floor at the wedding though. "I have to go, Mouse, time for my shift at the station, and I have an FBI agent coming in to talk to me about the break-in at Marcus's house."

"Let me know how it goes, Cat. See you."

He so much wanted and needed to get into that house. There was something not quite right about this break-in, and the FBI wanted to know what the brothers were up to now. Not that they didn't do good for their country or for the people who hired them, they just seemed to know things before the FBI did.

He introduced himself to the sergeant at the desk, asked to speak to the officer in charge of the Marcus McCloud case.

Caitlin came out from the bullpen and introduced herself. "Hi, I'm Caitlin Jones. What can I do for you, Mr. Franc?"

"I would like and need to see anything you have of the Marcus McCloud break-in."

Cat took him to her desk and explained there were only two detectives in the station, and she covered the street and one of the desks. She showed him the pictures taken at the scene, one of the dead men, whom they had not identified as yet, two or three of the holes in the ceiling, and of course the stab wound on Pablo's butt cheek. He was not happy to have that photographed, with promises no one but the St. Helen police would see it. Cat started to laugh. "Sorry, just the thought of being stabbed in the backside, then trying to sit on it . . ."

Franc had to admit as he laughed the image his mind conjured up. "That is going to hurt for one hell of a long time, and his job as private secretary to McCloud means sitting, don't you think?" They were both laughing then and being looked at as if they were disturbing someone's peace. "Would it be improper to ask you to coffee while we talk about this case?"

"No, not at all, there's a coffee shop just two blocks from here. We can walk if you don't mind. I need the exercise. I do the road checks, too much driving." The coffee shop was not a national-brand company but just a mom-and-pop shop that served coffee, tea, pop, and lots of donuts and sweets made by Martha, one of the owners; she wanted to be a pastry chef but opened this coffee shop instead, as she loved to be with people.

They sat at a table for two at the back of the shop, with coffee and, of course, donuts. "Did you get anything on Thomas McCloud, Caitlin? We have no prints or even his signature."

Caitlin told Franc, "All the officers' paperwork is Thomas McCloud's statement, and fingerprints are gone with all the rest of my casework. It is not there."

"This is not the first time I have been told this. Somehow that man manages to get anything he says, signs, or pictures of him, to just disappear from the paperwork completely. That includes us as well."

"I know he is slick and he is smart. Did you ever notice how quick that man can move for his age?"

"Caitlin, do you know how old he is? Because none of us at the FBI know, we cannot find a birth certificate on either brother. We know they are twins, and another brother is a drunk, but we cannot find any information on any of them. The drunk, Daniel—all we know is he is the youngest, but his age, where he was born, nothing. Even his marriage certificate is so blurred it's illegible."

"Wow, I knew he was secretive, but that is going some. Marcus told me that he would be home by twelve noon at the latest because they had a family breakfast meeting going on with his daughters and Mr. and Mrs. McCloud. I'll give Bertha a call to see how it's going.

"Hey, Grams, it's Cat. How's the meeting going? I have an agent here that wants to see Marcus and your hubby. Are they available to see him around noonish maybe?"

"Oh, hey yerself, Cat, 'tis done, the meeten, an' they jest left ta go ta Marcus's hoose. You can git them there."

"Thanks, Grams, love ya, bye."

"You call Mrs. McCloud Grams. Why?"

"I have known her since I was five or six years old. I went to school with her grandson Robert King, the pest. He loves to tease. We found out she was his grandmother when we went after Stewart King. He is, or was, her unwed son. She gave him up at birth, and he never forgave her for it, you knew that."

"Nope, did not know—it is not on this case, so I have not been privy to that. Do you know them well, Caitlin, or it's just a small town, and everybody knows everybody else?"

"No, I know them because I grew up in her kitchen because I was a scout in Robert's troop. I got whacked aplenty for picking on the boys because Bertha taught the boys they could not hit girls. That's not to say she couldn't." They both laughed at that.

Coffee and donuts done, they headed over to Marcus's house, hoping to get a bird's eye view of the events of last night. "Marcus, Tommy, this is Agent Jon Franc of the FBI."

Tommy looked at him and said, "Aren't you the officer that worked the case in Washington for us about two years ago, Franc, or was it someone that looks just like you?"

"Yes, sir, that was me. I was a junior agent then, not even up far enough to get called special, if you recall."

Marcus replied, "Yes, but good enough to help us solve the damn case before your buddies did."

"I did do that, and for that, I got a demerit for helping you, not them." They all laughed.

"Sure you wouldn't like to work for us, Jon? We pay better."

"If I ever decide to move from Baltimore, I will take you up on that. Can you show me where the break-in happened, please, and Tommy, do you know where the report from last night on your statement and signature went? Caitlin seems to think that the unfortunate officer that took your information lost it."

"I didn't see it after I signed it, Cat, sorry, hope she finds it."

"Here's the hole where they came in. You have one in custody, don't you, Cat? The other fell and broke his neck, and I admit to wrestling him to the floor. It is all in the report Maggie took."

"There are no other places they could have come in. Can I have a look around?"

"Sure. Pablo, would you mind showing them the main part of the house? I'm afraid the basement is undergoing abatement of asbestos now. They won't let you down there. They won't let anyone, for that matter. All I wanted was to put a gym in down there. Getting a little full around the middle, and I don't like it. Look at my brother, thin and no belly."

Cat laughed. "Wait, Marcus, he's married to Grams now. He will fatten up right nicely. I know I had to go to the gym after staying out there for two weeks."

Tommy gave her a hug. "You may be right, my girl, you may be right. She is making me chicken and dumplings for dinner with strawberry shortcake. Want to come for dinner? Bring Franc with you. He never gets a decent meal."

"You better ask Grams first there, Gramps. She may not want the company."

"When have you ever known her to make too little at any given time?"

"Just call, please, Gramps."

He did that right there. "Bertha, me love, is it all right with you if there are two more for dinner, Cat and her friend Jon Franc from the FBI?"

"Sure, I always have ta much anyways. Tell 'em ta come along fer dinner at six." Franc just stood there, amazed at how friendly he still was to him. They had not left friends two years ago. Pablo walked with a slight limp up the stairs and showed them where it all took place.

"Did you see any of this happen, Pablo?"

"No, Mr. Franc, I was on the first floor in the study near the kitchen when I heard the commotion. When I got there, the man fell through the hole while Mr. Tom was wrestling with the first man, the second stabbed me in the rear end, and no, Cat, I am not showing you where."

Franc had to put his hand over his mouth because he was going to burst out laughing as Caitlin was doing. "But, Pablo, I need a picture for my files." She lost it then; she burst out laughing.

Pablo gave her a look that would kill. He told them to follow him if they wanted to see any more of the house. If not, then they could meet the brothers in the front foyer, as they were getting ready to leave to get Mr. Marcus's daughters from the mall. They followed him downstairs.

Cat could not resist. "Which cheek did they reach you in, Pablo?"

He kept walking; not a word escaped his lips, but Franc was sure he had a few in mind for her right then. When they reached the car, he said to her, "I thought you said Robert was the prankster, or joker."

"He was, but I was just as bad, sometimes worse. That is why Bertha would whack me the most. My mother thanked her many times over for it. My mother was not a good mom. She was a drug abuser, and Bertha was there for me whenever I needed it."

"Can I pick you up to go out to the McClouds' for dinner as I have not a clue where they live?"

"Sure, I'll be at the station. Pick me up there, okay?"

"Sure thing, and why the name Cat?"

"Tell you all about it tonight. I'm sure Carol and the rest of the family will be there, with the exception of the honeymooners. They will be back next week."

They arrived just after five thirty. Marcus was playing gin rummy with his daughters. Robert and Denny, Bertha, Tommy, and Carol were in the most beautiful kitchen Cat had ever seen. "Wow, Carol, you outdid yourself. What a beautiful kitchen."

Bertha was beaming. "Tis a beauty, is it no? I jest love it, ner had so many a thing ta do me werk fer me."

Franc could listen to that woman talk forever; she spoke so melodiously. Carol turned around, and Cat introduced her to Franc. "Mouse, this is Jon Franc from the FBI. Jon, this is Carol Jones, more commonly known as Mouse. When we were kids, we were like peas in a pod, except I was always bold as brass and my best friend here was bashful. We became Cat and her Mouse."

Franc felt for this woman; her face was deep red, and she just stood there. "God, Caitlin, could you not give her a break now? She doesn't look like a mouse to me."

"Nor to me—hi, I'm Douglas Park. I work for Tom and Marcus in their financial department."

Franc thought, *Damn, someone who might shed light on this company's goings-on but not*. This guy would not tell you if they had two cents or two million dollars each.

Everyone chipped in to set the table and take the dinner into the dining room. There were so many people. Bertha was in her glory; she loved to cook, and she was learning so much from Carol about how to present the food so it looks too good to eat. Carol taught her about different seasonings and herbs for meats and vegetables.

She was grateful that Liz, Carol, and Denny had talked her into this large table that sat sixteen people; right now, there were eleven plus wee Bessie running around, getting treats from every one of them.

Bertha looked at Franc and told him, “There’s ta be nery a werd of business at me table. ’Tis a place fer peace an fellowship, ’tis all.”

“I agree, Mrs. McCloud, whole-heartedly.”

Bertha was looking at Cat and thought, *’Tis time ta give her a bite of her own.* “Caitlin, ya needs ta keep this’n on a leash fer yerself. Ya ner want ta lose a good man like this.”

Cat choked on her water and was beet red for the first time in her life. Not one person at the table felt terrible for her, but they did laugh at and with her. “Okay, Grams, I got the message: lay off Carol for a while. I get it.”

“Good, now eat yer supper.” Conversation was light and comfortable throughout the meal. The ladies of the house made the coffee and tea, and Bertha and the twins brought in the dessert.

“Anyone not wanting their dessert can pass on down to me,” Joanie told them. Everyone was in awe of the piles of strawberries on top of billowy whipped cream; somewhere under that was a simple white cake. They told Joan she was out of luck; they were not giving theirs up for anyone.

Cleaning up, the guys brought out the dishes, and the girls loaded the double dishwasher, one strictly for plates and cutlery, the other for pots and pans, roaster and the like, strong like the restaurant washers. Bertha loved it. She didn’t have to scrub the pots or fry pans anymore. Liz was jealous; she wanted one. Tommy told Carol to have it installed for Liz before they got home as a wedding gift.

They were just deciding if they wanted to play games or just sit and talk when the explosion shook the house. It felt like the whole town blew up; Bertha managed to grab a picture of her and Tommy at their wedding before it hit the floor. Joan held the lamp beside her; it was wobbling back and forth. Marcus and Tom were up and heading for the door along with Jon Franc and Caitlin. Her radio box on her shoulder squealed. She answered it. "Caitlin here."

"There has been a house explosion on the north side of the city. It's Mr. McCloud's house. We don't know if anyone was in it."

Cat looked at Marcus. He shook his head no. "Cat here, no one in the house. They are here at his brother's. His staff is off because of remediation of asbestos in the basement. He, his brother, Agent Franc, and I are heading there now."

They arrived only to find rubble left. Marcus was worried. Did they get the boy-man out of there before this happened, and did Zelda get away from their men and do this? He looked at Tom and saw he was thinking the same.

"Marcus, I'll go around back and check to make sure no one in the back of your property was hurt or any animals." Jon spoke up and said he would join him. They started around the side of the property, hoping that the sidewalk was still concrete. Jon asked Tommy if he was used to being in the backyard or side because it didn't look safe. "Yes, I have been. There is a dip in the walk just before you enter the backyard, but I don't know if it is still there." Jon took his flashlight out of his pocket and shone it on the ground; right in front of them was the dip, but it was now a hole, large enough to fall in. "Glad you had that flash, boyo. We both would have gone for a tumble."

"More than a tumble, Tommy, look." It showed the floor of the basement and a leg of someone, and it moved. "Hello, can you hear us? Can we get to you?"

It was Pablo. "Oh, I sure hope so, boss. I'm just under this large hunk of concrete. If you can move it, I can try to climb out."

"Don't move. That slab may not be stable, and it will crush you." Tom called Marcus and told him to get some men and machines;

Pablo was in the basement under a slab of concrete. Tommy crawled down to Pablo. He wanted to see how bad the man was and anyone else down there that the FBI should know info on.

"Jackson, are you okay? I mean, can you feel your leg, anything else stuck or broke besides your ass?"

"Funny, boss, ha ha ha."

"Are you alone down here? Have we still guests I have to worry about?"

"No, your other guest was taken to a home of Marcus's choice, and Zelda was taken on the plane for her drop to never-never land."

"Do you know if that trip was a success, Jackson, you know what I mean?"

"I sure do. If I could reach my phone, I could show you."

"What happened down here, then?"

Jackson pointed to the water heater; it was the new one Marcus had put in, three times the size of a standard house heater, but girls like long showers, and he hated cold ones. "It blossomed like a flower, and being that it was gas, it went up like a phoenix bird, all flames."

He called up to Jon. "There is only Pablo down here. He heard the rumbling and went down to investigate. The new hot-water heater just blew up. Can you tell Marcus to call the gas company to shut off the gas?"

Tommy called Bertha, asked if the girls could stay; it was terrible, the house was gone, and well, they were homeless for now. She told him it would be fine, but everyone would be sleeping at Liz's house as they did not have the beds for all three of them. That would be fine with him and with his brother, as he thought he would have to hire a hotel for all of them at this time of night.

Jon was not buying the hot water blow-up, so he called in their own men to check the damn thing out. He had a feeling things were not right. Caitlin came up behind him.

"Are you worried about the gas or something else happening?"

"I'm more worried there is something else going on, and I can't put my finger on it."

"You think the boys are up to something, and you either want in or catch them doing something you can arrest them for."

He laughed at her; she had the most incredible smile and the most beautiful eyes he had ever seen. Jon stood there looking at her.

"Have you memorized every freckle yet, or shall I stand here for a little longer?"

He gave her a light punch in the arm and turned red. "I just happen to like your smile and your beautiful eyes, that's all."

She walked toward the back of the house, and he grabbed her just before she fell in the hole. "Thanks, where did that come from?"

"I can't believe a water heater could do all this damage."

"Yes, they can and more. Marcus just told me he had the largest one made put in just before the abatement. Apparently, the girls love long hot showers. He does not like short cold ones." This made him roar.

"Nice, Cat, that was a good one."

"No, I am serious. Even Faye told me she felt bad for him. He would try to curse quietly while freezing in the shower."

"Are you laughing at me, Caitlin, because I hate cold showers? Not even after chasing a lady did I take a cold shower." Twice in one night, Cat's face turned red; she was glad it was dark on that side of the house. The gas people arrived and shut the gas off at the street. Pablo was grateful there were enough of them to help

Tommy and Marcus lift the huge slab of concrete of his leg. "Best take him to the hospital, sir, it does not look good."

"I'll take him," Cat told everyone. To her surprise, she got a response she was not used to getting.

"No, you won't. If I want to go, I will get there under my own initiative, thank you. I am not your charity case, officer." He held on to Tommy and limped away.

"Wow, I was just told off for no good reason."

Marcus spoke up and told her, "Pablo does not trust police officers because they arrested his sister for being a streetwalker because she was Spanish, and they abused her. She killed herself because she was ruined for her future husband. She was walking home from church when it happened. The two officers got a slap on the wrist as far as Pablo was concerned. They got three months no pay and were confined to their homes."

"Speaking of home, I had better get you there so I can find a place for my head tonight."

"You can stay with Bertha and me. Marcus and the girls are staying at Liz's house."

"Settled, then."

The three men spoke on the way back; Jon told them he felt bad not getting Caitlin to her home. "You would have taken her to the station. She would never allow you to take her to her apartment. She is still a little leery of men," Tommy told him. "Her fiancé was killed just over two years ago by a burglar, and she is what you call gun-shy of anyone near her home."

"Marcus, were you kidding about the hot-water heater? Because you made her face so red, I could feel the heat from it."

"No, I meant it. Those girls stay in the shower for half an hour or more each, mind you. I go in, and guess what? No damn hot water. A man of my age does not like cold showers unless it is absolutely necessary."

"Then you had better shower over at our house. There are three women over at Liz's right now." All of them started to laugh, until the next explosion hit so hard it shook the car.

Tommy pulled over and called someone on his phone. "Just what the hell just happened? A different house, what?" He started turning around and then said to the two men, "Your house just blew up again. This time, there is no hot-water heater to blame, Marcus." Jon thought, *What the hell was left to blow up?*

Tommy looked at Marcus and said, "It was number two that went."

"All right, what the hell is number two? And don't say shit."

Marcus saw no way around it. "The operative word here is a second basement that held cells for people of a threatening nature, so to speak, ones we needed to get information from. That is what went up, and I'll be damned if I know what caused that. There is no hot-water tank down there. Tommy, was Pablo down there?"

"No, he's the one I spoke to. Doc says his leg is broke, but he can manage on crutches in a few days, then he would put on a walking boot for him."

Jon was quick with that. "What doctor? He didn't go to the hospital, so what doctor?"

"What in God's name made you think Marcus would not make him go to the hospital, Jon? You know we have men all over, so yes, he was taken, and yes, he will be all right at my home this night. If you question him, you do it in front of me because he will not answer you otherwise, got it?"

Chapter Seven

BERTHA WELCOMED THE two men in and asked if they would like a tea or a coffee. Tommy and Marcus opted for tea, strong please, Bertha. Jon asked if she had ice water, please.

"When will Pablo get here, Tommy?" asked Marcus.

"Doc said as soon as the plaster is dry enough. Doc will bring him out, wants to say howdy to his favourite patient, Bertha."

"'Tis no true. He jest likes me scones, 'tis all," she remarked. "Jon, are you staying here as well? Ya see, he ner told me on the phone. Ya'll have the den, tis got a water closet fer ya. Marcus, yers does too. Now I'm off ta bed, an' tells Doc me regards." She left them alone. Bertha did not want to know anything of their talk this night.

Marcus explained to Jon about Zelda and the mentally challenged man. He also told him about his daughters and their mother and grandmother. He was hoping Jon knew something they didn't. When Marcus mentioned the grandfather, McKellen, he showed signs of real interest. "You do mean Walter McKellen, middle name Mason?"

"Yes, we do. Why?"

"He is wanted in ten states, as well as Canada, Australia, and France for the human flesh trade. His wife helped him, still does."

"You got that wrong, mister. My uterus was butchered in front of my sister, cooked and eaten while she had to watch while tied to a pole naked. Our grandmother was done the same. I had to watch that. It is his girlfriend, Zelda, who continues in this trade. She eats nothing but human meat. Zelda also runs money laundering out of Montego Bay for the mob and for herself. So no, his wife does not have anything to do with it. She was the housekeeper and cleaner along with our mother. We became the keepers and cleaners until I thought the FBI broke in to save a set of twins. They did not know the sex of the so-called twins, so they took all four of us. When they asked my sister, Joan, if she spoke Spanish, she told them no, we were not Spanish, and they just cut us loose, end of story, until Joan's boyfriend tried to kill Dad at Aunt Liz's wedding. Now, Mr. whoever you are, you got it straight?"

"Yes, Faye, I do thank you."

Marcus wanted to cry, empty his stomach, and crawl in a hole for what Jon said about her mother and for the horrendous pain she and her sister had to live through. Faye turned to her Dad. "Can you come speak to Joan? She is having trouble sleeping." He walked with her to Tommy's house. "Anything left of our home, Dad? Is Pablo okay?" She was crying and shaking. He pulled her to him and held her, and explained what happened. She didn't say a word, but he knew what she was thinking: the first home, real home, they had, and it was now gone. They crossed the back lawn, and he told Faye how Pablo was and that they would search the rubble if there was anything of value she wanted or that Joan wanted. "All I need is the blue boxes. They hold every case and every sale of meat that she made. All her returning customers, everything you need to know about Zelda and Walt is there."

Pablo arrived with Dr. Kline. He was not surprised Bertha wasn't around. "Tom, does she know I work for your organization?" Dr. Kline asked.

"No, Mark, and it stays that way. She abhors violence, and we keep it away from her."

"Pablo said to give this to you and Marcus. It's the sealed boxes. The rest are in my car."

"It's Faye's. She will be glad it's safe. I guess she kept records of the old man's doings."

Marcus came back; you could see his cheeks were wet and his eyes were red. He was surprised that the boxes were there. "Pablo told him that he knew how important they were to her, so he put them in one of the cells just in case."

"In case I went down the first basement?" Jon asked.

"Yes, she was so protective of them. When I asked her about it, she told me it was Master Walt's whole life, from learning how to butcher until she was rescued."

Jon thought, *How can anyone stand it, living through such horror?* "Marcus, are the girls okay? You know what I mean."

"As Faye put it, she is almost sane. Joan, on the other hand, may never be right again."

Denny announced that she and Robert were getting married in a small chapel outside Baltimore and honeymooning there. "The immediate family will be attending. We don't want a large affair like Mitch and Liz had."

Bertha hugged her and kissed both of her cheeks. "Congrats, me darlin', where's me grandson so's I can give him a hug an' a kiss?"

"Sleeping, of course, Grams, I just couldn't wait for his highness to arise from bed to tell you."

"Why the rush now, me girl? Three weeks—'tis a short time."

Denny whispered in her ear as she hugged Grams to her, "Because Jeffery's little sister or brother is on the way. The pill the doctor gave me did not work. Robert is so proud of himself. We are not telling anyone else until Mom and Dad are back tomorrow. Richard is walking me down the aisle. He says he's the only one that can give me away."

Everyone enjoyed the feast of a breakfast. Jon was not used to eating like this, but he tucked in and did his best. "Bertha, these buns, they are fabulous." He got a swat for calling them buns.

"They are scones. 'Tis no a bun. Ner call a scone a bun."

"Okay, scones it is. They are great!" After the clearing up, Bertha asked the men to take their conversation into the den.

Marcus called to Faye. "Can you follow us and help Pablo along with his crutches?"

"I don't think I will ever get used to you being called Pablo. Did Dad ask you to?"

"No, I am of Spanish heritage. No one pays attention to Pablo clearing off plates when the McCloud brothers leave the room. That is why they call me that, and I play the shy Mexican doing my job and keeping my nose clean."

"I missed you after you ran away from the house when I was a young teen. I wanted to go with you, but I couldn't leave my family behind."

Pablo said, "I know, Faye, but I had to get out of there or go insane, and what they were doing to me and you and Joan, I—oh, I can't talk about it, Faye. I'm still not right."

"They are all gone now. If Dad and Uncle Tom use those boxes, they will catch all the other meat traders."

Joan was following her and Jackson. "Why are we going to the den to talk to Dad, Faye?"

"Joan, can you keep Auntie B and Denny busy while the men talk and I run errands for them, please?"

"Sure, Faye, and I will get her to show us how to make tea and coffee, then when you want it, I will have made it." Faye nodded and watched her walk back to the kitchen.

"Will she ever be all right, Faye?" Jackson asked.

"This bombing was not just the hot-water tank, although it was set up to look like it was. There must be someone trying to take over Zelda's operation. I sure as hell hope not. People will die over this, and there will be a lot of them. He or she can build the business back up from her losses."

It was a mouse in the corner that answered the question. "It's the brother that acts like he is mentally disabled so he can learn all he can from the people in the room just like Jackson does. I watched him. He writes it down and gives it to Zelda. She reads it to herself and tells Walt, or not, depending on what it is. Then she throws them in the garbage. I have them all if you want them." Joan was so quiet no one heard her come in.

Faye asked her, "Where are they, sweetie? I'll go get them."

"I never put them down. I keep them with me always in my head, and I repeat them to myself every day and every night. Sometimes I can't sleep because of them."

Faye asked for pen and paper from her uncle. "Can you write them down for me, please, Joan? You didn't tell Jason about these, did you?"

"No, I knew you would be angry with me if I did." She sat at Auntie B's desk and wrote and spoke to herself as she did; she filled four sheets of paper with all the notes he passed to Zelda. "Here they are. I won't have to repeat them anymore, will I, Faye?" she asked.

Faye was trying not to cry. "No, my sweet sister, you won't ever again. You can forget whatever they say."

"Okay, did anyone want tea or coffee? Auntie B taught me how to make it." They all said they did.

The first thing Tommy did was to contact the hospital Marcus sent the man to. "Could you tell me if the patient brought to you by Marcus McCloud is doing all right?"

"He was released the day after he was admitted. He was normal, passed every possible test we threw at him. There was nothing wrong with him. He told us he did it because his sister made him do it, and now, he didn't have to because she was dead."

"He is on the loose, and we have no idea what the hell his name is. We don't even know if he is from the same place as his sister."

Jackson said, "Oh, but we do. In the boxes of Faye's were visas for Zelda and her brother, Walt, and his wife. The brother's name is Zion Bertram—age now would be forty-two, born in Holland, New Jersey."

Tommy kissed his head. "Way to go, Pablo."

"Not me. Faye—she collected all this shit, not me."

Tommy looked at her. "Why, Faye? Did you hope to use it someday against them and for what?"

"So I could put them in jail for all the things they did to people and my family. That's why. Look at my sister, talk to Jackson. He was there. Did you not know that we all suffered daily, some more than others?" She was referring to Joan. "Every day without a memory is a blessing, every time one of them dies is a blessing. So don't think we do not understand what the hell is going on. We go get that son of a bitch, and he flies just like his sister."

Jackson said, "No, Faye, he was Walt's brother. His sister promised him that he would become the new master when Walt died. He liked little boys to play with, and then he would eat them. Now how do we find him, and who would protect him?"

The answer came from Joan, the one everyone was worried about. "You can find him in his parents' home in Florida. They stay there all the time. He talked about it to his playmates. It's just outside of Lakeland, near the baseball parks. It is on Hall Avenue, third house on the left side of the street. He keeps his souvenirs there. Every playmate he had has a bone. He usually favoured a finger."

Marcus and Tommy went into Tommy's office and decided to capture Zion. Then he needed to fly like his lady friend. They needed some normalcy in their lives. Marcus went into the kitchen and asked Carol how soon could she start his new house and what amount of cash she needed down. He told her he would take care of the basement because they were being cleared of asbestos. He would do everything up to the main floor. If she could draft a two- or three-story house for him, he would be thrilled. Carol was excited to do this for Marcus.

They got the call: "The newlyweds will be landing at the airport in the morning at nine fifteen. Please be there to pick them up."

Robert and Denny were at the airport for eight forty-five just in case the plane was early. "Robert, do we tell them about the wedding, then the baby or baby then wedding?" She was so happy; things were going to work out for them finally.

Robert said, "Let's take it one step at a time. First, we see what kind of mood they are in: good, overtired, you know what I mean. Suppose things look like they are happy to be home and they are in good moods. Well, we blab everything all at once." He kissed her and hugged her to him. She was his life; she made all the bad go away.

The plane landed on time. Mitch and Liz came off the ramp, looking happy and refreshed. Robert brought the car up, and they loaded the luggage in the trunk. Liz and Denny got in the back, and Mitch got in the front with Robert. "Nice to see you, son, sure missed you and Denny. We brought you some cute things from Canada eh."

Liz said to him, "Stop that. Not all Canadians say that, just the ones that work in the stores."

"You look a little tired, Denise. Are you all right?"

"I'm fine, Mom, ready, willing, and able to get married."

"What's this about, Robert?"

"Pull into a restaurant, and we can talk without Bertha wanting to know how everything was." Robert chose one that was not crowded and had tables, not booths. "We are planning on getting married in three weeks just outside of Baltimore, in a pretty small chapel, Mom. It is what we want, just the family, not a lot of hoopla and carrying on."

"The reason for this, son?" Mitch asked.

Denny answered him, with a big smile, "I'm pregnant, and I'm only about five weeks. So we want to do it before Mother decides to start her crap again and lose our baby. I found out from my doctor why I lost Jeffery, and Mother is to blame. So please, can we do this our way?"

"Yes, of course, it's your wedding, not ours. We will do whatever you two need."

Denny hugged her and cried, "We are getting married in three weeks. Can you handle that, Robert?"

"Yes, my love, I can."

Everyone was at the house; they had planned a breakfast party for the family and the attendees except the kids; they were in school. Mitch grabbed a large mug of Bertha's tea and chugged it. "Nothing tastes like your tea, Mom. Sure missed it."

Bertha, Tommy, Carol, the twins, and Pablo made the most enormous breakfast ever, even a dessert. They were talking to everyone all at once. Liz said, "High tea at the Empress was so special, like having tea with royalty: small tables, your waiter making your tea, and each of us getting our own pot and timer. Mom, he timed it for the strength of the tea and so many petits fours on a three-layer plate."

"We even got to feed their dog that roams around the front desk area," Mitch told them. "We went whale watching, and one went right under our boat. Liz got pictures of them on her phone. She would not cross the swinging bridge with me though, had to do that myself. We did so many things and saw so much. It will take us forever to tell you all about it." They carried on for nearly four hours before Liz said she needed another coffee.

When she left the room to get her coffee, Tommy told her of the bombing and that they had house guests, as well as they did. "When did this happen, Tommy?" Liz asked.

"Two nights ago, but the girls have been used and abused, so if they seem rude or abrupt, forgive them, please."

"Bertha knows little of what the girls have been through, so don't ask her. She is having a hard time with Marcus's house being blown up not once but twice."

Marcus caught Mitch letting Bessie out for a walk and explained what had happened and as much as he could about the girls. "Holy shit, Marcus, do we know who?"

"Yes, and we are working on it, but I want everyone safe. The kids don't know, and I thought it best they didn't."

"Denny just told us she is expecting again, and they are getting married in three weeks. So that is the deadline: three weeks, and this is done. I do not want to lose another grandchild to stress, fear, and nerves. You tell Tommy, Marcus, I mean it."

Marcus knew Mitch was more upset than he thought he would be. Tommy was right, Mitch would help, but he would want it done ASAP. Bertha knew some but must be kept out of all other plans. "I am getting too damn old for this crap, and I know it," he told himself.

Chapter Eight

DENNY SHOWED LIZ the dress she had found; it fit like a glove, and she didn't have to wait to get it. It was a plain satin, with some lace at the neckline, and at the bottom of the gown, it had a train of about six feet long. It suited her to a T. "Grams made my veil and headpiece, and it is so beautiful. Mom, I cannot wait." She was floating on air.

"Who do you want to walk you down the aisle, Denny? I know Mitch would love to, so would Tommy."

"Richard is walking me, Mom. He told me it was his job as my brother and the fact that he loves us so much."

"Oh, Denny, that's so great. Does Mom know about the baby? I know she will worry about you day and night until this little one is born."

"Grams knows, and she is so happy for us."

"Who is standing for you, Denny?"

Denny replied, "Carol is my maid of honour, and Caitlin is my bridesmaid. Robert is having Stan and Doug stand for him."

They would not have a big rehearsal dinner or anything like that, just dinner with the family. On the day of the wedding, they were going to a restaurant just outside of the chapel so they could have dinner with them and a cake to cut. They were going from there to a B and B for three nights and then coming home.

Liz said, "You two have it all planned. Let us know what you want us to do. We would feel bad if we couldn't help out." Liz and Bertha kept their promise: only after-five dress, no gowns—this was to let the bride shine.

She wanted to be the only one. "Please, Mom, Grams, just the bride in a long gown and train, okay?" They had agreed, so they were off looking for an outfit.

Bertha nudged Liz to go behind the dress rack. "Liz, 'tis herself, Margaret Foubert. I canna go another roond of badness out the likes of her." They stood there and heard what she said to the other woman: "I heard through my hairdresser that Denise and that cheap imitation of a rich man are getting married. I asked Richard, but he refuses to speak to us. They are not getting married here in St. Helen. She is probably pregnant again, can't keep her legs closed." Margaret and the other woman walked to the exit of the store. Margaret had a dress covered by her coat over her arm. They walked to the store's door marked "departure" and left.

Bertha wanted to report her, when the store clerk said to the cashier, "Dress number 10711 costs two hundred ten dollars, charge it to his account. If he refuses, this time I have pictures, and I will charge her this time. This is the tenth dress she's taken."

Liz would have loved to report her to Caitlin, but Denise did not need any upset, not now. The clerk came over to them. "I'm sorry, Liz, but she thinks her son is going to pay for that dress. He has told us no more. He has paid for her stealing all over town long enough. That dress will cost him a lot of money. We feel for him and his sister. Denny did the same as Richard for years until she moved out of her parental home. How is she? We never see her anymore."

"Oh, Moreen, she is fine, going to architectural interior design school, seems she has a flair for it."

"Is it true she's getting married to Robert? I sure hope so. They make such a lovely couple."

"I can't say, Moreen. I don't know. Nothing has been told to us about it." Liz never lied like that, but for their sake, she did with no regret. News like that would fly through the town like wildfire, making Margaret the star attraction once more.

"Moreen, 'tis true, then, she may be leaven our wee toon? I hered that jest yesterday wit Tommy at the greengrocer."

"I hadn't heard, but you may be right. Their son has bought out all their holdings. It seems his father was proven to be involved with Tony Detello."

They left without buying anything. Bertha decided to shorten the dress she wore for Liz's wedding. She liked it so much. "Mom, I'm going to Baltimore with Mitch next week. I'll look there. Do we tell Denny what we heard before someone else does? Her baby is more important than her parents, and they are not going to do it again to that wonderful girl."

Bertha told her, "We leave wit no a truth, so's we have no a word ta repeat."

"Good enough, Mom, let's go do lunch with the kids."

"No, we're ta meet the twins ta help git dresses."

"Okay, then home for a tea and coffee. Do you have any scones left from breakfast?" Liz sulked.

"Ya know I do. Are ya daft?" They both laughed as they headed for the car. They were meeting Faye and Joan at the mall.

They were outside of the store, all excited. "Auntie B, look at this, please, look at the two dresses, say they will be suitable." Bertha and Liz looked in the window. One was a deep-emerald-green knee-length, taffeta and lace, the other was a navy-blue knee-length with three-quarter sleeves and a sweetheart neckline, belted at the waist.

"Why, they are gorgeous. Let's see if they have them in your size," Liz said as she headed for the store entry.

Bertha said, "Bet ya wee dollar, green's fer Joan and blue fer Faye."

"You're on, Mother dear. I thought the opposite." Liz was sure she had just won her bet with Bertha.

The girls came out of the changing rooms, Faye in the straight but elegant blue dress, Joan in the emerald. Bertha put her hand out to Liz. "Well, damn, you won again," Liz whispered. "The two of you look absolutely beautiful in those dresses, and they are perfect. They need no work at all."

"Auntie B, do you like them?" It was Joan who needed the extra approval.

"Yes, dear, I do. Tis jest right fer ya colour an' style. We ner so lucky."

Faye took Bertha's hand and took her to a mannequin; it had a soft yellow dress with a jacket. "Try this on, Auntie. You would look great in yellow."

Bertha remembered what Tommy had said, how he fell for her when she was watching the kids learn to swim, her yellow dress floating around her knees in the water. "I will. I love it, Faye. Let's see if they have it in my size." They did, and Bertha bought it without a second thought on it.

Joan showed Liz a mint-green straight dress, long sleeves and a darker green belt. "What do you think, Aunt Liz? It is so like your eyes. I was attracted to it because it reminded me of you." The four left the store happy they had their dresses—no hemming required.

Chapter Nine

BERTHA HAD DONE some fine sewing on Denny's gown. When she showed her, Denny was surprised. "Grams, you added the lace from my veil to the bottom of my gown. Oh, it's so beautiful. Thank you so much." She was hugging and kissing Grams.

"Stop yer slobbering on me, child." Bertha had tears as well.

Liz stood there, looking at Denny in her gown. "You are the most beautiful bride, so elegant. Mom, you made her look like a princess." Liz was happier than she had been for a long time. Time had finally healed the wounds.

They all had rooms at the bed and breakfast for the day before the wedding. The couple running it were so grateful that they had a full house at this time of year. Bertha offered to help cook for her crew. They accepted; they had never had a full house since opening. It was terrific, all of them on holiday together. They were staying for two nights, and the wedding couple were staying for three.

Denise and Robert had the honeymoon suite. The rest had large rooms done up in antique style. Liz loved it; so did Bertha and Tommy. Mitch was a more modern-style type. There was doubling up as there would not have been enough rooms. Dugan and Richard were bunkmates. Doug, Marcus, and Jon were together. They did not seem to mind; they got on okay. Bertha and Tommy had a room next to the girls. The girls had the largest space for beds; they were all together: Carol, Caitlin, and the twins. Liz gave strict orders that they were not to get the twins drunk, or they would be answering to her and Bertha.

They went to an Italian restaurant for dinner the night before the wedding. The reception was to be there as well. They had decided to have the small hall attached to the restaurant for the reception. That way, they could dance and have fun without bothering the rest of the restaurant patrons. They enjoyed a wonderful meal and left to go for a walk through the town as it was still light enough to see. Denny told Tommy that she would love to have pictures taken in this park of the wedding party, but a photographer was not in her budget. Tommy made a quick call to a photographer friend; one would be there for tomorrow for his grandson and granddaughter's wedding. He told Bertha after they went back to their room what he had done.

The next morning, Robert was kicked out of his room to go get dressed in the boys' room; he would not see the bride until he was supposed to. "Robert, you know I love you like a son. To me, you are my son. So I want to give you and Denny a good start. I hired Carol to build you and your new family a house right behind ours. There are two acres of land back there, and I bought all of it. You tell her where you want the house. Your mom is paying for all the furniture for your house as her wedding gift, as you would not let us give you a big wedding. No arguments, we love you two so much," Mitch told Robert; soon they would have a grandbaby to love and spoil.

"Thanks is not enough to say for all you and Mom are doing for us. We planned on staying in the add-on until we could afford a house, one that would house two or three kids, we hope, and us.

Thank you, Dad, thank you so much. I will not tell her until we are all together. That way, she cannot say no." They laughed together. It was time to get ready.

Robert, Dugan, and Doug were standing at the small church's front, and the organist was playing the wedding march. First came Carol, then Caitlin, and then the beautiful bride came toward Robert; all he could see was his princess walking toward him. She was so gorgeous, his Denny, and now she would be his forever.

She could see nothing but her man standing there, waiting for her. He looked so grown-up to her now. She always teased him that he had a young face and looked ten years his junior. He was the most handsome man she had ever met, and now he would be hers, forever and a day.

They said their vows, and of course, Mom and Bertha were crying. Robert went down and kissed them both and gave them hankies. Everyone laughed, Denny and Robert exchanged rings, and then they were pronounced husband and wife. The minister gave them a gift. It was a cross in a frame with their names on it and the date of their wedding.

Outside the church, the photographer was waiting. He caught them coming out of the church. He had been in the church and taken secret shots of all that he could. He suggested they go to the park for the photos. Denny looked at Tommy and smiled her thanks. He nodded to her. They stayed at the park, getting many pictures for all of them, even the sniffling uncle.

Their dinner was excellent, Italian American; it was all delicious. The band came in just as dinner was finishing up. Everyone was having a great time.

The garter was hunted after and found, Robert being cute and going under her gown to find it. When she squealed, he came out with it. He knew not to throw the one he had taken off her leg. It matched her gown and veil, and he knew Grams had made it. Robert threw it from the small stage out to the men in the group. Jon Franc caught it. He just stood there. "First time, I have tried at so many weddings to catch one of these. I will frame a picture of this on the lady who catches Denny's bouquet." She tossed it from the stage as Robert had, and Caitlin caught it.

"Now what?" Caitlin did not know what to do; she was a little scared. Usually on duty, she kept the unwanted out of the receptions.

A chair was placed in the middle of the floor, and she was escorted up to the chair. "Now wait a minute. My dress is not that long!" Everyone was cheering Jon on; they knew he liked her and she him. He took her shoe off first and slowly ran his hand up her calf; she was so red, and so were her arms and chest. He placed the garter over her foot and slowly, very slowly moved it up her calf to her knee and just above, under the edge of her dress. He reached up and kissed her on the lips to whistles and cheers.

"How's it feel to be so embarrassed, Cat?" Carol yelled at her.

The music started, and they started to dance. "I will get you back, Jon. I told you I am a tease, but I did not know how much a tease you were. Maybe Grams is right. I need to get a leash for you."

Doug asked Carol to dance with him. "Sure, are we showing off for the locals, Doug?" He smiled and walked her to the dance floor. The band saw him and played his song. They danced a salsa that had everyone hooting and clapping for them. All Carol hoped was her dress did not rip or slide up her legs too far.

There was a surprise for Tom and Bertha; a young man dressed in his dress uniform walked in and kissed Bertha's cheek from behind her. She turned about to swat whoever had done it, when she saw it was her boy, Michael. Tommy was up hugging him, slapping him on the shoulder. "You made it, son. Denny and Robert will be so pleased."

Bertha stood and hugged him to her. She was lost in his dress jacket as he was so much larger than she. "Have ya eaten, me boy? There's food aplenty fer ya."

"I will get a plate after I say hi to the bride and groom." He walked up to them and gave Denny a kiss and Robert a huge hug. "Congratulations, both of you, so glad for you. Robert, you didn't run up the aisle in the nude, did you?"

"No, thanks for bringing that up, now Dugan will not leave it alone until he knows what that is all about."

"So right, Robbie, now who is this soldier?"

"May I introduce my uncle, Sergeant Michael McCloud, Grams' and Gramps' son. I'm sure he is on leave to be here."

"Nice to meet you, sir. Now tell me what that was all about, naked up the aisle, where, when? Is there a picture of this?"

"No, and you will never get that information from me. My family would disown me if I were to divulge such information."

Michael started to laugh, and so did Robert. "Now, if he ever gets me mad at him, Dugan, you may just find out from me."

"Denny, would you like to dance with me?" Robert took her onto the floor and away from Dugan.

Michael took his mother's hand and danced with her. "Mom, I didn't tell you and Dad I have retired. I am no longer in the service. With my years in and my savings, I will be able to take care of things until I get a job, I hope in St. Helen. I know right now it is a slow time, and things are tight for everyone in complex right now, so I'll stay at the hotel and see what I can do, maybe construction. I do know how to swing a hammer."

"Ya'll do no such a thing. I got Carol ta build ya a place fer yerself. She calls it a guesthoose. I gits ta see ya every day an' feeds ya as well."

"Mom, that is so kind of you. Can I help pay for some of that?"

"Try ta give it ta yer dad, jest try."

They all headed back to St. Helen first thing in the morning. Michael went with Tommy and Bertha, as he flew into Baltimore and cabbed it to the bed and breakfast. "Dad, are you still working, or are you retired now?"

"Well, according to your mother, I am a man of leisure, but I still have my hand in once in a while."

"Need any extra help?"

"Tommy, he's jest now come hame. Leave it be."

"You heard the lady. Rest, enjoy a few weeks' R&R, then we will talk, okay?"

Mitch was surprised that Liz was still a little weepy; she cried at the church and cried when they said goodbye to the couple before they left. "Liz, are you upset that they got married as they did, quietly and without pomp and ceremony?"

"No, this is silly, but I just realized as they were saying their vows how bloody old I'm getting." She was weeping again.

Mitch laughed at her. "Come on, Liz, you are not even fifty, and we can enjoy ourselves for the next three days in an empty house."

"I know, my baby has flown the coop, and I won't have him there every night to eat dinner with or chat with." Now she was crying harder, and Mitch was laughing harder. She punched him in the arm and told him to stop laughing at her. She would tell Bertha he made her cry. She was half crying, half laughing.

"Do you want to stop for something to eat or go straight through?"

"Let's ring Mom and Dad, see if they want to join us. I would like to talk to Mike, see how he is doing."

"Sure." He used his car phone then. "Anyone want to stop for a bite to eat? Liz and I thought it would be nice for us to be together."

"Sure, me tummy is rumblen an' 'tis time fer lunch anyways."

Michael was glad Carol had found someone that made her happy and brought her out of her shell. He only hoped he could find someone that would fill his world like that. "Mike, your lady will walk up to you and say hello. That will be that. She will have a ring in your nose for the rest of your life."

"I don't know about the ring in my nose, but I would like to meet her that way."

"She will make you speechless and stutter your words when it happens, my son," Tommy told him. "You can all stop laughing at me now," he said with a red face.

Their order came, and all chatter about Mike finding a love life was over as they were enjoying a hearty meal before going the rest of the way home. "Tommy, does ya tink I can git a tea ta go?" Bertha asked.

"Sure, love, I'll get it for you."

"'Tis his birthday in a fortnight. I wants ta have a party fer him, but I no have his age fer the cake."

Mike said to her, with fingers crossed, "I don't think anyone knows his age."

"I'm sure his brother can tell me. I'll have ta ask Marcus," she said as Tommy came back to the table. This was going to be a problem. Bertha thought he was around the same age as she, not so, and Mitch knew it.

"Shall we all visit the little boys' and girls' rooms before we head out on the road?" Mitch asked. He gave Tommy a sign that said, "Come with me." Michael said he would be fine and would take his mom to the car. Liz said she wanted some air, so she would be just outside.

"Tommy, your wife wants to know your age, and she is about to ask your brother, so you had better clue him in."

"He already knows Bertha thinks I'm around her age." Tommy started to laugh. "He likes the fact that I look older than him, but he hates that he has to pretend to be as old as Bertha thinks I am. Tell her I'm one year older than my teeth and hair and too young to care."

"I will not tell her that. It gets me a swat I do not deserve, and she can hit damn hard when she wants to."

"I know, Mitchell, I know. I have been on the end of that swat a few times myself."

They went out to the cars. Liz asked Mitchell, "Well, did he tell you his age or not?"

"Liz, I know his age, and well, I'm not telling her on the promise to him. He is eleven years her junior, and she would probably not like that too much, do you think?"

"I think we never tell her that, Mitch."

They arrived home around dusk. "Mitch, do you think it's too late to go and get our little girl Bessie? I miss her."

"Let's. I miss her too." They drove over to Cat's friend's house, and Bessie nearly wagged her tail off. Liz thanked them and paid them for babysitting her, and they left for home. Bessie went from Liz to Mitch to give kisses and get hugs. She was glad to be going home. They were delighted to have her back.

The house seemed so empty, Robert and Denny not there and Mom and Tommy living next door; the place had grown. Liz turned to Mitch. “Let’s adopt a few kids. I just hate the house being so empty.”

“No, we are not adopting. We will soon be grandparents and be asked to babysit for the couple, for whatever reason they can think of to get a break from the sweet child.”

Liz swatted him a good one. “Yes, we will be babysitting but not like you said. The baby will be sweet but not the kind of sweet you mean. You are going to be wrapped around that child’s finger and you will love it, so stop it right now, Mr. Crabby-ass.”

Robert danced in front of her, then danced around her, then knelt in front of her. Moving to the beat of the music, he lifted her gown higher and higher. Robert dove under her gown and tickled her legs, making her laugh. He finally pulled her garter down her leg, and he switched it for the one in his pocket. He wanted to keep it for her because Grams made it.

Chapter Ten

THEY HAD TAKEN a four-day weekend, and now it was time for all to go back to work. Carol called Mitch and said she would need his help with specs on the house tonight. Would it be all right for her to come out to the house? "Sure, sweetheart, come for dinner. Liz is feeling the empty-nest syndrome, and I think it would help to see you."

"Okay, Dad, can I bring Doug with me?"

"Yep, love to see him." Mitch told Liz that Carol and Doug would be coming for dinner and that she needed specs on the house. "So let's have Tommy and Bertha over also."

"I'll call Mom and ask. I am sure they would love it. What about a barbecue for dinner?"

He agreed to that, then stopped. "Wait a minute. That means I'm cooking dinner, not you."

She laughed and handed him a grocery list she just finished. "Want to get this on the way home, or would you like Mom and me to do it for you?" He left the list on the counter, slapped her butt, and kissed her goodbye.

Liz walked next door with Bessie to ask if they would like to have a barbecue with them and Carol and Doug. Bessie was up on Bertha's lap with front paws on her chest, kissing her face and ears. "Ya wee thing, ya no canna washes me away." She was laughing and enjoying Bessie's love. Bessie went to Tommy next, but because he hadn't shaved, Bessie did not like the picky face.

"Want to come for dinner, guys? Carol and Doug are coming to take the measurements for the house. Mitch thought it would be nice for all of us to be together. He is barbecuing. What do you think?"

"Sure, for me, I'll help him on the barbecue, Bertha, want to?"

"I would like that a lot. I'll help ya wit the salads, Liz."

"I have to shop, so want to come with me, Mom?"

"I'll go, have some grocery buyen ta do."

"When would you like to go, Mom?"

"In aboot an hour, okay?"

"I'll pull in your lane and pick you up."

"Did ya have a chat wit Mitch aboot Tommy's age, Liz?"

"Yes, and he really does not know Tommy's age."

They were just outside of the city when the explosion rocked the car. Liz pulled over; she was frightened. "Are you all right, Mom?" Bertha nodded; she was. She was too shaken to speak. Liz's phone was ringing. "Liz here."

It was Mitch. He told her the apartment that Carol was staying in just blew up. Could she come to the complex and see to Carol? They would be right there.

They found Carol in her office with Mitch, Allen, and Shantelle. She was so upset she was in need of a doctor. Liz told her she was going whether she wanted to or not. Doug came flying into her office. "Is she okay, Mr. Maxwell? I heard, and I came as fast as I could."

"Liz just took her to the hospital to get a sedative or something. She is that shook up."

"I'll go there and see her."

"Bertha, would you like me to take you home or something?"

"I dinna know, Mitchell. I canna shop fer Liz, but are we still gonna have a barbecue?"

"Yes, we are, so let me take you shopping. It was some explosion. It shook this building as well. I will have it inspected to make sure all the walls and floors are still up to strength."

"Are Carol's things all gone, Mitchell? She gonna need furniture and clothes and things?"

"That, Mom, I don't know yet. I have an inspector over there now. They are making sure no one was in the building when it happened. But it was the top floor that got the worst of it, seems it went up a shaft or something, from what the fire chief told me."

They reached the store and went in to get the shopping done. They heard that an older man living in the basement had been killed in the blast. Mitch felt bad. He knew the gentleman; he hired him to do odd jobs around the complex.

Bertha did her groceries, and Mitch grabbed all that Liz had on her list and a bottle of wine as well. They headed home. Mitch thought of the older man and who would take care of his funeral. He knew if there was no one to take care of his arrangements, then he would.

Although the sun was shining, no one felt sunny; the warmth of the day was seeping out of their bones, as Bertha would say. Carol and Liz arrived home with Doug behind them. He was out of his car and over to Carol to help her into the house. Mitch came to Liz. "What did the doctors say about her, Liz?"

"They said she was having an anxiety attack and she would be fine. They gave her a shot to calm her down. She begged me to drive by the apartment. There is nothing left of hers. Two floors remain, and they are in bad shape. I told her she could live with us. She belongs with her parents until things get straightened out." They walked arm in arm into the house. Mitch returned to the car and got all the groceries for them and for Bertha.

Michael called Mitch. "What just happened? Mom and Dad's house just shook. Did we have an earthquake or something?"

"Or something, Mike, the apartment building Carol lives in was bombed. There is extraordinarily little of it left. We will be home soon. We are having a steak and lobster barbecue, so don't overeat now."

"See you soon."

Mitch and Tommy had just finished the barbecuing, gathering their hard-earned meal to take into the house when Dugan pulled into the lane. "Mr. Maxwell, can we have a chat?" Dugan asked.

"You can, but it will be after we eat. We just now finished with this, and I'm going to eat it, right, Tommy?"

"Right, boyo, we are, steak on the barbie, nothen better."

Dugan followed them into the house. The ladies had set the table, and Doug was pouring the wine for everyone but Carol. He offered Dugan one, but it was refused. Dugan sat, had a bite of food and a coffee, and waited until the ladies had started to clear the table when he began to talk about the apartment.

Mitch stopped him. "Not until Carol is out of earshot. She does not need to be any more upset than she already is." Dugan nodded; he understood. He had been told that she was in rough shape.

Mitch and the other four men went into the den; Liz, Bertha, and Carol stayed in the kitchen, having a second cup of coffee. "Mitch, may I may call you that, sir?" Mitch told him he could.

"It was not the new water boiler's faulty valve. The fire department and your inspector found bomb fragments left with what was left of the boiler. The janitor and his helper were not in the building, so we want to speak to them."

"Dugan, I gave them a week off. They are in Florida, on their twentieth-anniversary honeymoon. They will be just as devastated as we are when they return. At least there may be some of their things left in the rubble."

"They were a married couple taking care of the building?" he asked.

"I hired them as they needed cheap rent. I needed someone I could rely on. They had experience in cleaning buildings. What do you want, Dugan? I can give you their resumes and applications if you want."

"Yes, sir, I do. Someone did this, and I intend to find out who." He left then. He had really thought that maybe they had done it for money, and he would have it all wrapped up.

Mike did not like how Dugan had decided that it was the janitorial people so quickly. Why would they? What reason would he have to blame them?

Mike approached Mitch. "Does Dugan know the people he seems to think did this, or he just feels they were up to something?"

"Mike, I'm not sure, but I don't like the way he wants to put the blame on them."

"Would you mind if Erica and I walked the site, just as observers? We will see something others missed. We are trained in this kind of crap. I have nothing else to do right now, Mitch."

"Go ahead, I will let my investigator know, and Dugan so he won't bother you."

"Could you leave telling Dugan about us? We don't need him following us around while we do a hunt-and-seek kind of thing."

"Sure, I guess, but I will tell Andy. You won't get shot, okay?" Mike nodded. He was already calling Erica on his cell.

Mike was suspicious of Dugan; why did he push Mitch to think that the couple might be the ones who bombed the building? He called Erica. She jumped at the chance to work with him and his family. She would talk to Mr. McCloud about what Michael should or should not know.

Erica arrived at Tommy's house, and she and Mike made a list of possibilities. She brought up an idea to the father and son. "What if whoever killed Stewart at the wedding is the one making the family pay, or they are connected to the mafia laundering run by the late Tony Datello?" This gave Tommy the chills.

"If you are right, Erica, there is more to this than a bombing. Mike, you and Erica fly out to Florida to talk to the couple that Mitch hired. See if anything strange was going on, be careful not to set off suspicion if Dugan is right."

"Dad, I don't think he is right. He wants to solve this and get it over with fast. So his town is back to normal."

Bertha made a large dinner of roasted chicken and dressing, potatoes, and veggies. Carol made a Cobb salad. Liz brought home the dessert, a tiramisu cake.

They all joined at Liz's house; she had the largest dining room. Bertha's was large but not large enough to fit this many people. Carol asked Liz if she should stay at Caitlin's to ease the pressure in the house.

"Absolutely not, you are the one that is keeping us sane, and you are our daughter," Mitch told her, with a huge hug.

Mike told Carol he and Erica were leaving after dinner to fly out to check on something for Tommy. "Is there something wrong, Grams and Gramps okay?"

"Oh, yeah, Tommy said he wanted to make sure the property was closed up, and for sale, as he had requested of his realtor agent. The house was broken into, so we are going to check it out, that's all."

Carol told Mike about Doug and how he was helping her come out of her shell.

"Yeah, I saw that at both weddings. I'm glad you seem so happy."

"He makes me feel strong, Mike, like I can do anything. " He gave her a hug and went to pack.

He and Erica were traveling on Tommy's jet, which meant they could talk and make plans openly. "Mike, do you think this is related to the shooting of Stewart?"

"Yes, I do, there is more to it than a single bombing, and I want to find out about it. I am so out of the loop. Did you know about Marcus having twin girls?"

"No, and from what Mom said, neither did he. His daughter Faye wants to be trained to be a sharpshooter and learn how to fight. Her dad is not happy. Joan wants to be a mother and raise a large family that she can shower with love and affection while protecting them from harm. Mom told me they got her the best psychiatrist to work with her right at home because she won't leave her sister."

Erica saw that a car would be available when they landed, and the pilot knew when to pick them up. They found the couple with no trouble. They were at a well-known resort, enjoying their holiday. Jim and Nora had not heard about the apartment explosion. They had promised each other no television, radio news, or computers until their return to St. Helen. After Erica and Mike introduced themselves, they asked if the couple would mind answering some questions. Jim told them they would help if they could. "Nora and I had nothing to do with any bombing."

The new owners told them they were to stay away from the elevator tool room. There were now new people in place to take care of the elevators, and their equipment was off limits to them and the whole janitorial staff. "Have you ever been in the room after you were told not to go in? I mean, did you see anything out of place or added to the room?"

"Nora went in to get our equipment out. We paid for it, so we figured we should have it," Jim told Erica.

"Nora, did you see some of the things in the room?"

"She went in to get the things that belonged to her dad. He was a carpenter, and they meant a lot to her. She noticed a large safe built into the floor and one in the concrete wall. So we just stayed out of there," Jim told them. "One of the new janitor staff got a beating for going in the room. After that, a guard was placed on the room, twenty-four seven. We did not know the apartment was bombed. We for sure did not do it." Mike told Jim to take Nora to the private airport. They would be taken to a new resort at Mr. Maxwell and Mr. McCloud's expense. They were not to worry about the new owners.

Chapter Eleven

WHEN ERICA AND Mike returned to St. Helen, they went directly to Mitchell's office, and Tommy met them there. They told them what they had learned. Mitch no longer owned the building. He checked with the financial department regarding payments made to Mitch's company and paychecks being paid out. All was in order as if he still owned the building. They took the two of them out of earshot of anyone not involved. "Look, they saw two large safes in the elevator repair room, but after the young janitor got beaten and the guard was put in place, they decided to stay away and go look for other employment," Erica told them.

"Mitch, Nora was afraid that Jim would get hurt just like the others that used to work there. They didn't like working for her."

"We got our pay just as before, once a week from Taraco Corporation," said Nora.

Mitch told Nora and Jim their paychecks would still be there for them every week. "I want you two to take an extended medical leave. We will have the doctor okay it, say it is due to stress. They agreed, and Mitch had Tommy put everything in action: plane, hotel accommodations, car, and cash to spend. Tommy knew he could not tell Bertha any of this, but he had to tell her something.

"Bertha sweetheart, Mitch has just found out that people from the mafia have hijacked his companies and his holdings."

"Are ya goin' ta help him, Tommy?"

"I'll do me best, love. I will give him all the help I can."

Erica and Mike knew there was extraordinarily little to go on. Erica looked around the area where the couple lived. She found practically nothing but partially burned photographs and clothes. Erica watched the guard as she poked around, looking and taking things and putting them in her knapsack. The guard approached her. "What do you hope to find, little lady?"

"I hope to find some memories for Jim and Nora. Their lives were here. Did you know them?"

"Nope, didn't know them, but I need to get a coffee and use the boys' room. Want a coffee?"

"Sure, black, two sugars, please."

"Be back in about fifteen minutes." This told Erica he would be back in less than five minutes. She ran to the door, picked the lock, and got in. She snapped pictures of every corner of the room, floor to ceiling, and got out of there, making sure to relock the door as it was.

Erica was digging out a jewelry box when the guard came back. "Still at it, holy shit. Here's your coffee. Take a break." The guard was surprised she was still there.

"Thanks. What's your name? Mine's Judy."

"I'm Paul." He sat down beside her.

Erica smelled her coffee for additive; one or two sips would tell her if there was a sleeping agent in it. "Paul, did you get this at Cora's Coffee Shop? It's fabulous."

"Thanks, I did. It seems to be the best coffee shop in St. Helen."

Erica asked him if he always worked as a guard.

Paul said, "No, I usually do investigating into legal cases. Taraco Corporation hired me to make sure no one disturbed the evidence they have on someone in that room, in two safes. A real pain in the backside, but I better get back there. The boss is on her way. If you like living, you will get your ass out of here. I like you, so go while you can." Erica thanked him, shook his hand, and left. She looked back in time to see him empty her coffee on the rocks. He shook his head, laughed, and got rid of the cup; he said out loud to no one, "I liked her, so I stopped her. She would have died if she drank it all, now just a headache." He laughed again to himself.

Marcus had one of his people investigate this Taraco Corporation. The name rang a bell; he could not put his finger, but he knew it sounded familiar. He prayed it wasn't what or to whom it belonged.

"Michael, do you remember when Steward got shot at Tommy's and Bertha's wedding? It was a woman. Tommy's brother Daniel said it was a woman that pitched a gun in the bush where he was sleeping. He thought her underdressed for the wedding," Erica asked him.

"Yes, I traced her back to Parker, the old man the FBI was after. Why?"

"I think it's her. She has taken over for her father."

"If that's the case, call in a few favours from the FBI and see what they will tell us, most likely nothing, but try." They both laughed, but they knew if she was Tara Parker, Mitchell was in for the ride of his life. She meant business, and she was far too savvy in the ways of business and finance not to know how to beat Mitchell. She had to have taken over from Parker after his death, doing the laundry for the mafia. "Erica told me the guard at the building was Paul Simon. He is a hit man for hire, highest price paid gets him. Whatever he is, his job is to protect and guard the so-called evidence on who bombed the building. He most likely did it himself."

"Marcus, if this is a revenge game from her, whoever she is working with, we are all in for a long hard road back to normalcy. Get the masked man over to the building tonight. We can set him on this before we speculate on what to do. Let's make sure we are on the right road."

"Tommy, are you sure? He is not only expensive, he can be working both sides."

"One thing I know about him, he works for one side only. If they have already hired him, he would not show up. It is his way of letting you know where he is at."

"If you are sure, then I will place the call. Oh, dear brother, you are taking Faye to the shooting range today. What is with that?"

"She wants to learn how to use a gun, Marcus. She is just like you were at an earlier age. Give her a chance to prove herself."

"Right, and become a rescuer just like us, is that what you are saying, putting her life on the line for a stranger just as we do?" He was getting upset.

"One step at a time, Marcus. Who said she is going to have your talent with guns and manipulation of people's minds?"

"Make sure she doesn't, Thomas. I mean it!" He left his brother to go out in the yard, where Bertha was digging up the tulip bulbs to put away for spring. He saw her kneel and fall over to her side; she wasn't moving.

"Oh God, not again." He yelled for Tommy and ran to Bertha. Marcus screamed, "Bertha's shot! She's bleeding from front to back." Tommy was there in seconds, but to Marcus, it seemed like forever. "She's shot, Tommy, a through and through."

Two young boys from the yard behind the new house came running. “We are so sorry Mrs. P got hit. We were practicing with our BB guns, and well, we both hit her.” They stood, heads down, whimpering.

The ambulance came as Bertha came around. “I no can stand, Tommy, an’ I feel sick to me stomach.”

“Rest on my arm, sweetheart. These two youngins have something to say, don’t ya, boys?”

“Oh, Mrs. P, we are so sorry we thought to hit the fence and scare you, but we missed and hit you. We are so sorry.” Now they were crying.

The boys’ parents came over to Marcus. “What is going on? Why the ambulance? Did Bertha have a heart attack? Should the boys leave her alone?”

“Your boys shot Bertha with their BB guns. She has a hole through her side. They are attempting to say they are sorry to her.”

Their father spoke up loud enough for his sons to hear him. “They will be sorry when I get done with them. What was Mrs. McCloud doing when these idiots shot her?”

“She was digging up the tulip bulbs to store for the spring.”

“Well, my guess is Mrs. McCloud is finished. The kids will finish to her liking, then clean the yard and rake all the leaves and bag them as I know she never burns them—she composts them. Get started, boys, and I’ll take those guns.”

Bertha was taken into the hospital ER and patched up. “I’ll no stay in the sick hoose, Tommy. Ya takes me hame, ya hears me? Ya take me ta me hoose.” He kissed her on the forehead and told her he would. He also told the doctor to have a nurse come by to change her dressings. At home, he helped her to bed, and she soon was asleep. "Marcus, look at these shots. Do they look like BB shot to you?" They were .22 pellets, not shot from the boys.

"Tommy, your wife has been targeted. Tommy, she is being used to get to you. You are going to have to tell her the truth."

He knew he had to tell her something, but as to how much, he was afraid even to attempt to tell her the truth. Her husband was no rich bartender that stayed at home to care just for her. He knew she had an inkling that something was not what it seemed. She woke a few hours later and asked for him. "Tommy, we needs ta talk, and I needs to know the truth. Are ya the man I married or someone I don't know?"

"We will talk, Bertha, but let us get you a cup of your favourite tea."

Carol was coming toward them to see how Grams was. "Carol, love, would you make Grams a cup of her favourite tea, please."

"Sure, Gramps, I'll do it right now. Meet you in the kitchen."

"Will ya have one with me, Carol?" Bertha asked her.

"Sweetheart, when we can have some time in private so we are not overheard, I'll do my best to explain what is going on. Will that do?" Bertha nodded and leaned on him to get to the kitchen. She was in more pain than she cared to admit. While Carol and Bertha were having a cup of tea and taking her pain medication, Tommy slipped out of the kitchen to speak to Liz.

He asked her to get the ladies to follow her up to the chalet, using the excuse to decorate the place for a gala party for Christmas and Bertha and Tommy's birthday. "Does Mitch know what is going on, Tommy? Because he has never told me anything, and I know he cannot lie to me."

"He knows there is a problem, but as to how bad or how deep this goes, no. I need you to do this for me, Liz, to save the family from anyone else getting shot. Liz, it's because Bertha got shot that I ask this of you."

"Yes, I'll do it, Tommy, but you keep me in the loop, my friend. Bertha means the world to me, so do you," Liz told him.

Tommy was getting worried; the ladies were not stupid, and they soon would figure something out even if it was not the whole truth. Mitch wondered how much Liz had figured out. She seemed to know what to do to get the ladies to do what Tommy wanted. While they were shopping and making lists, the men were planning how to eliminate this Taraco Corporation. Joan opened up to Marcus and Tommy about the ruin of all his businesses and his best friend, Bertha. That lady brought him and Liz together all those years ago. He had a horrid feeling Liz knew he was involved with the rescue business. He wasn't sure, but his inner senses were tingling.

Faye talked to Joan in their room. "When did you first start memorizing all that information from his books and files?"

"Right after the punishments for not doing his friend's bidding. I planned on killing Master Walt myself. You and I were taken by mistake by paid rescuers for the Spanish boys. We started our lives over, hoping to become part of society. That is when I decided to be a child. He bought it and left me alone."

"When you plan to stop being a child? I would love to have you back as Joan, the smart one, the one who could figure out every problem."

"Not going to happen, Faye, I trust no one. Thanks to Uncle Tommy, several of the double agents are gone, but more will come. This isn't the first time. Parker had men infiltrate this rescue crew regularly. Read the books, Faye. It may surprise you." Joan handed over all the books and folders she had. "I trust you, Faye. Read them and return the books to me. I trust no one in this chalet." Faye nodded her consent. She had every intention of reading them with her father and uncle, making copies of them to study so she could return the books and files. "Faye, I know you will give them back. I also know you think I'm stupid enough not to realize you will copy them. I'm not, but destroy the copies when you, Dad, Uncle Tommy, and Charlie are done with them. Promise me."

Faye felt like the idiot now; for so long, she was the smarter of the two—not anymore. "I won't have to. Dad and Uncle Tommy will do it, but what has Charlie got to do with all this?"

"Charlie runs the organization. His father, Yee, started the rescue operation seventy-five years ago. He lost three sons and a daughter to the Oriental organizations. He, his wife, and Charlie made it to Canada, then, just before the separation of nationalities, they made it to the States. The rest you can get from Dad or Uncle Tommy. Yee saved their parents, brought them out of Scotland. Faye, there is so much you do not know, nor do you need to. I will let them know how much I know if needed, but until then, no one should know."

Faye agreed. "Never play the village idiot with me again, you promise. Most of my hate comes from the fact that Walt destroyed you."

"I am, Faye. I would never have married Jason; he would have died before that happened. I did not stop him soon enough to save Aunt B from getting hurt. So Uncle Tommy took care of him. Do not bring those out if there is any chance someone other than the leaders is there." She went over to the window. "Faye, I will probably never marry. I don't think my body is well inside. I have not had a monthly in over a year. If they need me to explain what I found out, I will. Other than that, I will not talk about it." She walked back to Faye, hugged her, and walked her out of the room. In a very soft voice, she told Faye, "I will always love you and protect you even when you don't know it."

All three men stood there, staring at Faye after she finished her speech. "Joan told you all this after she gave the books and files to you?" Charlie asked her.

"She knew that it was your father who started this rescue business and the McCloud family were among the rescued."

"Tommy, is she safe?" Charlie asked him. "She knows more than any of our men, and she knows which ones are not loyal and true to just us. I worry someone will take her out."

It was Faye that answered. "Charlie, have you talked to her? I mean in public, with the whole family around."

"No, I have not even met your sister, Faye. All I know is that she is your twin. Marcus says if you dressed identically, we would not tell you two apart."

"This is true until she opens her mouth, then you for sure know the difference."

He looked at her like she had two heads. Marcus and Tommy got it. "Charlie, can you go ask her if she would like mac and cheese for lunch?" Tommy asked him.

Charlie walked with Faye toward the main family room. "Joan, I was looking for you. Would you like mac and cheese for lunch?"

"Oh, Charlie." She started to dance with him hand in hand. "It is my most special lunch ever. Can we have tomato soup too, and hot chocolate?"

He swung her around and told her she could have whatever she wanted. She asked if she could help with the hot chocolate and maybe make some junket. He left the family room in wonderment. Joan was so childlike, so simple-minded no one would even think she was able to make up her mind.

Charlie entered the kitchen to see Tommy put a man in the back room, probably dead. He told Marcus she was a child, a simple-minded child. How could she know what she knew? Tommy returned to Charlie from the back room and told him, "Charlie, she knows how to hide in plain sight. Yes, she still needs help, but Joan is capable of giving us all we need to shut Tara down. Make sure you make her mac and cheese, with tomato soup for her lunch, Charlie, just not for us."

Joan entered the kitchen as Tommy said Charlie was to make the mac and cheese for her, not the rest. "Uncle Tommy, don't you like macaroni and cheese? Faye and I just love it. I'm helping Charlie make it, right, Charlie? Aunt B said she would not mind it at all."

"Mac and cheese it is, darlin'," Tommy told her. Charlie told himself he would have to learn her and know when he could trust what she said.

Everyone enjoyed the childlike lunch; Robert remembered when Grams made it for him and his pals for lunch and a nighttime snack when they slept out in the backyard in his tent. Denny told of how it was a Saturday ritual for her and Richard; they made it for themselves and had food fights because there was no supervision. Carol had never eaten mac and cheese before and rather enjoyed it for the first time. Tommy and Marcus, however, had other thoughts of this horrendous foodstuff.

"Marcus, do you remember making the dog sick because we fed him too much of this stuff? The vet told us to lay off the M and C for poor old King was getting too fat, and it was making him ill."

"Yes, I remember we both got a damn good hiding for our troubles."

"Why would you do that to the dog, Dad?" Faye asked.

"We got mac and cheese every day from September through April, hot lunch they called it at the school. No exceptions, you ate it."

"So now you hate it, right?" Joan remarked.

"Not hate, Joan, just tired of it. We can have it once in a while. You love the stuff, don't you?"

"No, but I love making necklaces and bracelets out of it for gifts. It does taste good, and it is good to grow on, right, Faye? Mom used to say that, it's food to grow on." Marcus had tears in his eyes; that was his Margaret telling her girls this crap was good for them.

After lunch, the ladies decided to check out the decorations that the chalet already had. Charlie showed them the workshop and the head decorator and his daughter. They were busy making lengths of garland from spruce trees and wreaths of the same branches. Denny wanted to help, "Can I jump in and help decorate the garland and the wreaths, please?" Marta told her she could and gave her the planned layout for the wreaths. "You mean they are decorated identically for the whole chalet?" she asked her.

"Oh no, just the ones that go down the long drive. People seem to follow them up to the main gate," she laughed.

"I see. Well, I still want to help you," Denny told her. The ladies followed Marta's father, Hardison, to the workroom, decorations from floor to ceiling.

Whatever theme you decided on, it was there. "What theme would you ladies want this year?" Hardison asked of them.

Bertha spoke up. "One ah hame an' family, a tree as tall as the ceilen, wit all the trimmens. Hardison, has ya that in yer Santa bag?" He smiled at her and told her to look under the big tarp.

Those had not been used for years, not since the boys' mom was alive. "'Tis what I want, Liz, are ya right wit that?"

"Yes, Mom, I am. Hardison, are there any other things you need? We are only too glad to do the shopping for you."

"Never enough green, red, gold, and silver bells to put on the garland around the great room and front foyer—most have been broken over the years."

"Make us a list, and we will get it. Can we help put it up and decorate the tree?" she asked him.

He nodded with a great big smile. He thought it would be the best Christmas ever since Mable McCloud lived here, how she loved home-style Christmas. She so wanted grandchildren to spoil and to teach them of their heritage. He asked Bertha, "Star or angel for the topper, Mrs. McCloud?"

"Always an angel, she will watch over us and keep us safe, tis always an angel," she told Hardison.

Chapter Twelve

TOMMY, MARCUS, MITCH, and Michael all read the books and the documents. They sat in silence, not believing what they read. "Marcus, do you believe all that Joan shared with us and all she told us?" Tommy asked.

"I do because she told Faye she intended to kill him herself. They were grabbed along with the boys. What I don't get is why they were cut loose by whoever did the rescuing. Did they figure out they were not Spanish?"

Charlie commented, "It was a junior team, with not enough sense to bring them in as well as the boys. I paid them half of the fee and docked them for leaving the girls on the side of the road."

"We rescued my daughters and left them. What the hell, Charlie? We don't do sloppy work like that."

"Relax, Marcus, I have had my eye on the two men since, and well, one learned to fly a month ago when I found Parker's cell number on his throwaway. The other learned to fly just two days before you came up here. As for the girls, they were more than anxious to get away from the rescuers. Neither one mentioned a slow or childlike adult."

Faye came in and said, "Mitchell, Liz is looking for you, but before you go, I have to tell you what Joan said: He will lose his complex and all his holdings shortly if they do not bring her down. She is a control freak, loves sex more than money, but running things turns her on. Put a genius with a gorgeous body and a matching sex drive in her path. It will slow her down. I warn you, she is no fool. Don't play at it. It must be real. Set up your sting. After that, take out all her crew and men available to her. If you don't, they will come for you. They are not only paid well, they work for other organizations that want all your family gone from St Helen more than she does. Do not hesitate, she will take you out faster than you can plan to do her."

Liz was waiting for him in the great hall. "Mitch, is there something you need to discuss with me? Because I found these receipts in your suit coat. Are you buying Christmas presents early and not for the family because we don't need gun scopes and life jackets."

"Liz, I—shit, these are for Charlie. He asked us to pick them up for him. He's good for the money, Liz." He was worried he could never lie to her, and he was sure he was a goner this time also.

"They are for me, Liz. I want to teach the boys how to use a scope to hunt eels in the lake, and the life jackets help them float," Charlie told her as he placed the tea tray down on the tea trolley next to her. He told them dinner would be ready in twenty minutes in the large dining room. Tommy wanted to talk to the whole family.

Bertha asked Liz as they were entering the dining room if she knew what was going on. All Tommy told her was they all needed to attend. "I'm sorry, Mom. Mitch didn't tell me anything either."

"It's all right, Aunt B, it's just dinner. I like dinner."

Bertha hugged her and thought, *Poor wee child, I needs ta love her all the more, fer she has no one but her sister. Marcus is always busy.* "Right ya are, me love, dinner it is." They soon were all gathered in the dining room. The table was set for fourteen people by Denny. All were chatting as they entered the dining room. Charlie brought in the first course of a Cobb salad, Tommy's favourite. A young girl came in and told Bertha there were people at the front entrance to see her and her husband.

"Thank you, Cora, we'll go ta see to it."

She and Tommy walked hand in hand toward the door; he stopped her and gave a huge kiss. "I love ya, me gal, with all me heart."

"Yer daft, Tommy, but I loves ya anyway."

To their surprise, Jon Franc and Caitlin were standing in the foyer. "Cat, yer welcome as all git oot. Mr. Franc, are ya here ta arrest me an me man or ta visit awhile?" She laughed to break the tension she saw on Caitlin's face. Bertha did not trust Jon Franc, but her husband seemed to.

"Mr. and Mrs. McCloud, is Mr. Maxwell here? Caitlin told me I would find him here."

"Yes, he is as well as his whole family. Is there trouble at his workplace?" Franc did not answer. "Follow us—we are about to have dinner. Join us. Bertha and Charlie always make too much," Tommy told them.

Cat spoke up. "Charlie make anything special, Grams?"

"Yes, your favourite, roast duck with rosemary stuffing."

"I'm in, Grams. Jon, you have got to try it." They all went back to the dining room. Charlie had Cora set out two more places for them. Everyone looked up at them as they entered. Mitch asked Jon if he'd come for a visit.

"No, Mitch, but it can wait until dinner is over. This looks too good to let it sit while we talk." He made it sound unimportant, so they all continued their meal. After a light dessert of strawberries and clotted cream, they were getting ready to leave the dining room.

"Are you going to tell Mitch that someone blew up his complex, destroyed all four floors, Mr. Franc, or just let him guess at it?" It was Joan who laid that on them, after which, she skipped over to Charlie and asked if he would help her build a snowman.

Jon asked Charlie, "Are you going to go with her to build a snowman?"

"Yes, I am, and she will tell me what I need to know. I will, in turn, pass it on to the family. If they deem it information you need, they will tell you." Charlie left the room.

Faye went to her Aunt B. "She is all right. She is trying in her own way to come back to us."

"Ya can tell her I'm here fer her whenever she needs me." Faye smiled and walked toward the door leading to the kitchen. Her father thought it odd she would go in the kitchen, even though she was following Joan.

She found Charlie waiting. He had her coat and her gun. Joan had loaded one for her and one for herself. "They do not need to know we are crack shots, Charlie, especially our father and that Franc fellow. Dad still thinks we can be normal human beings after what we have suffered."

"Faye, when the men told me of the condition the two of you were in, I knew we would see you again, here on the clean side or killing us from the depths of hell."

"We will be ready, Charlie, but until you have the head of the snake in your sights, no one knows what we are."

Charlie thought, *If they knew, they would fear the two of you. Tommy knows, and he is leery of you having a gun.*

"We are ready," Charlie's son said from the door. His son had no fear of the girls; he had worked with them and said he was amazed at their gun and weapons proficiency. He and the two girls followed Charlie's son out the back of the cellar door into a snow vehicle with treads instead of tires.

Tommy watched the snow tractor move away from the chalet, up the east side of the mountain. He also knew that his nieces were in that tractor. *I kept my word. Let's hope they do as well. They get to remove many of their grandfather's people and Tara's people in return for all the information they have of them and the gangs.* Marcus would not have allowed this. He wanted them to be normal young women hoping to marry and have grandkids for him to bounce on his knee—not going to happen. Joan was ruined with hot pokers and other terrible objects to please the audience watching; Faye—they took her female parts while she was frozen with drugs and able to watch. They ate them in front of her. Both girls were self-taught sharpshooters, able to kill without hesitation. They were trained in the use of other killing tools, such as the garrote. Charlie tested them, and they were better than his best men. *God give them sanity when this is over,* Tommy thought.

"The moon is low this night, love," he said as Bertha walked up to him.

"Aye, 'tis that, Tommy. Where's yer thoughts gone, my love? I can see ya mullen somethin' over 'tis a worry fer ya."

"Yes, it's the girls I worry about, Bertha. I know they have suffered more than any of us could imagine. They will never be like Carol or Denny—no children for them, probably no husbands either."

She wrapped her arms around his waist from behind him, resting her head on his back. "No, love, they won't, but they will do good afore they give up or die." She felt the sigh through his back.

Marcus asked them to join the rest in the great room to talk to Jo and Caitlin. Tommy nodded; when he turned toward Bertha, she saw the tears and gently brushed them away for him. "'Tis God's will, love," she told him as they followed Marcus.

"Mitch, two people were hurt, your secretary and her brother. They were just exiting the building when it went up. She's going to be fine—a concussion. Her brother may lose his leg."

Mitch swore under his breath. "Look, are we sure it is the same people as the one that blew up the apartment?" Jon handed him the letter.

> MAXWELL, YOU HAVE LOST YOUR
> BUSINESSES
> SOON, YOU WILL LOSE YOUR FAMILY
> ONE BY ONE, THEY WILL DIE
> UNTIL YOU ARE AS ALONE AS I AM
> THAT SCOTCH BITCH GOES FIRST
> THEN YOUR WIFE, GET THE PICTURE?
> YOU WILL BE AS ALONE AS I AM
> THE NEW LAUNDRY LADY

Mitch just stared at it. He knew what this meant; his whole family was in danger, his future grandchild, an unborn baby. He could make back the money he would lose, he could rebuild the buildings he lost, but he could not replace his family, not his wife, son, daughter, daughter-in-law, and most importantly, the woman that brought him and Liz together, Bertha. He stood to lose close to five million dollars; all he cared about was the family. Liz put her hand on his shoulder and said they would make it through. They had a strong family. She walked out of the room, found Tommy. "Tommy, you have a plan, I assume, because he is falling apart at the seams."

"Yes, Liz, I do care, so keep him busy and away from the city for at least a week or three."

"I will do my best. You are not going to tell me, are you?"

"No, the less you know, the less you have to lie about." She kissed him and left his office. Bertha was talking to Caitlin about how bad it was, when Liz returned to the family room.

"All right, ladies, here is what we are going to do." She laid out her plan; not all of them were happy, but they agreed. They knew what they had to do to help their men.

Bertha told Liz she would not leave her Tommy, so Liz should take the ladies and go. Liz was not surprised; in Bertha's place, she would do the same. Bertha wanted nothing more than to stay and be with her and Tommy.

"Are you ready, Mitch? The girls and I are. Robert is coming with us too. He wants to take Denny to Scotland to see the sights."

"Why in hell are we going to England to get ornaments for Christmas now?" Mitch sulked.

"Because I want the best, as Mom ordered, and they will sell out within the next few weeks, so we go."

"So we go, sweetheart." Bertha hated to see them go, but she knew it was for the best. Caitlin and the twins were still here, so she still had some female company. The twins had gone with Charlie and his son eel hunting. Why would anyone want to freeze to catch those horrid things? But his family loved them, and they only had these two weeks to get them.

Cora had asked her to teach her how to make the quilt she made for the baby Denny was carrying. She wanted to make one for her son. "Are ya sure ya wants ta do this, Cora? I'll teach ya if ya wants, but it takes some time."

"Oh yes, madam, it is so beautiful, and you did say we can make it for a boy as well as a girl."

"Aye, we can." Tommy had told Cora to occupy Bertha and keep her happy. Both her bosses would be in and out of the chalet, so would the twins; they scared Cora. Tommy had the head housekeeper hire someone to take over Cora's duties. Cora was not a bodyguard for anyone in the house. She was a housekeeper with no idea of how to use a gun or protect herself. The person taking her place did. They set up one of the guest rooms as a sewing room and got down to business.

As Bertha had asked her, she had gathered pieces of clothing that her son had outgrown and would be of no use to anyone else. For a backer, Cora had chosen a blue flannel that had little white sheep on it. Hardison had made them a quilting frame that Bertha was pleased with. "'Tis better than me own, Hardison. I'll treasure it, thank ya so much." Cora looked at the frame and could not see anything to treasure. Bertha taught her to measure and cut squares out of the clothing, then run them up on the sewing machine Charlie's wife lent them. This took them the whole of the first week: sewing and matching pattern and colour.

"Cora, we've been quilten fer nigh on a fortnight."

"Mrs. B, what is a fortnight?"

"Tis close to ten days, me girl." Cora smiled, not a word about the family being gone or that the bosses were gone as well. "Soon, me girl, we will be puttin' the top an' the bottom together." Cora hoped it would take longer than a fortnight because she enjoyed being with Bertha and learning a new talent. She had no parents, no husband, just one beautiful two-year-old. Mr. McCloud saved her from the Russian whorehouses. He helped with the cost of her baby's birth. She would work for him until she died, for all he had done for her and her son.

Marcus was so angry he was blood red in the face and shaking. "Why, Tom, why have you sent my girls to England to meet Liz? They were to stay here with me. I know we have had things to deal with, but—"

"Because they are just as much in jeopardy as the rest of the family." He handed Marcus a note.

THE PARKER TWINS MUST DIE
THEY GO RIGHT BEFORE YOU

"You get it now, Marcus? I want them safe as much as you, and your life is just as much my concern. If you can't keep your head in the game, you go into hiding as well."

"I got it, straighten up and fly right or lose your life." He didn't like it, but he would do as he was told.

The girls were no more than the length of the drive away. Hardison had given up his hut to them and was staying in the work barn. It had a small apartment above the storage rooms. "Will Joan need a doctor, Faye?" he asked her.

"No, I'll stitch her up myself. It's a through and through. She'll be up soon. Her side will hurt, but she has felt a lot worse."

"Charlie told me she cleared the apartment of six men on her own while you covered for her."

"Almost, she got seven before she got shot. I took out the last four. These men were both Parker's men and drug gang men. They needed to get some rest and change back into being the twins. Right now, they resembled two middle-aged men dressed in military uniforms. They gave Hardison the guns and asked him to let Tommy know they were here.

"He knows." It was Tommy. "Is she okay, unconscious or needing a doctor?" He had trouble looking at Faye; she was a man, one of at least forty.

"She is awake, listening, as usual—no doctor, I'll sew her up. Hardison has the guns. Destroy them for us, please. Here are all the paperwork, maps, and phone numbers we could get."

He went over to Joan. "It will be me doing the sewing. Do you need anesthetic, or do you want to watch?"

"I'll watch. I know I can trust you, Uncle Tommy, but I'm not there yet."

"Okay, I'll be right back. Faye can help you get ready." Joan nodded, never once opening her eyes. Outside the hut, he asked Hardison what they had told him.

Hardison told Tommy everything, gave him the satchel Faye had given him. "Sir, one thing, are they men or women?"

"They are twenty-two-year-old girls that have learned how to do what they do. They have at least four hundred kills between them. There is very little they won't do to get their job done, and oh, do not get on their wrong side, please."

Liz did not think she could keep Mitch here in London for much longer; Robert was climbing the walls but doing his best to keep Denny calm. Carol was done with London shopping; she hated the money, the rain. She mostly hated the food, being a cook. The greasy food did not sit well with her. Liz kept them from good restaurants to not be recognized, as Tommy had asked her to do. "Okay, we start in the morning packing all these Christmas ornaments so they will fly without breakage."

“Does this mean we are finished, we are going back to St. Helen?”

“No, we go back to the chalet, drop these off, see Mom and Tommy, then we go home.”

She knew they would not be going home unless the war was over. Liz could only pray it was.

Chapter Thirteen

HARDISON PREPARED THE operating table, just a cut-down metal kitchen table, narrow and long. They were getting ready to move her, when Bertha came in. She was quiet as a mouse; only Joan heard her. "Aunt B, you shouldn't be here," Joan said through gritted teeth.

"Ache, sweetheart, you're in need of a loven hand, an' I have one fer ya." Bertha took Joan's hand in both of hers. "You'll no be doin' this awake, me girl. I knows a thing or two aboot anesthetic, from werken with the first family. He was a veterinarian an' had me do the anesthetic fer him when he needed it." She looked at Hardison. "So no' just a decorator, are ya? I heard outside, Charlie calls ya Doc."

"Yes, Mrs. McCloud, I am your husband's doctor and surgeon. When you were poisoned, he had me consult with your doctor. When you were shot, again he did the same."

"So I'll help oot wit the anesthetic, a dog or a cat same as a human, right?"

"Yes, you are right."

"Tommy, we'll talk later. No, we all will talk." She stared at her husband, Charlie, and Hardison. She spoke quietly to Joan. "I'll no let go yer hand, love, till you're awake agin. Ya can trust me ta care fer ya."

"I do trust you, Aunt B. I have since that day in the dress shop when you showed me the right dress. I knew who you were then. I had to have a way to meet the family, meet my dad." She was ready, and Hardison called Dr. Lee to assist him after Joan was asleep and Faye was in the decorating barn, changing from man to woman. Bertha stood at her head while Hardison and Lee worked on her side.

"You missed a large bleeder, Tommy," Hardison told him.

"She will need a blood transfusion. Have we got any on hand?" asked Dr. Lee.

"Yes, I had the girls typed when they first arrived. Same as you, Tommy."

"We got that covered." Tommy put on gloves and retrieved it from the fridge under the operating table. Tommy hooked it up, ran the line to the injection site, and left for the doctors to take it from there. It was Hardison that did the rest.

"You can lighten it up, Mrs. McCloud. The surgery is finished. Can you bring her up slowly? I am afraid of her reaction."

"She will be fine as long as she hears my voice," Faye said. Bertha still had Joan's hand, or Joan had hers; she was holding on like Bertha was her lifeline. "Joan's awake and listening to us now," Faye whispered.

"You always tell on me, Faye." Joan was groggy but awake.

"You'll live to fight another day, sister," Faye told her.

"We cannot let the family know what happened. They think the girls were in England." It was Dr. Lee that came up with the solution. It would keep their father out of the hut and the rest of the family at ease. "We are going to tell the whole family that the girls contracted swine flu from England. They ate meat shipped there from China. It is highly contagious, and all the family will have to be inoculated for it. That includes all of you, so they know you have been cleared of it as well. Tommy says he doesn't need it. No one will be checking his arm for a needle mark."

"Afeared of a needle, are ya, Tommy?" Bertha said, with a smirk.

"All right, woman, I'll take the shot, but you better be ready to baby me for it." He laughed, but she didn't.

Dr. Lee entered the family room to inform them of the vaccination they were about to get. "Joan has swine flu! What about Faye? Does she have it also?" Marcus asked.

"Yes and yes, Marcus. Roll up your sleeve, as well as the rest of you." Jon Franc told the doctor he didn't think he would need to be vaccinated. Dr. Lee told him he did for the strain that the girls had. "This strain comes from England, where they imported pigs from China." The ladies were all lined up, ready to get their shots. However, Robert, Jon, and Marcus were telling each other to go first.

"Where are Mom and Tommy? Are they okay?"

"They are fine, Liz. They stayed with Joan and Faye until I got there, and they are helping them right now get things ready for their ten-day stay in the hut."

"Did they get inoculated? Are they safe?"

"Yes, Liz, relax. I took care of them first. They received booster shots as well. They should be in the house soon."

Bertha sat across from Tommy, Charlie, and Hardison; she said nothing but her face said a thousand words. It was Hardison who spoke. "Mrs. McCloud, how much do you actually know, and has Tommy told you anything?" Bertha just sat looking at all of them, with tears slowly making their way down her face.

Tommy went to her, held her, and kissed her. "I'll tell you, but do you want to know all of it?" He paused for a long time. When she didn't answer, he continued. "We are the head of a rescue team for hire. We do what we can to save children, families, and kidnapped people, even animals. It is not always easy. It involves nasty people, men who think they are gods, women who want to run and own the world and do anything to achieve it. Yes, there is killing and brutality involved, not always on our part, usually on the other. Right now, Mitchell's problems are caused by a woman just like I described. She was Stewart's woman. She blames our family for her loss, yet she was the one who killed him at our wedding. She did it because he beat her senseless for seeing another man. He damn near beat her to death."

"I no want to know the ugly parts, Tommy, but you must stop hiding yer doins from me. You, Charlie, ya are part of this as well as yer kids, and Hardison, me gentle-speaken decorator, a surgeon hired by me Tommy to care for him and his men and now our nieces. Ya can tells me of the twins so I know how ta help them."

All three men told her of the lives the girls had and what they went through. "They are more than full-fledged killers. Live for it. They are specialists in their field, learned at the hand of their grandfather, each taught through living through it."

Bertha was white, shaken to her very core. "'Tis the reason Joan plays the child. She's left ta herself."

"Yes, but that is how she learns what is going on. No one thinks her a threat, just a stupid childlike adult, a moron. She is brilliant, excellent memory retention. So she listens, learns, and tells us after she has taken care of the talkers."

She stood, nodded to all of them. "I'll get ready to help Hardison with the surgery. He needs ta stop the bleeder. I have the experience of a vet assistant. The people I worked fer first—he was a vet. I helped when he needed me. I will do the anesthetic for Joan and be there fer her when she comes around. Next time, Tommy, do yer job right." She went to Joan and told her she would be with her through the procedure right up to when she woke and longer if Joan needed her. She held the girl's hand, told her she loved her and would always be there for her. Hardison prepared the table and got the surgery ready. "Aunt B., thank you for understanding. I heard what the men said. I am sorry you had to listen to that horrible story. It was worse than their words. I will not hurt you or the family, I promise you on my life." Hardison had given her a shot, and Joan was asleep. Bertha never let go of her hand but kept an eye on Joan's breathing and heart rate for Hardison. He found the bleeder quickly. When she came around, she asked for Faye.

Faye was right beside her in seconds. "I'm here, Joan. Lie still and sleep. I will stay beside you and keep you safe until you wake."

Bertha asked Hardison if he had something cleaner to wear to the chalet. Hardison showed her where his extra cover-ups were. She covered her dress and went in through the kitchen and up the stairs. Liz stopped her in front of her room. "Mom, are you okay? You're white as a ghost, whiter than your hair, and you smell odd. What is it?"

"Hardison sprayed me so the vomit wouldn't smell so bad, an' I helped Dr. Lee fix Joan's side. She's okay now. She's no more in her tummy." Liz backed up from her; she wanted to get away from the smell. "If ya'll excuse me, Liz, I needs ta change me clothes."

"By all means, Mom, go right ahead." Liz thought she was going to lose her dinner.

Tommy and Charlie entered the kitchen, stripped, and threw their clothes into the open fire pit. "I will have the embers emptied tonight, Tom. Do you think Bertha is handling this well?"

"I don't know, Charlie. Time will tell, and a night in her bed, or not." A small closet in the pantry with a sliding door gave way, and the men had clothes to put on.

Tommy ran into Marcus, who wanted to know if his girls were okay and safe. "They are fair, Marcus. Dr. Lee gave them medication to stop regurgitation and bring down Joan's fever. They will be seen by him twice a day for the next ten days. We can't see them at all."

"I can't go see my girls, Tommy? I've had my shot, and Dr. Lee says it should keep us safe."

"It will unless you go into the hut. They are highly contagious, and Marcus, you and I are not young enough to ward this off. This is a killer strain of flu." Marcus shook his head and went into the study. Tommy knew he was hurting, wanting to see the girls, to see if they are healthy. He wondered if he should tell him the truth.

Bertha tapped him on the shoulder. "Ya will no tell him a thing. Let him think they are all right, still beautiful healthy girls. They ner be that, an' they will die young."

"Yes, love, they will, neither of them fully sane, but wanting to be."

Jon asked Dr. Lee if he could go back to St. Helen as he felt he could be of some help with the investigations. Jon was injected with a booster shot as well as the vaccine shot and released. Bertha told Tommy to make excuses for them so they could see the girls. "Liz, I'm taking Bertha up to meet Hardison's wife and daughter. We should be back by dinner."

"Before you go, Tommy, can we go back home soon? Denny is showing signs of stress."

"I know, Liz. As soon as we can, I'll get you back home. I know it's hard on you and the family. Just hang in there, my love. You are doing a great job."

Bertha and Tommy were sitting with Joan and Faye in the living area of the hut. Faye asked when they could be back in the field. "Not yet, Faye, your dad is climbing the walls, wanting to see you and Joan."

"All well and good, but Charlie and I have gone over the paperwork and maps. She plans another attack. We didn't get that info. The one guard threw it in the fire before Joan could stop him. She got part of it that wasn't burned. I kept it here because it would disturb all the family."

Hardison nodded then turned to Bertha. "If you are up to speed on the doings of this company, I will explain. If not, you should leave, my dear gentle lady."

"I'll do no such a thing. Tell yer tale, Hardison, and you, Faye, what'ere he misses."

Faye spoke up. "It's the map of the corner lot of your street, all that's left of it anyway—your house, Liz's, and the new one for Denny and Robert. The notes said all the properties were to be destroyed, making sure that the family members went with them. Charlie decoded a file Joan captured from the throat of one of them. It implies that the girls are to be drawn and quartered and sold for human meat. Marcus is to burn to death for creating the two abominations. This file is from our grandfather, Master Walt."

Hardison turned away from Bertha and the girls. His head bowed, and his shoulders slumped. “I have never heard of such people in my life. I left my practice to help here, fix bones, remove bullets, and set things right—not live in a horror movie, Tommy. More and more of this is happening. It has to stop! Or I will have to leave. I enjoy working in the decorating shop, but I can do without this to live quietly. I’d like to grow old sitting on my porch in the mountains. Marta sees one of the gardeners. Please tell me he is just that, a gardener, not a gunman.”

“He is my best gardener, knows his plants,” Tommy told him. He felt so bad for Hardison. He had promised him a quiet life up here on the mountain, at the chalet.

“We cannot let the family go back to the city. We don’t know when she is planning this.” Faye spoke up abruptly. “Look, there is a bookkeeper that works for her as well as the drug cartel. Info from the people around him says the drug cartel wants her gone, but they are unsure where her information is coming from. Let me go put a little pressure on him and see what I can find out.”

“Not without me, you don’t. You’re slow, I’m not. You overthink, I don’t. I have told you so often, Faye, once we set the plan in action, move and move fast, do not rethink it, but you do. How do you think I got shot?”

“Sorry, I thought to take out the other guard first instead of after. I know I should have stuck to your plan. So plan it out for me. I’ll do just as you say.”

“We will do as she says, Faye.” It was Charlie’s son Peter; he worked with the girls, always at Faye’s side. He knew her faults but still guarded her. “We have to do this, Joan, and you have to stay, heal, and get strong. You plan it out, and we will follow it to the letter. If Faye starts to stray, I will stop her.”

Joan looked at Peter. She saw something she had hoped to see for herself. He loved Faye. He would take care of her. He understood she would never be right in the head. "Peter, I will take your life if anything happens to my sister. Tell your dad I need his help and Uncle Tommy's to plan this. Hardison, give me something to get rid of the fog."

"Are you sure, Joan? You are not in the best shape to plan this out."

"Uncle Tommy, I have been the planner for the two of us for longer than you know. Even to our meeting the family, I organized it so it was me they met first. I knew just when to do it. The apartment we had, we could have covered the rent. I held it back so we would be kicked out exactly when I wanted it. It cost me, but it worked. We lived with our Dad, we wanted it to last longer, but that's life. Now get me that shot, Hardison." Her look was enough to scare even Tommy. Bertha knew this would probably be the end of the twins she saw in Joan's eyes.

She had to stay on her back, but she had Faye hold the maps and papers she needed. Charlie gave her as much input as possible; he admired her ability to see what would happen in advance. Charlie was afraid for Peter; he was not as good as the twins but better than everyone else except Tommy, but he did minimal fighting since his marriage. He did do the rescuing jobs and some of the takedowns. "Look, you have all I can give you. You have to go in as an arguing married couple. Faye, you have to look like you are about seven or eight months pregnant, holding your stomach. You will be carrying the chemicals you will need to get the man to talk. He may be unhappy about Tara, but he will not spill the information without help. Peter, your man bag will have the needles she needs. Use it quickly. Get in and out in ten minutes.

That is all you have. The guard checks him every ten, on orders from Tara. She does not trust him, wants an excuse to get rid of him." She looked exhausted.

Faye kissed her cheek and said something both Tommy and Bertha knew meant more than just goodbye. "I will see you in hell, my sister. I'll wait for you there." Joan smiled and shook her head in agreement.

Peter hugged his dad and said something in his native tongue that made Charlie tear up and hold him longer. "I will tell your mother in your own words, Peter, this I promise." They separated, and he and Faye left. Charlie shook Tommy's hand and went as well. Joan had fallen silent. Bertha knew she was awake. She kissed her forehead and told her she would pray for them.

"Pray it's quick, Aunt B. I don't want her to suffer. Uncle Tommy, send back up in fifteen minutes after they get in. We need to get Peter out with the information." Bertha was shocked at how matter-of-fact Joan was. "Aunt B, Faye knows once she enters that man's den, she is dead. Faye will get the information and fight to get Peter out. She will need all the help you can give her. We have always known we are short-lived, Aunt B. We have lived longer than even we expected. We wanted to meet our family and be normal for just a little while. Uncle Tommy knew who we were the day I arrived at your home. We are well known among the underworld because of our grandfather, Master Walt. Did you know, Uncle Tommy, he was afraid of you and our dad? He wanted both of you gone so he could live without fear. Thank you for that—the bastard and his sister deserved everything they got." Bertha wanted to hold her close and let her know she was so loved. "Tell Dad after this is over that we loved him and there is a package for him in Montana. All he has to do is go get it. I left the address on the desk in my room.

Ask for Margaret. She is his granddaughter, Faye's girl born four years ago, one of my grandfather's experiments—Faye's eggs and one of your men's sperm. The child's DNA will tell you who the father was if you need to know."

"Joan, you will be here with us. You can tell him."

"Aunt Bertha, I won't be here long."

They went back to the chalet. This time, Marcus was grabbed by Bertha. "I need ya ta listen to me, not a word, Marcus. Listen then go like the wind." She told him what Joan said. She told him everything. "I'll go help Faye first, then go for my granddaughter."

"No, you won't. Tommy has gone fer her and Peter with his men. You get that child before Tara does. Go, go now."

"Can I say goodbye to Joan?"

"No, she is gone as well. Why are you hesitating, Marcus? Take the plane, go." Marcus held her for just a few seconds and ran toward the heliport.

Bertha grabbed Liz and headed for the chapel to pray for all of them. Liz was in shock when she heard Bertha's prayer asking for help with saving Faye, Peter, Tommy, and poor Joan. Bertha asked that the other men that went return, be saved as well. She asked that He watch over the family. Bertha continued to pray through her tears: "Lord, save our homes. Please save the people around our homes." Liz was crying as well as Bertha. The rest of the ladies had followed them and were praying also.

Denny said out loud, "God grant our family peace and all of us together. I promise to be strong for my baby. Please grant our family this." Cora came in and knelt beside Bertha. She prayed in her native tongue; Cora was German. Then she told Bertha Marcus was gone. He went into the hut to tell Joan he was going and loved her more than he could say. She started to cry. She told Bertha that Hardison said Joan was giving up and she was failing.

Bertha rose and told the ladies it was time to prepare a meal for when the men returned. It was then that Liz realized Mitch, Michael, Robert, and Doug were gone. “No, Mom, no, they didn’t go with Tommy, please, no.”

“Stop it, Liz. Each of us feels the same. Get it ta gether.” Bertha sent them into the kitchen under Carol’s supervision to start a large meal. She herself walked over to Charlie’s chalet behind theirs and asked his wife to join them.

She was teary-eyed but agreed to come and be with all the women. “Mrs. McCloud, I thank you for this. Waiting alone is hard, and bad thoughts enter your mind.” They went into the kitchen; Bertha introduced May-Ling, Charlie’s wife, to the ladies. They cooked up a storm. May taught them some Chinese dishes. The food was ready and warm, but no men returned. The house phone rang, and Cora answered it. She ran to Bertha, who grabbed the kitchen line.

It was Tommy. “We have Peter. Faye is in bad shape. Tell Joan she is alive, hang on. We are almost home, love, and we did what we had to and got the information along with the bookkeeper.” She told him Marcus was gone to get the child. Tommy was worried about that but said nothing.

Bertha told the family the men were all coming home shortly. May-Ling thanked Bertha for letting her be a part of the family—like Liz said, one of the ladies of the house. May-Ling and Bertha walked toward the hut. “I’ll leave you here, Bertha. I know you want to talk to Joan.”

Hardison met Bertha at the door. “Unless you have good news, please don’t come in. She will just quit trying.”

"'Tis good news, Hardison, truly it is." She sat down next to Joan, took her hand, and told her that she knew she could hear her. "Faye's liven. Tommy an' the men are bringen her hame ta ya. She took a beaten, but she's alive, so start ta fight fer yer life, gal. Yer sister will need ya." Although Joan said not a word, the single tear running down her cheek said it all.

Faye held Peter's hand on the ride home. He never let it go. She was bleeding internally, and he knew she was in trouble. They needed to get her to Hardison and Dr. Lee. He wanted to tell her how he felt, show her he didn't care what she was. They arrived within the hour. Peter took Faye to the hut. Charlie and Dr. Lee stopped him. "Take her to the barn. Hardison and Lee are waiting for her. If she is going to make it, they will transfer her to the hut. Joan's strength was returning since she was informed her sister was hurt but alive. Maybe one of them will survive."

"Dad, Faye is in rough shape, but she is going to make it. Give her a chance." Peter pushed past them and went to the barn and told them both to do a quick check; then he took her to her sister, who would help her pull through. They did as asked. They were not surprised at what they found. "Peter, she needs to have the internal injuries found and repaired."

If the bullets in her leg and shoulder were minor, she was in luck, if not . . . They rushed her over to the hut for X-rays and an ultrasound. Hardison prayed he would not need to go to a real hospital. She would die here before she or her sister would allow that. Faye's internal bleeding came from a tear in the abdominal wall that Hardison and Dr. Lee repaired while Joan watched. Hardison took the slug out of her leg and shoulder. He found three in her leg, two in her shoulder. "She is going to make it, Joan, so both of you will be back together again." Joan closed her eyes and said nothing. Hardison thought the child would return, and then horror for the two of them would continue. He might be giving Tommy his resignation very shortly.

Faye found it quiet in the compound. They were still working on the information she and Peter had brought back. Faye was still healing and trying hard to wrap her mind around how slowly Joan was recovering. She seemed so weak, unable to move around too much. Getting up to eat her meals and chat with family would drain her of whatever strength she had. Sometimes when Dad would fly in from a business trip, he would spend time with her, only to have her fall asleep on him. Hardison said it would take time to heal her heart.

When she thought about it, the time had moved past them. Joan had planned to meet Dad by running into Aunt B. in the wedding shop. She was good at that sort of thing, always one step ahead of Faye. They had worked hard to help Uncle Tommy and Charlie capture the information they needed on Taraco Corporation and the other organizations attached to her. Joan got hurt going after info their Dad and Uncle Tommy needed. Faye thought, *If I had not second-guessed Joan's plans, she would be fine. All this happened over the past twelve months. Our birthday was just weeks away. We became part of the family just before our last birthday.*

Before she and Joan were rescued, she thought there would be no life for them. Thanks to the Spanish twins' saviours getting all four of them out nearly three years ago, life had changed. They now had a chance of becoming human.

Chapter Fourteen

MARCUS ARRIVED AT the address Joan gave him. It was an orphanage. He called ahead to talk to the organization's head to determine if the child was still there. "Yes, Mr. McCloud, the children are still here. We are paid handsomely for their care and their keep." He gave the matron the paperwork he had. He asked for the children to be released immediately to him. She tried to brush him off by telling him to wait, and she would bring them out to him in the courtyard. "Stop right there. Is Margaret here? She is the one I was told to speak to."

"Why did you not say that in the first place? Come with me. They are in the junior kindergarten class. They are very quick learners." He still did not know if they were girls or boys, and he was told of one child. She opened the door and called to Mark and Mary they came to her. They looked like their mother. "Do you remember when you asked me if anyone wanted the two of you, and I said your day will come?"

They were staring at him but answered her, "Yes, Matron, we do."

"Well, this man is your grandfather. Do you think you would like to go with him?"

They both came over and took one hand each. "Yes, please, can we go now?"

Before the matron could answer them, Marcus did. "Yes, let us go now, shall we? Matron Wilson, do they have clothes or any special toys they need?"

"No, they wear uniforms that belong to us. If you pay for their outfits, they can go like they are. Toys are shared between all the children." Marcus walked out the door without one look back. Neither child looked back either.

First stop was a clothing store, winter clothes for the chalet. "Now, each of you picks out two or three toys you want to take with you." Marcus had to get the driver to help him with all the bags, dollhouse, dollies, crayons, books, cars, trucks, and Legos, along with all the clothes, of course. He threw the uniforms in the garbage; they were so worn and thin they would not do for any other child.

They were excited and scared to get on the plane. To them, it was large and frightening. It was a twelve-seater, so they could play after takeoff. Marcus nearly fell over the toys, going to the back for a coffee. He laughed at this, something he never had the chance to do with his children.

When they landed, the kids loved the snow, they ate in a small restaurant off the main highway: hot dogs, orange soda, and ice cream. He thought they were going to get sick, but they wanted to know if they could get candy to eat in the car. When they arrived, he found Tommy. "There are two, Mark and Mary."

Tommy stopped him. "I know. I'm the one paying for their keep." Marcus slugged him so hard Tommy landed on his ass. When he stood, he said, "Before I knock the hell out of you, Marcus, would you care to explain that?"

"They had no clothes, no toys, no information on their medical condition or if they had any illnesses. They were treated like animals. I had to pay fifty dollars apiece for their uniforms that our cleaning ladies would not use to clean the toilets with, and you act like you're proud of yourself."

"I paid that organization two thousand a month per child for clothing, toys, education, and medical care. I sent extra for Christmas, Easter, their birthdays. The clothes and toys they have I just bought. They have the price tags still on them."

Tommy took Marcus into his private office, pulled out the files, sat Marcus down, and gave it all to him. "When you are done, come to see me." The documents took up a full drawer.

"They are not the same kids as described here."

"What do you mean, not the same kids?"

"Come with me." They entered the great room; the kids were thin but alert, playing but not violent with each other. They spoke to each other but not meanly. Tommy walked in and sat down. Just a bit loud, he said, "Who made this mess?" just to see the reaction.

"We did, but if you don't use the paddle, we will clean it up real quick, won't we, Mary?"

"No, it's okay. I was only teasing you. Do you like your toys?"

"Oh yes, we didn't have toys because matron told us our patron didn't donate enough for us to have our own stuff. We sat in the hall on holidays while the other kids got presents. They didn't have to share. We got what they didn't want."

"Well, not anymore, okay? What you get is yours." Cora came in and asked if Marcus knew what the kids liked to eat. "Mary, what is your favourite dish you like?"

"When the others get turkey, we get what's left on their plates. I love turkey and chicken and brown meat when there is some." Her brother said the same. Cora left the great room with tears in her eyes.

The assistant cook sent out salad, potatoes, three kinds of vegetables with ham, roast beef, and chicken. The children ate until they couldn't put another bite in their mouth. They were falling asleep at the table. Marcus and Tommy each took a child up the stairs to their rooms. Cora came in; she changed them into their pajamas. It was seven in the evening, and Cora said they would sleep until at least six or seven in the morning. "What time does your little fellow get you up in the morning, Cora?" Tommy asked.

"Oh, he is up at six every day no matter the time he goes to bed."

"Marcus, set your clock and tell Chef they are early risers."

"Can we take turns on this morning thing, Tommy?"

"Nope, your grandbabies, your job until their mother decides what she wants to do."

"Bertha, they are the image of their mother."

"What do ya mean by that, Tommy? Faye had twins or no, 'tis one but with two heads?"

"No, two children, Miss Smarty. From what Hardison says, they have the same father, but the mothers are a little different, like they are related to each other and had their kids on the same day."

"Can Hardison say for sure at least one is Faye's?"

"Yes, he can, and he's 100 percent positive the other is Joan's."

"Can it be? She ner said she had a wee bairn, only Faye. She told Marcus ta git his grandchild. Canna we speak ta them? They still ta weak?"

"Dr. Lee said they could see us, so do let's drop in," Tommy told her. He crooked his arm so she could loop hers through. The girls were both sitting at the table, eating lunch. "Can we have a serious talk with you girls, or are you not up to it?" asked Tommy.

"Ask away, Uncle Tommy. We will do our best to answer," Faye told him.

"Did you know that there were two children, a boy and a girl, at the orphanage?"

"No, I knew nothing of the sex of my child, but only one," she told Tommy.

Joan sat quietly for some time then looked at Bertha with pleading eyes. "They took all my eggs before they used the pokers on me, said they were going to sell them to the highest bidder. Later, I heard they had fertilized one and wanted to see if baby flesh would be tasty. That would be a new market for the master. I never knew a baby survived from my eggs." She was crying. "Uncle Tommy, Aunt Bertha, do I have a daughter or a son?"

"We have to do blood work on both of you to know whose kid is whose." Bertha took his phone out and showed them pictures of the children together and separate.

"A boy and a girl, do they have names, Aunt B?"

"Yes, Mark and Mary, they could pass for twins. They look like true McClouds."

Bertha could see Faye was struggling with it. "I'm no mother. Look what I do, and enjoy doing. What can I teach my kid? Look, honey, this is how you kill the men and then you get out of there. Mommy teach you how to hide."

"Stop it, Faye, you know better." It was Joan. "What we do is what we do. If one or the other takes over, if we both buy the farm, we have a family that will take over for us. They will be raised right. I can teach them how to be childlike and listen and learn. You can teach them to second-guess what I tell them." That brought laughter from all of them.

"Are you strong enough to go up to the chalet and meet them?"

"Hardison said they could go as long as we do the blood work first, and I stay with them."

They were going to meet their kids. Joan was so excited; she wanted to be a mommy for as long as she could remember. Faye, however, was nervous; being a mother brought significant responsibilities. She did want to see them and to know which one was hers. She was not sure she wanted the house-and-home game. The DNA tests took a little longer to get answers, so they would just have to wait. Her leg was getting stronger, and she could finally keep some food down.

Joan was growing stronger slowly like something wasn't quite right, something missed. The next time Peter stopped by, she would have him take her to see Hardison or Dr. Lee and have them re-examine Joan, look and see if there was something they missed.

Tommy thought the same thing. Joan should be up and feeling her old self. It had been nearly three months since she was hurt. Hardison decided to redo her X-rays and ultrasound. Dr. Lee convinced Tommy they needed an MRI machine. So the machine was bought and shipped to the chalet—anything for the twins. At first, Joan didn't like the idea of being swallowed by this machine with all the noise it made, but after cajoling from Faye, Peter, and her dad, she finally gave in. When the results came up on Hardison's computer, he was amazed. She had a tear in her aorta that was leaking; this was not a good thing at all. It could be the reason she was not getting better and getting weaker. Faye demanded they fix it. "Not that easy, Faye—on the result of the MRI test, the tear looks small, but it is in the aorta. I'm not capable of that type of surgery. We need a heart specialist, a heart surgeon." Faye was frustrated. She was getting better daily.

She needed Joan to do the same. Marcus or Tommy needed the planner back on her feet.

Hardison sent out feelers for a heart surgeon that needed a vacation, if he or she only took a look and found out what they needed to do. Dr. Laura Werther, a heart specialist, jumped at the mountain vacation in trade to examine a patient.

Tommy was not happy about this, but Bertha was ecstatic about it, so he gave in to it. His worry was too many noses in the pot will smell something not quite right. She arrived Friday evening just before dinner. Charlie had outdone himself. He had investigated her food likes and dislikes. He prepared a meal of all her favourites. After dinner, she questioned Tommy, Marcus, and Faye about the patient.

"You need to speak to her two doctors, Dr. Hardison and Dr. Lee. They can tell you more."

Peter rushed into the dining room. "Come quickly. Joan is failing! Hardison needs you now." Dr. Laura grabbed her bag and followed Peter out through the kitchen door to the hut. Joan was extremely pale, and her heart rate was slower than it should be. Joan did not trust this new doctor. A woman doctor—well, if Faye wanted her to do this, fine, she would; she didn't have to like it. She felt tired all the time; going to the washroom was such a chore.

Dr. Werther started with an MRI at a higher level. Hardison was uneasy about that, but she knew hearts, or so her documents said she did. She showed him and Lee, not just a tear. A small metal object was jammed in a bend of the valve feeding the aorta, causing pressure and pain. It had to be removed and quickly. Joan didn't understand. If she had a bullet fragment in her heart, then why hadn't she died?

"You would have, Joan, but the small tear has kept the pressure down. We need to fix both, kiddo. What say you come to my hospital and we get this done?"

"Thanks but no thanks, I can't go into the city. It is not a safe place for me but thank you, Dr. Laura Werther. At least I know what is wrong with me."

"You plan on dying shortly, then?"

"How shortly, Dr. Werther?" asked Faye.

"If she is lucky, a week, ten days tops."

"You are going to have the surgery, Joan. I do not plan on losing you because you are stubborn," Faye scolded her.

"No, I am not. I would die young anyway, so sooner better than later."

"Again, no."

"I can do your surgery in any one of the many hospitals that are set up for heart surgery. I will get you a list of hospitals for you, but you have to decide quickly. Time is of the essence."

Joan went silent, acting like she was asleep, just listening.

"Stop it. You are not a child, you are not crazy." Faye was not letting her off the hook that easily. "What if you are a mother to one of the children?"

"What if I don't make it? You will have to be there for both of them. All right, but it's done here. Get the medical crap she needs. Hardison, I die on the table, so be it. I am tired, Faye. I want the killing stopped. Yes, I am good at it, but I hate it. I can plan better than any of you, but I go because of you, dear sister. You never listen to me, do you?" She lay down and turned her back to them.

Tommy explained it all to these doctors, hoping to convince them to do it. Dr. Werther told him she could die without proper procedure. "Joan knows this, and she still wants it this way. She trusts no one. My niece barely trusts me. Faye is the only one she truly trusts, and even that is iffy."

Werther made calls to manufacturers for specific equipment. "Yes, cash, no names, the medical supplies and equipment will be picked up by helicopter." It took her two calls. She had all she needed. She was amazed that it could be procured just that easily if you had the cash to pay upfront. Tommy made the arrangements for the money to be ready for her. "You will fly out on my helo. My bodyguard will be with you—not to make sure you don't take off with the cash but make sure no one hurts you."

"Thank you, Mr. McCloud, you and your wife have been so generous."

"When this is over, you will have to sign a privacy agreement. Are you all right with that?" She told him she understood completely; she had heard of the rescuer organization, and she was glad they were there.

Surgery was set for eight in the morning the following day. All three doctors made their plans and set out who was to do what. Faye was scared beyond belief. Peter told her he would stay with her and the family. Hardison had set up a surgery in the large meeting room off the kitchen. He had it scrubbed and sterilized twice before the operating room was acceptable to him. Everything Dr. Laura Werther wanted was in place. All they needed was the patient.

It took four hours to repair the tear in the aorta and remove the piece of a bullet. Joan was fragile, and her heart stopped on them twice, but she was alive and breathing for the moment. Joan was put in an induced coma to keep her calm and quiet. Faye sat by her side until Bertha made her go to bed with the promise she would get her if there was any change in Joan's condition.

Faye was called into Joan's room two hours later. She was failing, and her condition was guarded. Hardison knew Joan was dying. She wanted to be awake if this time came. Joan had made him promise to wake her so she could talk to Faye. Faye held her hand. With a weak whispering voice, Joan told Faye her secret, then let herself go. Hardison feared Faye's reaction. Tommy was standing behind Faye, a knife in his belt. "Uncle Tommy, I feel like half of me just died. I want to scream, cry, laugh. I can't stand it."

He turned her around and held her. "Faye, child, I can't tell you I know because I don't know what I felt when my daughter died, but that's me. Let it out, scream if you have to. I know it hurts like hell." The whole family grieved the loss of the childlike adult. Very few knew her as she really was.

Joan asked Hardison and her father to please have her cremated and throw her ashes to the winds of the mountains, for then she would finally be free.

Marcus, Tommy, Bertha, Faye, and Peter joined Hardison on the mountain. Tommy had the pilot shut down the helo. Hardison sang "How Great Thou Art" as per Joan's request. Bertha said prayers for Joan and for the family that they would grow to know that Joan was safe and healthy with her Maker. Hardison said in his native tongue, "Take her home, Father, so she can be with her mother and be at peace for the first time in her short life."

Faye yelled out to her, "Goodbye, my sister, my best friend, be happy. I will always love you."

Marcus quietly dropped the roses he brought with him over the edge of the mountain. "For you, my little girl, a rose for every year you were here. I love you as if I had you all your life." He wrapped his arms around Faye and walked her back to the helicopter.

Chapter Fifteen

ON THE WAY back to the chalet, Tommy brought up the children. "Faye, sweetheart, do you feel up to seeing the children? They know Marcus as Grandpa, Bertha they call Grams, they know me as old Uncle Tom. It's time to decide if you want to be their mother, Auntie Faye, or put them in care." Marcus was about to speak, but one look from his brother stopped him.

"Uncle Tommy, I'm not all that well, if you get me, but I'm willing to try, only if I am excluded from the organization. I can't go out, do what is needed, then come back and be Mommy."

"Then we need to get this over with so we all can go home and live a normal life, don't you think?"

"Be as normal as can be expected."

Faye cornered Hardison. "I need your help. Joan left me with a secret that only you should know if anything happens to me." She told him.

He sat down hard on his chair. "It can't be. He can't know this, can he?"

"Yes, he does, and I am sure he knew Joan knew."

"I will do as you say, Faye."

Uncle Tommy introduced the children to Faye. They seemed to know her.

"You are our mother. We had a picture of you, but the matron took it because she said we were bad."

"Yes, Mark, I am, and we can start being a family if you and Mary want that." Faye wondered if they were programmed like she and Joan were.

"We want to grow up and be teachers that don't spank."

"That's good, Mary, so we will have to get you two into school as soon as we can."

"We will get them a tutor for now, then school when we return to St. Helen. Liz and Mitchell will help you with that." Bertha was pleased that Faye was trying. Faye was having a hard time with it.

Tommy told Faye that Charlie had found out where Tara was holed up. "Can you plan this out with him to get it finished?"

"I can try, but we both know she is not the head of the snake. And like Joan said, when you and Charlie have the head of the snake, it will be done," Faye said.

"Yes, Faye, I know."

"Care to plan that job with me, Uncle Tommy?"

"No, not yet. Let's clean up as much as we can before I go after that. It will probably be my end like Joan."

"No, Uncle Tommy, we will do it together, you, Charlie, Peter, and I together. After the Christmas holiday, we will make the plans to finish this problem."

Hardison and Michael went out to cut down the tree for the great room. The ladies were bringing the fancy ornaments and bulbs they bought in England to the room. Bertha went to the decorating barn, asked Marta to help her bring in the rest of her favourite things she and Hardison pulled out from under the tarp. There was a large box Martha kept closed. It was a unique tree decoration that Hardison wanted to open for Bertha and the family himself. It would be a great surprise for the McCloud twins. Bertha, however, was in for a huge surprise. Mary and Mark were so excited. They were told that because they were good boys and girls, Santa Claus would make a special visit here just to see them. Mark was trying very hard to colour inside the lines so his picture would please Santa. Mary made him paper snowflakes with the help of Cora and childproof scissors.

Bertha, Liz, and the rest of the ladies had run garland around the room in scallops on the great wooden beams that ran around the ceiling. They had decorated it with red and green bells with gold and silver bulbs. The natural cones added to it being so beautiful. The garland filled the room with the pine scent of Christmas. Marcus found his mother's Christmas music, had it piped through the house.

Faye was sitting near the floor-to-ceiling window facing the mountains; she was stronger, and her therapy for her leg and shoulder helped relieve the pain. She would have to fight through the pain until she was once more at full strength. Faye saw something move near the east end of the chalet. At first, she thought maybe it was an animal. Then Faye saw the gun with the sight sticking up above the shrubs. Quickly she told the women to move away from the windows and get the kids out of the room. She herself could not move that fast. Peter grabbed her up in his arms and took her out of the room. He told her Charlie and two of the guards were outside.

Caitlin entered the house and said it was okay. She looked like she wanted to rip a strip off someone. "I am so sorry, Mrs. McCloud. We were following two men, did not think to warn you."

Charlie came in. "We have the two men you were following. They work for Mr. McCloud. They are the guards for the property. What did you want with them, Mr. Franc?"

"Oh, they can't be the men we were chasing. My intel said that we had a line on two of the drug cartel people." Charlie brought in the men. Franc looked at the men—same clothes, same height, and weight. They had the same shoes that Caitlin mentioned to Franc that they were wearing. "I am sorry, fellas. I swore you two were the guys." He showed Charlie the picture. Franc wasn't prepared for Bertha.

"Ya take this mess oot of me hoose now an' ner come back. Yer FBI is no welcome here, now go." With that, she stamped her foot. "Charlie, clean this trash oot of me hoose."

Charlie bit his lower lip. He did not dare laugh at her or Franc's face as he escorted him and his men out. "She will calm down, Mr. Franc, and I'm sure you will be welcome as a friend once again."

"Thanks, Charlie. Did I spoil something for her?"

"Yes, they were just about to decorate the tree, and Santa is coming to see the children." Charlie went into the kitchen, where his men were removing the gunmen's clothes.

"Charlie, I need to shower. That guy stinks, smells like marijuana. I don't even smoke cigarettes."

"Use this one off the kitchen, leaving his clothes and your underwear outside the door," Charlie said. "Anything on you can be used to track her. Sorry, I'll leave clothes for you, Barry. You do the same."

"Thanks, boss. We'll be quick in case you need us."

Michael and Charlie took the two men out of the house. As soon as they heard from their guards, it was clear of the FBI. They dressed them in housemen uniforms, never used anymore, but it worked.

Tommy made sure the ladies were settled and back to decorating. He got stopped before he could leave. “Ya better be back afore Santa comes, ya hear me, Tommy McCloud?”

She was still mad, so he promised he would. He headed back quickly. He passed Hardison on the way. “I’ll keep her busy. I delayed Santa for an hour. That should give you enough time.”

Tommy thanked him and kept going at breakneck speed toward the barn. Charlie stopped him. “They are actually the biggest chickens in the world. Mike took out the clamps he needed to fix the hole in the fence they had cut to get into the compound. They thought he was going to use the clamps on them. They told me everything. I’ll go tell Faye and Peter. I will fill you in after Santa leaves. I already called him back and told him to come on his assigned time.”

Tommy took fifteen minutes to change his clothes and pick up the little box in his sock drawer. “I’m back, Bertha. ’Tis time ta put the topper on the tree.”

The box that Marta brought in was opened by Hardison. He kept his back to the ladies, but mostly from Bertha. Tommy watched her. He knew she wasn’t prepared for what Hardison had in that box.

She was nearly three feet tall, and her wingspan matched her height. She was porcelain and dressed in lace and satin. Her halo was gold. Hardison held her close to his body as he climbed the ladder. The tree nearly touched the twelve-foot ceiling. He opened the clamps under her gown and attached her to the tree, plugged her into the lights. Her halo glowed, as did her wings and gown. “Oh, Hardison, she’s beautiful, a gift from Himself above.”

“My mother made her. She carved her body from wood. Her face is the face of her first doll. The body was sawdust and falling apart, so Mom repainted her face and made her an angel. She is at least fifty years old."

Bertha had tears in her eyes and couldn't speak. So did most of the ladies. Marcus walked over to Tommy. "Remember our mom saying she will always be on our tree until we come home no more?" Tommy nodded. The tree was beautiful, so colourful with gold and silver garland, multicoloured balls and bulbs, and ornaments. It had been at least six years since Tommy allowed a tree erected. Faye came in with the children. They stood open-mouthed, not a sound from either one. Faye gave each one an ornament to put on the tree. One was a large crystal-blue letter J. The other was an F in green crystal. "I will have your Grams have two letters M's made for both of you," Faye told them.

Mark said, "Can I have a red truck with the M on it?"

"I want a dolly with an M on her dress, please."

Bertha rubbed their heads. "Aye, wee bairns, ya can."

They heard a noise overhead, and they ducked down. "Mommy, what is it?"

"I think it's Santa coming to visit us. Are you ready to meet him? Don't be afraid. He loves children so much."

Santa came into the great room and said, "Ho ho ho." Mark and Mary hid behind Faye. Santa knelt so he was almost their height. "Can you come close and give me a handshake, my little friends?"

Mary grabbed Mark and pulled him forward. "He's a little scared of your belt Santa, that's all." They talked to Santa and told him what they wanted. Santa reached in his bag and took out a big box as tall as her, and it was a doll that walked and talked. Everyone was glad her dolly didn't wet. Mark got the largest fire truck ever seen. It had a siren, hoses, ladders, and firemen with helmets. He promised not to use the siren when they were in the house.

"It's fine in the playroom, Mark, as long as it's not bothering anyone," Santa said. "I have other boys and girls to see. But before I go, I must talk with Lady Bertha. Is she here?"

"Aye, I'm here, Santa. Ya needs me fer somethin'?" She walked over to where he stood in front of the tree.

"I know you have been brave and strong for your family and your man, so I have this for you." He handed her the box Tommy had given Santa. It was an antique locket with a diamond in the centre of the front. Inside were pictures of her and Tommy. Inscribed above the pictures was "I love you forever." She gave Santa a wee kiss and cried, "Thank you." She walked over to Tommy and asked him to put it on her neck for her, which he did. She told him she would love him as long as he loved her, and she would never take it off. She only hoped the gift she had made for him made him as happy as he had her. Only time would tell—six more days until Christmas.

Marcus played on the floor with the children as Liz took a ton of pictures of the tree and the children. She thought about when she and Mitch would be doing this with their grandchild. It would be a while before that happened. Maybe Mom could teach her to knit or crochet or even make blankets like the one she taught Cora to make. All this would be great if this horrible war was over. She heard Robert complaining to Denny that living the life of a rich man was okay, but after this long, the game was no fun. "Robert, this is no game. Your mother's home, Grams and Gramps' home, and even our new home are all in jeopardy. That woman wants us dead, no trace of the Maxwell or McCloud families left, and that, my beloved husband, includes the King family as well. I know there is more going on than the FBI investigating this, Robert. Listen to the conversations in the hall, with your mom and Mitch privately arguing. And Grams—she needs to put her armour on. She is ready to go to war. I tell you, Robert, you are missing the big picture.

"Joan was dying, getting the swine flu in England. I heard Peter say to Faye that Joan had a bullet fragment in her heart that they were going to remove. That's why Dr. Werther came to assist Hardison."

"Denny, are you having hallucinations? Everything is okay. Joan had a fragment, yes, but it was not a bullet. Those twins were scary—well, so is Faye. Marcus is happy to play with Faye's kid, although where they came from is still a mystery to me. They do look a lot like her. Mark called me Uncle Robert yesterday, and Faye told him he got it right. So now we are Aunt Denny and Uncle Robert." Liz wanted to interrupt this conversation. They were getting close to figuring some of the problems out. She would see what Mom had to say about what they knew and what she had pieced together through Tommy.

Mitch felt sick that his family unit was mixed up in all of this—Liz, Robert, Denny, and the unborn grandchild. He had to get this over with, for them. He loved all of them more than all the riches he had. He had to join the organization full-time and become one of the warriors. The lady that gave him his family, his best friend Bertha, already was a warrior. She tossed the FBI agent out on his ass. He would never let his buddy Jon live that one down. After all, she had stamped her foot at Jon, had raised her voice. She should have had a sword at her hip, the way she went at him. He would not forget Charlie having to bite his lip and escort the FBI out of the house. How did she put that—

He heard Liz calling to him and left the atrium to go to her. He was about to round the corner of the hall, when he saw she was being held by a hooded man with a very large gun. Mitch wanted to charge in but knew that was exactly what they wanted him to do. He backed down to the atrium, out the door, into the side garden, ran around to the back door, and quietly entered. Charlie was reading a cookbook. "Charlie, a hooded man has Liz in a headlock in the east wing hallway. He had a gun and was making her call for me."

Charlie put the book down, opened a lower cabinet, handed Mitch a gun, took one out for himself. "That weapon you have, Mitch, is loaded and ready. I know you can handle yourself. Can you listen and obey orders?"

"Yes, Charlie, I can. Where is Tommy?"

"He is right behind you," he told Mitch. "Peter is in the front of the house, working his way toward Liz. Faye put the kids with Bertha, and she is only yards away from Liz. She wants us to make noise from the opposite end of the hall like we don't know he has Liz. Faye will do the rest. She or Peter will. If she misses, it's up to both of us to back her up this time."

They moved toward Liz as they spoke. It was all over before they got there. Faye used her bow and arrow from the far end of the hall, got the guy in the back of the head. She was sorry she scared Liz, but the guy was about to cut her throat open. Liz stood there, looking at the dead man on the floor, arrow sticking out of his cheek. "That, my friend, is woman power, trained woman power. Thank you, Faye. I could have died. He was going to give me what did he call it, some kind of necktie." Liz hugged Faye and held on to her.

"Liz, are you all right? You are shaking like a leaf in the wind." Liz was mumbling something. "Let me take you to your husband."

Mitch was there before Faye could move. "You will take her to Hardison in the hut. He will look after her."

Mitch knew Hardison was a doctor of sorts, but not the full extent of his abilities. He portrayed the gentle decorator that Bertha admired for his skills. "Just why would I do that? She needs to rest."

Faye spoke in a tone he had never heard. "You will take her or Peter will. She is in shock. Dr. Hardison knows how to handle this. Do as you are told, sir." He lifted Liz into his arms and rushed out to the hut. Hardison was waiting for him. How he knew before Mitch got there confused him.

"We carry in-house phones, like a two-way radio system the kids used. Could you lay Liz on the examination table, please?"

Mitch was frightened. He did what Faye told him. She sounded strange.

Tommy and Bertha came in. "She's ta be fine, Hardison?" Bertha asked.

"Yes, Mrs. B, she will be. I'm going to give her a shot that will calm her down and one for pain in the neck region. I'll fix that when she is out cold."

Mitch never noticed the cut on her neck, which was bleeding like a slowly leaking faucet. Mitch turned to Tommy. "What the hell, right in our own house? She had nothing to do with your problems, or should I say ours. She does not deserve this. She is a gentle, sweet lady." He was getting louder. Tommy popped him on the chin. Mitch went down like a dropped paperweight.

"Now I have two to clean up, thanks to Tommy. Great guy you are." Bertha told Hardison she would straighten out Mitchell. Could he give him one of those tabs he was giving Faye to stay calm?

He shook his head no. "They are too strong for Mitch. I'll give him something to calm his nerves."

"Thank ya, Hardison," she told him as she and Tommy laid Mitch on the sofa.

When Mitch came around, he was confused at first. When Mitch realized what happened, he was ready to swing at Tommy. "Settle yourself, Mitchell. He did what's ya needed. I'da used a board."

Mitch laughed at her but knew she meant it. "How is Liz?" he asked.

Hardison told him she had a minor cut on her throat that did not require stitches. Liz would sleep for at least five hours. "She will be upset, Mitch, but she will work through it. Be grateful Faye had the strength to pull that bow. Her shoulder is still not up to where it needs to be. That arrow went through the guy's skull and came out his cheek. It takes great skill to do that. She saved Liz's life." Faye was standing next to Tommy, talking to him.

"Thank you, Faye, for saving my wife. I couldn't get to her as you did. Thank you from the bottom of my heart." He started to cry.

Faye was taken aback. No one ever thanked her for doing her job, doing what she did to save one of their own on the battlefield. She had never been thanked for it before nor seen the emotion it brought out. "I did what was needed, Mitch, no more. I'm glad she is all right, no real damage done." She left the hut with Peter. He told her, to non-combatants, saving a life as she did—well, that was next to heroic. She looked at him like he had two heads. "I did nothing, saved one of our own—that's all." He kissed her and walked her back to the chalet and the kids. He told her she was learning to be normal just like she wanted. She punched him in the arm and called him an ass.

Liz offered to take Faye with Bertha Christmas shopping for the children. Faye was excited to go. Bertha told her Cora was going to watch the kids with her little boy.

"Aunt Liz, what do I buy for the kids? I know, more dolls and trucks, but they must want something else."

"Let's see what the stores here have, but mostly for Mark, cars and trucks and dump trucks that dump stuff. Boys love that kind of thing."

"Charlie suggested we get him a sandpit for his playroom so he can dig with his trucks and dump the sand in piles everywhere. A sandpit in the house!"

"I guess your dad had one when he was little. He loved it. Your Uncle Tommy liked his drawing and painting books and sculpting things. Mary—I think anything ladylike would make her happy, but we need to get them clothes. Cora told me they need undergarments. They have three pairs each. Mary needs slacks and sweaters, jumpers, dresses, and oh so much more. Mark needs the same."

Faye looked at her. All she and Joan ever had were two dresses, no undergarments, and no shoes. Their mother was dressed the same. "I'm overwhelmed, Aunt Liz. Can I count on you and Aunt B to get me through this?"

Liz could see Faye close to tears. "Of course, this is the fun part, Faye. When they get older, their wants become more expensive." The ladies shopped the better part of the day. Some of the things had to be sent up to the chalet ahead of them. Faye had never seen such an amount of clothing and toys for two children.

They bought gifts for Robert and Denny and all the other men in the family. Liz bought a beautiful pearl set of earrings for Bertha and a pale-yellow cable-knit sweater set. Faye got her framed pictures of herself and Joan and one of the children playing in front of the tree. So much excitement from shopping, she was tired out, and her feet hurt from shopping in fancy shoes. She should have worn her combat boots.

The ladies set up the dining room to wrap their presents. Charlie told them they could have professional wrappers to do it for them. "'Tis no fun, that. I ner had ta have someone do it fer me afore, I no needs anyone now, but thank ya, Charlie, we'll be fine. Screw off." Liz was beside herself with that remark. They lined up all the rolls of paper in cardboard stands, the tissue in boxes, and boxes of boxes.

They spent two days wrapping and piling it all in large boxes. Charlie had all the gifts put in a spare room that he could lock. He knew what children were like. They got nosey at this time of year.

Faye asked Charlie to take her shopping to get unique gifts for the adults in the family. "Charlie, you know them better than I ever will know them. Would you stay with me and help pick out their gifts, please?" He told her he would do his best to help her. Charlie called Peter and asked him to relay to Tommy that he was in town with Faye and would be a few hours before returning. Peter told him Michael was there now, checking on something.

"Let's start with the easy ones." Robert was easy—a fancy chess game made of glass. Mitchell, a pair of kid-leather gloves and a grey scarf. Michael was just as easy. Faye found a bookstore that had a collection of books on historical figures in American history. Faye found a man's toiletry bag for her dad. Marcus always complained that the toothpaste tube would break, and his shirts or clothing would have to be laundered before he could wear them. Now Marcus would have no excuse about his clothing. He would not have to buy a new tube of toothpaste every trip. Every time Uncle Tommy sent him on a business trip, he would be prepared. She found the Best Chef in the World hat and apron for Charlie. Hardison got a book on the most challenging flowers to grow in mountain ranges.

Charlie pulled her over to a jewelry store window. "See the set at the back, Faye, just what you want for Liz." He was right—a white-gold snowflake on a delicate chain, matching bracelet, and earrings.

"They are perfect, delicate but beautiful." Charlie bought a sapphire ring for his wife. She was amazed he knew what size to get and how he wanted it wrapped for her. Grams was hard. She was an elegant lady, dressed moderately, never flashy. They were going past a clothing store, and in the window, both Faye and Charlie stared at the mannequin dressed in an outfit of pale-pink, almost-white pants and vest with a little darker turtleneck sweater. The clerk told Faye Mrs. McCloud bought at their store often, and they knew her size. Would she like it wrapped for her? Faye agreed to have it wrapped while she looked for something for Cora. She had told Faye once she admired the way Liz dressed. She found a pair of slacks and a blouse with a cardigan sweater for her. Uncle Tommy was last on her list.

"Faye, may I suggest something I know he will love?"

"Oh yes, please, Charlie, what?"

He took her to the art studio. "See that painting of the mountains with the cabin. Does it look familiar to you?"

"It's the one behind the chalet, isn't it?"

"Yes, your uncle painted that about ten years ago. He loves to paint. Why not give him the supplies to paint again?"

She bought a complete kit of paints, brushes, cleaners, and canvas to work. She intended to place a note in it to paint her a picture of Joan sitting on the hillside. "I want something special for Peter as well, Charlie. What does he love the most?"

"Besides you, he, like Tommy, is an artist. His medium is charcoal sketching and drawings."

She had the lady build a kit for Peter, with everything he needed to do his sketches. "Have I missed anyone, Charlie?"

"I don't think so." They headed for the car for the second time with their bags. Michael came up to them.

"Faye, can I borrow your shopping buddy for about an hour?"

"Why, what's up, Michael?" Charlie asked him.

"Several men and a few women are hunting for the two we have at the chalet. I heard one of the women say they checked the outside of the compound and scoped much of the grounds on the inside of the fence. Now they are searching the town. Those two have information for our boss's partner. He is waiting in the coffee shop for them."

Faye saw two people coming toward them, walking up the parking lot lane. Faye pushed Michael aside and leaped over him. As she did so, she told the driver to get down. Faye had the woman by the throat, her blade at her carotid artery. The woman squirmed under Faye's pressure until she saw Michael take his pliers out of his pocket. They were to twist the wire that would hold down the trunk of his old car. She started blabbing anything and everything she knew. Charlie leaned in to the driver and told him to call Tommy and tell him to meet Faye and himself.

Peter talked to his dad. "Michael is there now, Dad, so find him, and I will send Mr. McCloud."

"Michael is standing beside me, and tell Tommy to haul his ass." They put the woman in the trunk. She told them she was a bookkeeper and a purchasing agent for Tara. She let Faye know where and when she would be next. She begged Faye not to kill her. "Keep your mouth shut, don't scream, and maybe your boss will let you live."

Tommy arrived and asked Charlie, "Just what the hell is going on?"

"I think we have the head of the snake right here in the coffee shop, waiting for the two guys we have at the chalet."

Faye asked Tommy, "Is it who Joan said it was?"

"Yes, Faye, I'm sure it is."

Faye took the gun from Charlie. She was going to go for her bow, but Tommy stopped her.

"You would be dead by the time you aimed it. Use the gun, or your hands."

"Okay, how are we doing this?"

"I'll go in first, you behind me, as a backup, then Michael and Charlie as protection."

Faye told him, "No, I go in first as lead. You know I'm better than you or Charlie, no brag, just fact. Uncle Tommy, can you be right with me? We can pretend not to know he's there until we are right on top of his table. Charlie and Michael can come in through the takeout door on the side of the restaurant. They can warn the waitstaff to get people out ASAP. Then come up from behind when we have his attention."

"Great plan, Faye, will you follow it or decide to change your mind when we get in there?"

"No, I must do as Joan said, 'do what the plan says, no deviations.'"

They entered the front door, chatting about the Christmas party and decorations. When they were right on top of his table, Faye moved like lightning. She had her knife under his chin on his carotid artery.

"Just stopped in for a quick coffee. You could have come to the chalet. After all, your men are there. We have a few more of them there under guard outside the compound."

"Well, Tom, your cook over there does not serve my kind of food." Faye cut his throat just enough to bleed, not to kill. He did not show any signs he felt it. "Do you honestly think I would sit in the open like this unprotected? If you do, you are just as inanely stupid as I thought you were."

Charlie threw three ring fingers on the table, along with a watch and a necklace. "We had a chat with your friends. You are alone."

His eyes widened slightly, nothing else that showed he was scared. He felt the cold sweat run down his spine. He knew his time was up. He was not going to give away anything to Tom McCloud. "Faye, you should thank me for allowing those abominable children to live. They were on my menu to be my next feast when Marcus took them. How he found them was fortunate, wasn't it, Tom? After all, you have footed the bill for the last three years. How is Joan doing, by the way?"

Faye's blade cut a little deeper. "She is dead, asshole. You know that it is only by sheer will I don't do you right now."

"Mr. McCloud, I never use that name when speaking about you, Tom. I don't feel you deserve that title. After all, you were adopted, not born to it, were you not?"

"Sorry, I was born to it, so was my brother. Nada, my friend, it was you who was adopted, Jackson. Marcus will love seeing your dead body being fed to the wildcats of the mountains. You used his love because he loved Margaret. You used his daughter's. Well, she's going to use you. Go ahead, Faye. He is yours to do with as you please."

"He is not worth the effort, but I know he hates heights, Uncle Tommy. Let's teach him how to fly." Jackson told Tommy he would give him any information he wanted, everything he needed to find Tara, just not the flying lesson.

"We know where she is, Jackson, tell us where the rest of the snake is. And we know you have that knowledge."

"You drive a hard bargain, Tom, but I'll give you what you want—well, what I know anyway."

"Cut his throat, Faye."

"No, wait, I'll tell you."

Charlie came up, put his hand on Jackson. "Remember, I will know if you lie."

Faye looked at her uncle. He shook his head. Michael whispered in her ear, "Charlie feels the blood pulse in his shoulder. When he lies, it changes. He learns to read the pulses." Faye smiled.

"Well, tell me about Walt's kid. How is he doing?"

"Jason is living in his dad's house."

She looked at Charlie. "Walt never had kids, hated them. He would rather sell them or eat them. Lie." Charlie got it; she was helping him. He had both pulses now.

They worked on Jackson for nearly an hour. He would try to lie at first, then tell them the truth. He was so afraid he would fly if he didn't.

Marcus came into the café, and Charlie told Michael to stop him. "He will end this interrogation. He will not listen. Marcus will kill him."

"Come on, Marcus. I'll let you have a go at this bastard when my dad has all the info he needs."

"Get out of my way, Michael."

Michael put his gun in Marcus's chest. "One step, you go down, got it? I will not hesitate to do it. I want this over as much as you do." Marcus left the café and stood at the door, his gun in his pocket.

Tommy had all the information he was going to get out of him. He looked up at Faye. "It's time to go."

Charlie felt Jackson's heart rate go up. Charlie looked at Tommy. "It's time to go. Side door or front, your choice."

"Side, do it quickly." Charlie and Michael had him out the door and in the car before Marcus saw he was gone. Tommy told Faye, "Time to fly, my dear. Marcus can come only if he promises to keep his mouth shut and his hands to himself." She agreed and went to get her father. Tommy grabbed Marcus and told him to keep his hand and mouth shut. Marcus decided to meet them at the heliport.

Faye looped her arm through her dad's. "Let him die of fear. It is a long way down. The mountains have rough rocks." Marcus pretended to be all right with it. His Margaret deserved a better fate. She deserved to have Jackson drawn and quartered for what he did to her and his daughters.

Chapter Sixteen

PETER AND FAYE took the kids to see Santa, and Mary asked if he was real, because he never came for them before. "But he was at the chalet. Wasn't that him, Mommy?"

"Yes, this Santa is his helper, and you can tell him what you want for Christmas," Faye told her, with a smile and a tear in her eye. Mark stood like a soldier in line, moving up as the line moved. He was never speaking to Mary or the boy ahead of him. The elf tried, with no luck.

Peter went up beside Mark and asked, "What's up, buddy? Are you scared? Do you have to go to the boys' room or something?"

"No, I'm not scared of Santa. I don't have to pee. I am afraid of her. She works at the orphanage, and she's mean."

"Can you tell me which one without pointing at her?"

"Yep, she's the elf with Santa. She had that thing under her green top as Mommy has in her drawer and you have in your shoulder pocket."

Peter knew he meant their guns. "Can you pretend to have to go pee for me, Mark?" Peter asked him.

"Yep." He started to dance from one foot to the other.

Peter picked him up, grabbed Mary's hand, and left the line. "Faye, Mark knows the elf standing next to Santa. She has a gun."

"Yep, she does, and so does Santa," Mary said. They left the store. "How do you know them, Mary, Mark?"

"They work at the orphanage. One is a punisher manager. If you're bad, she spanks you hard till you have red marks, and sometimes you bleed. Then you have to be nice to her."

Faye knew how they had to be friendly. She was right, from what the children said. The man was a guard to keep the kids in and the evil people out.

"We already saw Santa at home, Mom, so can we not do that again, please?" Mark asked.

"We want to get you and Papa Peter something. Grams said she would take us," Mary said.

"Let me talk to Grams, and I'll set it up just for you two, okay?" She tickled them both. Peter had gone to Tommy and Michael with what the children had told them. Peter told Charlie about the encounter at Santa's Village. Charlie knew this was not good here, so close to home. He hated to talk to Tommy about this. Christmas was just a few days away.

"Can I have a peanut-butter-and-jam sammich, Charlie, please?" It was Mary.

"Is it okay with Mom, Mary?"

"She's sleepin', and Papa Peter said to ask you."

He smiled. Papa Peter—he never thought that would happen. Peter had a tumour in his lung as a child. The treatments sterilized him, but he was alive. "I guess you can, but you, young lady, will have to help make it." They gathered up the ingredients, and Charlie put Mary on a stool with one of his aprons. He let her spread the peanut butter on the bread and her hand and the counter. He put the jam on. He did not want that running off the countertop, down the cabinets. With a glass of milk and her sandwich, he put her at the kitchen table. Mark made the same request and did a little better job than Mary with the peanut butter.

He did the bread and hand, not the counter. Charlie listened to their conversation. He was surprised to hear Mark say he didn't like being in the barn. Mary said it was okay as long as the dark-haired man wasn't there. Charlie wanted to know, what dark-haired man? "Next time, Mary, if he is out there, come get me. I want to meet him, okay?"

"Sure, Charlie, can I have a cookie, please?"

He gave her two and two for Mark. He wondered why Cora or one of the ladies was not watching the kids. "Mark, is Cora watching you two today?"

"Nope, the ladies and Cora are being held in a room upstairs. We were in the playroom, so they didn't see us."

Charlie grabbed his phone and called Michael, as Tommy was with him. They were chopping logs for the fireplaces. "Code red, Tommy, code red here in the house, all the ladies."

"I'll call the others to get here fast." Charlie called the guards into the kitchen. Tommy and Michael came flying in the back door. Charlie was telling Paul to dress as a houseman and his daughter June as a housemaid. They were to take lunch up to the ladies' crafting room. "Tommy, you have to sit this one out. You are far too close to it."

"Not this time. Michael and I are going outside to come through the window."

"The window might be unlocked as they must have crawled in that way." They planned their attack, knowing whoever it was, they were expecting it. Their guns under the napkins, food on the trolley, they knocked on the door. It was the signal for Tommy and Michael to go in through the window. Bertha saw Michael in the window and unlocked it for him and stood so he could raise it halfway and crawl in along with Tommy. The food people were allowed in. All hell broke loose. The four men that had come in holding the ladies were down. Not dead, but hurt. The leader was whispering to the others. Bertha saw the pill and slapped it out of his hand, and the rest put it down. Michael looked at it. "It's not cyanide. It looks like a sleeping pill."

Faye took it from him, smelled it, then rubbed her finger on it. "It is to prevent them from feeling any pain or moving a muscle or speaking. Joan and I were given this."

One of the men looked at her, then said, "Faye, is that you? Could it be? They told us you were dead."

Faye stared at the man. "Are you Joseph the pantry boy?"

"Yes, I've been promoted to thug by Tara. She has taken over Parker's and Walt's organizations. Anything you want to know that I know, I'll tell you."

One of the others said, "We never touched your women. He did so. Please let us live a little longer." Tommy didn't understand this man. He had verbal vomit like a mockingbird.

Faye explained it to him. "Joseph was chained to the vegetable pantry. His job was to supply vegetables to the kitchen and order whatever was needed. He was used as we were, except they didn't eat his parts."

"Wrong, Faye. I can't have kids either." Bertha felt sick, and Liz lost her tea out the window. "They took my seminal sacs and sold them to the highest bidder."

The one indicated as the leader was taken to the hut; the others were taken to the cabin behind the chalet.

The ladies were all upset. Bertha told them they all needed a stiff hot toddy. "Charlie, me boyo, can ya make us a hot toddy fer ta calm our nerves?"

"Yes, Mrs. B, I can. Weak or strong, sweet lady?"

"Make it a wee strong fer me."

Paul told Peter that the one that was supposed to be the leader was dead. "I have no idea how."

"Hardison will know, Paul, unless his body is no longer here."

"It's here, and I'll have it taken to Hardison."

"My dad wants to see the body where he died, so leave it." Peter immediately called his dad. "Check the barn quickly, and watch Paul. I think I smell a rat."

Charlie and Michael ran to the barn. The guy was not dead but was close to it. He was in deep trouble; they carried him to the hut. Hardison did blood work real quick for poison and drugs. He found the drug compound and did a reversal.

"Can you save him, Hardison? We need some answers."

"One of our own did this. I'll need guards out here, ones you trust with your life, Charlie. This is too damn close to home for my liking. I sent Marta to her grandparents until I deem it safe. I may not be here much longer myself."

"I understand, Hardison. I feel the same." Charlie had Michael and June watch the hut inside. They were inside. Charlie and Peter were outside.

Hardison brought the young man around. He thanked Hardison, told him it was the dark-haired man. He thought his name was Paul but wasn't sure. Hardison called Tommy to come to the hut.

"I'm here, right outside the door. What is it?"

"Just get in here. I need my insulin shot."

"Okay, right away." What Hardison said was "We have a spy in the hen house. I've got a problem." Tommy went in with his gun in hand. "Who is it, Hardison? Things are coming to a head, and you, Charlie, and many others have family here, besides me."

"What colour hair does Paul have, Tommy? It's important."

"It's a dark brown, almost black. Why?"

"Charlie told me the children don't like being in the barn when the dark-haired man is there. This man was drugged almost dead by a dark-haired man maybe named Paul."

Tommy called Charlie to have Paul meet them in the barn to help find the drugs used on the man.

"Paul, can you help Tommy and me find the shit used on that creep in the barn? Everyone else is on duty patrolling the compound."

"Sure, I'll be right there." Four other guards had eyes on Paul. If he tried to leave or pull something else, they had him. He entered the barn, walked over to Charlie. "What's up, man? Everyone's got the jitters. That guy deserved to die. He had the boss's family. Not good, man, not good."

"No, it's not. Let's find the drugs used."

"Why would the drugs still be here? Wouldn't whoever did this take it with them?"

"Maybe, but maybe not. Boss wants us to look, we look."

"Okay."

Tommy watched as he poked around, not really looking but watching Charlie as if he was worried Charlie would find something. "Hey, Paul, what do you think that is up in the rafters?" Charlie asked him.

Paul looked at Charlie, not where he was pointing. "Now how the hell would I know? Damn, Charlie, I liked you a lot. Why in the hell did you have to find that?"

"I don't know, Paul. I guess because Tommy wanted me to find it. You should have hidden it better, Paul."

"Was it those damn kids? They squeal on me?"

"No, Paul, the guy you drugged did. He wasn't dead, he named you, described you, and told us who you work for, and it's not us."

"No, it's not. I've worked for Parker since I was sixteen, then for Walt, where I learned pain could be great for sex."

Charlie saw the flash of the knife. He moved before it got him. He watched Paul sink to the barn floor, with a blank stare on his face, two holes in his chest.

"Tell the kids that dark-haired man won't bother them anymore." Tommy held a pair of Mary's undergarments in his hand. "If he did what I think, Charlie, Faye could never know. You understand? She will lose it for good." He was shaking. Just the thought made him ill. Faye suffered enough. Her daughter didn't need to as well.

Bertha and the ladies were drinking their toddies by the light of the Christmas tree. Denny was drinking hot tea with no alcohol in it. They were calmer and more settled. Liz suggested they play a game. Carol suggested charades or some kind of team game, who or what they are by clues from their team. Liz had "Andrew Jackson" on her forehead. All the clues were not helping. She finally ran out of time. "Who put that in the bowl, guys?"

They were laughing at her when Tommy came in. "What were the clues for Liz?" They told him. "Oh, Andrew Jackson, right." She walked over to him and punched him in the arm. He feigned great pain and fell on the sofa next to his wife, who laughed at him.

"Yer no sympathy from me, ya poor daft man." They played for an hour or so when Charlie said Mr. Franc was at the door. Bertha was getting up when Tommy stopped her. "'Tis all right, love. I called him. I need him to see something Charlie and I found in the barn earlier today. You and the family enjoy the game. I'll not be long, I promise."

Jon Franc went with Tommy to the hut. The man that Hardison saved was only willing to turn state evidence to save his life. He had more information on the details than the FBI had. Franc told Tommy he owed him one. Tommy and Charlie told him about Parker's man infiltrating his guards and had been for a while. "We'll look for him, Tommy. Tell Mitch I said hello. Do you think this Taraco Corporation has anything to do with this, Tommy?"

"Jon, this is right in your backyard," Tommy told him. "That's why I called you. We may need your help to save our homes here and in St. Helen. My family wants to go home and get back to work and live as normally as possible. Jon, they don't want to celebrate Christmas here, not that it's uncomfortable, it's just not home."

"I get it. We're doing all we can to get the culprits."

"Have a good one, Jon. See you in the new year."

"Oh, by the way, Tommy, is your wife still mad at me?"

"Just a little. She's a Scot. It takes time for us to forgive and forget." Tommy laughed at Jon's face.

Mary had terrible dreams. Faye asked her if she was okay.

"Ya, I'm okay. I almost wet my bed 'cause I was scared by the noise, but I'm okay." Faye kissed her forehead and found it hot. She said she would be right back to Mary.

"Hardison, Mary is very hot. Can you come up to the chalet, please? I'm worried."

"Sure, Faye, I'll be right there."

"She'll be fine, Faye. She has a low-grade fever, probably a cold on the way. I'll give her a tablet to bring down her fever. If she's no better in the morning, I'll come back in."

"Can you swallow this for me, Mary, or do you want me to call for a liquid medicine?"

"I can swallow it, but I'm a good girl, so I don't want a spank again, okay?" Faye froze where she was standing.

Hardison asked her very calmly, "Who spanked you, Mary?"

"The dark-haired man, he spanked me, made me pee on his privates." Hardison gave her some water to swallow the tablet. She managed it. He turned and grabbed Faye and led her out of the room.

"He's dead. Tommy killed him. Do not make an issue of this, Faye. With luck, it's not happening again. She will forget it. she is only four."

Faye remembered it started when she was four, but it didn't stop. "Hardison, if we don't stop this, kids will continue to be used by maniacs like this." He held her while she cried. He knew she had enough; it must stop.

"Tommy, that bastard touched Mary, probably Mark as well. I'm giving them penicillin shots just to be safe."

"I know, Hardison, I found Mary's undergarment in the barn. When we captured him, he admitted to it. He worked for both Parker and Walt. He's dead, but I put Jon Franc on his case as if he is still alive, hoping to chase away any others snooping around. Hardison, I'm getting too old for this cloak-and-dagger shit."

"I agree, Tom, I agree."

When Hardison gave the kids their shots, Faye wanted to know why both, and why he was so concerned. He explained it was a precaution, that was all, better safe than sorry. She remembered getting those shots after things happened. She got it. "If he is not gone, I will get him."

"Faye, your uncle took care of him, and Charlie witnessed him do it, now no more worries."

Mary asked, "Do we get it in the arm or in the bum, Dr. Hardison?"

"Dr., is it? Well, Miss Mary, it will be in your hip. Will that be okay?"

"That's fine."

Mark just pulled his pajama bottoms down off his hip and stood there. "Not like we haven't had to do this before, right, Mary?"

"Yep, once a month, every month. Mommy, don't be sad. We like it here, and they can't take us away now that Grandpa got us. He was brave. He stood up to matron even if he dressed like a woman."

Faye knew she had to let Uncle Tommy know the orphanage had something to do with all our problems. Hardison looked at her. "I'll tell him, Faye. They all need to know."

"Who needs to know matron was a man, Mommy?" Mary asked.

"Gramps does, sweetie. It's okay."

"Papa Peter, we got shots today, and they didn't hurt at all."

"Well, I always cry when I get a needle. They hurt so much."

Mark told him, "Be brave and bite your lip. Then you don't cry."

"I'll try that next time, son."

"I'm your son, Papa Peter. I got a dad! Mommy, I got a dad."

Faye was going to tell him it was a term of endearment but just didn't have the heart. He was so excited and happy. He ran off to tell Mary they had a daddy. "Peter, are you okay with them thinking you are their dad?"

"You bet I am. I love those two kids, so if they want me as a dad, they got me. Faye, I had a tumour in the lung as a kid. The chemo treatments sterilized me. So for those two tykes to call me

Dad, I'm only too glad to take on the job." Faye gave him a big hug and a kiss that said more than thank you.

"Mommy kissed Daddy. I'm telling Charlie." They couldn't wait to tell the household they had a dad. "Charlie, Papa Peter is our dad now. Mommy kissed him, and he called me son."

Charlie wanted to cry and laugh at the same time. "Well, then I'm your grandpa Charlie because your dad is my son."

Mary stood still, working that out in her head. "Yep, that's right, Mark. We got a new grandpa too."

Tommy stood near the door with Bertha, listening to this conversation. "Well, we will have to see if we can get Faye out of the battle scene and into the Mommy scene totally."

"Do ya think ya can do it, me love? She's a fighter, quick ta action. I've seen her go."

"It will be hard, my love, but if we both work on it, then with the help of those two youngins, we have a chance."

Faye heard them. She was coming down the hall toward the kitchen to catch up to the children. "You take out the rest of that reptile, I will quit totally. I want to be like Aunt B and Aunt Liz. Get a job or just take care of my children. Peter said he wanted the job of being their dad. I would be honoured. Joan would be more than pleased, don't you think?"

"Yes, dear, I do. Ya deserves it." Bertha told her, with a hug.

The kids were so excited Santa Claus was coming tonight, and this time, he knew where they were and that they were good kids. Bedtime became a chore. "Mom, are you sure Santa likes chocolate chip cookies and milk? We could leave him a sammich and a beer."

"No, where did you get that?"

Mark heard Granddad say they did for Santa when they were little. "That's because Granddad and Uncle Tommy grew up in a place that sold beer and adult drinks."

"Well, they live here, don't they?"

"No, Mary, only children can leave something for Santa. Grown-ups have done their fair share of leaving food for Santa."

"Okay, if you say so, but I think all that hard work, he needs a beer," Mark replied as she tucked him into his bed. They still insisted on staying in the same room, but they wanted their own beds because Mary snored. They had to know where the other was. Faye and Joan were the same. Their mother was never allowed to stay with them. She was going to make sure that they never felt abandoned, that they were normal kids. All they had to do was grow and be healthy.

Peter came to say good night to them. He was surprised they hugged him and kissed his cheek and told him they loved him. Peter had tears running down his face. "Now, right to sleep because Santa will be here soon, and if he knows you are awake, he won't leave any toys for you," Faye told them.

Everyone pitched in to take the presents downstairs. It wasn't just what the kids were getting; here were presents for everyone. Bertha was beaming. "'Tis beautiful, I ner ha a Christmas like this me whole life." It looked like Santa Claus emptied his sleigh all around the Christmas tree. No one could touch its boughs.

The kids had everyone up at the crack of dawn. Charlie, his wife, and their family were there, as well as everyone else.

The Christmas lights on the tree and the room glowed with soft light, yet bright enough to see what they were doing. Cora got a note from Santa saying there would be something under the tree for her and her son. Three hours of oohs and aahs, "wow, would you look at that," and "I love it, thank you" later, everyone had opened their gifts. Bertha pulled Tommy aside to give him his present. He opened it and looked at her. It was a watch with a cover on it. Then he realized it was an antique pocket watch with "I Love Tommy, Your Bertha" on the back. He grabbed her and held her so close to him. "I'll treasure this for as long as I live, sweetheart. I love you more than life itself." They stood holding each other for a long time.

"Grams, does Gramps need you to hold him up?"

"No, sweet boy, he's holdin' me 'cause he loves me."

Mark wrapped his arms around both of their legs and said, "I'm holding you 'cause I love you too."

The big surprise came when they took the children to the playroom. A sandpit had been uncovered. It had been there from when Tommy and Marcus were little. It had new clean sand in it. Both Mark and Mary screamed with joy. They asked Cora if her little boy could play with them. She put Xzavior in the sand. He felt it, then picked up a small shovel and dug into the sand. He giggled. He liked it. Mary showed him how to fill his truck up and dump it. They played for two hours. Mary played with her dollhouse and her tea set, content to be on her own.

Cora told the family she would stay with the children if they wanted to get some rest. It was only nine in the morning. Bertha thanked her and left to rest. Only Faye and Peter stayed with her. They chatted about the kids and what Cora hoped for her boy Xzavior. She told them she was saving for him to go to university and be whatever he chose. Faye felt the same way. It amazed her she could think like that about children. She thought of Joan, how she would have loved this, being a mommy and taking care of their two beautiful beings. She held her tears back as best she could. Peter squeezed her. "She does know, Faye, through you."

The children went to bed grudgingly. They so wanted to continue playing with their toys. Faye and Peter were sitting by the tree, looking at the lights. Peter took a small box out of his pocket and got down on one knee and asked her, "Would you be my lady, my forever and ever, would you be my wife?"

She held out her hand and said, "Yes, oh yes, Peter, I love you so much."

Chapter Seventeen

BERTHA WAS THE first to be told about the engagement; she was elated for Faye. She never thought this would happen for the girls. Faye asked Aunt B to come with her to tell her dad. He wasn't too fond of her being with Peter. He was a warrior, like her, and that made him ineligible for marriage. Bertha told Faye, "He can say he's no good a man, but ya make yer own choice." Marcus was not pleased but congratulated her anyway. He hugged her and told her how happy he was for her and Peter. The children would have a proper family. He was so afraid one or the other would get killed fighting to save the family homes, and that would break the other's heart and the hearts of the children.

Liz and Mitch were happy for them. Liz prayed this was the beginning of the end of the long war for Faye. Mitch told Liz maybe they would soon be going home. Things were looking up for the family. It was growing again. He explained to Liz that Carol and Doug talked about getting a house together instead of wasting money on two apartments. Maybe another engagement was in the offing. Liz said, "Are we ready for a wedding or possibly two when Denny is so close to having our grandchild?"

"No, but who cares? It looks like things are getting better."

Tommy got word from one of his scouts that the information they got from the two men was on point. They had her headquarters pinned down. The cartel she was working with had dumped her ass because of her inability to listen and follow orders. They wanted nothing to do with her vendetta toward this family. The head of the cartel was willing to meet with them and work it out. Payment for damages, etcetera, no hard feelings between the cartel and the McCloud family. Charlie, Tommy, Marcus, and Michael sat in the hut with Hardison. "What do you think, Charlie?" asked Michael.

"I, for one, do not trust this at all. It could be a ploy to infiltrate our defenses and take us out. We still do not know if this information is 100 percent on the money, do we?"

"No, Michael, we don't, but we have to put our boys out there to find out if they are on the up and up," Marcus replied.

Michael waited until Tommy and he were alone. "Dad, why not send Erica and me in? I know her husband George might not like this too much, but we could nose around find out what we can."

"Why not send George and Erica? Tara knows you, Michael. She saw you at our wedding. George she has never seen. Erica is a master of disguise. She can handle whatever we give her. Let's talk to them and see what they say."

"Check out this cover story," George told Tommy. "Hey, boss, I'm okay with this. We'll call it our honeymoon, make out like young lovers."

"Young lovers, George? Lovers, yes."

"Boss, that is going to cost you. Our cover story could be, we are rich. We own several gold and diamond jewelry stores. We are on the first vacation we've had in many years. We will spread some cash around and gamble some. The cartel likes to gamble and take in the sights, show off that they have the money to throw around. A few drinks, bingo, 'loose lips sink ships' type of thing."

"Set it up, Erica. You and George just became millionaires."

"George, if only we were, my love."

"Get the info we need. You may just be that, richer than you think. Your bank account will grow substantially. Retirement could be sooner than you think."

Erica knew Tara could have seen her at the McCloud wedding. She worked out hard, dieted, and got down two sizes. Erica dyed her hair ombré from burgundy to blonde. Her hubby did not like that at all. She was not a heavy woman to begin with; she was slim and shapely. Now she looked like those stupid movie stars, skin and bone. And that hair, Lord forgive her for that! Her beautiful rich dark, black-brown curls were all gone. She did not look like his wife at all.

She took him shopping for clothes that yelled, "Rich man walking here, step aside." He was embarrassed, to say the least. He never owned fourteen pairs of pants and the same amount of shoes, all kinds of shirts, jackets, suits, and golf shirts and shorts. Erica made sure he had the best imitation men's jewelry ever. He refused to take off his wedding ring for the phony one. They were ready within a week.

Michael and Charlie met them at the heliport. Neither of them recognized Erica. George's face was familiar, but he had a goatee; his way of walking and holding himself looked different too. The hired limo arrived, their massive amount of luggage was loaded by the driver, and they were on their way.

They arrived at the airport, heading for the private jet arranged by Tommy. They were going to Las Vegas for a month. Here anyone and everyone were welcome. Many of the cartels' leaders were here on business-trip vacations, precisely what Erica and George needed to infiltrate as stupid rich people wanting to have fun.

They had rented a penthouse floor in the largest hotel they could find. There was a danger in this because, as Erica knew, these rooms could and would be bugged. They had to stay on their guard at all times. Outside of using their first names, everything else had been changed. They spent the first week letting people know they were there, see us, know we are here, pay attention. After that, they both went to work. They were talking with the wealthy leaders of the black market. They even spread around some of the more expensive jewelry to see if they could get better prices. Black-market dealers were attracted to Erica and George's illegal ventures. They were in. Information was trickling down to them without asking for it.

It was when Tara herself showed up that they got excited. She had the penthouse in the next tower. They gambled together. Erica invited her and her number one to have dinner by their pool. Erica asked the newly rich and famous friends as well as Tara and her people. Tara liked the almost-naked waitstaff. She also enjoyed the company she was in. She cozied up to George, asking where he made his millions, whom he had to lay to get there, and how long he was married to his wife. This was what they were working toward. Tara was a nymphomaniac. George was one gorgeous man, muscled to the nines. She had to have him. She flirted openly in front of Erica, who ignored it as though this was normal. Tara slipped George a key to her penthouse. He winked at her. Erica contacted the people in the cartel for backup. They were ready. The leader, Mr. Sabastian, met Erica outside the penthouse on the balcony.

"Look, we can't be named on this, but I personally will guarantee as many men, drugs whatever you need."

"All I need from you is to make sure none of her guards get in our way. We need more than her gone. She has her hand in many pies. We need that information."

"That, my dear, I will supply gladly. We want her and her people out and gone. No charge. I'll have it to you in the morning." Erica thanked him and took his arm, and walked around to the party side of the pool deck of their penthouse. She was all over the man. Tara took it as this couple had an open marriage, so she nearly had George right in the pool. Erica left an hour later with the good-looking leader. It gave Tara free rein over George. Her invitation to join her in her penthouse came speedily as was expected. George picked her up and carried her across the bridge between the two penthouses. He told her he would bend her over the edge of the bridge and take her right there. She squealed with delight but told him she preferred it her way. So they continued into her bedroom. She turned her back on him long enough to drop her swimsuit. That was Erica's cue. The needles were shoved into her butt so fast she couldn't move.

Tara looked at Erica. "What is this?"

Erica smiled. "A threesome, darling. I like you too. He has to share. So you get a little relaxer, then we play."

Tara was surprised, but she was feeling loose and ready to play. She answered all their questions. Erica got all the documents, maps, accounts, and plans for the McCloud family. George had all the answers on a throwaway phone.

Tara was found sprawled on her bed, regurgitation from her mouth beside her. It was made to look like she choked to death on a piece of meat. She was never checked for drugs. The cartel made sure of that. The information they supplied was close to what they found. This George and Erica didn't share.

They were back on the jet within hours, telling the hotel people that tragedy next door was just too much for them to stay there any longer. They paid for the month they had rented it for and left.

Tommy could not believe another part of the snake was gone. The information was worth every penny it cost and more. The heads of the organization were trying to sort everything Erica and George had found. They decided that a lot of what they got from the cartel was misinformation. Tommy had Erica and George come in to help decipher them. She told him, “Look at these two documents, Tommy, notice the code written on the side of each. The documents are the same. The code is not. Do you know whose document is whose?”

“Yes, we marked them so there would be no confusion. Why?”

“Look at the dates on them: 10-10-18, on the other 20-12-19. These numbers mean words. We have to figure out the words. We first learn the language, then work on the documents, maps, and files. The phone numbers can’t be disguised. I tried one, and it worked. I threw away the phone right after.” It took them many tries and failures and weeks of frustration. Mitch was looking at a map that was a duplicate of Tara’s; he saw a similarity. The codes on each were nearly the same. They overlaid the maps. Sure enough, there was the apartment building and notes in code on the sides. Mitch told them his secretary Miss Fibbs was great at codes and puzzles.

“What say we bring her in? She needs the work. Her brother is her dependent now, and well, she needs the help. She won’t take a paycheck she hasn’t earned.”

“Can you trust her, Mitch? We haven’t brought people in that are not trained.”

“First, let me talk to her to see if she is interested in being part of this organization. We do good work as well, Tommy, most of it is. Janet’s brother was hurt because of this, and we all know it is because of Stewart. Let’s see what she thinks.”

"You know she will have to sign an agreement of silence."

"Yes, we all did. Are you going to make Bertha sign one also?"

"She did just before we married, Mitch."

"Liz should be read in as well. She is on to us more than you know."

Mitch was shocked. "Liz has an idea what's going on? How did I give it away?"

He asked Liz if she thought Miss Fibbs would be good at decoding the material that Erica and George brought back. He wanted to see how she would react. "Sure, Mitch, she is good at codes and puzzles, but make sure she knows what she's getting into. You never read me into it. I just figured most of it out myself."

He stood there, looking at her. "Shit, Liz, you could have told me."

"Why do you think I made everyone go to England to buy ornaments and decorations? Tommy asked me to get you and the family out of here to protect you. I did."

"Do you want to know the whole of it? Because you will have to sign an agreement of silence."

"Mom did before her wedding, so did I. Do you think Tommy would let me into knowing the family was at war?"

"He never told me, and you, playing like you didn't know what was going on."

"Hey, wait, I do not know. Neither does Mom. It's like this: I will help, but I do not want to know the nasty, bad things. Mom is the same."

"So you want to know who and what we are?"

She put her arms around him. "Yes, dear, so calm down. Yes, I am a lady, but I'm not weak. I'm strong and can handle more than most. Yes, I get frustrated at some things, but the one thing that gets me is the half-truths. You know you cannot lie to me. I let you think you get away with a half-truth, but it hurts me."

He spent the next hour explaining the inside out of the rescue organization. She was pleased to know and a little frightened, but not as frightened as she was being held by those men and to hear Jason say what he did to Faye. "We will work together, Mitch. I need to go to Tommy's gun range and practice."

"What for, Liz? You don't need to carry a gun."

"No, had I had one that day, Tommy, Michael, and Faye would have had more backup." She had him.

"Okay, I'll take you or Charlie will."

Faye heard them as they were walking down the hall. "Aunt Liz, you want to go to the gun range? I'll take you. The kids are with their new tutor, learning how to put to paper the numbers and letters they are using."

"Okay, let me go get my things, and I'll meet you out front."

"Back door, Aunt Liz, Peter and I will take you." Liz surprised Faye; she hit the centre of the target eight out of ten times. "You use a gun a lot, Aunt Liz?"

"No, why?"

"Your accuracy is fantastic."

"Yes, but my fear level would probably change that."

"No, if anything, it gives you more purpose to be accurate. Wow, you are good. Peter, what do you think?"

"I think she hunted when she was young."

"You would be right, Peter. My dad and I hunted deer when I was young. I hated to see my dad kill a deer or any animal. I would purposely miss the deer or rabbit or whatever he saw."

"That's why you are so accurate. You practiced missing. It's the same as aiming to kill. You did it to miss," Faye told her.

Miss Fibbs was overwhelmed at the size of the chalet. "Mr. Maxwell, it's beautiful but so large."

"Yes, but it is home. You and your brother will be staying in the chalet as well. Our Dr. Hardison wants a look at his leg if that's all right with him and you. I know they said it might have to come off, but let Hardison have a look, will you?"

Tommy had promised Mitch that he would have Hardison look at the kid because Carol said she thought he had potential, and Mitch wanted to help him so much. "Hardison will be honest with you, Dave. He thinks the leg can be saved. We will do it for you."

Mitch introduced Miss Fibbs to Tommy. "Janet, this is Tommy McCloud. He is one of the head people of our organization."

"I'm pleased to meet you, sir. I hope I can be of service to you."

"Name is Tommy. May we call you Janet or Jan?"

"I go by Jan. That would be fine."

"Once you and your brother are settled, we will talk some more."

Charlie showed them to their rooms. Both were close to the elevator. "My name is Charlie. Anything you need, let me know."

"Are you part of this organization, Charlie?"

"Yes, Jan, the other head person, but I'm also the cook, so you see, there is no formality here." He walked back down the hall. He stopped, turned, and said, "Jan, Hardison will be up to see your brother this afternoon. He is a nice man. You can trust him." He took the elevator down to the basement. "Tommy, she seems to be a little skittish. The size of our home threatens her. We will have to make her feel comfortable. Do you think you can have Bertha and Liz have a wee tea party with her, say in the sunroom off the dining room? I think that will help if she gets to knows Liz and Carol."

"Can do, Charlie. Bertha will love it. I'll call her now."

"Sweetheart, can you help make Jan Fibbs more at ease? She seems intimidated by the size of our little chalet. Ask Liz and Carol. She knows them. Have a wee tea party in the sunroom—it's cozy."

"Only ta happy ta help ya, me love. When ya want me ta do this?"

"Tomorrow, if everyone is alright with it. By the way, it's Charlie that suggested the wee tea party."

"Thanks, Tom, now she's going to be on me."

"Better you than me."

Mitch thought the study would be best for Janet to work. It was quiet. "Think you can work here Jan. I feel funny calling you Jan, so you had better call me Mitch. I will do my best to remember to call you by your first name.

"This is a lovely room. Yes, I can work comfortably here."

He laid out a few of the documents, showed her how the duplications had different numbers or letters. Think you can figure this out for us?"

"I can only try, Mitch. These look like the plans for the apartment building you lived in the penthouse. Then you moved Carol into the same apartment, am I correct?"

"Yep, you are. Sorry, we have two children here, and that word is their favourite, yep. Yes, it is, and we need to know what those codes are if they lead to whoever did it and what they are planning next." Mitch knew what was planned, but did they get rid of the problem, or was there more involved in this?

"If you want a coffee or anything, just hit 4 on the house phone. Charlie will get it for you."

"He's one of the bosses, but he's the cook. I don't get it, Mitch."

"He loves to cook. He loves this chalet; his family has been here for many years. There are other chalets on this side of the mountain. His wife, son, and daughter live in one with him when he's not here."

"Just leave me with these documents. I'll do what I can." She was using all the code breakers she had; it just would not give her any answers. Her brother came in. He looked at it and said it reminded him of the cereal box code when I was little. You had to send in so many box tops to get the decoder ring. He laughed then said, "That first set of numbers and letters say *apartment shaft*."

"What is this, Janet?"

"Sit down. I have to call Charlie."

He came quickly to the study. "What is it, Jan? Is something wrong?"

"No, something is right. Tell him what you just told me."

"Okay, it's no big deal. The first code says *apartment shaft*. It's the same code I played with on the cereal boxes when I was a kid."

"Jan, can it be, for sure?"

"Yes, I went on the computer and requested the codes and decoders, and there it was, all of it. The code is off the cereal box, and all you need is the decoder ring to figure it out."

"A decoder ring, Jan? How do we get more?"

"We have one right here. My brother used the one on his key chain and told me what it said." They were laughing, and Charlie was dancing Jan around the study.

Tommy came in. "Can I have the next dance, Jan? Looks like you discovered something."

"Her brother broke the code. It's off the kids' cereal box, and if you have the decoder ring, you can crack anything on the box. In this case, on the documents."

"Well damn, that is incredible." Charlie said lunch was ready in the sunroom, but Hardison wanted to see Dave in the hut. "Okay, if you will show me where to go, I'll do my best to get there."

Tommy knew pride when he saw it. "Dave, can you walk about a half a mile on those sticks?"

"No, sir, I can't. Why?"

"Well, how about you use this? Charlie can ride behind you to show you the way." It was a moped, a small one. It would take two people on it. Dave smiled, thanked him. He knew this man understood. When the two of them had driven off, she thanked Tommy.

"He is so proud. He doesn't like to be a burden on anyone."

"I saw it in his eyes. He's young, he'll learn, if Hardison finds a way to save that boy's leg. And before you start on the cost, Hardison is our doctor, one of the best. So you work for me, and apparently so does Dave. His leg work is on us. Let's go to lunch. My wife hates it when I'm late." He took her by the arm, and they left the study.

Tommy introduced her to Bertha; she knew Liz and Carol. The rest of the family introduced themselves. Jan was fascinated by Bertha's accent. "How long have you been here in the States, Bertha?"

"Well, let's see, fer too many years ta count. I was in me fourteenth year when I came ta this country."

They chatted, and Jan settled in nicely. Marcus kept looking at her. Do you work for Mitchell, Jan?"

"Yes, until the building collapsed. I was his private secretary."

"I remember talking to you, and you were so kind to me even though you didn't know me."

"I hate to say I don't remember you, but that is my way. I treat people like I would want to be treated."

"Are you related to Mitch?"

"No, I'm Tommy's brother. I work in the offices away from here. I travel a lot."

"Maybe I could help with your travel plans."

Mitch intervened. "He travels by private jet, Jan. Other than letting his drivers know he's coming, that's about all you could do for him."

"Now, Mitch, she was trying to be helpful and friendly toward me. I appreciate that."

Jan turned red. Liz told her not to worry, you get used to the men banter back and forth." She kicked Mitch under the table. He got the message. Marcus was flirting; he liked Jan.

Hardison took an MRI of Dave's leg. The bones were trying to knit, but they were out of alignment. He would never be able to walk on it. Sometime down the road, the leg would have to be taken. "Dave, I'm calling a friend of mine. The bones in your leg are out of alignment, and they will never mend properly. Will you let me call my friend and between us straighten your leg? It's not going to be easy, and it will be painful at first. Then you will need to have us work on therapy to strengthen it. Tommy told me he has put you on the payroll so your medicals are all covered, so what do you say? Or do you need time to think this out or talk to your sister?"

"Oh no, I want you to do whatever it takes to save my leg. I do have to help with the codes, though, so can we do this?"

"Yes, we can. Ready for lunch, Dave?"

He gave the decoder ring to his sister. "I'm going to be very busy with Hardison, so can you do this without me?"

"Yes, Davey, I can."

"Could you call me Dave, please? I rather like it."

"Okay, Dave, I will." He got back on his scooter and headed for the kitchen to talk to Charlie. "Would it possible for my things to be transferred to the hut? Hardison told me after his friend arrives, I won't be able to get back here."

"I'll move them this afternoon, Dave, good luck. I hope to see you walking real soon."

Dave smiled. "Me too."

Marcus started helping Jan decode the information that they received from George and Erica. It had been a week, and they had managed to get the information on what was in the elevator tool room. Tommy had Erica, Michael, and George go in and retrieve it. Things were chaotic as no one knew who was boss now. Taraco Corporation was falling apart at the seams. The FBI was making arrests every day. The laundry lady's business was falling apart daily.

Michael walked into their office and said, "Okay, we are moving everything in that room, and I mean everything. You guys get gone. The feds are on to us now that Tara Parker is dead. The cartel has left the country. Anyone who is owed money tells me now." None of the men had been paid in a month. He figured it out. "Okay, line up. It's payday." He paid them one by one from the money Tommy gave him. Tommy knew they hadn't been paid. The guard that usually did the paying was dead. He didn't learn to fly well enough. Everyone paid, one man stood back; he knew Michael had more money. "If you think you can, come get it. But is dying for half of what you just got worth it?"

The man went for his knife; he got an arrow through his chest. "Told you it wasn't worth it." Michael turned and left the trailer, got into the car with Erica, and George drove them to the dilapidated building.

Erica picked the lock, George opened the doors, and all used the combinations that Jan had decoded and opened the safes. Money, documents, maps, and plans all had the same code on them. "Let's not stay long in St. Helen. Go straight to the airport," Erica told them. "I have terrible feelings." They did as she asked. They were back at the chalet in no time. "Mike, do you know this guy? I have never seen this pilot before."

"No, I get it. Kiss George and tell him to be ready." They were about to take the bags off the plane; they were heavy. The pilot put a gun on Erica and told her to heave the bags where they were.

"Put it down. I have my blade two inches away from your nuts, man. I am quick. Kill me, lose your manhood." That was all it took for him to look down to see she was using her finger. The board that hit his head was real. He went down.

"Great, now I have to carry this piece of shit to the truck." George was not too happy about this. "Did you figure on his size, Mike? He's as big as me. I'd say two-fifty at least."

"I'll help you, but let's do it now. I want him tied up so we can question him back at the barn."

George nodded. Erica and Mike finished emptying the plane. Michael called his dad, told him what went down and that they were entering the compound now. "Take the pilot to the barn and tell Charlie to meet me there."

"I'll take the money to your safe and the paperwork to the study."

"No, let them work on what they have. Don't make them overwhelmed with the amount they have to work through. Each document they get done is a day sooner they can go home."

Tommy and Charlie met the pilot in the barn. "Hello, and who might you be? I don't recall hiring you to fly my planes."

"I worked for Tara, and now I work for her husband."

Bingo—they had the other end of the snake. With the help of Hardison, they got the information they needed. Soon they would end this damn war and return home, start living as they should be. But he thought Bertha was loving living here on the mountain. She might want to stay up here.

Jan continued working on the codes; there was so much to do, and only she and Marcus as Dave was still out in the hut with the doctors. "We need more help in here, Jan. I wonder if there is another ring we could get so we can get more done."

She went online, saying if anyone had this toy ring, the purchaser would pay handsomely for it as it was a collector's item. "Let us hope we get some responses." They had five, all with hefty price tags on them.

Marcus said, "I will have Charlie check these people out and see if we can at least get one."

Charlie came into the study two days later with Liz and Mitch. "Here, we have two new decoder cadets, Jan. They have their own rings and are ready to decode for you." They laughed, but it meant more work would get done. As they decoded, Jan input the information into the computer.

The four of them were left alone to work on this, hoping to get to the bottom of it all. Jan commented that absence of true love, regardless of what kind, can cause people to want revenge to the point of tasting the pain they inflict. Mitch thought about that. Could Tara have been past the point of sanity she couldn't stop and had no clue as to why she continued?

"Jan, can you check this for me? I'm not sure, but is this how she planned to blow our whole block? It's like taking out the neighbourhood four houses each way of our homes."

Jan and Marcus went over everything Liz had done. It took the better part of an hour. "Your work is right, Liz. This is or was what Tara planned."

Marcus was following a scribble; it ended with more code on the back of the document. "Good Lord, her husband still intends to do it! He has set a date. Look, Jan, it's only two days from now!" Sure enough, it was correct; now they needed to figure out who he was and quick.

Tommy put a call in to Franc. "You still have that guy from here, Jon? It's important."

"Yes, but he's not giving up anything other than what he already has. Why?"

"I need to talk to him, and in a hurry." Tommy explained what they had found out without giving away how they did it.

"Tommy, I owe you big. I know that, but how am I supposed to pull that off? He is in a safe house awaiting trial. They don't even know what the formal charges are, other than working with the cartel and the Taraco Corporation."

"Just tell me where I will take care of the rest. I will leave you totally out of it and your buddy Mitchell. What do you say?"

He didn't give it a second thought. There were children, old people, and a lot of parents in that area. He gave Tommy the address.

"Thanks, Jon, between us, we may be able to put a stop to all these horrendous goings-on."

First, he had to kidnap the bastard or just knock out the agents or both. Damn, this was not the bush league. He went to Faye and

Michael, told them what was going on. "Can you see a way to do this without harming the agents or that idiot?"

Faye spoke up and made everyone in the room silent. "What if he is the husband? He has set things in motion but can't be blamed for it because he is, after all, a guest of the FBI."

Michael finally spoke. "Are the men in the cabin his? Yes, then they know who he is and what his name is." It took them no time to get to the cabin.

Faye stopped them, gave the signal to listen. They stood close and did just that, listened. It was the youngest of the bunch they heard first. "We should be grateful we are here and not on the crew set to blow up part of St. Helen. Jack Reed is just as nuts as his wife, Tara. He only married her because he knocked her up. Then she got rid of it. He still believes she lost it. Padro, you helped her get rid of it, didn't you?"

"Yes, she was damn near five months. It was a developed baby. She told me the only reason she let herself get pregnant was to make him marry her in the first place."

"She needed his ability to plan out things, and her mind didn't work like that. Facts, figures, and sex—that was her."

"When is this shit going to happen, Padro?"

"It is set for two days from now. They will use the sewer system to put massive amounts of charges, enough to blow up a whole town under six square blocks of housing. Then call in all the fire departments and the EMTs. When they are just about there, they blow it. No one to help the people, because they are dead too. He had all the police call codes, firemen codes, and all the paramedic codes, no 900 calls for them."

Faye nodded. They went in; she grabbed the young one. "So you all knew his plans, and you sat there, being fed, clean clothes, medical, and a bed to sleep in." She pulled her knife and put it to the kid's throat; he felt it. He wet his pants.

Tommy pointed his gun at the one sitting on the bed, writing something. "Give me that."

The man replied, "Yes, sir, but it's my confession to my Maker for being the person I am."

"Well, I'll give you a chance to change which direction you're going: who, when, and how. Right now."

Faye still had the kid. "Please, miss, that's my son. Don't kill him, take me." It was Padro who spoke.

Faye pushed the kid at him. "I had no intention of killing him, just making him mute."

Padro told them about Jack Reed. "He worked for Parker as a planner of laundry systems. Tara's husband also planned the touchy hits for him. He knew Tara and Stewart. He helped Stewart with many jobs. When she killed him at his mother's wedding, it was to humiliate her, make her feel bad for not loving her son. It backfired on her. His mother was pleased he was gone, out of her life. Her mother was used and abused. She needed to know her real name, where she was born, her real name. Stewart said he knew. He didn't but Jack Reed did—he told her. Things just went from bad to worse after that. All Jack and Tara wanted were to rule the underworld, take over the drug cartels that were going out of the country, take down anything or anyone attached to Stewart's family. She wanted them destroyed as her family had been in Cuba. Her mother was taken from a drug lord as payment for some attack on the Parkers' land in Cuba. She was forced to be his daughter and do as he demanded. When she died of cancer, he buried her in an unmarked grave in the back garden of his house in St. Helen, no coffin, no nameplate, nothing. Tara had her put into a coffin, buried in a cemetery, with the headstone with her real name on it, Consuela Cortez, her dates of birth and death on her stone with the mother of Tarrisa. That was why she went after the cartels and anything Parker had going. Jack was glad Tara was killed. He said he was free of her. He would do this last thing for her. Then he was leaving this country for good."

"One question, the man I have in my barn, is it Jack Reed himself?" Tommy asked.

Padro answered yes. He planned it that way to get caught doing a stupid thing then work from there. He had placed timers in that barn to blow it up. "You are part of the family, no?"

"Yes, I am," Tommy shot him for smiling as he answered.

"My dad was Jack Reed's brother. His real name is Ricardo Hernandez. Please just put the rest of us in jail, not in the grave."

Charlie and Michael got everyone out of the barn. They moved all the equipment, horses, farm stuff; everything they could move was out. Then they moved Hardison, Dave, and all the medical equipment to an empty cabin. Tommy, Michael, Marcus, and Charlie tore the barn apart. They found six timers and seven detonators attached to charges. They followed them. Sure enough, they had little time left before they were to blow. Charlie had the house cleared as well.

Tommy had never been so scared in his life. His family was in jeopardy no matter where they were. He got ahold of Franc, told him everything. He could have all the men he captured, but he had to make sure Reed was still at the safe house. Tommy was sure he was gone. "Tom, I'll go myself. Are you okay up there?"

"No, but I will be. If I have to kill every damn one of them, I will get the rest of the information on who and when."

Liz told him, "Tommy, look at me. I know you are as frightened for the family as we are, but we can't give our hand away. We are playing poker with the asshole. Go to him, and he sees your hand. No way will you bluff him then. Call Franc, have him in solitary confinement on some trumped-up charge. He can do that, can't he?"

"I can try, lassie. I thank you for knockin' some sense into this old man." He called Franc back if Reed was there and what he needed him to do.

"Already done, Tom, the bastard had just killed my people, a woman and a man, both full agents. Both had kids. We got there before he could get out. He is in solitary confinement for the criminally insane."

They went back to the documents. Bertha had joined them. "No, Tommy, 'tis time I do me share. I'm no lady in waiten. I'll help, an' if ya no like it, ya can kiss me tuther end." He kissed her and told her the FBI was coming to take the other men away. "Good, ya needs ta let us help. Ya no can do it all yerself." She handed him a sheet she had decoded. It had to do with the sewage plans, where they ran and where they emptied.

He picked her up and swung her around. "Bertha, me love, you just found the key to it all. I love ya so much." He gave Charlie, Marcus, Michael, and Peter the information. "Can you get the city plans to figure out when this is? Once we know, we can get in there and take the charges out. The neighbourhood needs to be evacuated. We can claim a gas leak. Help the people leave, so they see the gas company jackets."

Mitchell said, "We get them out, less chance of death on their end."

Charlie said, “That is easy. Peter and I will dress as gas-meter readers. Each house gets a stink bomb, small but enough to put the odor through the neighbourhood. We will them get out until they find it and fix it.”

“I agree, but not you, Charlie, or Peter. I need you here. Doug and George are here, aren’t they? Well, it’s time Doug told Carol who he works for.”

“Tommy, she loves him. Will it end it for her?” asked Liz. After all, she was their daughter. They gave her the papers for Christmas.

“Liz, did ya stop loven yer man when ya learned what he was aboot?”

“No, Mom, I didn’t, but I was angry he didn’t tell me before. She will be too.”

They set the plans, but the gas readers turned out to be Doug and Carol. He had to teach her how to set them. Her practice tries had the barn stinking awful, but she got it. “Doug, I am sad that you didn’t feel you could tell me, but it doesn’t change how I feel.”

Chapter Eighteen

DOUG AND CAROL were sent into the town that afternoon. They went from house to house through the neighbourhood as fast as they could. The smell was like dead skunk and fuel oil. It emptied the houses quickly, each family not wanting to pack a thing. There was one exception: an elderly couple, the first people to live in this area. She walked with the aid of a walker, and her husband was in a wheelchair. The lady who lived next to them told Carol about them. "Mr. and Mrs. Donaldson are handicapped. Can you help them?"

"Yes, ma'am, we will for sure. You get to safety now."

Doug carried Mr. Donaldson first, while Carol took his wheelchair and the walker. Doug carried Mrs. Donaldson to the car. They took them to their daughters on the other side of St. Helen. Carol was glad to be done with this job. "Doug, we stink like dead skunks. No one will want to be near us."

"Good, want to shower together for the rest of the day?"

"Get real, my boy. Tommy will have more for you or me to do. I am scared. Doug, our homes, the houses of all those people . . . By the way, one of the boys that live behind Grams, you know, the ones that shot their BBs at her—well, I think he recognized me."

"Won't matter, his parents are not interested in if the kid knew who the meter readers were."

The FBI and Tommy's men talked with the city officials to get permission to enter the sewers. They needed maps of the area that were not available on the computer. Franc told the smart-ass city planning officer to get the maps and revisions ASAP before he had the mayor fire his ass. The city planning officer decided to do as he was told. His job meant too much. He could talk to his boss later.

One of the men from the sewer department came forward. "Mr. Franc, I'm Paul Kelly. I worked on building that sewer system, and I know the area. I live there. If I can be of any service to you, I'd be only too happy to help."

Franc wanted to kiss him. It was the first help offered, instead of arguments and stalls to getting things done. "Yes, please, we need the help." He explained the situation to Paul Kelly and what the time limit was.

"Sir, your people need a sewer guy to guide each one of you. They know the sewers like the back of their hand." Kelly knew what the men had to find. He trusted them to do it. "How many men will you need? I'll get them in short order."

Franc called Tommy over; he was trying to read the damn diagram. Franc told him what Mr. Kelly told him. "My name's Tommy." And he shook Kelly's hand.

"Mine's Paul. We will do what is necessary to get the job done, Tommy. How many men will you need? I have six plus myself, Franc. What do you have?"

Franc told him he had four, counting himself.

"That's ten of ours, Paul. Can you get that many men to volunteer right now?"

"Give me twenty minutes. Do we have that much time?"

Tommy shook his head. "We do if we can get the manpower, no if not." Kelly took off toward the shack beside the office. He wasn't gone long, not nearly the twenty minutes he had asked for, and came out with twelve men. "We have equipment for you and your men as well. You will need gas masks and headlamps. All of you will need vinyl suits. There is stuff down there that will burn you as well as melt regular clothes and shoes."

"Holy shit." Franc was shocked.

"Did you think it was clean like your office, Jon?" Tommy was laughing at him. Kelly helped them get ready. He also told them they should plan out what men should go into each section.

"I know we have twelve pairs to work, but there are over twenty divisions down there, branches like a tree. Some go to the recycling plant to clean it for drinking water, others to the sewage plants for composting or destroying." Franc wanted to be ill.

"Are you still in, Jon, or do we get someone else? You look sick."

"I'm good. Shit, right, Tommy? That's what we are walking through."

"Yes, my friend, that's it exactly. Did you think it was just bathwater or laundry drainage?"

"To be honest, I never gave it a thought about what goes on below our little city, water, soap, etc. How dumb is that?"

Kelly patted him on the shoulder as he handed him his suit and gear. "Most people don't even know what a sewer system is. They think it's the rain runoff from the road."

They were dressed and ready to go. Kelly took lead, as he helped build it and still worked in that section of the sewer. He laid out what groups went where. Soon they were ready when the police showed up.

"Sorry, sir, your people can't go there."

Franc was head of the FBI department here. He stepped forward as best he could in his yellow suit. "Listen, officer, I am Jon Franc, head of the FBI here in St. Helen, and we are going to get your men and cars out of the way."

"It's a union matter, sir. They put a stop to it. They say you have no authority to go into the sewer to look for strange fish called chargers."

Franc damn near lost it. Tommy took the officer away from the union rep and told him, "The chargers are not fish. They are connected to detonators set to blow up a section of our town, approximately six square city blocks. Now we have removed the people on the pretense of a gas leak—the skunk smell. We have less than twenty-four hours to get these explosives out of the sewer system. These men have volunteered to work with us, the FBI. Let us do the job. So you get them smart-ass union people the hell out of our way."

The police officer shook Tommy's hand, told him he would clear the area. "If you need more men, here is my cell number. We will step in. Sir, our city means a lot to us officers. I'll tell Captain Dugan he will help keep people away. Thank you for what you are doing, sir." He started shouting at the union people to get in their cars and get out of the area. He did a quick explanation to his men. They too got to work, removing people and the gawkers. He stationed four men at the gates of the sewer station.

After all the people were suited up and paired off, they started down the tunnel that led to the neighbourhood sewers they needed to go. Doug stopped his partner. "What does that do? I mean, it looks like some ventilation pipe."

"You would be right. Why?"

"Radio your guys. I'll call mine to check every opening to those vents." They worked endlessly, finding detonators, and charges more than they thought. They had barely done half the tunnels when the count had hit over fifty explosives.

Kelly found something he did not want to see. "Tommy, can you come over to my side? I need you to see this."

Tommy sloshed his way over to where Kelly was standing. "What is it, Kelly?" He thought, *Not another type of explosive.* It was a rat-chewed woman or girl; they were not sure. A note was attached: "for my Tara, she is yours now, you bury her." It would take DNA testing to know who she was. This did not help them at all. He radioed it up top to have someone come down and remove the poor lady. Kelly was crying. "What is it, Kelly?"

"See the bracelet. Look at the name."

One side said Bridget; the other said, "Love, Dad." Tommy felt sick. *Oh God, not his kid.* "She's yours, isn't she?"

"My granddaughter, she would have been thirteen tomorrow."

Tommy punched the wall and swore. Kelly called and told them to get ahold of the coroner and his son. The body was Bridget. He turned to Tommy. "Let's keep going. The bastard must have more surprises for us to slow us down. I'll grieve for my girl tomorrow." They walked on, still finding, disconnecting the detonators from the charges and collecting the explosives, both Paul and Tommy praying, *No more bodies.*

Doug and his partner were near the exit when Doug stopped his partner. "Bob, wait, look at the way that iron gate is leaning. We move that, I'm sure it will blow if moved. The charge is set so if someone was chasing you, you moved it, you would die on the spot." They approached it slowly. Sure enough, a large bundle of dynamite was attached to a sensor. "We do not touch this—bomb squad only on this one." He called Franc, told him they needed a bomb squad from the outside to clear the iron gate of dynamite. Franc told him they were on their way. Doug and Bob turned to go back when Bob grabbed him.

"Doug, is that a hand floating by my foot? Please tell me it's not."

Doug bent down, took hold of the bloated hand, and gave it a gentle tug; a body was attached. "It's a man, and he's been here for a while." He called Franc again. "We have another body: male, been here a while, not a transient, normal clothes."

"That makes three. One of my men found a boy but a little fresher."

They went back to the tunnel junction and followed the map toward the other exit on the sewer. They ran into Charles and his partner Gayle, and they had two more sections to do. "We'll give you a hand," Doug told him. Charlie told Doug the body count had risen to six. There were four females, all under fifteen years old and two men in their thirties, and Tommy found Kelly's granddaughter.

Gayle turned to Bob. "Did you know it was Bridget they found?"

"No, I wish I didn't know now."

The four continued finding more explosives, praying they found no more bodies. They came to the exit. Doug did the same thing he had at the other exit, and sure enough, it was rigged to explode. He stopped Gayle before he could touch it. "It's charged to go if you touch it. There is enough dynamite to blow all of us up." He backed away toward the wall. Charlie made the call for another bomb squad. They had been at this for nearly ten hours. Bob sat down on a ledge at the side of the tube. He was exhausted. Doug told Charlie he would stay with him. "We will all just take a break then continue later, okay, Bob?"

He shook his head to the negative. "I was Kelly's son's godfather, and now his baby is gone. Who would do such a thing, a child? Please, God, she didn't suffer horribly." He was crying.

"Buddy, this is Kelly. Stop your blubbering, get the job done. We will all mourn tomorrow, hear me?"

"Yes, boss, I got ya, I'm going." They walked onto an open drain with a field in front of them. Both Charlie and Doug stopped their partners from running out of the opening. Charlie whispered, "There is a detector wire across the opening. If we brush it, boom!" Doug followed the wire. It ended buried in a sack of sand. There wasn't any way to know where it was attached. They had two chances: go back until the bomb squad got there or crawl on their stomachs under the wire. Charlie might make it, Doug would, but Bob was a big man. He wouldn't make it. Gayle—it was iffy. "We go back, or we wait. There are no other choices."

Gayle said, "If we take our suits off, maybe we can."

"No, you can't." It was Kelly; he was on the other side. "Sit your asses down, in your suits, Gayle, and wait. It will be about thirty or forty minutes. Do you hear me?"

"Yes, I see. Sit on my ass, I got it."

Tommy would love to have a man like that in his organization. "Ever think of leaving the sewer for a better-paying job, Kelly?"

"Yes, but I've had no luck, not what you would call educated past high school."

"Can I ask your age, Kelly?"

"Sure, I just turned forty-six last week. Why? Got a job for me?"

"Yes, after this, we can talk."

The bomb squad came, and it was a little trickier. They asked the men to back up and go around the turn in the tunnel. They heard a muffled explosion. “All clear, men, come on out.”

They had covered the sandbag with a steel shield and pulled the wire. Gayle flew out of the drain; as he passed Kelly, he said, “I quit. I will never go down there again.” Kelly understood; he patted his arm and let him go.

Bob stood by Kelly, his arm over Kelly’s shoulder. “I’m afraid it’s me too, Kelly. I never want to go in there again.” He left.

Tommy radioed Franc. “These men will need therapy and in a hell of a hurry. They are leaving their jobs because of this.”

“On it, Tom.”

Kelly thanked him for that. “I’m afraid those two will never be able to work in there again. It was hard on Bob for the last five years. A cave-in kept him down for two hours, and now this. He is done. Gayle—he’s only six months from retiring. I’ll see if we can keep him up top in the yard until his time is up.”

“Will he lose a lot if he leaves now, Kelly?”

“Yes, six months would cost him about forty bucks a month on his pension check. They cut you big when you leave early. Go before fifteen years, you get zip, nothing.”

Tommy thought about it, and he would talk to their boss, keep Gayle up in the yard. He would pay his wage if that’s what it would take.

At the end of nineteen hours, they had all the explosives out. A second crew was scanning behind them. They were coming out as Tom and Kelly were talking. This part of the snake was dead.

Charlie prayed, *Please let this be the end of the war. Let the organization go back to rescue.*

Tommy gathered all the men together, and they had food and coffee, tea, hot chocolate for everyone. "I want to thank each and every one of you personally for the work and effort you put in today. It has been a gruelling twenty hours for all of us. The man who set this in motion is in a criminally insane hospital, in solitary confinement. He is a killer who enjoyed his work. Again, you have saved hundreds of people: men, women, and children, along with their pets and the wildlife that live around these parts. An elderly couple who would never have made it to safety would have died where they slept. Again, thank you from the fullness of my heart to you."

As he was stepping down off the makeshift stage, an explosion rocked the front of the company's entrance. A truck blew up, hurting two people with it. It was a company truck used to transport parts and men to job sites. They rushed them to the hospital to save their lives.

The men gave him a thank you back for saving all their jobs because if that sewer had gone, it would have been years before it was replaced because without homes needing sewage, they would not rebuild the sewer. That was the city for you.

Tommy found Kelly with his son Gary, and he heard his son say he would have to borrow the money from his dad to pay for Bridget's funeral. It was more than he and his wife could afford. Tommy excused himself and asked where Gary worked. Kelly's son replied that he was a doctor, and his wife was a nurse.

"What kind of doctor, if you don't mind me asking, young man?"

"I'm a general practitioner. Why?" He felt defensive, and he didn't know why this man was asking personal questions at a time like this.

Kelly told his son Tommy was the man that knew what was in there, and his men went in along with them. "He was my partner in the sewer tunnels, Gary. He was with me when we found her. Mr. McCloud felt it as I did."

"Gary, my name is Tom McCloud. I would be honoured to cover any and all expenses for Bridget and offer you a job and along with your wife, but we can speak about that later. Kelly, I want to hire you at twice your pay and full benefits. Here is my card. Take care of Bridget, then get ahold of me, okay?"

"Yes, Tom, I will."

They arrived back at the chalet by morning. Tommy and his crew slept on the plane. Charlie told Tommy, "No one getting flying lessons today, boss."

It brought a smile to his face. "Charlie, there's a young doctor, a general practitioner. Does our little town on the mountain have a doctor other than Hardison?"

"No, he's pretty much taking care of them. A midwife did the babies, but she retired before Christmas."

"I want to bring him up here with his wife. I don't know if they have any other children, but it was his daughter Kelly and I found. I couldn't believe how Kelly took charge of his men, feeling the pain of losing a grandchild. Do you think Hardison will be slighted by this? He has been our doctor for so many years, and maybe he might appreciate the help."

"Hardison would. He told me this horror had to stop, or he was leaving—he was getting too damn old for this shit."

"I agree, Charlie, I agree. Wake me when we land, please, Charlie."

When they arrived, Charlie nudged Tommy and told him they had landed. "Tommy, we are here. Tommy, wake up." He wasn't moving.

"Mike, get a wagon. Tommy's not waking up, and I need to get him to Hardison ASAP."

Michael didn't go for a wagon. He picked his dad up in his arms and yelled at Charlie, "Start the car. I'll hold him, you drive, no one else in the car."

Charlie called ahead to Hardison; he was ready for him. Michael carried him into the hut, for Hardison threw him out, or he tried to. Neither Charlie nor Michael would leave. "Call his wife, Charlie, get her out here."

Charlie called Bertha, then went on Dave's moped to get her. "Please, Bertha, get on and hold tight to me. It's Tommy. He's in the hut with Hardison."

She grabbed Charlie around the waist, and they flew out the chalet to the hut. Bertha went in, scared to death.

"It seems Tommy's in a deep coma-like sleep, he's exhausted. How long did he work, Charlie, in that swamp-like condition?"

"Twenty hours, Hardison, then he spent time talking to all the men, thanking them. He also talked to the father of the little girl we found. She was Tommy's partner's granddaughter. It took a lot out of him. He told me it did. He could not bear losing any of his family."

"He needs to rest, and I'll give him some booster shots to help him."

Tommy stirred. "Shots? Like hell you will, Hardison, you know what I'm like." He couldn't raise his head; it was too much of an effort.

"If ya think ya can stop us, me boyo, yer daft, my love. Do ya need his butt or his arm, Hardison?"

"Woman, you are not undressing me here."

Hardison said, "We only give them in the butt. They will work faster."

Tommy was trying to get up; every muscle ached worse than a beating. He quit trying, and Bertha kissed him, whispered, "Only in your hip, love, I'll no drop yer pants."

"Thank you, sweetheart, no need to see my scars."

Hardison knew about the scars, but he doubted Charlie or anyone else did. The booster worked within an hour. They were calcium and vitamin E and C, all to relax his muscles and give him some strength. "You can stay here, or Charlie can, or Michael can carry you up to your bed."

"I'll take ya, love, on this here thing. Let's go." They put Tommy on behind Bertha, and Charlie told her to slow down before getting to the elevator. She smiled, and she was gone.

They heard Tommy, "Let her rip, love. Hot damn, this is fun."

Bertha got to their room and helped with his clothes. He never slept in nightwear, so she covered him up and stayed until he was asleep again. Hardison met her in the great room. "Bertha, he has had a slight stroke, nothing bad. He won't feel any heart pain, but he has to slow down. We can manage most of it with medication that he will be told are muscle relaxers or vitamins."

"He will do as I tells him, Hardison. Do ya know his age?"

"Of course I do, Bertha. Do you not know his age?"

"No, I tried fer the whole time we been wedded. He keeps it a secret."

"If I tell you, you must never let him know, and I know why he doesn't want you to know."

"Ya best be tellen me."

"If he does, he'll not have a job. Hardison, no!" Tommy bellowed from the balcony.

Hardison kissed her cheek. "When I retire, I'll tell you."

Tommy was standing at the balcony railing, looking down. "Is it so important, my love, that you know my age?"

"'Tis yer birthday in a fortnight, and I wanted ta put it on yer cake, 'tis all."

"Well put. I'm old as my toes and younger than my teeth."

She laughed and said, "'Tis daft but I will. Can you give me a reason yer hidden yer age? Are ya that old? I no believe that I sleep with ya." And her cheeks went red.

He came down the elevator, sat on the sofa with her, and said, "If I told you my age, you would never have dated me, let alone married me. I've been in love with you for longer than you know—before my daughter died, but I told you that. So I'll tell you my age only if I have your word and promise not to leave me or repeat it." She gave him her word. "I'm eleven years younger than you are, dear. When we started to date, you were so shy and nervous. If you knew, you would not have dated me, correct?"

"Yer right, but ya look older, love. Marcus looks younger than ya do."

"We are twins, and he was saved by Mother giving him to my auntie away from my dad. He was raised with a gentle hand. My mother wanted to send me as well, but the old man wouldn't have it. I worked in the bar from the age of six, cleaning up slop buckets from empty glasses and bottles. I did what I was told, as did Mom. He beat her as much as he beat me. One day, I had enough. I heard alcohol poisoning could kill. I put rat poison in his drinks by using a special bottle of booze just for him. It took a month, but the son of bitch died. I aged leaps and bounds. I looked like a small twenty-year-old."

"I loves ya, I'll ner leave ya."

"I talked to a young doctor whose wife is a nurse. Hardison could use help in town. The midwife retired before Christmas, leaving Hardison to do the birthing as well. I thought I would give the kid a job, and his wife. What do you think?"

"Talk ta Hardison. If he's abiden it, I can go along too."

Paul Kelly gave Tommy a call. "I'm interested in talking to you about that job, Mr. McCloud."

"It's still Tom, Paul. Are you afraid to fly?"

"No, why?"

"I'm up at my chalet, so I need you and your son to fly up here if you could, at my cost, of course."

"Well, okay, when?"

"Tomorrow too soon?"

"No, where do we go, Tom?"

"I have a private jet at the airport. Do you remember Charlie, my coworker?"

"Yes."

"He'll meet you at the airport. We'll have you home in time for dinner, Paul."

"See Charlie at eight in the morning. I'll be seeing you tomorrow."

Hardison was pleased to have a general practitioner working in the town, and he brought a nurse with him. Hardison was so happy. "Are we going to bring them into the organization, Tommy?"

"Let's see if you like him first, Hardison, and for his dad, yes. I need a man who has nerves of steel and can command as Charlie does. Even Charlie says we need new leaders as the organization is growing so large. Charlie would like to be just the cook and grandpa Charlie and to be with his wife and family for a while. I think Paul can take over the other stuff for Charlie."

"We will have to see what Charlie thinks first."

"Does that mean I have no say?" Marcus inquired.

"No, but do you know Charlie's job? Can you plan out the rescues like him or order what we need from whatever suppliers he uses?"

"No, and I don't want to, you know that."

"So why do you want a say in this?" Tommy was getting angry.

"I don't. I just would like to be included, that's all."

"You are, every time you take care of the money end of things, the business ventures we are involved in. By the way, Mitch would like you to slow down on the flirting and the presents. You are making Janet uncomfortable, and she's needed here again."

"Got it, although I do like her."

"She's not a weekend release, Marcus, and she's a forever kind of girl like Bertha. So if that isn't what you want, back off, okay?" Hardison wanted to knock him on his ass. Marcus saw it and left, told his brother he was flying out to the city of Quebec that afternoon.

Paul Kelly and his son Gary arrived just before ten o'clock. They were chatting with Charlie on the drive up to the chalet. They were shocked at its enormity. "Charlie, the way Tom spoke, I thought he lived in a chalet-like house."

"Well, it is, sort of just larger. To us, it's home."

Tommy greeted them in the foyer and asked them to follow him and Charlie to the study. They had to step over a few trucks to get there. Paul laughed. "Just like I remember coming home after work, stepping over your trucks and cars. You have little ones, Tom?" Paul asked.

"No, they belong to Mark and Mary, who are my niece Faye's children. We're so used to the caravan of vehicles, and we just step over them. Their mother is always trying to get them to pick them up."

They talked about Paul first, and then he went with Charlie. He was definitely interested, and now that his wife was gone, he was free to move. "Sorry about your loss, Gary. When did your mom pass?"

"She isn't dead, just gone. Dad went to work one day when I was at college. When he came home, she was gone, so was everything in the house. They divorced a year later. She was seeing his best friend, and she married him."

"What about you, Gary, you and your wife willing to move?"

"If it means I will be able to work as a doctor, yes, we are. She is doing a waitress job and working two shifts at the hospital. I had a patient that thought she knew better than I did about what was wrong with her. When I refused to prescribe the medicine she wanted, she let all her friends and the people of the town know I was a quack, and I did not know how to diagnose a nervous condition or breakdown and prescribe the proper medication she needed."

"By any chance, was her name Margaret Fobert?"

"You heard the gossip up here?"

"No, her daughter Denise—we call her Denny—is my grandson's wife."

"Robert King is your grandson? Man, I felt for him. She crapped on that young man."

"We have an opening for a doctor in our town. Hardison—you will meet him shortly—is our doctor up here. The town comes to him. The midwife is retired, and so we do need help. We would supply a home, a car, and pay you until you get on your feet. The house and car will be yours. You eventually won't need me to support your family. I heard great things about you from a doctor at the hospital in St. Helen. He felt like you did for Robert. Your office may need work. I don't think it's been used since old Doc Howard died. You would be working for me, so if you say yes, we will move you and help you get set up in whatever way you want."

"I talked to Dotty, my wife, before I came. We agreed if this meant a practice for us, we were ready to move. Bridget was our only child, and we had her cremated, so if we had to move, she would come with us. When would you need me to start?"

"Yesterday," Tommy said.

He shook Gary's hand and walked him out to the hut. He left him with Hardison and caught up with Charlie. "How's it going, fellas?"

Charlie told him. Kelly was anxious to start, liked being on the mountains. He could breathe clean air.

"Well, Kelly, what about the organization we run? Can you handle that?"

"I have heard of your rescue group, and I never knew it was this large or this busy. My sister was taken from us for a ransom, which, of course, we couldn't pay. Dad contacted a man named Yee. Two days later, Beth-Anne was home. Dad made payments of fifty dollars a month until he paid Mr. Yee the five hundred it cost to get her back. It also stopped him from drinking and gambling. Is this the same rescue group?"

Charlie answered, with a tear in his eye, "Yes, Yee is my father. We go by our last name. My name is Char Yee."

"Where do I sign up Tom? That way, I can continue to pay back for my sister."

"You will have to sign an agreement of silence, which means you can never talk about us or who you work for."

"Okay, not even my son, got it. Got the paper for me to sign?"

Tommy handed him the paperwork; he signed it and handed it back. "Welcome to the organization, Kelly. You will be moved tomorrow by my men. I need a list of what you want out of your house. Your son can pack the rest for you. You are staying here if you don't mind," Tommy told him.

"Why is that?"

"I need you to go to work getting a group of ten men in handcuffs down to the heliport. It will be you leading and four of your men helping."

"Okay."

Hardison took Gary into town, and he showed him the offices.

"They do need a lot of repair work, but it's a large office, great examination rooms."

"Then what do you think?"

"I think we are moving. I hope my dad will be okay with us being so far away."

"He will be right here with you."

"Dad likes his privacy."

"He was hired by Tommy, and he will have his own place." Dr. Kelly was going to set out his shingle.

"Bertha, my love, it's been a good day. Paul Kelly has joined us, and his son, Dr. Kelly, will be setting up shop in the town. Hardison is real happy about that. No more baby-delivery business." Bertha giggled at that.

Chapter Nineteen

BERTHA LOVED THE idea that young people were moving up to the mountain town. The seasons were different, but spring, summer, and autumn were her favourites, except the snow on Christmas. After the holiday it could go away. The children loved it so much she couldn't begrudge them their fun. At her age, it was dangerous. Tommy made her walk with a partner, just in case. A fall could be worse on her old bones than the youngens.

Liz asked to see Tom privately; she needed some fatherly advice, not motherly right now. He told her he would meet her in town at one for lunch. Would that work for her? "Yes, Tommy, but you mustn't tell Mom we are meeting. She will want to be there."

"All right, Liz, I got it, whatever it is, just between us." He told her if he wasn't there to wait for him, he was ordering materials with Dr. Kelly for his new office. "I know, don't invite him to lunch."

"What is bothering you, Liz? I'll do my best to be on time."

It took him a little longer, but they got all the supplies they needed. Tommy hired a carpenter and a painter. He also brought in an architect to make sure everything was done to code. Carol appreciated the business. Dr. Gary Kelly was already getting calls from people needing his assistance. Charlie set him up in one of the empty chalets until his office was ready. Dr. Gary was so busy. Hardison felt just a little sorry for him, not enough to help, but he did feel for him. Dotty took care of the minor things—cuts, bruises, cough due to colds—which helped him. Gary couldn't be happier. Denny was one of his first patients. She was close to her due date. "Dr. Kelly, I was hoping to be home in St. Helen before the birth, but, well, you know what's going on."

"Yes, and I also know stress is not good for you. Hardison told me about your condition now. Is your stress level high or low?"

"It's about four."

"Not bad. Most mothers at this stage of their pregnancy will be nearly five and a half or six. You still have just under two months to go, Denny, but the baby sounds good. Do you want to know the sex of the baby?"

"Hardison asked me that, Robert, and I want to be surprised."

"I'll see you in two weeks and from then on until you leave, or we deliver your sweet bundle."

Tommy was about ten minutes late to meet Liz. One look at her and he knew there was trouble brewing, let's hope, not in her marriage. "Okay, honey, I'm here; I'll listen to you talk."

"Let's get a coffee or some lunch so we won't be bothered, all right?" Tommy ordered tea black and an egg salad sandwich. Liz got vegetable soup with crackers.

"Okay." She grabbed his hand, tears flowing down her face. Liz said in a whisper, "I'm expecting."

He sat there stunned; what the hell, she should be happy—wait, her son is having his first. "Are you afraid of having this baby, Liz, or is it that Robert is going to be a father before his sister or brother is born?"

"I'm afraid the whole family will tell me to abort the child; I'm too old to have another child."

"Liz, you are about the same age my mother had our half-brother Duncan. She managed with our help."

"Robert and Denny may think Mitch and I are stealing their thunder. First baby born into the family. This baby will be younger than his or her niece or nephew." She was weeping hard.

Tommy slid over to her and held her. "Liz, are you sure? Did you see Hardison?"

"No, he would tell Charlie, and so on down the line."

Tom knew she was right. "Let's go see Dr. Kelly. His wife, Dotty, and Dr. Kelly are working out of one of the chalets. We can say you wanted to introduce yourself and welcome them to our town."

"Okay, but I'm sure it's not menopause." She had him on that one. He could not give her an answer for that. He didn't know what the hell that was.

They went to see Dr. Kelly. "Hi, Tom, and who might this be?" He could see she had been crying.

"This is my daughter-in-law, Liz Maxwell. She needs your help, but it's on the hush-hush until she says so."

He took Liz into a makeshift examining room. Dotty gave her a gown and asked her before she changed what the problem might be. "I think, no, I know I'm expecting." She started to cry again. He had Dotty go in and help her, first to get the tears under control and then get into the paper gown.

"Liz . . . I may call you Liz?" Liz told her she could. "Are you past fifty years old?"

"No, I'm forty-two."

"Okay, then it could be menopause."

"No, Dotty, I am regular as clockwork. Mitch and I had . . . had, well, you know, midcycle. I never worried about it before. Until now. I'm two months late." She held her tears as Dr. Kelly came in.

Dotty held her hand, talking to her the whole time. "Well, Liz, there is a swelling in your uterus, and your cervix is closed. This usually means you are pregnant, but I took a sample, and I will do some bloodwork to be 100 percent sure."

"What if my family wants me to abort this baby?"

"Have you even told your husband yet?"

"No."

"I think that comes first, dear," Dotty told her. "I am a change-of-life baby, Liz. My mother was forty-seven when I was born. I was their only child. Do you think because of their age, they wanted to get rid of me?"

"No, I don't; you are here."

"What I meant was you and Mr. Maxwell will make that decision, but in reality, Liz, it's yours to make—your body, your life, your baby. See what I mean." Liz thanked Dotty for her talk and Dr. Kelly for his help.

Liz felt better when she met Tommy outside the chalet. "Okay, Gramps, here we go. I have to tell Mitch first. Then we will tell Mom, and you be surprised for me."

"You bet I can. Unlike your hubby, I can manage a white lie to Bertha."

She hugged him. "I like Dr. Kelly and his wife. They are common-sense people. She made me understand that it's my choice, no matter what anyone says."

"They are right, Liz; only you can decide the fate of your child—you and the good Lord."

Liz waited until after dinner, and the adults went their separate ways. "Mitch, will you go for a walk with me?"

"Sure, honey, but it's cold, so bundle up."

"We can walk down the lane then sit on the wooden bench for a while."

"You have something on your mind, sweets, that we need to be in private for you to talk to me?" Mitch was a bit worried. Is she ill or dying or something?

"Yes, but it's not dire. I'm not ill or in jeopardy." She laughed. She could read him better than a love story novel.

Denny and Robert asked where they were going. Could they join them?

"Denny, I'm going for a long walk to lose a few pounds. Can you manage four or five miles, dear?"

"Oh no, Mom. Robert and I will walk over to the barn and get some wood for the fireplace then. See you later." Liz knew she was disappointed, but this time she needed to be with Mitch alone.

They had walked for ten to fifteen minutes without saying a word to each other. They reached the end of the lane. "Well, are you going to talk to me or what?" Mitch asked her. She sat on the log bench and patted the spot next to her. He sat down. Liz took his hand in both of hers and kissed him like she just came back from a trip, or she was leaving on one. He looked in her eyes and saw the tears. "For God's sake, woman, spit it out, I'm dying thinking my world is ending."

"We are going to have a baby in about seven months." That's all she said.

He fell off the log into a pile of snow, and he didn't try to get up. "Mitchell, get up and talk to me. Tell me what you think." He rose on his knees and faced her. "I think it's wonderful. Are you all right? You've seen a doctor . . . oh, what am I saying? Of course, you have. Yes, oh, yes, a baby, do you know what it is?"

"Mitch, I'm only a little more than two months. They can't tell yet."

He hugged her, got her up, and danced around on the road. "Who knows besides us, I mean," he asked her.

"I wanted this to be our moment in case you didn't want the baby, and then it would be up to me."

"Oh, Liz, I want this so much. I know we are older parents, and Robert's nose may be out of joint, but he'll come around. Mom and Tommy will be so happy. Little Bessie will love it. She is here, by the way."

"I have something I want to ask you also, but it can wait; let's tell the world our news." Liz laughed, relieved he was happy. "Well, at least the family for now."

Robert and Denny were piling the wood on the iron rack beside the fireplace when they came in. Mitch asked them, "Where were Grams and Gramps at?"

"They are on the balcony watching the stars. Why?" Robert asked.

Mitch said nothing and went and asked them to come in. Tommy could see he was elated at Liz's news. Time to play happy and surprised, he thought.

When Mitch gathered everyone he wanted, including Faye and Charlie, he asked them to sit, please. Little Bessie was all over Liz, licking her chin and smelling her clothes. "We have some exciting news to tell all of you. Liz, you should be the one to tell," he told her.

"Mom, Tommy, all of you, I'm expecting our first and probably only child."

The room went completely silent. No one said a word. Faye was the first to speak, "Congratulations, Aunt Liz, Uncle Mitch. I'm so happy for both of you."

"Well, I'm not." It was Robert. "Do you realize I'm nearly twenty-three years old? Denny and I are expecting our first. This child will be its aunt or uncle, younger than ours." He went to walk away.

Before Mitch could grab him, Tommy did. "You selfish, ungrateful, spoiled brat. Your mom is expecting, yes. What has that got to do with your child? This baby will be your sister or brother, and you don't like the idea of not being an only child? Grow a pair, Robert. You are a married man. Life may throw a curveball your way when you are older. Take it like a grown-up."

Tommy let go of him, and Mitch laid him out on his ass. Denny looked at him and said, "Robert, you deserved that. Your mother is crying because of you. Sleep on the bloody sofa, you son of a bitch."

Robert realized he was childish. He needed to think this through. Should I take Denny and go back to the city? It's safe now. Or does he eat his words and pretend he was sorry. Thought about his job. Maybe he should leave St. Helen and start somewhere new. He was standing in the study when Bertha walked in. "Ya needs ta tell yer dear sweet mother yer sorry even if ya denna feel it or means it. Robert, she is all ya have, an she will love ya no matter what. Robert, have yer babe. She and Mitchell will have theirs. If ya no want a relationship wit the barin, fine, ya canna stay oot of the kids' life, but not yer mother's. As fer what yer thinken, stop. Ya know yer job is good. Denny won't be willen ta leave her brother. Wake up, child, wake up." She smacked him in the back of the head.

Bertha came back to Liz. "Ya no mind the brat. He'll be aroond soon enough." She held Liz and Mitch's hands. "What's yer plan fer the future now that there's a wee barin commin?" she asked.

Liz knew what she wanted, but she didn't know what Mitch would think. She told Bertha, "I'm not sure yet, Mom. Mitch and I haven't discussed it yet."

"Well, I'll be here fer ya. So will Tommy."

"Charlie told me he wants ta congratulate ya as well."

Mitch looked at her. "What's on your mind, Liz?"

"I was going to suggest we give Carol and Doug our house and move up here. I love this place—the peace, the quiet, and the people of the town. The schools here are good, and well, college is too far away to think about."

"I was going to ask you the same thing, honey, for exactly the same reasons, only now more so with our baby on the way." They went out on the balcony where Mom and Tommy were. "Can we live here with you until we build our chalet?"

"You can stay here forever. Raise the baby here with built-in babysitters." Bertha was so happy. "We are giving our house to Carol and Doug if they want it."

"Tommy an I are stayen as well. I ner felt so safe as here. We ladies of the hoose have ta stick ta gether." Liz and Bertha went to the sunroom to have a mother-daughter chat.

"Mitch, I overstepped with Robert. I'm sorry, I just couldn't believe his attitude toward Li after all she and you have done for him and Denny."

"I'm hoping he gets over his embarrassment because that's what it is. His mother is older. She should be preparing for her grandchildren, not starting a new family."

"You think that's what it is, Mitch? He's embarrassed." Charlie started to laugh.

"Of course it is; he's thinking, I'm twenty-three, married, and a baby sibling younger than my baby."

Tommy was quiet for a while. “I’ll go apologize to the kid now. I feel bad. I was awful to him.”

“I deserved it, Gramps. Charlie is right. My kid will be born before my sibling. I guess Denny and I could babysit for you guys.” Robert felt like a whipped dog, with his tail between his legs. He acted like a child himself, and his wife made him feel twice as bad. He thought he had lost his balls to the dog.

Mitch could have told him they were moving up here. He planned on turning the running of the business over to his best friend and his wife to run, and the import-export business to be run by Robert and guided by Mr. Giles, of course. Mitch would save that conversation for a later date. When he finds out everything, he wanted Liz at his side. Robert may not take it so well, now that they were moving up here.

Mitch and Liz took the young couple out for dinner in town. They were surprised to find out that they had purchased a cabin from Charlie. His oldest daughter had moved to be with her future husband in Boston. They liked the cabin. Carol and Doug paid Charlie cash for the cabin. “We knew Doug had to be close if Tommy or Charlie needed him. So we are staying on the mountain.”

“What about your architecture company, Carol?” Mitch asked.

“Can rent space up here and travel if need be. I want to do homes, houses for families. I’ll finish Robert and Denny’s house.”

“Well, we will have to sell it.”

“Could you consider something for me?” Carol asked. “Caitlin is a police officer; her fiancé is an FBI agent that has to stay in St. Helen. Could you think about letting her rent to own it because she loves that house, and she loves Grams and Gramps?”

“Sorry, love, they are staying here on the mountain as well?”

I'm so happy about this. Do Denny and Robert know about all this?" Carol asked.

Liz answered her, "He doesn't know. He had a hard time with our other news."

"What other news?" Carol wanted to know.

"We are having a baby in seven months, if all goes well."

"Oh, I'm going to have another sibling. I'm so happy for you two." She had tears in her eyes.

Doug shook their hands. "Can we babysit? I love kids, and I know my lady does as well."

"Thanks for the offer. You and Grams and Gramps can fight it out." They all laughed at that. "The kid will speak Gaelic before it speaks English."

Bertha thought about her home in St. Helen. She did love it, but she loved it on the mountain. "Tommy, canna we keep our hame in St. Helen? I want ta be able ta go ta the city, an stay where I'm comfy."

"Sure, love. I didn't want to sell it either. There will be times when we have to talk with clients. You are now a part of this, so yes, we keep the house."

What a wonderful gift to her, she thought. She never had a home of her own, and now she had two to choose from.

Liz contacted Caitlin to congratulate her on her engagement. Caitlin thanked her but was sad. "What's up, Caitlin? I thought you would be excited like Carol is."

"I would be, Liz, but Dugan says I may have to leave the force if I stay engaged to an FBI agent. I may leak information to Franc that the police don't want the FBI to have, or he may tell me something I shouldn't know about and repeat it."

"That is ridiculous. Many police officers are happily married to FBI agents, and they are fine. Is Dugan upset that it's not him you're enamored with?"

Caitlin laughed. "Dugan never showed that kind of emotion toward me ever. When we were younger, I had a crush on him, but that was after cadet school. Now he's a chief, and I'm a sergeant."

"Well, pay no attention to that crap. He may be just playing with you."

"Yes, but let's face it, the prices on homes are so high, and nothing is rentable. That is a decent price, and the ones we can afford are not rentable or clean or falling apart."

"I know of a nice place, has four bedrooms, three washrooms, and a fenced back yard that has a great price."

"Oh come on, Liz! Where, TIMBUKTU?"

"No, my home, silly. Mitch and I are staying up at the chalet on the mountain until we can build our own house. Are you sitting down, Cat? I'm expecting in about six and a half months."

"Congratulations! I'm so glad for you and Mitch. How is Robert taking it?"

"He's coming around to it. Denny will box his ears if he doesn't."

"Are you sure about your house, Liz? I love that house. Do you want rent, want a mortgage? Liz, tell me!"

"We want you and Jon to be happy. It's our wedding gift to you and Jon. We will stop in and see you once in a while if that's okay."

"Oh, it sure is. Does Carol know how lucky she is to have parents like you two?"

"Will you tell Jon?"

"I think you can do that, can't you?"

"I can, but I think it is better coming from you and Mitch. Can we meet for dinner?"

"Yes, but out of town, please. I don't care to see anyone just yet."

"I'd like that spot we had your bridal party at, but I don't think the guys would like the service too much."

Liz laughed and remembered that night with fondness. "No, I don't think they would."

"Let's go to that restaurant on the highway just up from there. You know the one, I mean, we can have a few dances and that after dinner."

"That sounds great; when you set it up with Jon and let me know, Caitlin."

"Right. I thank you so much, Liz."

"Bye, Cat."

Robert overheard Grams telling Charlie that Liz and Mitch were staying on the mountain. He went to Denny. "Did you know my parents were planning to stay up here?"

"No, I did not, but what has that got to do with you being upset again."

"Well, who is going to be living in my old house?"

"Robert, we are moving into a new home, one Carol and I designed. One I love. It has everything we wanted and more. So what the hell is the problem now?"

He shook his head and walked away. "It's my childhood home. I was raised in the house, and now strangers will live in it. I'd rather it burn down than see that." He was telling Peter that when Charlie walked in.

"They are renting it, I believe, to Caitlin and her fiancé, Jon Franc, not some strangers. Robert, this has to stop. You are an adult, married, and a child on the way. If you want that house, tell them. Simple as that. Make sure it's what your lady wants also."

"Charlie, you do have a way of making me feel like an asshole."

Denny talked to Liz and was so happy her friend Caitlin was going to be their neighbour. She was afraid she would be alone. All her friends from before had deserted her because of her parents. Richard was still there for them, but he was so busy now he was running everything. Her girlfriends very seldom called, and if Denny called them, they always seemed to have an excuse.

Robert saw his mother knitting something on the sofa by the fire. "Are you renting or selling our house to Caitlin and that Jon Franc?"

Liz remembers what the doctor told her: to stay calm and answer him like an adult. If he acts like a child, treat him like one.

"Yes, we are, Robert; Caitlin is engaged to Mitch's friend, Jon Franc. They both have jobs that won't let them leave the city. She would be company for Denny and a babysitter if ever you needed one."

"No, Robert. We are staying with her. You have a beautiful home that is being furnished as we speak. Are you telling me you want to live in our old house with fewer bathrooms, fewer bedrooms, and a leaky basement?"

"No, I guess I'm not. They can have the problems. We will be leaving at the beginning of the week." He turned on his heel and left her.

Liz did not like his attitude toward her, Caitlin, or toward his wife, Denny. What has happened to him?

Denny went to Charlie; anyone related to Robert would only jump all over him. "Charlie, do you have a minute to talk? I have a problem, and well, I can't go to the family with it?"

"Sit down, Denny. A cup of tea, to start with, then we talk?" Charlie took her to his favourite spot, a breakfast nook just off the kitchen, quiet and, best of all, secluded. It's where he does his best thinking. "All right, darlin', what's got you so upset this early in the morning?" he said to her with a bright smile.

"Robert slapped me for telling him he needs to get over being jealous of his mother's pregnancy."

Charlie had to put both his hands under the table. They had turned into fists. "Are you all right, Denny? No pains, no bruises?"

"No, I put cold compresses on my face as soon as he left the room. It doesn't look swollen or bruised, does it?" She turned her face for Charlie to see the side he hit. There was redness in the shape of a hand on that side.

His anger was rising. This girl was trying her best not to cry or show the hurt. "This isn't the first time, is it, Denny?"

"Once before, just after the business with my parents started, him losing his job, they put him down as a no-good person to any and all who would listen. I lost our first child because of it."

"I think he needs to cool off a bit, and then I'll have a small talk with him. No sense bringing in Tommy, Mitch, or any other family member. It will only anger them and start a rough go for him."

"Thanks, Charlie. I know he needs help. I guess I'm not the right one for the job." She finished her tea and just sat there. Charlie left her sitting there. She was a very pregnant, perplexed woman. He was going to help, but not in the way she thought.

"Kelly, you know anything about boxing?"

"No, Charlie, why?"

"I need a boxing ring set up in the barn as fast, and I mean fast. We have to teach a person not to hit women."

Kelly growled. "That's easy, knock the shit out of him."

"No, I'm going to knock some sense into him. He is going to learn to defend himself. After all, a wife with child on the way, the time is now. He needs to know this."

"Charlie, I like your methods. Where do I get a boxing ring?" Kelly asked.

"Order one ASAP, Kelly, like yesterday."

"On it, Charlie."

Tommy found Denny sitting in Charlie's quiet place. "Good morning, Denny, up early today?"

"Yes, just wanted a cup of tea before everyone came down."

Tommy saw the mark. He knew what it was, and he'd seen it too many times on his mother's face.

"Had a chat with Charlie. He likes company in the morning."

"Yes, he does; that's why I came down."

"He said he had to tell Kelly to order something."

"Thanks, love. I'll go find him."

Tommy wanted to tear Robert apart, limb from limb. First, a slap. Or a shove, then I'm sorry, but the next one is more challenging, and so on. She is a gentlewoman. She's seen enough, been through enough. He found Charlie walking back from Kelly's cabin. "What are you doing about Denny's problem?"

"She tell you about it?"

"No, I saw her face. I know when a woman's been slapped, seen it too many times on my mom."

"We are having boxing training. Robert is first, whether he wants to or not. I personally will knock the crap out of him all while I am teaching to defend himself. If this doesn't get him to see the light, then we humiliate him in front of his parents and family."

"Can I help teach the little bastard?"

"Tommy, you have to get in line. So does Kelly."

Charlie found her still sitting in his breakfast nook. He placed a mirror in front of her. “Look, but don’t cry; get angry, Denny. This is your first lesson on defending yourself.”

“I need to defend myself from what?”

“This is going to escalate if we don’t work together to teach Robert to strike out is wrong.”

“Do you honestly believe he will do this again? Oh, Charlie, this frightens me!”

“I know, sweet child. That’s why you are going to help me teach him to keep his hands to himself.”

“My brother had a temper when he would get angry. He would strike out, usually at his poor wife. Now he hits a punching bag, not his family.” She put her arms around him. “Charlie, what am I to do? The family will see this. Tommy already has. He went looking for you.”

“He found me, and you are going over to my chalet with my wife and daughter. May-Ling will take care of your face, so the red does not show. She will also show you how to cover the bruise that will come and when to cover it.”

“What does that mean?”

Peter came on a golf cart to get her. “I’ll tell everyone you and June are shopping for baby things. Now go.” Peter helped her into the cart but only said, “Hello, chilly, put this around you.” She was so embarrassed she couldn’t speak for fear she would cry.

When they got to May-Ling’s home, Peter helped her down and hugged her. “Don’t be afraid to learn the lessons Mom and Dad are about to teach you.” He needs to learn you are a person, not a personal whipping post.”

He walked her inside. May-Ling put a cream on her face that cooled it off quickly. "Denise, was he angry with you or something that was said?"

"I said he needed to get over his jealousy of his mom's baby. He closed his fist then turned and slapped me. Told me to mind my own business when it came to his family."

June shook her head. "Next time, and there will be, hit him back across the face as hard as you can and run from the room. He won't chase you; he'll be ashamed to admit he hit you first. Will you try that, please?" May-ling said. "I want you to start wearing loose dresses that make it easy to move in and lets him see how pregnant you are."

June put a mirror on the table in front of her. They showed her how a lighter shade of foundation would hide the slight discoloration of her face. May-Ling gave her a notebook and pen. "Every time you write it down—when, where, why. Write it down, Denny. WHEN, WHERE, WHY, HOW YOU FEEL, WHAT YOU WANT HIM TO FEEL. Next, don't stay alone with him. Try to be in the family's company, if he asked you to go somewhere you don't feel up to it. You are too uncomfortable with being so close to delivery. If he tries to corner, you call out to anyone nearby. He will soon get the message you do not trust him, and you are not going to give him the chance to do it again, no matter how many times he apologizes afterwards. It's not going to happen again," June told her.

"Denny, this is going to be hard for you. No more holding hands, close embraces, unless you are in mixed company. If he gets your hand, he can pull you away and embrace. He can lift you and you are no longer in control. I know it's a lot, but it will save you from another slap or even a beating if his temper gets the best of him."

They taught her how to take her hand back before he gets ahold of it, how to turn on the embrace so he can't get ahold of her. She had a good cry and got hold of her emotions and thanked them.

"One question, May-Ling—Charlie's brother: did he stop hurting his wife?"

"Yes, the things we taught her and Charlie gave him boxing lessons like he is going to teach your Robert."

Two days later, the equipment came. More of the men wanted to spar, but only to show off their prowess. Charlie cornered Robert in the great room. "We have a boxing ring set up in the barn, Robert. Do you know how to defend yourself or your wife if you are attacked?" Charlie asked.

"No, I don't, Charlie, and I don't care to spend time in a boxing ring learning how to punch someone."

Charlie stood close and said to him, "Only female someones, Robert. We all saw Denny's face." Out loud he said, "Come on, Robert. I'll see you out there this afternoon. Wear sweatpants and shirt." Quietly he said, "Be there, or I'll come to get you."

He tried to get Denny alone, but she wasn't having any of it. "You never want to be alone with me anymore, why?"

"You know why, Robert. You will never be given the opportunity to use me as your scapegoat when you are angry like you are right now." She walked over to Grams and talked about what Dr. Kelly said at her last visit.

He changed his clothes, thinking he would let Charlie show him a few moves, then he would leave. He was angry but at himself. His wife no longer trusted him. She stayed away from him. She had started sleeping in another room and locking her door. He felt like an unmarried man with a pregnant wife. He wanted to ask Tommy if that was normal, but he was afraid of the answer. Everyone seemed to know he hit Denny, but no one said anything, so did they? He would die of embarrassment had she told everyone. If she told his mother, she would have said something, more like screamed at him. His grandfather taught him you never hit a woman, so Mom would have blown up. Mitch would have stopped talking to him. Gramps might have asked him to leave. So how did Charlie know he hit her. Denny went to Charlie; no, she would go to a woman, not a man.

He went out to the barn expecting more than Charlie out there. "Get in the ring, Robert. I'll bring the gloves."

He put the gloves on, and they stood looking at each other. Robert had a slight smile on his face. "Do you know why you are here, Robert?"

"To learn to take care of myself and my family."

"No, you are here to learn to manage your anger—what to do with it when it rises to the point you want to strike out. She didn't tell anyone. I saw her face, your handprint on it. She said not a word, asked for a cup of tea. I wanted to hold her and comfort her as I would my own daughter. You will learn to manage your anger, or you are going to lose her. I see her pulling away from you now. So what's it going to be, Robert? Lose her and your child or learn to manage your temper?"

They started slow, Charlie allowing a few to get to him. Then he struck Robert in the chest. It made him angry. He swung wide, and Charlie deflected it. He was trying very hard to hit Charlie but didn't connect. Robert was drenched in sweat when Charlie called a halt to the first lesson.

"What did you learn, Robert, from this lesson?"

"Don't lose control because you get nowhere when you are angry."

"Can you apply that to you and Denny now?"

"Don't take it out on her because she is there and you need to vent. So go hit the tree outside or run and get away from the problem and her."

"Good. See you tomorrow for lesson 2, but you go write down what you have learned. Next time you get angry, read it. Even if you don't want to, do it. If you are still angry, read it again and again until you calm down."

Each day Robert boxed with Charlie. Each day Robert opened up a little more, always felt he had to take care of his mother, and how even when she started dating Mitch, it gave him breathing room. When they married, he was elated—he had a dad, and he would be taking over looking out for his mother. Then the trouble with Denny's parents. Denny losing the first baby. All felt like they were his fault. He was in seventh heaven when he found out about this baby. He understood why Mom and Mitch kept the war at home away from them. They did it to protect Denny and the baby. "Charlie, I swear when Mom said she was expecting, it tore my guts out. All I could think about was they are older parents who are going to take care of the kid—me, that's who. All over again, I'm responsible for another person, a brother or sister, along with my child and Denny; it was too much. So when she told me to get my jealousy under control, I hit her. I felt so bad, but Charlie, that's the second time over angry words I've hit her. I love her so much. What is wrong with me?"

"Anxiety, frustration, and overcharged feelings all can cause this. I'm going to introduce you to your new best friend."

They walked over the far side of the barn, just before the stable area. There hung a punching bag.

"This is your new friend, and you give it a name. From now on, you feel these emotions creeping up, don't wait to change. Come out here and talk to your new best friend while you punch out these angry feelings."

"Charlie, will it work? God, I hope so. She won't even sleep with me."

"You have to earn her trust back, Robert. It's going to take time, but if you work at it, she will come around. Are you still writing your journal as I asked you to?"

"Yes, and I read it every time I get antsy and before I go to bed. I've started adding to it as well as the rules you gave me. I can't thank you enough for helping me. I think I'm finally growing up."

Charlie sure hoped so. His wife is tired of the hot epsom salt baths every night to soothe sore, aching muscles.

Charlie found a box wrapped up in silver paper with a blue bow tied on it.

"Because I love you and thank you." He opened it. Inside was the family photo of his family—all his family, he didn't remember it. It hit him. Denny asked him if he would stand on the hill for her to get the right light, and slowly his family gathered around him, wanting to know why he was standing there. They knew. Denny did it for him; he loved it. He loved it so much he wanted to hang it in his breakfast nook but thought it might be a bit selfish not to want to share it with the family. Then Charlie saw the second one in the box—a little smaller, just right for his little nook. He hung it up so he could see it from the kitchen and admire it when he sat in the nook. She didn't need to do this, but he loved her all the more for showing her gratitude for their help saving her marriage.

Robert asked his parents out for dinner at the café for an Italian restaurant. Liz was excited about it. Mitch wanted to go as well. They drove down together in Robert's car. He didn't say much of anything on the way. Denny told Liz she was getting Braxton Hicks, like pre-delivery pains, but they are not so bad she needs to see Dr. Kelly. Mitch pleaded with them to stop. They were ruining his appetite. They laughed at him.

At the café, they ordered their meals. A family-style three-course dinner. Pasta with meat sauce, chicken cacciatore, and dessert. Robert told his mother he was sorry about how he reacted to becoming a brother to the baby. He went on to explain it to them as he had to Charlie. Robert even told them about his boxing lessons and his new best friend. They were glad to hear he worked out being a brother. No one mentioned the hitting. After dinner, he told them why he took boxing lessons and his journal he writes in now every night. Liz told him she keeps a day planner by her bed and writes in them every night. They were enjoying a glass of wine when Denny's water broke, and her labour pains started right away. Robert called Dr. Kelly. He told him he would meet them at the hut. The new maternity part of the office was not done.

Hardison was only too glad to defer to Dr. Kelly when it came to babies. He was prepared for them when they got there. Liz and Robert helped her undress and get into a gown. Dr. Kelly arrived, and Denny relaxed. He prepped, and Dotty set out his instruments. She told Denny they were only there if needed and to cut the cord. She told Robert to get into a gown and scrub up. He was going to help Denny deliver this baby.

Her labour was relatively long; she was getting weak when the baby finally decided to make an appearance. A beautiful boy, he weighed in at six pounds and six ounces. Mom, Dad, and grandparents were overjoyed, and both Mom and baby were all right and healthy. They named him Robert Richard Mitchell King after his dad, his uncle, and his grandfather.

Chapter Twenty

EVERYONE WANTED TO hold JR. he seemed to love all the attention. When Bertha took the baby, she cooed to him in Gaelic, which no one had heard before. It was a lullaby she sang to his dad. Robert seemed to know it. He stood behind Grams and started to sing it with her. For the life of him, he didn't know where the words came from or what they meant. Liz watching, snapping pictures on her phone. Tommy remembered the lullaby from his childhood. JR started to fuss. Bertha handed him back to Mommy. "Tis ta feed the wee barin, an JR's nappy's wet, dear. Denny got it, time to feed the baby, but what did he have on that was getting wet besides his diaper? What's a nappy, Grams?" Liz told her it was his diaper. She looked at Robert. "You sing a Gaelic song to our boy and didn't know what a nappy was," she said laughingly.

He smiled at her, "And I honestly didn't know. I just knew the song."

Denny wondered when Robert was going to tell them they were going back to the city, now that Carol says the house is finished. She had all the things that were bought for Jeffery set up for JR, so his room is ready also. Carol showed her pictures of every room. Denny was happy with it. They rented a small tag-a-long trailer for all the things they bought in England and all the lovely Christmas things all three had received. Robert handed JR to his grandmother and said, "We have an announcement. We are going back to the city as soon as Dr. Kelly gives us the go-ahead for JR to drive that far."

Bertha was sad she would not see little Robert grow. Tommy kissed her. "So is life, my love. They will come to see us, or we will go there to see them. JR will know his great-grandparents."

Charlie came in and went to the great room. "You have to see this, oh my Lord, this is bad." They had missed two of the charges. Robert's house and the house next to them were gone; all that was left was a gaping hole. "The family had gone to visit the kids' grandparents, so no lives were lost."

"Thank God for that," Bertha said.

Denny was glad all their photo albums were at her brother's; he was putting them on CDs to save them. Furniture can be replaced. Memories are always with you, but lose a picture, and that memory is gone. We lose memories as we age.

They would start again. Robert was amazed at himself for not losing it and getting angry. He didn't need to go see Bert the bag. Tommy called Franc. "What really happened, Jon? I know we did a thorough investigation, and the sewer crew did also."

"It wasn't the sewer, Tom. Those houses went up because they were targeted. Carol made it out with her life. She's okay with temporary deafness. It will pass. Carol was just getting into her car to leave when the house blew up, taking the one next door with it. She's flying back to you right now. I put her on the plane myself, I called Doug, and I was just about to call you when you reached me. Keep the family up there, will you? Caitlin and I just moved into Liz and Mitch's house, now with broken windows and pictures off the walls, but we are okay. As soon as I know something, I will let you know."

Tommy did not tell the family the truth. "We missed a couple of explosives, Robert, and Denny's house as you saw is gone. The house next to them also. I'm sorry, kids, you'll have to stay here a while longer until we can rebuild for you one more time."

Mitch spoke up and told Robert he would be running the import-export part of their business; could he do it from here? They could get people back to work in that area.

"Sure, Dad, I can, but where?"

"I rented some buildings just outside of town on the downside of the mountain. We ship to there, but staffing is limited; the people that we had been all but moved on with their lives and new jobs. Well, all but Mr. Giles."

"Please, Dad, the man and I do not get along, Mr. Giles thinks he is the best at his job; he's not. There was a lady—her name was Snowdon, Vickie Snowdon. She did all his planning, his meetings. Giles may have thought he ran the office, but she did. Mr. Giles, I don't even know his first name. Isn't he old enough to retire?"

Mitch knew where Robert was going. No one in that department liked Giles. He was the one that turned Liz down for a receptionist job. So yes, Mitch got it loud and clear. He understood.

"Okay, what about manual labour? Are any of our people left, or have they gone as well."

"I don't know, but I will get in touch with Ms. Snowdon. She will know."

"Are you really moving things up here?"

"Some of it, Robert. Your mother and I are staying up here, so I will work out of the officers up here. The legal departments will be rebuilt in St. Helen and here because we need them in both places. Carol and Doug have bought a cabin up here, and she plans to open her architectural offices here."

Denny started to laugh. "I dreamed we would be living on the mountain. I was working for Carol, and you were working for Dad. What do you think? I know Richard will be upset, but he can fly up to see us, right?"

"Are you sure because I love it here as well?"

Bertha grabbed Robert and danced him around the room. "I'll ner miss me, boys. They're here to stay wit me."

Liz laughed at her, but the tears of joy ran down her face. JR would grow up with his family around him.

Tommy called Charlie, "Do they know anything at all?"

"No, our boys are with the FBI going over everything for some kind of clue. Franc said he let me know as soon as he found something."

"Start checking all the vacant buildings on the downside of the mountain Mitch is going to rent or already had for his import-export business. When will this shit end?"

"Ms. Snowdon, this is Robert King. Mitchell Maxwell is starting up the import-export department of his business and wants to know if you are available to work for him again or are you employed?"

"Only if I do not have to work for or with Giles. That pompous ass. I know I should not say such things. He is a five-foot-seven-inch dictator that no one likes to work with."

"I know, I had to work with him. He expects everyone to grovel at his feet and thank them for his mistreatment. . . . There is one thing—we are relocating up on the mountain. Can you do this, or would it be too far?"

"My parents live on the mountain in a small town called Hargood. Is that anywhere near you?"

"Yes, it is. Can you fly up here Monday? We will have our plane bring you up, and do you know if there are any of our people who worked for us needing to work?"

"They have all settled, Mr. King. It has been a long while."

"All right, we start from scratch. Have you any records of our business with other companies and associates?"

"Giles has them."

"Mr. Maxwell would be the only one able to get those; he will have to get in touch with Giles."

"See you Monday. The plane will take off from the airport at 8 a.m. in the morning."

After talking to his dad, he went to check on the baby and his wife. JR was asleep, Denny was reading a book from Tommy's library. "The book any good, sweetheart?"

"Yes and no. I'm just waiting for Robbie to wake up. My chest is getting heavy and sore." He snuggled with her until Robbie woke up, wanting to be fed.

Robert changed his nappy for him and laughed. "I changed his nappy and put a new one on."

"Good, give the clean kid to me."

Mitch did get ahold of Giles; before Mitch could suggest he retire, he was told that Giles was not coming back to work. He wanted his retirement money paid out in full with full medical, dental, and optical benefits. Giles angered Mitch a little—not the retirement, the medical demands.

"Well, Giles, it's like this: you want a full payment, that's fine. I want all the kickbacks you took while you worked for me. Don't deny it, I know. As for your medical, you cover that with those kickbacks. I expect all the company records sent to me express.

And yes, I will have them examined. Good day, Giles. Have a good life."

He let Robert know that Giles would not be returning. "Robert, did you make an appointment with Ms. Snowdon yet?"

"Yes, she's coming up Monday."

"I will need a new head of the department—someone who gets along with the employees, mainly you."

"She is very nice and easy to speak with. You will like her, Dad. Denny likes her; they got along when they met at the complex. So let's hope she fits the bill. I know I am not ready or know enough yet to do one-half of the job."

"You will one day, Robert, you will."

Liz overheard Bertha talking to Tommy and Charlie. They discussed the house bombing, and it didn't sound like it was missed explosives in the sewer. When Bertha came out of the study, Liz grabbed her. "Mom, I know you talked with them. Now talk to me. Are we still at war? What trouble is it now."

"They canna tell yet, Liz. Robbie's hoose was done on purpose. Yer hoose got a wee shook up, winders blowed oot pictures off the walls. Carol's shook up, an she canna hear nothin, but tis only fer a wee while."

"Mom, do they know who is doing this?"

"No, Liz, ner figured it oot yet."

Tommy came up to them. "As soon as I know, Liz, I'll let you know. We didn't tell the family on purpose. They had enough upset and fear to last a lifetime. Myself included. We thought it all over, back to being normal people again."

"Let us know if we can help you. Mitch and I are only too willing to help get this over."

"Not you, Liz. You have a new life coming to protect. That's a job on its own."

Little Robbie was being rocked by Great-Grams. Denny was having a short nap on the sofa next to her. Charlie came in quietly. "Tea for my lady?" he whispered.

Bertha nodded. "He's a right beauty, is he not."

"Yes, Bertha, he is. They are lucky to have a sleeper," Charlie told her.

"Yes, his daddy ner let us sleep till he was all but four months old."

Charlie left to bring in the tea tray. The chalet rocked. The noise was deafening. Charlie grabbed Denny off the sofa and rushed Bertha with him out of the great room. The windows around the fireplace blew inward.

"Bertha, we are going to the kitchen; it's the safest room in the house."

"Where's Tommy, Charlie?"

"He's in town with Mitch and Michael."

"I'll call him when I know you, Denny, and the baby are safe."

Faye was already there in the kitchen with the kids. Cora had just left to shop for Charlie. Robert flew in the back door. He was heading in to get his wife and son. She was standing next to Charlie, white as a ghost. Bertha held the baby protectively in her arms. Charlie told them to head out to either the hut or the barn. "No, the barn is gone; the hut is okay. We are safer right here until we find out what the hell is going on."

The men arrived at the chalet. "They are saying it's a tremor of sorts. I don't think so."

"Robert, have you tried the radio or your phone?"

"No, but I will now."

"They are saying part of the far side of the mountain had a landslide, the ice is too heavy, and it is moving."

"Are we close, Gramps, to the Slide?"

"No, we felt the release of the earth," Tommy told them.

Robert took the baby from Grams. She looked like she should be sitting. "Grams, please sit down at the table. I'm sure Charlie has some tea brewed for you." At least he hoped he did. Charlie moved, helped Bertha sit, and brought her a cup of tea.

"Tom, I need to check my family."

"I already did. Peter is bringing May-Ling and June up here as we speak."

Charlie was grateful. "Thank you! I was scared."

"You did for me. I did for you, my friend."

Michael and Mitch came in. "Where is Liz?"

"Mom, she was with you, wasn't she?"

"She was in the hall, Uncle Mitch, with Grams before Denny gave her the baby."

"I ner seen her after Mitchell," Bertha told him.

All of the men headed toward the great room. "Mitch, check the study, Robert go to the sunroom. Charlie and I will check the upstairs."

They were calling to each other. "Not in the study . . ."

"Not in the sunroom . . ."

Charlie yelled, "I found her! She's on the floor of her room. Somebody call Hardison now."

She was unconscious and very pale. Mitch was going to lift her onto the bed. "No, Mitch, let Hardison see her first, just in case, okay?" Mitch knelt beside her, holding her ice-cold hand. Hardison came rushing in. "Sorry, I had a man with a head injury. Did she fall, what?"

"We don't know, Hardison; we found her like this. The rest of us were in the kitchen." He made Mitch move out of the way and sent the rest of them out of the room. After checking for broken bones and listening to her heart and the baby's, he had Mitch help him lift her to the bed. She had a big red lump on her forehead. "What could she have fallen on or what came at her to cause this lump?"

They were looking around when Mark said, "Could this be it? I picked it up and took it with me when Mommy called me to go with her."

It was a round stone, smooth, but one side had words carved onto it. "I have a job to finish, and she's the first."

Mitch sank to the floor and started to cry. "I can't take any more of this."

Tommy came in and looked at Mitch; Hardison handed him the stone and pointed to Liz, who was still unconscious. "I need a stretcher. I want to get a better look at that lump. Mitch, do I have your permission to do an MRI on her head? I want to make sure there are no blood clots."

"Yes, you do."

Tommy radioed for a stretcher. Hardison told the men to take Liz to the hut. He set the MRI up so he could check her head. Blood clots could kill her. Robert stayed with Grams and Denny. He was worried sick about his mother and, for the first time, his unborn sibling.

Charlie was examining the rock ball with its message on it. "This was done with a dermal drill, and there is moisture on the sides, possibly from whoever hand that held the ball while it was being carved on."

Hardison told Charlie to see if there are any prints on it besides Mark's and his own. Hardison put Liz through the MRI;

he watched as she moved through; she had a large swelling, no broken skull or cracks, which was great. She never woke up during the procedure. Mitch stayed right by her side. Hardison decided to give her something in hopes to bring her around. Still no results. He called in Dr. Kelly because of her pregnancy. He didn't want to give her any other drugs. Dr. Kelly examined the MRI, then Liz's head. "What did she hit or get hit with?"

Charlie showed him and said he was checking for prints. "Did you think to check for chemicals on it that would cause her to stay in this catatonic state?"

Hardison swabbed the rock for a chemical compound. He showed his results to Dr. Kelly. They both knew what this meant: Liz was poisoned. Between the two doctors, they found a reversal to the chemicals on the weapon. Liz was draggy and sick to her stomach. Dr. Kelly gave her a mild pain reliever.

"I was heading for the hall when the house shook, and then a man was standing outside the window. He broke it and threw something at me. That's all I remember."

"Can you remember what he looked like, what he was wearing? Anything, Liz?"

Bertha touched Tommy's arm. He lowered his voice and tried to sound calmer. "Was he young or old?"

"Remember he looked like a kid, no more than fourteen or fifteen. He had a red winter parka and black hat and gloves. Why would a kid do this?" she worried about the baby.

Kelly knocked on the door. "I have a kid held in the barn, red parka. You looking for one?"

Charlie and Tommy were out the door and ran with Kelly toward the barn. Charlie told Tommy to calm down. "We will not get anywhere with you like this."

"I intended to scare the shit out of him, not kill him, Charlie, and you are going to pretend that you can't stop me."

"Kelly, your job is to hold him like you want to do him in for hurting your boss's wife."

"You got it, boss," Kelly told him with a grin. They got to the barn, and the kid was fighting off one of the guards; the other was out on the floor. Charlie jumped him from behind, and Tommy sucker-punched him on the chin. He went down.

"Tommy, that's no boy. It's a girl or a woman."

They put the woman or girl in a chair. Kelly held her by the shoulders. When she came around, she tried to struggle.

"Don't bother; there are more of what you got if you do." Tommy asked who she was and worked for. She spat on him, and it warranted her a slap across the face. "Shall we try again?" Tommy's voice was a lot sterner.

"No, we won't," she told him.

Charlie noticed her eyes. He spoke to her in Chinese. She answered him in English, with foul language. "Your choice of words only shows you are a child," Charlie told her. Tommy doubled his fist and slugged her in the stomach.

Charlie meant it when he told them to stop it right now. "This bucket of shit will get you nowhere."

Tommy was surprised at him but turned to him, "You would suggest?"

"Removing her jacket to start with."

Tommy thought, *Has he lost his mind*? Strip the kid?

"Kelly, do it." He held her. Charlie started removing the jacket. She tried to kick him. Kelly hugged the chair and her and wrapped his legs around hers. Tommy pulled the jacket down her arms and let it hang on her waist. She had an explosive strapped to her chest.

"What the hell is this! You have exactly ten seconds, young lady, and I will personally kill you and dump your body off the side of this mountain."

She started to cry. "Look, I was told to hit the blonde with the granite ball and put the explosive in the chalet. They would release my parents and my brother, that's all I know!"

"Who told you to do this?"

"A man named Giles. He wants the Maxwells dead."

"Where are they holding your family?"

"In a cabin about ten miles to the northeast of here. The man was the one responsible for the tremors and slides."

"Get Mitch on the two-way. Tell him what's going on. Also, get the rescue crew up and ready."

Charlie did as he was asked. Tommy told the girl they would rescue her family and get rid of Giles.

"Please be careful. My mother has cancer and is bedridden. My dad and brother are tied up at the end of her bed. He beat my brother for trying to stop him from blowing up our small barn. He shot my dad for trying to defend my brother and me."

They gathered in the rescue cabin, planning what they needed to do. The girl drew a picture of the cabin. Charlie, six men, and their equipment moved out. Tommy told him to bring Giles here. Mitch needed to see the son of a bitch.

"Sir, can I go with them? My mother needs me to give her the pain injections. That's all my family can afford for her."

"No, but I will make sure she gets all the medical attention she needs. Our doctors and any cancer doctor to help her, would that be okay?"

The girl, crying, thanked him. "My name is Diane. He was using my dad so he could store heavy boxes in our barn. He paid for the medication and the doctor for my mother. That is why we did what we did."

"We will undo what he did."

Charlie surrounded the cabin with listening devices. They could hear what was going on. Giles was yelling at the father, "What the hell is going on? Why is it taking so long! She should be back by now. We should have heard the explosion!"

The rescue crew threw gas bombs through the windows, then stormed their doors. Giles tried to shoot his way out. Kelly slapped him and took the gun. He couldn't have shot anyone as the safety was on. He was bound and gagged, treating him the same as he handed out to this family. It took less than fifteen minutes after arriving at the cabin.

"Tommy, we have him, the wimp; he couldn't even fire a gun. He left the safety on. I need the helicopter. This woman is dying from something, but not cancer. The family needs help."

"Copter on the way, Charlie. Do you need Hardison to meet you at the heliport?"

"A means of transport for the family that is not a car."

"I'll send an ambulance."

"Thanks, Charlie, out."

Hardison found the woman to be suffering from an inflamed gallbladder that was close to perforating. Hardison and Dr. Kelly operated on her and got her out of pain. Dr. Kelly told him they would take her to his new facility, where he and Dotty could care for her. The family was taken to town after the father's bullet was removed from his leg with Dr. Kelly and a guard. The daughter wanted to stay with them and work off whatever payment was needed for the help they gave her family. Tommy asked her where she learned to fight as she did?.

"My father had a dojo where he taught my brother and me. He does not teach others. He is old and aches from sore bones."

"Can you teach Louise, or can your brother?"

"Yes, we both can. Why?"

"For payment, you teach the men I give you. You must do this here as I do not trust many men."

"Yes, sir, I will live in your barn."

"You will live with Charlie's family. His wife is May-Ling. Their daughter is June, and their son is Peter. They will treat you like you are one of their own, right, Charlie."

"Yes, we will."

She asked Tommy how he knew Charlie was behind him. "I, too, have your training."

Mitch went into the barn. Giles was sitting like a king even though he was bound and gagged. "So you wanted to kill my family. Did you think you would succeed?"

"Yes, I did. I would keep my due bounty and get medical coverage along with my pension. You never knew how to run a proper business. I do, so fail if you like, but not on my time."

"You have no time, Giles. These two men are taking you on a plane to St. Helen, but you will not get a cent from me."

"Mitch, does he get a free flying lesson?"

"Yes, he does."

"What, I don't need to learn to fly a plane."

"No, but you are going to get one."

"This solved the problem up here. Did it solve the one in St. Helen?"

"Hey, Giles, did you know I had a son? You don't, and you only have that woman, so don't try telling me he gave me away because you would be dreaming."

"No, doesn't solve the one in St. Helen. He went back to Liz and his family. "Thank you, Tommy. Let me know when the bastard learns to fly, will you."

"Sure will, Mitch, and he could have killed that woman. Some drunk played the doctor. We got him."

Liz was feeling better but had a headache that was worse than she had ever had. Mitch helped her back to the chalet and their room. "Mitch, what did Giles expect to win by hurting me and trying to kill you?"

"All the money he ever wanted. It didn't work out that way. Michael had Erica and George go to his condo. He had all the books on our import-export business for the last ten years. All the money he took on kickbacks and merchandise he sold without it being on the books. That's the reason he never allowed anyone close to him or near his computers or books. We have them all now."

"Will Robert and this Ms. Snowdon be able to figure everything out so they can get it all back on track?"

"Yes, I'm sure of it."

Bertha told Mitchell she would sit with Liz if he needed to go to see Tommy.

Tommy came into the chalet, and Charlie was with him. "Do you think she can teach a select few young men as we are trained, my brother?"

"I can only hope she and her brother can. Did you meet their father, Charlie?"

"No, should I have? Is there something I need to know?"

"Yes, go to town and see the father and brother. Call me when you are done. I have told Diane she can stay tonight with your family."

"What are you not telling me?"

"I think you need to go, Charlie, for yourself and May-Ling. Now go."

Charlie took his truck and went to town. He first went to the doctor's office, where he was told the husband and son were staying at the lodge three blocks down as there was no place in the facility for them. He walked there all the time, trying to figure out what Tommy was telling him. He arrived at the lodge and asked the lady at the desk where the people Dr. Kelly brought were.

"Are you here to help them? Because unless the doctor pays for them, they have nothing."

Charlie took three one-hundred-dollar bills out of his wallet and gave it to the lady. Her attitude changed and she had a worker take him to them. The boy answered the door, looked at Charlie, and backed up with a look of awe on his face.

"You have no reason to fear me, young man."

"You are Uncle Char Lee, are you not?"

"I'm who?" Then Charlie saw why the boy said it. "Am I seeing things, Chee? Is it you? Am I seeing you for true?"

"Yes, my brother, it is me, I am ashamed to say."

"No reason to be ashamed, Chee. I have missed you. We thought you dead. We were told you were killed. Parker's men said they left you and your family for dead and laughed. They are dead now."

"They thought we were dead because we played dead. I injected them so they would look dead. Instead of the fight, I took the coward's way out. They had broken most of my ribs and both my legs I was useless to them." He bowed his head in shame.

"Chee, you were so lost to us. Why did you not come home to us? May-Ling loves you. She thought you died. She mourned for years."

"To ashamed, my brother, I cannot look at you."

Charlie lifted Chee's head and kissed both his cheeks. "You have nothing to hide from me. Come, we are going home. Your daughter is in my home."

When Chee tried to rise, his son lifted him so he could stand. Charlie lifted Chee in his arms and carried him to the truck. "You drive, young man? What is your name?"

"Yes, I can drive. I am named after you; I am Chuck."

"Good." He placed Chee on the seat of the truck and gave Chuck the keys. He held his brother all the way back to the chalet. He called May-Ling to meet him at the door with Peter.

She was standing there with Peter when they arrived. Charlie got out and turned to get Chee. "Why have you got us out here in the cold, Char Lee?"

Charlie turned with Chee in his arms, and May-Ling fainted. Peter caught her. "Father, are my eyes deceiving me?"

"No, Peter, it is your Uncle Chee. He needs Hardison. Can you get him?"

Peter ran as fast as he could. He told Hardison, Chee was in their home, in bad shape. "Please come." Hardison grabbed his bag, and they went back in the gulf cart.

Hardison could not believe Chee had been found. He ran into their home with Peter. He stopped when he saw Chee, a broken man, not just his bones but his spirit.

"Chee, we are brothers, one of one. Can you ever forgive me for not being with you when you needed me?"

"You could not have known. I hid from my family, from all of you."

"No more. We are one, we will always be one."

Tommy came in and wrapped his arms around Chee. "We are one, my brother. Stay with us."

Hardison gave him a shot to ease his pain. He turned to Louise. "What happened, and please just what they did to him. I need to know so I can cure him." Diane told him what she knew. Chuck told him the rest.

Charlie turned to his wife. "I am ashamed I did not look longer for my brother."

"Now he is with us once again, Char Lee. That is what matters."

Hardison got him back to the hut. Charlie, Dave, and Hardison worked on Chee. His bones were realigned, and he was placed in a body cast and put in a drug-induced coma. He told his wife Lori they would save him. "Please make sure my daughter is safe. She is safe. She is with her Aunt May-Ling and her Uncle Char Lee. We are home. We are one."

Chapter Twenty-One

PETER ASKED HIS dad, "What is this, 'We are one, we are brothers, we are one' that you, Mom, Tommy, and Hardison say to Uncle Chee?"

"It is the mantra of our dojo from the time Tommy, Marcus, Chee, and myself were young. There were four more, but they are gone."

"Is Louise one with you, Dad?"

"I am not sure, but Tommy believes she is, so maybe her brother too."

"Why did you not teach us? June and I would have only been too glad to work with you."

"Would you have died in my place if I asked you? Would you have taken a beating for me when asked?"

"If it meant saving you, yes, Dad, I would."

"I would not let you, to be one of one. You are beaten close to death and must not ask for mercy, must ask to die in place of whoever you have taken their place."

"You did that, Father, for who?"

"I did it for my father, and he did it for his father. I would never ask you to do it for me. I will teach you all I can but never ask you to do as the old ones did to prove loyalty, strength, and honour."

Peter knew his father believed his son would give his life for him. He did not need to ask him to be beaten close to death to prove it. He told Faye all about it but told her it was to stay with them. She understood; she was amazed that both her uncle and his best friend were of the one. One day she will tell Peter that she and Joan are one of the one. She was standing by the window watching the kids with Aunt Liz and Grams playing in the snow. Faye thought of how great this was to be free of the filth, the pain, and the killing. She would never let her children know such a life. Tommy was three steps away when she said, "Hello, Uncle Tommy, hard day. Your steps are heavy."

"It was hard watching Chee trying to walk out without aid."

"He is vital inside, Uncle Tommy, and he'll make it. He had Charlie and Peter as well as the girls to lean on."

"And you, Faye, are you going to hide from me much longer? I know you are my sister as one of one, so was Joan. Parker bragged about how he forced the two of you to die for each other. When it backfired on him, he beat both of you senseless."

"That was then, this is now, I am one of one brother, and I will always be, but I do not want Peter to know. He feels cheated that his father did not teach him this."

Tommy wished Faye was one of the ones openly, because of her mental and physical ability. Mark and Mary would be her first priority now. If he badly needed her to defend the family, she would stand and fight. Tommy had no doubt; this he knew in his heart.

"Tommy, did I hear her correctly? Faye is one of the ones, a sister," Charlie asked.

"Yes, but I have given my word. Peter must never know. If the family or organization desperately needed Faye, she would stand with her family. She is one of the one."

"Who trained her, Tommy? I must know."

"You do know without me telling you. He was forced to teach the girls and only the girls."

"Can I forgive that? I do not know?"

"You can, and you will, Char Lee, because you know why he did this. He had no choice; your father saved your family and the family that will come. He was willing to give his life for your family lineage, and so, my brother, you will forgive."

"You are right; I've no reason to blame my father for what transpired. He did what he had to."

"He taught the girls the true meaning of loyalty, strength, and honour. They used to defend themselves as much as possible. They were warriors then; Joan gave her life for the kids and us. We will honour her wishes."

Peter had Mark and Mary out for a play day in the snow; they built a snowman and his family. "Daddy, can we build a snow person for everyone in the family?"

"We can try, Mary, but it's cold, and your little fingers will soon be frozen."

"We can come back out tomorrow and the next day until we have the family."

"That is providing sweets; the sun doesn't melt it all away."

"Can Grandpa Charlie put them in his big freezer?"

"I don't think so, but you can ask."

Liz was off to see Dr. Kelly for her check-up. She was beginning to have a little tummy. She watched her weight eating as Dr. Kelly told her, but she had a strong urge to eat peanut butter and banana sandwiches dredged in beaten eggs and grilled. This she did not share with Dotty or Dr. Gary Kelly. The scale said she was gaining about a pound a month; right now, that was fine. She was four months along and doing just great.

Bertha had made four knitted blankets and crocheted two sweater sets for the baby. She had also made Mark and Mary sweaters with snowpeople on them. Mark had a boy snowman, and Mary had a girl snowman. Tommy wore his snowman sweater whenever he took them out to play in the white stuff.

Denny had learned to knit and was making little Robbie a blanket for his carriage. Robert worked with Grace Snowdon every day, rebuilding the import-export business. She was glad to be back on the mountain and working. Grace was born up here, left to go to school and find work. She stayed in the city when she did. They got along fine. Each learning from the other, they soon had a working model and the books in order. Grace had figured out how much Giles had stolen, and from where he took it, Robert was doing his best to reconnect with the overseas contacts. Most spoke English. He told Mitch they would need a translator for a few of them. He surprised Robert and spoke directly to the ones Robert could not. Mitch was fluent in six languages.

By the end of the week, Grace had the basics of the company up and running. Robert had made four overseas appointments, and they were all connected within three days after landing in Prague. Danny was glad to stay home. Mitch had talked to his best friend Allen and his wife Shantelle to find office space for the law firm to start up and get running again. Shantelle hired her secretary Stephanie back to work with them also. She had been running her cases from home. Her husband would not. He needed a staff, people to do tracking on computers, investigators to do the legwork, and secretaries to carry out a legal office's daily grind.

They were getting back to everyday living. There were no problems for the family as a whole; their daily life was happy. They were looking forward to the Easter Bunny's arrival. Mark and Mary had heard about this rabbit that brought candy and eggs of all colours to them to find.

"Even outside, we still have some snow out there; the candy will melt." Mark was concerned.

"No, Mark, he will hide it all over in the house, even sneak in your room and hide some in there."

The kids got to colour eggs with Mommy and Daddy in the kitchen, and Grandpa Charlie stayed well away from all the coloured water and mess. "Fair warning, Faye and Peter, you will clean up this mess when the children are finished helping the Easter Bunny."

Liz shopped for cute Easter outfits for the children. She just couldn't resist buying some baby clothes and toys and, of course, bedding and blankets. Bertha had to put a stop to her shopping. "Liz, me girl, are ya no gonna leave some fer us to buy fer yer shower? Ya near bought the whole store." She made Liz put back half of what she had in her basket to buy. Bertha told the clerk when Liz walked away, "Put it all on me charge and sent it ta this address."

Bertha bought candy for everyone, unique things for the kids like giant furry stuffed rabbits and teddy bears. She had asked Charlie if she could bake the kids a special cake. He agreed to help her. He had thought she was going to cut a rabbit out of a flat cake. She baked a white layer, a chocolate layer, and a strawberry layer. She made a very creamy filling that tasted of sweet lemons. When she had finished stacking the cakes, it was nearly a foot high. "Charlie, do ya have an extremely sharp carin knife? Tis a long blade I needs and a short one." He did, and he gave them to her. She noticed that they were mismatched and old, probably his favourites. She carved the cake into a lop-eared rabbit holding something that was not there.

"What is this creature holding, Bertha?"

"When tis done, he'll hold a big chocolate egg full of candy."

"I got the egg when I was oot with Liz. Tis fer you ta cut it open fer me ta fill, then we'll use a hot knife ta seal it up agin." He was amazed at Bertha's ability. When finished, the cake looked just like a white furry rabbit holding a giant chocolate egg decorated in all the Easter colours of yellow and green, pink and blue and mauves. It was beautiful, the flowers and leaves, the vines and swirls; all perfect.

"Bertha, you have done this before."

"Charlie, I've been doin' these here cakes fer Robbie fer years."

"Well, I need lessons. My wife and June would love it."

"I'll do ya one if yer willin ta help me."

"Yes, my lady, I will."

"What a gift to give, made with love, and you can eat it."

They worked together, Charlie learning how to make the creamy filling and then the special icing Bertha used to make the fur.

"Ya will have ta git a egg ta fill, Charlie, I ner bought two."

"Will this work Bertha?" It was a small yellow basket with green cellophane inside.

"Tis a right thing, Charlie."

They filled the basket with candy and little strips of paper with notes on them in Chinese. Tommy came in; he wanted to steal some candy and got his hand slapped and a kiss on the cheek.

"Bertha, my love, they are so beautiful; they look real."

"Charlie helped make one fer his family."

"That one with the basket and notes, right," Tommy told them.

"Yes, and ya no tell on him either."

"I promise if I get some candy now." Charlie threw him a small bag of jelly beans.

Charlie wanted her opinion on what to serve with the ham.

"The usual, Charlie, wait! I gots an idea." Bertha called Carol. She was at her cabin. "Hey, love, ya comin' fer Easter dinner, right?"

"Yes, Grams, Doug and I will be there. Can I bring something?"

"Ya canna help Charlie plan this dinner, yer a far better cook than I."

"Does Charlie know you are asking me this?"

"I do, Carol. I could use the help. I have never done Easter. We don't do this holiday."

"Well, you are now. I'll be up this afternoon, and we can lay out the meal, then figure a dessert."

"Dessert is covered, Carol. Bertha did it."

"Okay, see you soon."

Chee's wife was doing so much better. She was walking around and helping May-Ling with chores in the chalet. Chee was to get his last hydrotherapy treatment. He was walking slowly on his own now. She hoped he would gain some weight back.

"We are having an Easter dinner at Tommy's chalet. All of the families on the compound will be there."

"How many, May-Ling, will there be?"

"About forty people, but only two children."

"Would it be all right if I made something special for the dessert?"

"Check with Char Lee. He'll let you know."

Instead, she walked up from the chalet to the big one on the hill. Lois went to the kitchen door. Charlie answered it and let her in.

"What can I do for you, Lois?"

"Would it be possible for me to contribute to the dinner, Char Lee? I would like to make a special small dessert for everyone," Carol and Bertha heard her.

"Yes, you can, Lois, please, this is a family gathering. Let it be a meal everyone will remember."

She told them she would make it at Char Lee chalet and bring it on the day of the dinner.

Everyone had their designated chores for the Easter feast. It was left up to Liz to figure out where and how to sit forty people. Bertha had a better idea. "Let's empty the great room. Tis large enough, Charlie; we needs a roond table ta fit all of us."

Liz thought it an excellent idea for everyone together. "Yes, let's do that."

All Charlie thought was who the hell was going to move the furniture and where he would put it. He called a company in the next town that supplied tables and chairs for weddings and large functions. They told him, "Yes, we do have a table for that many people and the chairs. Do you need a table covering for it and in what colour would you need it?"

Charlie talked to the ladies of the house about what shade of tablecloth they would like and whether they wanted the dishes to match.

Liz said to Charlie, "Let's get the dishes, flatware, and serving pieces brought in. That way, they take them out dirty, and we don't have all that cleanup afterward for forty people." Charlie wanted to kiss her; for years, he and his wife, Tommy, and a couple of the men did all the cleanup. It would take hours.

Liz and Bertha chose pale-yellow cloth with mint green and white dishes. They couldn't wait for the day. Tommy asked Charlie, "Where in the hell do you plan on putting the furniture?"

"In your study, in the sunroom wherever it will fit."

"Call a container company to have them deliver a furniture container with covers."

"Will do. Can they move all the furniture too?"

Tommy laughed. "We do that, my brother, we and whoever we can rope in to do it."

Lois and May-Ling decided to make enough for each person to have two of the dessert. They were making *lao po bing* or wife's cake. This was made for the men going to fight by their wives during the Yaun and Ming Dynasty. It was crusty flakiness on the outside and layers of flaky sweetness inside. The men could carry it with them. The ladies worked all day and made ninety-five of them. May-Ling and Lois took samples of this to the chalet. Bertha, Liz, Carol, and Char Lee tried them, each moaning at this fantastic dessert, so delicious and delicate.

"Lois, you've done a great with this," Bertha told her.

Liz explained to her, "Bertha means it is the best ever."

"May-Ling and I made them together. It was not just me," Lois said.

"Thank you both; how many did you make, ladies?"

"We made ninety-five, but there is still enough for each person to have two."

"Not if I find them, there won't," Tommy told them. "They are so good, Charlie; why haven't you made these?"

Very indignantly, he said, "I do not make wife's cake."

They all laughed. May-Ling said, "We would call them lao po bing."

Charlie hired kitchen staff and servers to help out. Dinner was to be served by the wait staff. Charlie and Carol had laid it out for them in advance. Extra platters of ham and veggies were brought in on trollies for the servers to put on the table. Those wanting more could reach it.

Tommy stood, asked everyone to hold hands as he gave the blessing. "Our heavenly Father, we thank you for this bounty of food and for the hands that prepared it. We ask this in the name of Jesus Christ. Amen." They all repeated Amen.

Mark asked Great-Grandpa if the Easter Bunny made dinner too.

"No, Mark, Grandpa Charlie, Great-Grams, and Aunt Carol did. May-Ling and Lois made a small dessert, and Great-Grams made you something special, so eat all your dinner, and you can have some."

Everyone enjoyed all the special ways Carol, Charlie, and Bertha had done the vegetables. Mary wanted smashed potatoes instead of the funny fanned-out ones with brown edges. Charlie knew what she was like and brought them to her, just made for her. It took nearly an hour of eating and chatting before the main part of the dinner was over. They brought the bunny cake, which was surrounded by the lao po bing. The children ran to Bertha when they brought the bunny cake in. Bertha gave them a large soup spoon each and told them they could hit the egg with their spoons. Mary and Mark just looked at it. Tommy whispered in both their ears, and the spoons flew as did the candy inside the egg. All the guests applauded them. Mary and Mark bowed at the waist and grabbed some candy. Everyone had cake and lao po bing.

All Bertha wanted to do was sleep. She was so grateful that they only had to do the few leftovers and not all the dishes. Carol and Doug took their box full home, as did many others of the guests. Charlie had put ham and veggies away for the family and sent some home for his family. Hardison told him he would be back tomorrow for a plateful. Everything was so good; if he had room in his stomach, he would have eaten twice again.

The kids were tired. They had hunted for candy and eggs in the morning and put them in the baskets Great-Grams had given them. They played with the new toys until dinner. It was bedtime, and they did not argue. Each with their stuffed bunnies, they jumped up into bed. Faye prayed they would not get sick from all the goodies they devoured.

Faye and Peter were sitting on a bench outside of the kids' room. Peter asked her if a spring wedding would be okay.

"Sure, next spring would be great. The kids will be a little older."

"No, Faye, this spring, May is a beautiful month up here. We could be married under the cherry trees. The blossoms are so bright with colours of red and pink with green leaves. We don't need a big wedding, do we?"

"No, just big enough to fit both our families and a few friends we have."

"So what do you think?"

"I'm sure Tommy and Bertha can persuade your dad to be here for that, and the kids can be the flower girl and ring bearer."

"Peter, what is the rush?"

"My family feels uncomfortable with us living like this. I'm here part-time, at home part-time. Do you see what I mean?"

"Yes, Aunt Liz has been hinting, and Aunt B has as well."

"Yes, let's do it."

"Where will we live after, Peter? Can we take the kids away from this now? Do we live with your family or build a place of our own?"

"I have spoken to your uncle and my dad; they are in agreement, we must stay here for the sake of the children."

"Okay, we set a day in May, preferable near the end."

Liz and Bertha were so excited—a wedding here. They loved the idea of an outdoor ceremony. They told her they would help her with everything. Faye was overwhelmed. "I have no idea about a gown or veil, Aunt B. Who do I choose to stand for me? How many? Gosh, I should never have said yes to this wedding."

They sat her down. "Let's keep it small. Are you close to Denny and Carol?"

"I'm close with Carol and Erica because Carol is teaching me to cook, and Erica, well, you know why."

"Okay, we ask them to stand. Do you want a long gown or a dress?"

"Peter told me May-Ling wants me to wear a traditional Chinese wedding ceremonial robe."

"Have you seen it yet?"

"No, she said I had to bring you and Aunt B with me to see it and try it on. It's a tradition that my parents come with me, but Dad is never here, and well, you and Uncle Tommy are the closest I have to parents."

"We will go with you, love, an if ya needs Tommy, I'll drag his wee ass along too."

"You will take my butt where, woman?"

"Faye has ta try on a robe, an her parents are supposed ta be there fer her."

"Count me in, Faye; I want to see this gown or robe too."

She laughed at him.

Bertha was surprised when they entered May-Ling's home that they had to remove their shoes at the door. May-Ling gave them slippers to put on. She showed them into her sitting room. June, Lois, and Louise brought out a trunk and opened it. "Faye, will you please stand on the stool for me?" Faye did so. The girls put a screen around her. Faye was asked to remove her outer clothing. Faye was not happy about this, but she did it. They gave her a long white slip of silk to put on. When she had that on, June and Louise went into the screen area with Faye. She was given a red silk blouse with long sleeves; it had flowered cuffs. Then a red over-blouse with Chinese designs was added to the first one. Then she had to step into a pantlike skirt made of satin, red with pale gold floral designs on it. An overskirt of panels of transparent red silk with embroidered flowers and leaves. Next, a three-quarter-sleeve red jacket, with oval patterns on the front of flowers, and on the sleeves, same as the front. The cuff was split to fit over the blouses. The collar of the jacket stood up with a gold design to match the front of the jacket. They placed a headpiece on her that was beaded flowers with long beaded tendrils.

Faye felt beautiful; regal, in fact. They took the screen away; May-Ling had tears. She told her, "This was my mother's wedding robes, and it was mine. It will be theirs one day as well." She was referring to Louise and June.

Bertha, Liz, and Tommy could not believe how absolutely gorgeous she was. May-Ling took her hand and had her step down, and her feet were showing. The girls lowered the main skirt to cover her feet.

May-Ling explained, "Chinese women never show their feet because they are not pretty. Faye has large feet that need to be covered as well. They will have to have white stockings and red slippers. What size shoe do you wear, Faye? I will have to order them."

Faye looked at Liz. "I wear an eight." She was embarrassed; they had little feet.

May-Ling said, "Then we don't have to order."

Lois brought out a pair of red satin slippers, size eight. "These are mine; I have big feet also. I only wore them down the carpeted walkway. You are welcome to them." Faye thanked her and put the slippers on.

"Now, after the Chinese wedding ceremony, you will go change into your white gown and get ready for the American ceremony because legally, the Chinese ceremony is not recognized here."

Faye wanted to pass out. "I have to do it twice?"

"No, you can do it in your white gown, only if you prefer."

Faye could see it would hurt May-Ling. "No, I want to wear this, so I guess it's a two-for-one wedding." They smiled, and the girls giggled until May-Ling gave them a look.

The next day she was hauled off to a bridal shop in Boston.

"Aunt B, Aunt Liz, Carol, Erica, and Denny, listen—one shop, we get the dress or gown, and we go, all right." They agreed, smiling but agreed.

Bertha, Liz, and Denny took Faye wedding gown shopping. Faye was put into a strapless, one-shoulder mermaid, see-through full-shirt by the store clerk. She was exhausted. The girl brought in a three-quarter-length sleeve gown on the A-line style but slightly fuller. It had a round neckline with lace over the bodice and around the bottom of the skirt. It had a train of about three or four feet. It was simple but beautiful. The girl put a veil on her head, and she went out to the ladies. Bertha could see this was the one; Faye was lit up. She looked fabulous.

"This is it, Faye," Liz said. "Oh, how great it fits; no alterations are needed." The girl said if she didn't want the train, they could fix it. Faye told the girl it was perfect just the way it was. She was staring at herself in the mirror. It was her, Faye, in a wedding gown. She turned to the ladies. "What say you, my family?"

They went up to her and hugged her and told her how beautiful she was. She left the showroom floor to put her clothes on. Liz and Bertha split the cost, and by the time she came out, her gown and crinoline were bagged and paid in full. "I have to pay for it. I hope they take payments. It's more than I thought it would be."

"It's paid for. Here is the bill. Have a great wedding! Aunt B and I paid for it for you," Liz told her. Bertha said she had to make a stop at a material store. She'd be just a minute. Liz knew. She kept Faye out of the store, looking at flowers along the street.

They were back by dinnertime. Liz asked Tommy if there was a unique headpiece that his family wore or a traditional headdress. He took her to the office, opened the safe, and took out a wooden box. He handed it to her, and she opened it. "Why, Tommy, it's a tiara; it's beautiful."

"It was my grandmother's. Mom never wore it. She wore a white sapphire tiara; this gold-and-white diamond tiara is more Faye. Bertha wore this at our wedding."

"Will you take it to her on the day of her wedding?"

"Bertha and I will, Liz. She is like a daughter to us."

Faye and Peter talked to Charlie about the food. "Would it be possible to have a light lunch after the first ceremony while Peter and I and the rest of the wedding party change clothes for the second ceremony?"

"We can, but how many for the luncheon, Faye," Charlie asked.

Peter spoke up, "We want just the families at the first wedding."

"Are you or Faye ashamed of your heritage, Peter?"

"No, we feel that the Chinese ceremony is more important, special, Dad. We want you and Mom, Bertha, and Tommy as Marcus told Faye he would not be able to attend. The rest of the families around us."

"Your mother will be so pleased that Faye wants this. I am sure her family will also be. I will contact the monks of our church tomorrow." To Charlie's pleasure, the Lama said he would officiate the wedding with the help of the monk.

At the American wedding, Faye asked June and Carol to stand, and Peter asked his dad to be his best man and Doug to stand with them. Carol asked Li if they should give Faye a bridal shower.

"Yes, we do, but not in the true sense of the word. We will get her personal things instead of houseware. We will have to tell May-Ling this. They will be living here."

Faye went to May-Ling and asked her if she could teach her the tea ceremony for the parents before the wedding. "Faye, that is kind of you to think of that."

"I know it means the unity of both our families."

"I would love for you and Charlie to take part in the wedding as Bertha and Tommy will be there for me."

"We are honoured, Faye, you would want this. You are not of Oriental descent. I love that you care."

"I have never been a part of a family or family tradition. This Christmas was the first time I had a tree, gifts, a family to share it with, so yes, I want all the family traditions to bring us together."

Faye was so surprised that the ladies gave her a shower. She received many fancy nightgowns and lingerie outfits. "I'm sure Peter will enjoy these." She got cookbooks and bathrobes for both of them. Liz gave her a pendant with matching earrings. Carol gave her a pearl necklace. June gave her a bracelet with their names and wedding date in Chinese symbols on it. May-Ling gave her a beautiful wooden chest. In it was a handmade wedding blanket and silk sheets. "They are to keep you close together because silk sheets are cold and the blanket is warm." Her face turned red, and the ladies smiled and laughed at her. "They will need to keep warm, won't they."

May-Ling spent two days teaching Faye and Peter the wedding tea service. Charlie went to the Lama to find out where he could get a Chinese wedding tea set. He wanted to surprise the wedding couple. He was surprised when the Lama gave him a box and blessed it for them. "This is the tea set of our forefathers. It is my gift to them. They must pass it on to the next couple, so it continues its journey bringing young and old together."

When he gave it to Faye and Peter, he explained what the Lama had said to him. "I will do that; it will be passed on in our family for many generations."

Faye asked Liz to check the little tables that May-Ling and June had ordered to see if they could fit under them. "What are they for, Faye?"

"Before we go out in the garden to marry under the cherry blossoms, we are having a wedding tea ceremony in the great room. Peter's parents and Uncle Tommy and Aunt B will be my parents. The rest of the family will be there with settings for each family. Would you and Uncle Mitch take care of Mark and Mary? They will probably not like it, but I want them there."

"How many will be at this ceremony, Faye?" asked Liz.

"Only our families. Same for the wedding in the garden—only family. It is a special thing for us, and we want only the family there with us."

Liz hugged her close; she whispered, "I couldn't love you more if you were my own daughter, Faye. I am so proud of you."

"Thank you," was all she could manage as her throat closed with emotion. Faye had never known such love before.

The morning of the wedding, June came over and asked for Liz and Bertha's help. It was a surprise for the wedding couple. Bertha thought it wonderful. Liz was hoping Mark would not give them a hard time. It took about twenty-five minutes to dress the kids. They were in Chinese dress outfits, as is tradition. Mark wasn't too keen on the hat, but he said if it was for Mommy and Daddy, he would wear it. They were adorable. Liz took so many pictures of them.

June and Carol helped Faye into her outfit; Faye was shocked when May-Ling and June did her face in white, with the other black and red colours to shape the design on her face. May-Ling put her headpiece on. She was not expecting the dark veil to come down over her face. She could see out, just barely. "It will be lifted by Peter just before the tea ceremony when the Lama calls the couple forward. He told Dad that he would do it in Chinese and English for both sides of the family.

"Oh, June, what if I make a mistake with the tea."

"Mom or Dad or the Lama will help you. You will do fine."

Both families were there standing in front of their tables. Peter met her at the door as Bertha and Tommy brought her in. Tommy and Bertha gave each of her hands to him. "I accept this woman as a wife," he led her to the center of the room. Each set of parents came and knelt at their tables. The tea set was there. Peter led her to the Lama and the monk. "I am here to ask for a joining of this woman and myself at this ceremony of families."

The Lama told Peter, "Raise the veil that I might see this woman is not a child."

Faye's vail was lifted and laid over her floral crown. "I accept your choice."

Faye and Peter knelt on each side of their table, and she proceeded to make the tea, lifting the wooden ladle and spoon as May-Ling had taught her. Only using the wooden whisk with gentle strokes not to bruise the tea but create a flavour for enjoyment. Peter served Tommy and Bertha, and Faye served May-Ling and Char Lee. Then to the surprise of the family, Faye served all of Peter's family and he all of hers. Faye brought a special cup forward for the Lama with a bowed head. "I am not of your bloodline, nor worthy of you honour. Please accept this humble gift of tea in a cup I made of clay for you."

He took the cup and drank. "I will treasure this honourable gift as you have enlightened my heart and my mind. You are truly one of the ones, to become part of our family."

They all rose. The children took their parents' hands. Faye smiled at them and blew kisses. They walked out the doors to the garden to stand under the trees full of cherry blossoms, and the Lama, with the help of the monk, performed a short but beautiful ceremony. Peter was given the words in Chinese to repeat. That he would protect, feed, and care for his wife; he would love her, honour her and be with her forever. He repeated it in English. They were all shocked when Faye said her vows in Chinese first, then in English. The children were asked to give their blessings to their parents. June and Louise had worked with them since Easter. Mark and Mary knelt in front of them, raised their hands open, and said to them in Chinese, "We guard your love in our hearts as we give you our love to guard in yours." Then they said it in English. Peter and Faye picked them up and held them. Mark looked at his mother, "Please don't kiss me with all that stuff on your face."

No one could hold it in; even the Lama and the monk were laughing. So ended the ceremony.

Charlie was going to head to the kitchen to get the light lunch out for the family when Tommy stopped him. "You go change, you and May-Ling. We will get the lunch out on the tables. They will be longer than you two getting ready, so change and come back for a bite to eat before the next party starts."

Faye wished this was it. They could just be family, and she was now Mrs. Peter Lee. No, here we go again. Carol and June helped her get the make-up off. Her hair was redone. So was Faye's make-up. The ladies helped her put her gown on. Bertha and Tommy came in. Bertha placed her veil over her head and down her back to the floor. It spread out in a semi-circle. The lace at the bottom was a perfect match to her simple gown. "Non yer tears, I make ya veil as I made Liz's." Tommy placed the diamond tiara on her head to hold the veil. She looked like his mother when she was young. "Marcus will be sorry he missed this."

"You look like our mother." June put her bracelet on her wrist. Carol added the pearls she gave her. Bertha gave her a blue hankie to put in her bosom. Tommy told her, "Something old, something new, something borrowed something blue. You have my mother's tiara, it's borrowed, and it's old. You have the bracelet and pearls; they are new, and you have a hankie that is blue."

She hugged them but didn't let go. "Please help me continue to be a good human and not a killing machine. I will always be your sister, as one of the ones, but I also want to be a daughter, a mother, and a wife."

"You will always be a daughter, a mother, and a wife. You have come a long way from your past. Faye, I know if I called upon you to protect our family, you would, but for now, you are a beautiful young bride."

The church was not large, so it was full. The families took up half the church. Friends of the bride and groom and the family friends took up the rest. Tommy was on the phone. He was waiting for the bride to arrive. "What the hell is the matter with you, Marcus? She's the only daughter you have. Why are you not here? She would have loved nothing more than you walking her down the aisle."

"Do I have a choice, finding that mother or leaving this to walk her down the aisle to marry out of her heritage? Why Peter, an Oriental, when there are so many Americans to choose from?"

"So that's it. She's marrying Peter, a Chinese person. He goes so against your mindset. You did not give her a chance to make up her mind when you asked her. May-Ling's sister loved you. You just couldn't wait to bed her, that's why she said no. I have to go; the bride's here."

Tommy helped Faye out of the car. She was a vision to be held. He gave her his arm. "Ready, sweetie?"

"Yes, Uncle Tommy, I am. I had a strange talk with May-Ling's sister. We will talk after about it?"

"Yes, are you upset?"

"No, just disgusted. I thought better of him."

"Faye, forget about it. For now, a man is standing at the front of this church that wants you for you, not whether you are Chinese or black or white or American. To him, you are the love of his life."

"I know, and he is mine. Thank you for understanding that love doesn't choose creed, colour, or race."

Bertha met them at the back. When the girls and the kids were ready, Doug walked Bertha up the aisle. The music started, "Mom, do we have to marry Daddy too?"

"No, dear, he is your daddy now. Mary, remember to plop flowers on the floor for Mommy to walk on."

"I know!"

Tommy looked at Faye. "Shall we walk up the aisle on the plopped flowers?"

She smiled. "Yes, Dad, we do." They had a traditional ceremony, neither one wanting to do their own vows. Peter and Faye walked back down the aisle carrying the kids. All four of them happy.

Chapter Twenty-Two

EVERYONE ENJOYED THE reception in the great room. It was a self-serve meal and a dance afterward. Faye and Peter practiced a dance that Doug had taught them. They danced to great applause. Charlie put the wedding gifts in Tommy's study and locked the room.

When the kids were falling asleep on Grams and May-Ling, it was time for them to go up to bed. Faye and Peter took them up.

"Are we all married now?" Mary asked sleepily.

"Yes, sweet girl, we are," Peter told her.

"Good night, Daddy, I love you," she told him.

He whispered back, "I love you too."

Mark was asleep before they got him into bed. He got kissed by both parents. Faye turned the nightlight on for them and, as always, left the door open.

The night nanny came in to sit with them until all the company had left. "Please call us if there is anything. They did overeat the sweets."

The party carried on until after one in the morning. The bride and groom finally got to say good night to the last guests. Liz and Mitch had gone upstairs to their room for the night. Robert and Denny were still dancing. Bertha said to Tommy, "Tis time to go, they'll no leave if we are here."

He let the couple know it was time to shut the lights off. Charlie and May-Ling kissed them and were heading out when Liz screamed, "The kids are gone! Someone has taken the children. Nanny Barbara is dead!"

Tommy hollered at Charlie, "Get the forensic crew in here now. No one goes in the room." Faye crumpled to the floor. Peter lifted her to the sofa.

"Bertha, could you call Hardison, please."

"I'm here, Peter; give a few whiffs of this. She'll come around."

Peter used the smelling salts as he had been told. Faye came to quickly. She started crying. She knew who took her children. He would pay, or he would die.

The forensic team went over the room several times. Only the children's prints were found. They found a piece of cloth. It looked torn near Mary's bed. It wasn't from either one's nightclothes or from Nanny Barbara. "I will tell you who did this so you can prove it."

Tommy held her. "Are you sure you want to say this out loud?"

"Yes, not only could he not accept our wedding, he takes the children. No, I want him found. I will personally take my children back, and if not, I will take him out."

"I will do it, Faye, not you, not Peter. He is the children's grandfather. Better they hate me than you."

"They will know I care enough to save them," Faye told him.

Charles spoke to his crew. "They have a head start. I know Marcus, and he had help. Look in the staircase, or look in the back parking lot. He will go out in the darkest area of our compound."

Kelly took his group out the back, spreading his men over the whole dark parking lot and gardens. They found footprints and again a piece of material. This time it was off Mark's pajamas. He was leaving a trail. Kelly found another piece in the back of the garden by the gazebo. Charlie followed the trail to the heliport.

"Damn it. They are gone." Kelly heard Charlie's cry and felt his pain. He knew he would have to tell Tommy and their mother they are gone.

Kelly walked with Charlie back to the chalet. "I will stand with you, Charlie, I feel your pain, and I know you feel for them." Charlie put his hand on Kelly's shoulder and thanked him. They walked into the great room, the floor sounding hollow, echoing loudly.

"I'm sorry, Tommy, Faye, he got away in a helicopter." Charlie lost it. He cried out loud, sobbing how sorry he was he couldn't catch him. Tommy and Berth went to him and held him. All three crying.

Peter held his wife and quietly said to her, "Walk slowly to the elevator. We change. We go find our children."

"Yes."

Tommy saw them and knew what they were going to do. "Not without us and the rescue crew. You are not equipped to take Marcus on. He is not just a money counter or a bookkeeper, Faye; he is an appointed killer. He takes out the holder of the captives. He also takes them out before things happen. He is good at his job, very good. His crew is trained as snippers, and he will take even you out if they are told to do so."

"Faye, we have to plan to get prepared for the war he has just begun."

Faye turned to her new husband, "I prayed for a normal marriage, a peaceful, happy life with our children. No more fighting, no more killing, Peter, I have to go to war. Promise me you will take care of our children."

Bertha wrapped her in her arms and just held her. "I prayed fer ta same thing, Faye, fer you an Peter ta be happy and free of all this. Ya must promise yer old auntie ye'll be careful an come hame ta me."

Hardison was asked if he could put her in a coma until this war was over just to keep her safe. Hardison told him he could not do it, not only for ethical reasons, but her mental and physical state would suffer. Plus the fact that she would kill him upon being revived.

"Charlie, do I call you Dad now?" Faye asked.

"Only if you wish to, Faye," he told her.

She grabbed him, held him, and he let her. "Please, Dad, help me find my babies. They are all Peter and I will ever have. They are yours and May-Ling's grandchildren. Please help me."

"I will, my daughter, I will. Tommy and I are working on a plan. Why don't you and Peter change clothes and met us in the rescue cabin in ten minutes."

"Do I have your word as a brother of one, you will wait for us?"

"You do. I will wait."

"And you, Uncle Tommy, your word please."

"My word and my bond, sister of one."

She left the room moved like lightning. Peter had trouble keeping up with her. He could only imagine how fast she could move if she was not in her wedding gown.

They met the rescue crew in the cabin. Faye knew most, and some were new. Kelly gave her a quick hug but said nothing. Charlie told them to quiet down. "This rescue is not going to be easy. Some of you already know the grandchildren of Tommy and Charlie have been taken by no other than Marcus. Yes, he is their real grandfather, but he has no right to Faye's children. We are going to rescue these kids. Little Mark left us a trail to the heliport. I pray he has done the same from wherever they landed." Kelly stepped aside. Faye fought her tears. No way would she cry here in front of all the crew.

Tommy came in. "The copter landed just outside Boston at a small airstrip, not on any registration. We go now." Six choppers were waiting, engines running. Tommy, Charlie, Peter, Kelly, and Faye were in the front copter. The rest followed with equipment, guns, and ammo. They arrived at the small airport, only to find they had taken Marcus's private jet. Hardison was called upon to help loosen the tongue of the owner of the airport. He looked familiar to Tommy.

"You are Bruce McCormick, are you not?"

"Yes, I am."

"Then you know where he went, don't you?"

"He's my boss. What am I supposed to say?"

"He kidnapped my grandchildren, a boy Mark and a girl Mary. I want my family back."

"What are you talking about? The kids called him grandpa."

"They call me Grandpops, that help you any, dumb ass?"

"All older men are grandfathers." Hardison let the guy see the needle, "If you don't tell us without help, you will with this, and then you die."

Bruce got a bad case of verbal vomit and told them Marcus's next flight plan if he doesn't change it. "There are two places for him to land. One is in the outskirts of the Dakota Mountains. The other is a small town near Los Angeles. Its population is twenty-five or so people. If he wants to hide, either place would work."

"Why is that, Bruce?"

"All the people in each small town are his people, trained to do just what you are doing now."

"Are you one of them, Bruce?"

"Yes, sir, we just got a woman and a girl out of a bad house. The husband is no more." Charlie knew about this rescue. Marcus told him the woman changed her mind. They were turned down. Just before Hardison put Bruce to sleep, he said something that made Faye sick to her stomach. "He often had us do jobs for Parker and Walt, but not for a while now." Hardison jabbed him in the neck, and twenty seconds later, he was out.

"Tommy, none of us knew. How could we—he kept it well hidden." Charlie was trying to appease Tommy until he saw Faye's and Peter's faces. In their minds, the man was dead, ready to be fed to the zoo animals. Instead of leaving, they tore all the records out of the small office and loaded up the helos.

"Charlie, take half the crew go to the Dakota town. I'll go to the rinky-dink town outside of Los Angeles."

"No, Tom, he will go to the LA town there. He has a trained team, and they are killers."

"Okay, if you are sure we go."

"Faye, told it is the only place he will feel safe for a short time. He will go overseas with the kids as soon as he can get them to do as he wants. They have to be able to convince the border police they are who he says they are. Walt could never get Joan and I to do it."

"He will use drugs on them. I know he will. If he worked with Parker and Walt, he will for sure."

"We have to fly out of range of detection."

Kelly was not going to talk to Tom; he would go to Charlie. "Charlie, could we not have vans met us about fifty miles out."

"Not just vans, cars, motorcycles. They won't be expecting a collection of different vehicles to pass by or through this town. Not all at the same time, spread out unevenly."

"Get the idea, Kelly. I'll tell Tommy."

Tommy took the motorcycle with Faye on the back and Peter in the sidecar. He had all their weapons and extra ammo, along with Faye's bow and arrows. As she put it, quiet but efficient.

Marcus thought Bruce would feed them misinformation, before Tommy or Hardison could shoot him up with drugs. Tom and that chink are on their way to Los Angeles.

He was safe here. When Marcus felt he was safe to return to the mountains, he would contact the slut he was sleeping with to get the kids. Marcus had made enough money off his side jobs and the companies they ran. He was retiring. He could watch Mary and Mark grow up like he should have Faye and Joan. He would be able to take them to school, watch them play sports, or learn to play an instrument. He would be able to see them do all kinds of things. A little voice in the back of his head said, "But you will never see them marry." He got up and poured himself a second cup of coffee. Polly came in, her gun hanging on her hip. "You want something to eat?"

"No, but you can stay for a while."

"No thanks, I'll send in Suzy. She likes to screw you."

He didn't say anything. Suzy would occupy him for a short time, and then he would sleep. Sex with Suzy was like having sex with a pig. She grunted the whole time. He rolled over and went to sleep. He told her to wake him at seven in the morning. He wanted to survey the land behind the deserted town.

They arrived just after midnight, and the next vehicle of men was due in thirty minutes. They would all be there by three in the morning. Faye told Tommy and Peter to rest. She would watch the town for movement. "Not happening, lady, you and Peter rest. You had a hard day, two weddings and a reception, I got to sleep during the lunch break." They leaned up against a boulder and cuddled. Faye let Peter think she was sleeping so he would rest. She was too wired to completely relax enough to sleep. By three o'clock, everyone was there.

"Charlie, did most of them rest before they left to drive the hour in?"

"Yeah, they did. Kelly has a way with the crew. Have you noticed he can be stern and quiet at the same time, or he will be loud and funny?"

"I watched him with his crew in the sewer. He could handle anything thrown at him."

"We needed a man like him; good job getting him."

Faye stood. "Let's set out what we plan on doing. The kids should be sleeping, so they would be out of the way."

Kelly said to Faye, "He will expect his brother if Bruce blabbed, but not you. Do you think you can confront him without killing him right off?"

"Why?"

"Because if he has hidden the kids to safeguard himself and kids."

"What the hell are you talking about, Kelly?"

"Faye, if you have done this job of rescuing children, women, families, and abused husbands, would you not safeguard their safety?"

She walked in a circle several times. "Son of a bitch, you are right, Kelly. We didn't find any bits of cloth at that airport nor out here. He's hidden the kids." She started walking toward the town.

Kelly stopped her. "We need him, so we know where he put them. Faye, use your head, darlin', we need you alive to raise them when we get them back; you don't think I'm going to do it, do you?"

Kelly was being dragged along with her. She stopped and looked at him like she had just woken from a bad dream. "Kelly, thank you." She went back to Peter.

Tommy thanked him as well. "Have you always been this wise or just fast on your feet, so to speak?"

"My mom made me join the debate club, the chess club, the math club, and the public speaking club. Do I need say more?" They both laughed but quietly.

They were ready to go. All the men were in position. Peter and Charlie had the rear of the town with six other men. Marcus or his men would not get out the back past Peter and his crew. Four others were sent to collect the rest of his men and or women. Kelly, Tom, and Faye entered the cabin where they knew Marcus was sleeping. As they approached the front, they heard two women arguing as to who was going to ask the SOB if he wanted anything to eat. Finally, the one called Polly said she would ask, but she definitely was not screwing that old man's ass. She went into the back of the cabin. "Marcus, can I get you something to eat?"

"No, but you can stay and keep me company until I fall asleep."

"Nope, I'll send Suzy in. She likes to screw with you. Are we leaving in the morning or hanging here for a few days? If so, someone needs to do some shoppen', if you know what I mean."

"I am going to survey the back of the town in the morning. If it's clear, we are staying put for about a week."

She left cursing to herself. This place stinks, the men are pigs, and so is he. If I can hitch a ride, I'm out of here.

Kelly pulled Faye and Tom back. "Listen, we can pick her up on the road and see what we can get from her, as long as you let her live long enough to tell us, Faye."

"We could, but she may be a screamer, and where would that leave us?"

"I got it. I'm just learning, Tom, I'll get there." Faye told him she thought it was a damn good idea.

One of the crew grabbed Tommy and waved at Faye and Kelly to follow. They went behind one of the buildings. Jake said to them, "Listen, Dawn is in no shape to try and run the road. We also have three little ones under thirteen. I have seen other scouts out there, and they are looking for the old asshole. We can help them or stop them, but either way, we get a ride out. Are you in or out?"

They all agreed, but the one called Dawn, she didn't speak. Faye tapped an SOS on the wall of the cabin once, and she waited, then again SOS. This time there was an answer.

"If you are here to help, go to the back door." That was it.

Faye met the girl. She looked no more than twelve to her, but she spoke like a grown-up. "How old are you?"

"How old do you want me to be?"

"I want you to be your proper age, not something he trumped up."

"I am twenty-four years old. I have a disease that stopped my growth but not my ability to think. It's rare, as far as my asshole parents knew, myself and two other kids in America had it. It is not like the ageing disease where you age faster than your body can keep up with it."

"So he made you act like a kid for clients that wanted to be with little girls?"

"Yep, you know him too."

"Let's gather your stuff and get you out of here. We have a way to save all of you."

"Lady, there are twenty kids here. Think you can take that many?"

"Yep, I can, but you have to gather them as quietly as you can; you can do that? We will be ready at the far end of town by the boulders, okay. There will be a guard to go with you."

"See you soon."

"What are we going to do with that many children?"

"We will find them homes or find their parents. Our organization is what we do, Faye. We rescue people. We don't usually set out to kill a family member."

"Take Peter and lead all the kids back to the dugout rocks, then come back here to Charlie and me. We will be waiting for you."

"Charlie, Faye has a good point. What in the sam hell are we going to do with all the children?" Tommy asked him.

"Tommy, we will feed, clothe and put them up in the extra cabins. Hardison can check them out. May-Ling had wanted to help, and she is a trained therapist. Let her have a go at the kids and see if she can find their parents."

Faye and Peter returned and told them the kids were used as pons in a child pornography ring. "All I want is my kids back and that bastard dead."

Charlie told Kelly, "It's a go, get your men in position. The crew has all of Marcus's men and the two women he had here."

"We go in."

"Yes, we go."

Charlie and Tommy were first in the cabin. It was dirty and unkempt; not his style of living. He was sleeping, not a care in the world.

All four surrounded his bed before he moved like lightning, but not as fast as Faye. She had his gun out of his hand and her other around his arm. "Care to tell me where my children are before I cut you up for zoo food?"

Marcus said, "Kill me, and you will never find them. You don't deserve them, Faye, maybe before, but you married him; he's not even white."

"You are supposed to be one of the ones. Are you not, Marcus? Well, tell me who trained you. Don't bother, I know."

"Yes, and I hated him for making me do what I had to do for him."

Tommy grabbed his legs and pulled his naked body out of the bed from the bottom. He lay on the floor, and his arm pulled so high over his head the shoulder socket popped.

"You did it for yourself, not for me, and I knew that going into it. I was honest and true to my training. I did it to save your miserable ass."

"Where are Mark and Mary?"

"Find them yourself if you think you can."

"I know they are on the mountain, and I intend to get them back. You have choices. Tell us where they are or fly or die right here. Pick one."

Faye was not kidding, and Tommy felt she was going to go for it. She had a manic expression on her face, one he had seen on Joan's coming back from an attack.

Kelly spoke to her, "Darlin', I'm all for cutting his nuts off and feeding them to him one at a time, but we still need the bastard alive for just a short while." He led her out of the room, away from the scene, to calm her down some.

The guard that was supposed to be on the second door watching him stopped her. He was with Suzy. "They your kids, lady?"

"Yes, they are."

"Save me, I'll tell you right now where they are."

"So tell me." She pulled the hooker off him. She had nearly bitten his penis off, and he was bleeding badly. He opened his mouth to speak and died. "Son of a bitch." Kelly kept her walking out the door.

She found another hut full of children under the age of six. They needed medical attention. She radioed to Hardison, "I have about six to eight kids that are in bad shape. Can you come down here? We have him and his men under control?"

"On my way."

One of the men from their crew said, "Faye, that's my daughter, in the corner, she is staring into space."

"Hardison is on his way here now; we will get this sorted out."

Every building had something going on: women being held for sale, men being used for beating by other women and men then having sex with them. One was a lawyer that worked for Tommy. Marcus said he had just up and quit.

Peter asked Faye to go back to the cave area or work with Hardison. She was getting more upset than ever.

The last cabin was just what they did not need to find—women with babies just born, women ready to give birth, and women holding dead babies. The women were weak, abused, and in need of help. One woman grabbed her, begged her to kill her, and take the baby far away, where no one will find him.

"I have a cabin full of women with babies, some alive, some ready to be born, some I am not too sure about."

"Put a guard on them, and I will get to them, Faye, I promise," Hardison told Faye. "I will be there shortly and do what I can while we are here."

She asked the woman if they had eaten anything recently. They all said, "We get fed as soon as we give the baby to them."

She sent Peter to find some food. He was back with soup and some kind of meat that he did not want to know what it was, but they ate it. Hardison had called in three copters to take the kids and now the women and their babies and the men out of here. The girls he found were another matter. Tommy was shocked, but he did not want Faye to know until they got them back to the chalet.

Marcus had stopped talking to anyone. When they were very close to home, he said to Tommy, "I want out over our mother's mountain."

"No such luck, my friend. You have ten minutes of life or more. Depends on you."

He took a choice. "They are with a woman I sometimes sleep with when I am back at the chalet."

Faye felt her muscles contract; she wanted to push him out right then. "What is the woman's name and where in the town does she live?"

"I'll tell you that when we land."

Kelly said, "He means Bela Richards. I followed him one night it was late, so I figured he needed protection. When I saw where he was going, I left. She is the town hooker."

That's all it took; her knife went deep between his testicles, and she was not going to stop. Tommy opened the plane door. "Goodbye, brother. It hurts me to think you would do such a thing to your own family." Kelly pushed him out so Faye and Tommy would not feel at fault.

They landed on the plane and found a piece of material stuck to a tree next to the road they were to take.

"Faye, as much as I would love for you to be the one to pick up the children, you need to change your clothes. Our kids are not going to buy that it's catsup," Kelly told her. Peter nodded in agreement.

Tommy said, "Let Peter go. He had no blood on him, and they will be okay with their dad." She agrees. "One thing: they will still be sleeping. It is only six in the morning. You can have them back in bed before the sun comes up."

Peter went with Kelly to get the kids. When he knocked on the door, Bella answered it. She knew Marcus got caught.

"They are sleeping; nothing happened to them, I promise."

Kelly picked up Mark, and Peter picked up Mary.

"Thank you, Bella, for taking care of them."

"I would never hurt a child. I thought he was wrong, but I needed the money. I'll give it back."

"No, Bella, you did what was asked of you. You earned it."

They took the children home and put them to bed. Faye came into the room. It was nearly time for them to wake up. The time came and went. They waited for another hour; still they didn't wake up.

Faye screamed. "Peter, get Hardison! This is wrong."

It took about fifteen minutes for Hardison to get there. He picked each child with a needle, with no response at all. Hardison took blood from both of the kids and ran. He shouted, "Bring them to the hut; if it's a toxin that will kill, I need them right next to me."

They didn't hesitate; they grabbed the kids and ran. Tommy, Charlie, and Kelly were coming in.

"Move, the kids have been injected or given something. They won't wake up." All the men ran in front of them. Held open the door for them.

"Hardison, have you any idea yet?" Faye asked.

"Not yet, Faye, but I will keep the kids in an upright position. That will slow it down, at least I hope so." It took Hardison thirty minutes to find the drug.

"That bastard, he used the date rape drug on them." Hardison told them it was terrible because they both were so small. He gave them both the anti-toxin. All they could do was wait. "All we can do is pray," he said through his tears.

Mary woke up and started to cry. "Mommy, he hurt me. Grandpa Marcus hurt us."

"I know, sweetheart, that's why Mommy and Daddy went to get you."

"I tore Mark's jamas so you could follow us, but he slapped me and said if I did it again, he would hurt Mark and me."

"He won't ever hurt you or Mark again."

Mark stirred and looked for Mary, then he smiled. "We are at home again. He was a bad grandpa. He hurt Mary and made her show her privates to the truck driver. He told him to look, don't touch."

Faye had tears in her eyes. All this just to punish her for marrying Peter. "Please put it out of your mind, kids. We will do our best to never let anything like that happen again," Peter told them.

They took them back to the chalet and their room.

"Are you guys tired, or do you want your breakfast?"

"I want to eat, Mommy," Mary told her.

Mark was right with her. They got dressed and headed for the kitchen. "Grandpa Charlie, can we have breakfast cakes, please."

"Yep, right away." They got the knives and forks that Charlie kept for them and the napkins for chin wiping.

"Dad, what are breakfast cakes?" Peter wanted to know.

Faye smiled and winked at the kids. "They are the early worms that come out just before breakfast, and Grandpa Charlie chops them up and makes flat cakes with them."

They were giggling as Peter made a terrible face and acted like he was going to be sick. "Be brave, my son. The children love them. So will you. I promise not to put too many worms in yours."

When Charlie put breakfast down for all of them, they bowed their heads and asked for peace and well-being. Mary added, "And Mommy and Daddy stay together forever like the rest of our family."

Charlie approached his wife and Louise about the children that they found the night before. Some so little they weren't sure of their own name. May-Ling said they needed more therapy than she could offer them.

"Wait, May-Ling, we can start by just making them feel safe and slowly work toward getting them back to sanity. Look at our Faye. No one would ever believe how she was a year or so ago. Look at her now, a wife, a loving mother, and a caring daughter-in-law."

"Charlie, I will need the rescue cabin. It is the largest. I will need bedrooms built, so they feel more human."

"We can do that for you. Why not ask Carol to help you design it into a homey dormitory and one of the other cabins into a schoolroom? Let's get them back on track with accessible at-home early education."

"Yes, I agree. The older ones can do a little more therapy and maybe remember where they came from and if they want or need to go back. I will talk with Hardison after he and Dr. Kelly are done with the medical checks. If these kids can use your help, we can bring in another therapist to help you and Louise."

"That would be great, but I need just loving, caring people that the kids will want to open up their thoughts. People like Bertha and Liz are such open and loving people by nature. Maybe they can help you as well. Talk to them, Char Lee, do you think they might help?"

"I think you could, Liz could, but Bertha is easily hurt, and her love goes out to all that are in need or in medical help. She may be of help to you in a different way. Let me speak to her for you."

Carol met with May-Ling, and they walked through the cabin. "I understand what you want, May-Ling, but I need to know a budget for expenses."

"There is none. We do it and get it done. These children need this, as Char Lee said, yesterday."

"I need to know when you want me to start."

"Again, Carol, now, this morning, if possible."

She took Carol for a walk over to the cabins the children were in. They were small and cramped, and very much as they had. The children were still huddled into small groups; even though they had food and fresh clothing, they felt they were being herded for the slaughter.

"Okay, I will start by using the two cabins on each side of the large one and join them. We will turn one into a large kitchen that will feed all of them at one time—the other a playroom with television and games and desks and study areas. The large cabin we turn into an open therapy area and then the bedrooms into private therapy rooms. We still need dormitories for the kids to sleep."

May-Ling grabbed Kelly. "I need space for sleeping dormitories for the kids and the woman and babies."

"I'm on it, May-Ling, Charlie told me to get you whatever you needed. Could we take those old cabins on the back of the property that Tommy uses for storage? We could redo them into dormitories for the kids and the woman and babies?"

"I don't see why not, Kelly."

While they were talking, Carol was drawing on a piece of paper she took off Kelly's notepad. When Kelly left them, she turns to May-Ling. "How long has this rescue organization been here?"

"You would have to talk to Char Lee and Tommy-son."

"I will, this afternoon, but right now, let us get things on the go."

The work started as they were standing on the path leading to the main chalet. Denny and Robert were taking the kids for a walk up the hill for a special breakfast.

"Denny, where are they going?"

"We are going to have a pancake breakfast on the lawn at the chalet. Bertha, Liz, Cora, and us will help them, don't worry."

"How long will they be out of this cabin?"

"How long do you want them gone?"

"Give me at least six hours if you can."

"Will do, May-Ling. We can try some of the games to get them ready to have a nap on the lawn."

Carol called Doug and they, with two other men and the ladies, tore into the cabin. Each room was changed into dorm bedrooms with clean windows, bright curtains, and proper beds. They had a furniture store send all the single beds and bed linen they had; all made up by the rescue crew and their families. They needed to change a whole layout in such a short time. In two hours under Kelly's direction, four bedrooms were fitted out with three single beds and three small dressers. The kitchen was dismantled and turned into a four-bedroom for the four girls close to being teens. Kelly suggested to Carol that they leave the living room as a play area or television room. They had the other cabin done differently. This was for the mothers with babies and ones who were expecting. The lady that had held the dead baby was taken directly to the hospital.

May-Ling and Louise were exhausted, as were the other workers, but by bedtime, the kids had finished two meals and played out, the cabins were ready for them, so was the mommy cabin. They would keep improving, but they had a happier place to stay.

Carol told May-Ling she would have Kelly and his workers start on the main cabin in the morning. The add-ons would be first as a priority. Tommy thanked Carol personally, "They are great-looking rooms for the kids and the moms. Thanks to Carol for all you did."

"So now, my friend and almost great-granddad, you give me the papers, and I get read in. You must know I was not born dumb to this kind of thing."

"Figured as much. Douglas gave you no hints at all."

"No, but I'm nosey and a quick read."

"How did you acquire so many children and those poor women."

"Sign this, then we talk."

She scanned it then signed it.

"Marcus turned to the bad side of things. He was running sex games for hire. You wanted a child, okay, boy or girl. You want to beat a woman or man your choice. You want sex with the same sex; we have that too. You want to do it with three people and a child, well, okay."

She wanted to throw up. "Every one of those kids has been abused in some way, Gramps?"

"Yes, Carol, Hardison has diagnosed many sexual diseases in them. He has brought in the health authority to help in this area. Tommy led the fight to keep them here instead of institutionalizing them in isolation. He and Dr. Kelly are treating them with shots and oral medication. Soon they will be healthy in body. Then the hard work comes. May-Ling is a trained therapist as well as Louise in that area. She and Louise will start working with the trauma they have suffered."

"They are like Faye and Joan were?"

"Yes, Mark and Mary as well."

"Oh Gramps, I thought this kind of thing had been stopped a long time ago.

"No, dear. It is more rampant today than fifty years ago. Some of those babies were born with all kinds of venereal diseases. Some won't live another month. The mothers, well, some don't want the children; others just want to die themselves."

"If they need me to help them, I'll be there, Gramps."

"I figured you would, Carol."

"Does Grams know about all this?"

"Yes, as does Liz and Mitch. Denny and Robert were just read in as we needed their help."

"Can you tell me what Doug does for you in this organization?"

"No, and he can't tell you either, so please don't hound him. He is strong, and we don't want this to come between you two."

"Kelly doesn't know what half of the crew does. He does his job, and that's all. Get it."

"Got it," she told him.

The one patient that did not stay in the cabin was one special girl and her friend. They stayed in the hut. Today they were going to meet someone special. It was going to be hard, but the blood work told the story, and blood doesn't lie.

Chapter Twenty-Three

CHARLIE SPOKE TO Peter. First, he wanted him prepared, just in case there was a backlash. The girls were going to be hard for both of them. Peter could not get over the similarities. The smaller one was blood tied as well. Her demeanour was slightly different, but the attitude was there.

Faye had to be told and shown. Hardison had explained it to Gayle. She was frightened of the fact she and Dawn had a connection here.

Faye and Peter were to meet Tommy and Charlie at Hardison's hut. She didn't know why but thought, "Maybe he wants me to let some of the kids play with Mary and Mark." She just wasn't sure what it was all about.

They went into the hut. Tommy and Charlie were waiting for her to get there. Hardison and Dr. Kelly were there waiting for her as well.

"Faye, please sit down, will you?" "Hardison asked her.

"What's up? You don't pamper me, Hardison. Why start now," she told him.

He tried again and faltered, "Faye, there is something you need to know, and of course, it's me; it's just that, you see . . ."

"Oh, stop this. My name is Gayle. You and I spoke briefly at Marcus's happy camp, I believe."

"Yes, we did, so what is it I can help you with?"

"Do you understand blood DNA, Faye?"

"Of course, I do. I'm not an idiot." Faye was getting angry; she could sense something.

"All right, here we go. Did you get a real good look at the girl that seemed to be attached to my arm?"

"No, she had her head down. She wouldn't look at me."

"Meet your sister Dawn. She is your quintuplet, and I am her sister made from your mother's eggs before you and the three girls."

"What the f—k are you talking about?" she was on her feet.

"Calm down, Faye, come on." She took her over to the medical table. "Give me your arm."

"No, I won't."

Dr. Kelly came up. "I'll do it, Gayle; I know you can, but I will." He took blood from Gayle and then from Dawn, who still as of yet not looked at her.

They were put into Hardison's centrifuge. Five minutes later, his computer spits out that all three blood types were a 100 percent match to blood relatives. Faye plopped down on the chair, then stood, walked over to Dawn, and lifted her face. Dawn looked at her. She was a mirror image of Faye except less strained.

"Can you talk, or do you rely on Gale?"

"I can speak. I just never did in front of him or any of the people who worked for him. He kept calling me a freak and Gayle a miscarriage gone wrong."

"Have you ever seen my sister or me before?"

"Yes, when you were about five or six, Master Walt allowed Gayle and I to play with you and Joan but only for about an hour. He laughed and told us we would never see our sisters again. Then Marcus took us to his sex camp. We have been there ever since. Gayle has been cured twice of sexually transmitted diseases. I also have Dr. Kelly monitoring the baby to see if it's going to be all right."

Faye passed out. Dr. Kelly used smelling salts, and she came around quickly.

"Are you saying that you can and are having a child?"

"Yes, not that the father is around, but I am about six months along."

"You do not show at all. Why?"

Gayle interrupted this, "We didn't get fed on a regular basis, Faye. We are both malnourished. So is the baby. Marcus didn't know she was, and we hid it. He would have had her uterus torn out as he did to the other girl that died."

"Gayle, are you strong enough to handle some bad news?"

"Sure, my whole life has been bad news."

"Your father, my father, was Marcus, and he is dead now."

"Well, what do you know, prayers are answered," she told Faye.

"This doesn't bother you that he was your father?"

"Oh, we knew. He told us when he brought us from Grandfather's. You have one advantage over us. We never got to see our mother. It was forbidden for her to do anything for us. We could hear her outside the door talking to us, saying that she loved all her children. Even her son that they took from her at birth. She would come once or twice a week and talk to us. We knew not to talk back to her. The man would come and beat her and chase her away."

Faye put her arms around Gayle and then Dawn. "We are sisters, we are one."

"No, Faye, we are sisters; only Dawn is of the one. She was beaten to save me."

"Tommy, what can we do? They are related to you as well."

"I know, Faye, but we had to see how you were going to handle this news. Not only two sisters but a baby on the way and a brother out there somewhere."

"If we can go through their records, maybe we can find him. Marcus always proclaimed our mother as his long-lost love, that he hated Grandfather for taking her away and not telling him she was having his babies."

Gayle spoke up again, "I have a letter she shoved under the door just before they took us. Here, read it for yourself. I do not want to say these things out loud."

> MY DEAREST DAUGHTERS
>
> I AM SORRY I COULD NOT BE A REAL MOTHER TO YOU.
>
> YOU HAVE TWO SISTERS OF THE SAME FATHER AND A BROTHER
>
> I HAVE NEVER SEEN, HE WAS TAKEN RIGHT AFTER I FEED HIM THE FIRST TIME. I WAS TOLD HE WAS SOLD. I KNOW IN MY HEART THAT THE LORD WILL SOMEHOW BRING MY CHILDREN TOGETHER
>
> I LOVE YOU NOW AND ALWAYS
>
> MAMA

"I have no proof that he took the boy. What you don't know, Faye, was he was in on the whole show. He wanted the bar ruined because Tommy was with their mother, and he was not. He hated her for choosing you over him. Marcus hated his father for being a weakling. He mostly hated the fact that your mother managed to save the bar, so whenever he got the urge, he came to Master Walt and paid to beat Margaret and have sex with her any way he wanted. The result was four girls and two boys; one died at birth. Probably because he beat her just before he was born, he wanted to see her howl while she delivered. He wanted to eat the baby boy in front of her, but Master Walt wouldn't let him because he had sold the baby's body already. Walt wanted your mother so bad, he tried to buy her from your dad, and Marcus tried to convince him it would save him the money and his bar. Walt was too afraid of the new friends you had. Mr. McCloud, you did not know your brother for the fowl man he was. He hated anything and everything you did. So I'm sorry for your loss, but your loss is our gain. No more beatings, no more sexual abuse."

"I am your true Uncle Tom or Tommy, whichever you decide. I answer to both, and you have an Aunt B. Her name is Bertha. Once you meet her and get to understand how she speaks—she has a Scotch brogue—you and she will become great friends."

"Will she accept me? I look so much like Faye."

"You look like me, and Joan and Faye, and she will call you Faye, or Joan, by mistake and call me Dawn by mistake, and we will laugh at it because it was just an honest mistake."

Dawn started to cry. "If only I would live long enough to see and feel all of this."

Dr. Kelly jumped in, "Dawn, Hardison and I are curing your problem, and you will live to see a ripe old age like your uncle here."

"Watch the old age, Doc. I may look older than I am, but I'm not ripe yet."

"Ya no, me boyo, what are ya hidden from me now?"

"Bertha, meet Gayle and Dawn. They are Faye's sisters, all the same age."

"Yer shitten me, are ya!"

"No, Aunt B, we are quads, and we have a brother."

"Tommy, move yer arse. I need ta sit doon."

Dawn asked Faye, "What did she say?"

"She was surprised, and swore, then told Uncle to move his ass. She needed to sit down."

"Okay, got it."

"Gayle, are ya no growed like the rest?"

"Ya has the look, ya jest wee short, tis all."

"Yes, I know. It's a genetic disorder. I don't mind. It's okay."

"I like the idea yer wee like me. Call me Auntie B. Tommy, are ya no goin' to bring them ta our hame ta live?"

"When Hardison says they can, we will move them into our home, dear."

"Is that what she said, Faye?"

"Do ya no understand me, child?" Bertha asked Gayle.

"I am sorry, but I only got some of it. I promise to learn to understand you and learn your language. I speak six languages now."

"I canna teach ya, Gayle, if yer willen ta learn Gaelic."

The family group chatted for about an hour or so. Dr. Kelly came back. "Dawn, I have a new serum for you to try. The people at the Johns Town Hospital sent it for you to try. It worked well on all their patients with the infection."

"You have to stay on it for a while." He took her into the private examination room.

"What is wrong with Dawn, Gayle?"

"It's a type of herpes that just won't stop, and with her having a baby, we don't want her to pass it on to the child."

"Let's keep that to ourselves for now, Gayle."

"Fine with me."

Tommy wondered if it was a good time for the girls that Kelly and Charlie had gone through the paperwork and found where their brother was. He had hoped he had been sold to a decent family. No, not his luck, he was sold to work a farm. Cattle, dairy farm. A large dairy operating with over a thousand head of cattle.

He never moved up. He was a worker, cleaning, milking, birthing all of it. He slept in a room built off the barn. There was no love between him and the farmer's family. They did not share meals together. When he turned twelve, he was relegated to the room of the barn. He was told he had an enormous debt to pay off. Until such time, he would work the farm. His food and clothing were added to his debt. He was known as Boy. No other name was given.

Tommy had Charlie look into this debt—what was the debt, to begin with, what was it now. He would love nothing more than to bring his family together. He was part of this family. He had Doug check out what kind of man he was. Did he have his father's cheating, stealing, lying ways, or was he a decent young man, worth the time and effort to save him, or do I save him and straighten him out.

Kelly called him on his cell. "Yes, Kelly, What do you need?"

"I need a private conversation, ASAP."

"I'm coming."

He met Kelly on the back lawn. It was warm, and the blossoms were gone, but the pine smell filled the air.

"What is it, Kelly?"

"The boy has been put in the hospital. He was made to go after a rampaging bull that the farmer didn't want in with the heffers. They left him there. They told the hospital he had no coverage. Do what you can for him, and if he dies, so be it. It's God's will."

"What hospital and how fast can we get there."

"If you take the jet, you are there in half an hour because you have to drive to the hospital. If we wire ahead to the hospital, you are coming, and you are there in fifteen because you will land on their heliport."

"Do it and I'm gone. Bertha, I have to fly out right now; it's an emergency."

"Be careful, love."

He landed on the heliport, jumped down, and was heading to the elevator, where he was met by an intern.

"Sir, the young man has no coverage, and he is being held in the emerg. I'm afraid no one wants responsibility for him. The poor bastard doesn't have a name."

"His name is Thomas Charles McCloud, of the McCloud family, one of the richest families in America."

"You, sir, who might you be?"

"I, young man, am the Thomas McCloud, and that young man is my long-lost nephew. Now get the hell out of my way. He is coming with me."

"He has a bill of twelve hundred dollars, see."

Tommy handed him two thousand dollars. "Pay the bill. Bring me the change."

He entered the ER and asked about the boy. They directed him. He had Charlie and Kelly put the young man on a stretcher and start for the heliport.

"Stop right there; that patient hasn't been released." It was the hospital guard.

The intern ran up to Tommy and gave him the change and the receipt. "He is now. His bill is paid, and I just signed the release forms. Get out of this man's way."

Hardison was on the copter waiting for his patient. He could not believe they just let him lay there in so much pain. "Not to worry, son, we'll have you home and in good shape with your real family shortly." He just stared at Hardison and then closed his eyes; he was dreaming again.

Tommy took his hand. "You won't be going back to the dairy ever again. They will be paid whatever is due them. You are a member of my family, and you will be staying with me until you want to go or do whatever it is you want to do."

He looked at Tommy. "You look sort of like the farmer, but not. Am I dreaming? Are you real? Am I flying in a helicopter or just dreaming again?"

"No dream, son. You are flying. Sleep now. Soon you will have a new life and a family that will love and care for you. You do have a name, and it's Thomas Charles McCloud. Can you remember that?"

"I'll try, sir." He fell asleep.

They landed, and Kelly drove the gulf cart back to the hut. Charlie and Tommy hung on to him. He was groggy from the pain medication, but he knew he was being moved. Hardison told him he was going to take X-rays of him to see where he was hurt. Then he was put in a big machine that clunked; the MRI gave Hardison all the rest of the information he needed. The X-rays showed he had three broken ribs, a fractured femur, and a lump as big as a goose egg on the back of his head. The MRI showed bruised lungs, stomach and bladder swollen, but no real damage to vital organs. His femur was in a plaster cast. His ribs had to be wrapped tightly to hold them in place. Hardison had him placed in the bed next to his sister Dawn.

Gayle spoke to him quietly, "Do you need a blanket or a pillow, Thomas?"

"I, ugh no, thank you. My name is Thomas, for sure?"

"Yes, it is, Thomas. My name is Thomas. My name is Gayle, and the girl in the next bed is Dawn." She was told not to tell him yet about his sisters.

The next morning Thomas was surprised by an older lady with a tray full of good-smelling stuff. "Now yer gona need a helpen hand ta eat this here food. So ya needs ta sit up a wee bit."

He looked at her for a second or two, and he answered her in full Gaelic. Dawn and Gayle did not get what they were saying at all. Neither did Hardison. Bertha was in her glory. Somebody understood her.

Tommy came in and heard them. Before he went close, he radioed Charlie, "He speaks pure Gaelic. Check the family heritage out." He greeted Thomas with Gaelic as well then switched to English so no one in the room would be offended.

"How are you feeling, Thomas, ribs giving you much pain?"

"No, sir. They hurt some, but not as bad when I hurt them and not got bindings." He was eating like it was his last meal. "Slow doon, son, yer gona choke on it."

Gayle and Dawn's breakfast came in just as large, and they were told that they had better eat it all.

When he was done eating, he prayed his thanks for his food. That told Tommy he was raised by old-school Scots. Gayle smiled at him, and Tommy could see Faye's eyes. "Both of them are my sisters?"

"Yep, and you have another one that will be here soon."

"I have three sisters. Do I have any brothers?"

"No, you are the sole male in this family group."

Faye came into the hut. Thomas looked at them. Then Faye told him, "Me, Joan, Dawn, and Gayle—we are quads. Gayle has a genetic disorder that has caused her to stay small, but she's one of us."

"How will I tell you apart and where is Joan?"

"Joan died last year, Thomas. I brought you a picture of Joan and me with Uncle Tommy."

"Was she ill long?" He seemed to actually care.

"No, she was shot, and a bullet fragment got stuck in her heart."

"Oh Lord, it must have been hard for all of you to lose a sister."

Gayle knew this was getting too deep for him. "Yes, it was. We all miss her, and we are glad she is with her Lord."

Thomas said, "Amen, my sister, be with Him."

Faye put her arm gently over his shoulder. "You will see differences in each of us. I tend to walk fast and say very little."

Gayle told him she tends to learn as much about everything as she can.

Dawn told him, "I hope to be the best mom in the world, Thomas. I will be a mommy in about three months."

"Wow, so much to learn, so much love from all of you. The only love I knew was my pet cow Beasty. She was a large jersey cow and had big calves. She would lean on me when I fed her or come to me in the field."

Faye wanted to cry. A cow—that was the only love he knew. "Well, look out, Thomas, all the women in our family like to love and hug and kiss their nieces and nephews."

"I will always have a red face, but I have to admit it sounds wonderful to be cared for like that."

The door opened, and two little people came in, Mark and Mary. "Is he our new uncle, Mommy?"

"Yes, he is. This is Uncle Thomas. Can you say hello to him?"

"Sure." Mark climbed up on the bed. "Hello, Uncle Thomas, does your bones hurt a lot?"

"Yes, Mark, they do. A boy cow stepped on me and kicked me."

"Well, why would he do that, silly old cow," said Mary. "Hello, Uncle Thomas."

"Hello, Mary."

He was showing signs of being tired, so Faye thought to take them out. "Mark, do you have crayons and papers to draw on?"

"Yep, we do. Want some?"

"Yes, I'll trade a picture I drew for some?"

"Okay."

Thomas gave Mark a picture of a pasture and low hills covered in grass and flowers and a few cows.

"Uncle Thomas, this is real cool. I'm gonna get Mommy to frame it." It was a fantastic rendition of the pasture.

Hardison came in and said, "Okay, family, time to leave my hut."

"Oh gee, Dr. Hardison, I was just getting to know my uncle."

"You can come back tomorrow, Mark."

"I'll bring you a bunch of pencils, crayons, and markers with papers to draw on when I come back tomorrow."

"Bye, Mark."

"Bye for now." Mark blew him a kiss, and then he waited, staring at Uncle Thomas. Faye whispered to him, "You have to blow a kiss back." Thomas blew Mark a kiss. Mary had a sad face. She was almost in tears. "Mary, what is wrong?" Faye wanted to know.

"He doesn't like me. He didn't give me a picture or ask me if I wanted to help him, and I was nice to him, wasn't I, Mommy?"

"Yes, sweetheart, you were."

Thomas quickly told her, "I will make a picture for you as soon as I have papers and pencils, Mary, and I do like you very much," and he blew her a kiss.

Faye and the kids left the hut. Thomas lay back and dozed off. Dawn got up and went to talk to Hardison.

Hardison checked Dawn's baby. It wasn't time, but the baby was turning, preparing for birth. "Dawn, are you sure about your due date?"

"I didn't figure it out; one of the other women did."

Hardison asked her, "Could we do an ultrasound? Your baby is turning, preparing to be born."

"Yes, please, I'm not ready. I don't want to give it up yet." She started to cry.

"You are not giving your baby up. If you want to keep this baby, we will help you. You have a family that will be there for you. Faye will help you; she's a mom." They did the ultrasound. "Dawn, your little girl is fully developed. She is small, but she is ready to be part of this world."

"Am I in labor, Hardison?"

“Not sure yet, Dawn. It could be false labor. We will know by morning.”

Gayle came back to them. “Thomas is sleeping, but he is making a gurgling sound.” Hardison all but pushed the girls out of the way. “Thomas, can you hear me?” Thomas nodded. Talking was too hard. “I am going to do an X-ray, then we will see what is going on.”

He pushed his bed into the operating room and set him up for the X-ray. Thomas was going in and out of consciousness. “Gayle, can you help me?”

Gayle helped him with the X-rays, and while Hardison put Thomas on oxygen, Gayle called Dr. Kelly and Uncle Thomas. Dr. Kelly said he’d be there as soon as he could. Tommy was on his way to the hut. So was Faye.

They were before Dr. Kelly. “What is it, Hardison?”

“His lung has a tear in it. I didn’t see it before, but the tear has gotten bigger. I need to operate. Dr. Kelly is on his way.”

“Tommy, you and Charlie are going to have to scrub up. We are going to need all the help we can get.” Faye was holding his hand. “I will be right here. I won’t leave you. We are family, remember that. Fight for that, Thomas. Never let go. We need our brother.” She was crying, her tears soaking her blouse.

Gayle came up to him on his other side. “You have to fight. Dawn is in labor. You are soon going to be an uncle again.”

He squeezed her hand back. He thought to himself, “If I die, I will have known true love.” Dawn grabbed his good leg. He looked at her, “You will live and know the love of a woman and the love of your children. It is not your time.” He felt her words. He wasn’t sure if she spoke them. The darkness came.

They scrubbed, and Hardison and Dr. Kelly went to work. Hardison hated to crack open his rib cage. He had broken bones and cracked ribs, to begin with. The surgery lasted over three hours. Faye helped Gayle with Dawn. Her labor was getting stronger each hour.

"Faye, what happens if they are not done when Dawn is delivering?"

"We do it, Faye. We don't have a choice. Dotty is delivering a baby in town, so it's up to us."

Bertha came in. She had another lady with her. "Dawn, this lady is a midwife. She'll help ya if ya needs ta push."

"My name is Martha Radcliff. I've been delivering babies for thirty years. You're in good hands."

Dawn started walking the floor. She never made a sound, just rubbed her tummy and walked. Finally, she stopped. Her eyes grew large, and a puddle appeared between her feet. "I think it's time," she said between clenched teeth.

Martha got her settled on the bed, put extra sheets under her, and put the bed in a sitting position. "Bertha, can you hold her up and help her push when I ask?"

"I canna do that."

Martha looked at Faye. "She can do it."

Gayle held her hand, and Faye was told to open a clean towel and put it across her hands. Just stand there. Dawn gave a push, then rested.

"Dawn, this baby is small. All I need is one really hard push. Bertha, raise her shoulder when she pushes."

It was only seconds, and Dawn growled. Bertha lifted, and a little girl was born. Martha put the baby on Dawn's chest, cut the cord, and told Dawn, "We need to get the baby warm and get her breathing." She put the baby in Faye's hands. "Wrap her up and bring her to that table; Gayle, watch for the afterbirth. Let me know when it comes."

Martha aspirated the baby's nose and mouth. The baby was breathing, and she had lungs to prove it. Dawn could hear her crying. "She's crying, I hear her." Gayle, she's alive. Our baby is alive."

"Your baby, Dawn. Your daughter. Someday maybe I'll have a baby, and you can be the auntie."

Faye brought the baby, and Martha went back to her patient. "Dawn, you are going to have to push. The afterbirth is not coming."

Bertha lifted her, and she pushed. A tiny baby boy came into the world. "Oh Lord, it's a baby!" She cut the cord and rushed to the table. She didn't think she could save him, but she was damn well going to try. He couldn't be more than two pounds. She put the oxygen on him and pumped his tiny chest. There was a weak little cry, and he stopped. He was breathing but just barely. She made an oxygen tent out of gowns and pumped in the oxygen.

"Faye, put the girl with him. If he feels her, he may fight harder." Faye thought she was nuts but did it. The babies turned to each other, the bigger cuddling the smaller one. "It seems to be working!" Dawn wanted to see the babies, so afraid they would die.

"Ya ner can move, love, til yer afterbirth comes." Dawn pushed so hard she cried, and it came. Gayle helped Bertha clean her up, and they could not stop her. She was up and heading for the back. Bertha grabbed a wheelchair and told her, "Sit, and I'll take ya ta see um."

She stared at the babies. "Will they live, Martha?"

"I don't know, Dawn, only the good Lord does now."

Dr. Kelly came out of the surgery, surprised at the sight. He changed his gown and gloves. “Okay, young lady, back to bed.” When she didn’t move, he said, “Now, I have to save these babies.”

Dawn moved out of his way, and the women made her go back to bed. Gayle had changed the sheets, and it was clean for her. Bertha placed a soaker pad under her to sit on. Tommy and Charlie came out, stripping off the gloves, masks, and gowns, only to see Dr. Kelly working on an end table.

“What the hell,” Dr. Kelly said. “Two, not one. Two. Would you look at this? They are both breathing and fully developed. No parts are missing. They are doing better than I had thought one would have done.”

“Are they girls or boys?” Tommy asked.

“One of each, Tommy. Look at this. The girl is holding the boy. I have never seen this, never.” Bertha had to see. She put her hand on Dr. Kelly and one on the tent. “Heavenly Father be kind ta these babes an there wee mum. She ner asked fer this but she’ll love’m with all her heart. Amen.” All of them repeated that: “Amen.” Hardison was the last to see the twins. “Two, holy shit.”

Bertha hit the back of his head, and they all laughed. Gayle yelled, “She’s bleeding bad.” Both doctors ran. They had to pack her. It took giving her a direct transfusion from Faye to her. The bleeding stopped, and she was still with them. Faye felt light-headed and weak.

“You can’t move right yeat, dear, not until your levels go up and stay.”

Peter was told by two-way radio that she was okay, but she would have to stay put a little longer. Hardison brought out an old incubator. They cleaned it up, and the babies were placed inside.

"Hardison, I've never known babies that small to make it, but they have one thing going for them—they were full term. Both have all their parts working. I hope Bertha's prayer works."

"Me too, Dr. Gary. I don't want another swat. She hits hard."

They went to see Thomas. Tommy was with him, as was Charlie. He was having a rough go breathing, but he would make it. He was strong.

Dawn was not capable of breastfeeding, so they were feeding the little ones with baby kitten bottles. Hardison managed to get them from the vet in town. They were like baby birds—mouths wide open every time someone touched them. Dawn could not believe how fast they were growing.

Gayle asked Hardison, "Is he big enough to do a blood test on for a genetic disorder?"

"Not yet, Gayle, but I understand. I will as soon as I can." She could only hope he didn't have what she had.

Dawn was getting stronger every day. "When can I hold them, Hardison?"

"You mean out of the incubator, don't you."

She told him yes. "When they reach at least five pounds. I know it seems like a long way off, but it will go fast. Have you chosen names for them, Dawn?"

"No, I wanted to see if the family would help me. I would like them to be named after people in the family, so they know they belong."

Faye had heard her say this before to Gayle. "Dawn, why not Margaret after their grandmother, and Charles after their uncle, Thomas Charles?"

"Oh, Faye, do you think it would be all right?"

"I know it would. She was my mother too, and I am sure Thomas would be proud. Why not ask him?"

Dawn looked at the babies. "Margaret and Charles, that's who you are from now on."

She went into the next room and told Thomas. "I am very proud to be his namesake, Dawn. I have prayed for your children ever since they were born." They visited for twenty minutes, and she had to go. Doctor's orders—no more than twenty minutes. Thomas didn't let her. He was so afraid they would not make it because of their size. Baby calves that are born small very rarely make it but one or two months.

Faye would read stories to him about the world and the people in it. He was amazed at all the things he never knew existed. People had colour television. He had heard of television but never see one. Moving sidewalks that were like a miracle. How did they work. He fell asleep thinking about air balloons.

Three months had passed, and the babies were being weighed, hoping they had made their five pounds. Both looked almost the same size. "Here we go, boys and girls. Let's see how big you have grown since last week's weigh-in."

Margaret weighed in at a healthy five pounds two ounces. Charles weighed in at five pounds on the nose. Dawn danced around the room with Gayle. He told her to sit, and he would bring them to her. Hardison placed both babies side by side on her arm and lap. She felt their weight and was glad. She kissed each one. "Hello, Margaret, Charles. I am your mommy. This is Auntie Gayle, and Uncle Thomas is in the other room. And the big man with the gentle hands is Uncle Hardison. He saved you for me." Hardison turned his back to get a small blanket so she wouldn't see his tears.

Tommy, Mitch, and a waddling Liz came in. "They both weigh five pounds," Dawn proudly announced. Bertha asked their names, and Dawn thought about what Faye had told them. "Margaret Faye, and he is Charles Thomas. They are named after the family." She told them they would never know how they came about. "I had Hardison test to see if they were of mixed race, and they are not. They are like us. They would have had to been told if they had another race inside. I want them to think that their dad died and never came back from the sea."

Bertha told her, "They ner have ta know from where or who jest their daddy didna want them."

"Hardison, when can my family move up to the chalet?"

"Soon, Uncle Tommy, about a week."

Liz went to rise as she and Mitch were going to go for her daily walk up and down the lane. Her eyes got big, and water flooded the floor. "Gayle, call Dr. Kelly. We have a baby on the way."

"Liz, do you want Mitch to take you to town or wait for him here?"

"Wait for who to get here." It was Dr. Kelly who came to the hut with Hardison about a case he was having trouble with.

"Dr. Kelly!" she screamed.

He turned and saw Liz. "Okay, lady. We do it right here."

"Mitch, the girls will show you how to scrub up, and Gayle and Dawn will be assisting us to bring her baby into the world."

"What am I supposed to do?" It was Mitch. He thought his job was to wait with the guys outside until they heard the baby cry, then pat the others on the back once they knew the sex of the kid. They took Mitch to the back and put a gown on him, a pair of surgical gloves and hat and mask. He was ready.

"Liz, have you had any heavy feelings like the kid has slipped down?"

"Yes, about a week and a half ago. I was going to tell you tomorrow at my visit."

"Well, this one won't wait for that, but you will be a while."

He no sooner said it, and she let out a good bellow. "Let's get her into a bed and prepped. Can you call Bertha for me, Tommy?"

"Bertha, love, Liz is having her baby. Doc wants your help."

"I'm on me way," which meant she was riding her moped through the chalet again.

Liz didna look too good. "Are ya no feelen good, Lass?"

"Mom, the baby seems to be pushing into my back."

Mitch told Hardison, and he brought out the ultrasound to check the baby's position. "Okay, Liz, this is cold, and it may make the baby jump, so be ready, all right." She nodded. "Dr. Kelly, come see this. The baby was breach. They could try to turn it, but the baby was already in the birth canal."

Hardison went to Liz. "It's like this, sweetheart, the baby is backward. You know what I mean?"

"Yes. Breach."

"We can try to turn it for a natural birth, or we do a caesarian cut to save you from an extreme amount of pain. It's up to you and Mitch."

"No, Hardison. It's up to me. My body. I make the decision."

"Liz, I don't want to lose you. Not now. We have a family."

She touched his face. "I can do this, Mitch. You can help."

Hardison explained to both of them how they would proceed to turn the baby, and Mitch would have to help.

"Bertha would have to help Liz try not to push and bear down until we get the baby in the right spot."

Thomas came up to Liz. "Can I try something? I know it will hurt, but not as much as what they want to do."

She told him to do it. Thomas picked up the bottle of breast milk and told Hardison to squirt some up inside, maybe once or twice. Hardison looked at him like he lost it, but he remembered he birthed big cows.

"Okay, here we go." One squirt, nothing. The second one started the baby turning on its own. When it stopped, they gave it another squirt. It took nearly an hour and a half to get the baby in the right position. Liz was white as a ghost, but she was hanging in there.

The real labor started that baby wanted out. The contractions were coming at a rate of every five minutes and spending up quickly. Bertha was wiping her forehead with a damp cloth, and Gayle and Dawn were giving her ice chips. Dawn left and joined Thomas in the back. They were down on their knees, asking God to save the child and Liz as she was a great lady. "Amen." They heard the cry and went to see. There in her father's arms was a very large chubby baby girl. Dr. Kelly asked Mitch if he wanted to cut the cord. He shook his head yes, and handed Bertha the baby. He cut the cord, and he took the baby to the examining table to have her checked out. Hardison aspirated the baby's nose and mouth, and she let another cry to let them know she wanted her mother. She was hungry. They weighed her at eight pounds six ounces.

"She is one healthy baby girl, Liz."

The baby latched on right away. The men backed out of her cubby to give her privacy. Bertha was going as well.

"Where do you think you are going, Grams?"

"Patrica Elizabeth is done. You get her. I need to sleep. She was not easy on her mommy."

"No, lassie, she wasna that. Patrica, ya say."

"Yes and no arguments, Mom. That is her name." With that, Patrica burped and went to sleep. Grams went on gramma duty right away.

Mitch was slightly ill but managed to brag a little that he helped Liz with the delivery of their daughter, Patrica Elizabeth. He hoped he could convince her to add his mother's name on the end of that. After everyone had left and it was just Liz and the baby, he asked her, "Could we add a name to the name you chose? I like it, don't get me wrong, I know it's Bertha's middle name and yours, but could we add my mother's name on the end? It's Victoria."

"Patricia Elizabeth Victoria Maxwell, I love it. Too bad the shower's tomorrow." They laughed.

Bertha came in and asked if Tommy could bring the bassinet over for the wee one ta sleep in.

"We don't have a bassinette, Mom?"

"Ya do. I bought it fer yer shower. Now ya need it."

"Oh yes, please, Mom, that would be great."

"Could ya give him a hand?"

"Mind ya, don't forget the bedding." They left, and Gayle and Dawn came over to the bed to see the baby.

"She is huge, Liz. Were you eating for an army to get her that big?"

"No, but I didn't tell Dr. Kelly I was eating peanut butter and banana sandwiches dipped in egg wash and fried, at least twice a day."

They laughed until they saw the look on Dr. Kelly's face. He did not look pleased. "You were eating Elvis Presley's favourite sandwich twice a day?"

"Yep, they were good."

He laughed and said he would see her tomorrow and left. Hardison told her she would stay with them for two days and she could leave to go back to the chalet. The girls said they would help her move; they had already moved over. She thanked them, knowing what a clutz Mitch was as it would be a great help. Everyone was gone except Grams. She had no intention of leaving. Hardison gave her a pillow and clean sheets for the next bed and said, "Good night. If you need me, I'm at the back."

Thomas was leaning on Dave, using his cane. "We can do this together, my friend. We will have you walking by yourself in no time."

Each day Dave took him out in the summer air. He had set an easel up for him to draw on, the children brought him pencils and sketchbooks. Tommy would not believe his artwork. He had two of his sketches framed—one for his office; the other for their bedroom.

"Thomas, can you do portraits?"

"You mean like people's faces?"

"Uncle Tommy, yes, but I have only done cow faces."

"Could you do the babes as they are now?"

"I can try. They change so much every day."

"Yes, they do."

"Would you like to go to an art school, study different styles of drawing or painting?"

"Uncle Tom, I can barely read or write. Gayle and Faye have taught me how to write my name. I can work here, can't I? This is such a beautiful place to live. I'm strong, and I'm sure Kelly or Charlie could teach me how to do something."

"Yes, they could, but there is a great big world out there that is waiting for you to see."

"It can wait until I'm ready, I guess. I have worked hard from the time I could walk. I don't even know my date of birth or how old I am."

"I will get you something that will show you who you are and how old you are and when you were born." Tommy kissed his head as he walked away. "Damn you, Marcus, you bastard. May you rot in hell as your body is on the mountainside."

"Doug, what did you find out about that family, and do they know anything about his date of birth?"

"Yes, I know a lot about the family that bought him. He's not the first. There are two girls and another boy. All bought from Marcus. The boy is in a mental institution, stomped by a stampede of cattle. Never cared for after that. The two girls work as field hands, slopping pigs, feeding chickens, tending the main garden for the family table. The same thing—they all owe an enormous debt and must work it off. The girls are twelve and sixteen. I think the teen is pregnant, not sure. The family has a husband, wife, and four grown boys who do nothing. The father is classified as a cattle barren. McGregor has four ranches, they range from meat cattle, stock, and dairy. The wife plays at being a lady of a high standard. They are from Scotland, both from the streets. He came over when Walt Parker needed someone to tend his meat distribution. He brought her with him.

"Neither one is educated but pretends to be. The four boys may or may not be their legitimate kids. As for the debt, there is none. Walt and Marcus decided that the cattle ranchers would pay free meat to them for free labor. All they had to do was raise them. They are filthy people, but clean up on Sunday for church."

"Did you find out his date of birth or when he was bought?"

"I have some record that I am tracking now. Tom, there are two other children, small, on another ranch, boys. They look like Thomas. Could be his. I know they are not because he has never been off that damn ranch until he was hurt. I was in his room off the barn, and the walls are covered with drawings, fantastic drawings done with stones. Mostly pastures and cows and one cow that he drew several times. I'll keep looking."

"Doug, let Charlie know where the kids are, all of them. We will rescue them, and maybe treat Farmer—wait, what the hell is his name?"

"It's McGregor. Manchester McGregor."

"Well, we may teach Farmer McGregor a new dance, 'How to Dance with a Bull.' What you think?"

"I think we dance, boss."

Doug sent all the records to Charlie. He, in turn, asked Faye and Peter for their help deciphering all of it. Some were Walt's. Some were from Marcus.

"Peter, let's separate them into their piles and work through them."

"Great idea. What one do we start with?" They were sitting in the breakfast nook. Robert said to do it by date, not by what company.

"What do you mean, Robert?" asked Faye.

"Look, this is dated 1990, right. So anything in all the mess in, say, from 1990 to 2000 in this pile, some may go together. Get what I mean."

"Yes, we do. Sit, join the club. It's called find out when Thomas was born, his date of birth."

"All right, I'll help, but first we need an okay from Gramps or Charlie."

"It's got my okay. Good enough?" It was Charlie.

"Peter, can I speak to you in private?" They left.

Robert asked Faye, "Did you sign some papers for Gramps?"

"Yes, and you don't talk about it unless, of course, you want to die."

"No, I just wanted to know I was in good company." She hit him.

They worked all morning when Mark and Mary arrived to say they were going with Dave out to see Uncle Thomas.

"You guys are doing the same thing Grampa Charlie and Great Gramps are doing."

Faye kissed them and told them to watch Uncle Thomas's leg. When they were gone, Faye excused herself and said she would be goin on a bathroom run. Robert nodded. He was so engrossed in the paperwork.

Faye found them in the study. "Care to fill me in, guys."

"No, but you're here, so there are more kids on the SOB's farm, and he has a few more ranches. All with kids owing a large debt. None of them have names. We are going to get them, all of them."

"Oh, I'm not invited to the party. Is Peter . . . they knew she was angry. All Peter is doing is planning it out with Kelly. He is NOT leaving here. I promise."

"Uncle Tommy, if you need us, we will be there."

"I know, Faye. Have you found anything about the other children?"

"I guess the ones you are going for, but not Thomas, not yet."

"Keep looking, please. He feels he is not a person, no name, no date of birth, no parentage."

"I got it." Faye was thinking on the way back to the kitchen, "Robert, grab that stuff and put it in the boxes. Don't mess up what you have sorted out. I don't want the kids to get into it."

"Okay, why?"

"We are going to talk to my sisters. They are getting ready to move up here. I need some info; want to come?"

"Yes, you bet. I miss Robbie and Denny, and they have only been gone two days."

"How long are they gone for?"

"A week, but it feels like forever." They saw the kids sitting side by side talking to Thomas, and Faye realized he was drawing them. When they reached the hut, Uncle Hardison had the little ones in a double stroller walking down the lane.

"Gayle, Dawn, can we bother you for a bit?"

"Sure, what's up."

"Do you remember other kids were taken from where you were, young babies or a little older?"

"Yep, I used to mark on the floor when they were born and when they were taken. Why?"

"Our people have found out where four, maybe five, of them are, and they are going to get them."

"Send someone to the horrible place if it is not burned down. The dates will be there, girl . . . born . . . died. Boy . . . born . . . taken. That's how they will see it. Look under the floorboards of his bedroom; he kept a book of dates. I'm not sure what they are about, but have a look."

"Hello, Robert, you missed the kids," Dawn said. She was in the back room.

"I will not get used to the way all of you look alike." They laughed at him.

Faye told Tommy what Gayle had told her. "It may lead us to all of their birth dates and who are their mothers."

Tommy called Doug and relayed the information. "I'll send four men—don't know what's there now, if anyone, but better safe. Talk to you later, Tom."

Bertha heard most of it. She waited until they were alone. "Are ya jest looken fer Thomas's of birthdate Tommy?"

"No, love. Marcus sold four or five more kids to the same rancher. We are going for them—two girls, one twelve and one sixteen, possibly pregnant."

"Put him oot with his cows in the shit."

"We will, love." He smiled at her. "You know you would do that, wouldn't you?"

"Yes, I would." She left him then. If only that would stop all this. But they would stop this one.

Doug and four men entered the deserted town. They found the floorboard with the dates and deaths on it. They also saw the blood on the floor and walls as well. Doug took pictures of the floor. "Doug, are these dates of women or kids?"

"Just kids, Tim."

"We need to check each cabin for signs of this. I'm going up to the head cabin. Come with me. Send the others to check the floors of the other cabins."

They tore up the floor under the bed and the table; at first, they didn't see it, then Tim said, "Doug, look, it looks like a briefcase or bag of some sort."

Doug pulled it out. "Jackpot, look at this. All the mothers' names, sex of the child, and the fathers with dates of birth of the children, even certificates. Can't be real, but there is one—wait it's real. This one was taken after the kid was born."

They found forty-five in total, all with the child's mother and sex and when and where they were sent. Some had a dollar price on them.

Two of the men came back with more books and pictures of girls that had been sold. They could not believe that Marcus had little boys under the age of three were photographed for sale.

"Doug, I have to get the hell out of here. Doug, this is worse than a war camp."

"What are you talking about, Jack?"

"I found a burial ground where they were burned—the poor unfortunate people—and left their bones to rot in the sun."

Doug couldn't bring himself to tell Jack what he and his men had found was not a crematorium. It was a barbecue pit. They flew back to the compound.

"Tom, you need to come with me. No one else."

"Okay, Doug, where, the hut?"

"No, I mean alone."

"Kelly, I need an empty cabin. We got one?"

"Yep, up on the ridge. The one Bertha likes to use for her picnics with the children."

"I'm going up there. No one goes there—no one, including Charlie, knows where I am."

"Got it, boss."

"You trust him that much, Tom?"

"Yes, with my life."

He handed Tom the pictures of the floor and the kids, and then he said, "Sit, because what you are going to see will break your heart."

The first list was taken out of the case, and this one Tim found just before they left the cabin. The list had names on them. At first, Tommy got it: mother . . . child . . . death . . . wait, father—Marcus. Sixty children born to him twenty years all sold or died. The mothers, some Tommy knew the names. He got up, went to the door, and threw up.

"What else, Doug? Tell me now. How many of them are alive and findable."

"Twenty are alive; they are older, range from thirty-five down."

"He was at this long before Margaret, wasn't he."

"Yes, him and Margaret's dad, who happened to be Master Walt's brother."

Tommy slumped in the chair. "Do they have a life, these older ones?"

"They live in a compound, on the other side of the mountain. Most have jobs: some are builders, some are painters, some do clothing, that sort of thing."

"Are any of them married?"

"No, oh God, I had hoped you wouldn't ask. All the ones I just told you about are sterilized at the age of five or six. They were sent there to wait to be sold. Some sold, but the rest just got too old, and he left them there to die off slowly."

Tommy burst into tears. They were all related to him, and there was nothing he could do for them, put money into their compound, send food, clothes, what. He felt like a defeated man.

"Tom, you did not do this. He did. Tom, you didn't know what Marcus was into or who he was dealing. He liked what he did, behind your back, laughing at you. None of my men know that it was a barbeque pit."

"Here is Thomas's date of birth; he is thirty years old next month on the tenth. He was born on September 10, 1990. Thomas was listed as not for sale. He was Marcus's toy. Whenever Marcus was angry with you, he had him abused. Margaret had another son she thought was born dead. He isn't. He is one of the boys you want to rescue; he is twenty-five, born October 31, 1995. The rest of the kids are not related to you."

"Bring the boys and girls here. If there are more, bring the FBI in, Doug, please."

"I was going on this rescue. I can't now."

"I understand, Tom."

Doug knelt and held Tom to him. He loved this man like a father; he saved him, educated him, and gave him a job he loved. Now he was about to marry his granddaughter.

Tommy rose from the chair, looking older than when he came in. "I need a stiff drink."

"No, you don't, do you?"

"No, a tea will do."

They left the cabin the way they found it. Kelly told him Charlie was looking for him. "Kelly, do you know why? Something about what Tim found. He wanted to give it to you and Doug."

Tommy looked at Doug. "You take care of it." He went to find Bertha; she was sitting talking to Dave and Thomas. "Sorry to intrude, dear. I need to speak to you urgently. Excuse us, please." She followed him until they were out of hearing range.

"Tis a bad thing, yea have fer me, love?"

"Yes, and I need to be held in your loving arms while the world goes away."

She listened, she cried, they cried together, and she held him until she felt the sobs stop and he was asleep. When he woke, she told him, gently, “We ner speak ah this agin, we’ll help those we canna, an live fer the family we have.”

“Did I tell you today that I love you?”

“No, tell me now.”

Chapter Twenty-Four

THE RESCUE WAS set for the next night. Charlie and Kelly were heading it. They had their instruction. Charlie was surprised Doug and his team were on this rescue. When they were in the air, he asked Doug, "What's up!"

He gave Charlie a quick version and swore him to secrecy. Tom was falling apart on this one. "We bring his family home; if we find more, then we are to bring in the FBI."

"How many are his family, Doug?"

"At least four, possibly five."

"Doug, are you one of the ones."

"Yes, that's how I met Tom. I was beaten so close to death for my mother that they left me. Tom saved me, cured me, educated me. Now I would give my life for him and for you, my brother."

"Then you must know, one of the children we are about to rescue is not Marcus's but his, and he does not know it; he thought his daughter was all the children he would ever have."

"How Marcus got him drunk beyond consciousness. He used one of his women, and Tommy gave him what he wanted—a whipping post."

"I believe he knows. That's why he never drinks. Have you ever seen him take a drink? Charlie, not even at his wedding, lift a glass, sure; pretend to drink yes; drink it, never."

"We are here."

Kelly put his hand on Doug. "Please, when this is over, can we talk?"

"Sure, Kelly."

The McGregors were asleep, so they rounded up the kids first. The girls were afraid to go. Kelly softly told them they were going home to where they belonged. They went with two of Kelly's men. Both boys jumped at the chance of leaving. The other ranch yielded three more—one girl and two boys.

"Charlie, it's time to talk to Farmer McGregor. Just you and I, are you good with this, or do we need Kelly along in case?"

"Kelly, come on!"

The fat SOB was naked on the bed; a woman slept in another bed in the same room. There was a young boy chained to the farmer's bed, curled up and bleeding. Kelly got him out then came back. He was holding a whip he found on the floor. "The kid said if he didn't do what he was told, the farmer used this." Charlie saw hatred in his eyes for the first time. He tapped Doug and pointed, "Oh shit, no, Kelly, not yet." Kelly lowered the whip.

McGregor was shaken awake. "As a result of this, you are served that Walt Parker, Marcus McCloud, and Tara Corporation are dead. If you or your people take a child for labor, we will come for you with a vengeance. There is money on that filthy table for the kids. I'd advise selling out and get gone before the FBI gets involved; you have twenty days."

"Go for it." Kelly let him know how it feels. Charlie and Doug heard the screams almost to the helo when it stopped. Charlie told them to start the engines. Kelly came up to the plane a little bloody but absently whistling a tune to himself. "Feel better, Kelly."

"Lots thanks, I'm keepen' this." He threw the whip into the plane before he jumped in.

Doug was about to get in when a man looking like Thomas asked if they could take Dummy. He took Charlie to a room with brass on the doors and windows. Inside was a man in dirty underwear sitting on the floor. No furniture. The man gave Charlie the key. He opened the door. The man took the other's hand and said, "It's okay, Dummy, we are going home. They found us. Marcus won't know until it is too late."

Dummy spoke, "He won't know we are gone, and he won't know who took us. I remember you, Charlie. I used to see you through the window of the basement. You and Tommy and Marcus did that funny stuff and got spanked. I remember."

"Why is he called Dummy?"

"Because he only speaks to me, and I never tell. Can we go?"

"Yes, we go." Kelly gave the man a pair of flight pants to put on. It helped the smell.

All the way back, he thought, "Is this Tommy's kid? He doesn't look like Tommy."

The man that asked if Dummy could come said, "No, he's not Tommy's kid. See that one over there kind of by himself not talking, face down."

"Yes. That's Tommy's kid."

"I'm Marcus's kid, so is Dummy."

The girls were so young. When they got there, Tommy had set up a cabin for all boys and girls and then put the girls in another place. "Tommy, come with me."

"No."

"Yes, now." He followed Doug, and there in the corner of the chalet of Bertha's was a young man; there was no mistake. He saw it right away. "How old are you, son?"

"I'm thirty-six."

"Do you know your mother or your date of birth?"

"My mother is dead, and she died at the hand of your brother right after my birth. He tagged me not for sale. That tag stayed with me until I was put on the farm you found me."

"Do you know who your father is?"

"Yes, you, he made sure I knew your dad lives like a king. You live like a bum."

"I never knew about you until today, I swear."

"Are there anymore related to you?"

"Dummy is. He's Marcus's, but he's not dumb. Do you want to stay with the group, or go get cleaned up, meet your family, what?"

"You are willing to acknowledge me, more than to be a part of your life."

He started to cry. He said, "You knew. He said you didn't care. He said you didn't want me." As dirty as he was, Tommy held him and let him cry.

Doug took them down the hill, gave him clothes, and showed him where the shower was. "What do you do now?"

Tommy said nothing. They were close to the hut, and Thomas came out and saw who was there.

"Well, Mac, did you tell him your story, that you were his son, and how Marcus had you believe he hated you?"

"Shut your face, boy."

"Not by you."

"I am Thomas Charles McCloud, and I have a birth certificate to prove it."

"Why did you let me run off at the mouth like a fool when you knew all along who your son was?"

Doug grabbed him. "Who are you?"

"I am Marcus's head boy. I know who everyone one of these assholes are, including Dummy."

"Dummy is not dumb; he is your father's last-ditch effort."

"Marcus is dead, so are all the rest. Only you and your merry band are left, Julius." He went to attack Thomas but was stopped short by an arrow through his heart.

"We know where that came from," Charlie remarked. He was shocked, and it was Peter.

"Dummy, do you have a name?"

"Yes, sir, Marvin Leslie, undercover agent, FBI. You could call my boss, Jon Franc, for me please."

"Is there anything else I should know?"

"No, sir, you did what I've been waiting for, for nearly six months. I don't think they knew."

"They were given misinformation."

"Kelly, get him cleaned up. I don't think Jon wants to see him like this."

"Sir, under the safes, you will find the information on the bombings. There are no new kids in town."

Tommy turned to Thomas. "You were born September 10, 1990, to Margaret. As you know, I am your father. I am pleased to meet you. I am the one who named you at the hospital, but if you have a name, it can be changed."

"I had no name, boy, just you found me."

"Why did you not tell me? Why hide from me? Did you think I would destroy you?"

Tommy was falling apart. Faye came. "He can't take this. Tell him if there are any more truths to be told."

"I wanted to be sure I was really a part of this family and you. You accepted me as if you knew me all my life. The girls accepted me as I was their brother. I never felt love before. You showed me. When you came to me that day on the lawn, offering me the world at my feet, education and training, wanted me to experience everything I hadn't, I knew true love, and my dad loved me for me. Then I was ashamed to admit who I was."

"Can you ever forgive me for not finding you sooner? For not knowing what he was up to."

Bertha interrupted this talk. "Time fer sorries are gone. Tis time ta love an be loved." Thomas hugged his dad for the first time.

Chapter Twenty-Five

HARDISON CAME TO Tommy. "Come with me."

"In a minute, Hardison."

"No, now, and don't argue with me."

"What is up your kilt, man!" Tommy asked.

Hardison was quickly moving away from him. "Go with him, Uncle Tommy. He seems to need to show you something or tell you something that only you can see or hear," Faye said as she kissed his cheek.

Tommy found him standing outside of what used to be the rescue cabin. "What is it, Hardison? You look like you saw a ghost?"

"I heard you ask Thomas if there was anyone other than him."

"Yes, he said to me. Marcus told him he was the goat to kick because I didn't know about him."

"Why?"

"Come in here and do not open your mouth or move from where I tell you to stand. Do I have your word?"

"Yes, Hardison, as your brother, I will not move or speak."

Hardison went over to a woman rocking a little boy. Hardison took the sleeping child and handed him over to May-Ling. He went back and sat next to the woman. "How are you doing, girl? Feeling better?" She nodded yes. "Do you know where you are?" She spoke softly, barely loud enough for Tommy to hear. "My father is a rich man that lives on a mountain."

"Does he know about you, girl?"

"No, he can't know; he's a bad man. He would beat me worse than Master M. does."

Tommy wanted to run. Is she my daughter, or did Marcus make her believe she was?

"Girl, how do you know Master M. wasn't lying to you?"

"He let me see my mother before he killed her in front of me. She told me that my father's seed was taken from him and Master used it to make me, my little sister, and brother. She told me to do everything Master told me to do, and he would let us live."

"Where are your sister and brother, girl?"

She pointed to the little boy and the teen now holding him. "They are right there, Dr. Hardison, but you know that."

"What if I told you that you have an older brother, and he is thirty years old, and you are how old, girl?"

"I am twenty-eight. 'Little Girl' is sixteen, and boy is five years old."

Tommy quietly asked May-Ling for a chair. He sat, and May-Ling held his shoulders. She whispered to him, "Hardison did blood work. They are yours, my brother, 100 percent. If you thought you would never have any other children besides Margaret Jean, you are wrong. It is up to you as to whether I tell them or let them believe you are a monster."

"I want my children, just as I wanted my son, Thomas." When he looked up, the three were standing in front of him.

"You are the McCloud, the father," Big Girl asked.

"Yes, but I would never do what Marcus told you. I could never hurt you or touch you as he did. You know he is dead, don't you?"

"Yes, we know. Hardison and May-Ling told us. He told us it was you and your people that saved us. The farmer kept us locked up in a house so no one but Marcus could see us. He would bring men and women to the house. We were to wait on them and service them. So we thank you for that."

"Would you like to meet your other brother?" Tommy asked. Forgetting himself, he stood. All three jumped back, screamed. "No, no, I would never do you any harm. I would never touch you as he did. I am so sorry; I scared you; Hardison told me not to move, and I did. I'm so sorry." He fell back on the chair and wailed. "I cannot take much more," and he fell off the chair.

Hardison was at his side in seconds. He and May-Ling checked him to see if he had the beginnings of a heart attack. May-Ling radioed Charlie to bring Bertha and Kelly, "CODE RED." The three watched as the people worked on him. The lady with the funny way of talking was saying something to him; she was crying. May-Ling said to the other lady she was sorry. She thought it would help the children to meet him and know he would not hurt them. Thomas came in with Faye. Kelly explained it all.

Tommy tried to raise his head. "Don't blame them; they didn't know, I was at fault." Hardison told him to shut up. It was too late. Tommy was unconscious. Hardison told Kelly to bring the Jeep; they had to take him to the hut ASAP.

"If anything goes wrong, Hardison, I will never forgive you for not letting me get to know my father," Thomas told him.

Tommy roused again; only then did he not speak. Big Girl went close, knelt beside him, and touched his cheek. "If you are who he says and you aren't lying to me, we would like to know our father."

Bertha fainted. Charlie caught her.

"May-Ling is this true?" he was angry at her for this; Tommy was their brother. Bertha did not need this told to her this way, nor did Thomas.

"Yes, the blood tests prove positive. All three are his, as Thomas is."

Hardison brought Bertha around with smelling salts. "Are ya sure, me man, an me, have four children?"

"Yes, Bertha, you do. This is Big Girl, Little Girl, and Boy."

Thomas knew how that felt—no name, no chance at life. He spoke to them in German, and they answered him. He told them he was like them, and their father found him and saved him. He would do as much for them if they gave him a chance. He told them of all the rest of the family. Then he switched back to English. "Sorry, I picked up on the accent. I worked that farm when I was young enough to hold the horses and big enough to work the cornfields. The farmer wanted me gone. McGregor's daughter was becoming my friend. So I was sent back to the cattle ranch."

"You learned German there?"

"Yes, if you did not speak their language, they beat you."

"Did you know about the kids in the house?"

"No, nobody was allowed at the back of the farm."

They rushed Tommy into the hut, and Hardison started working on him. "Ya have but one chance, boyo, I'll do ya in meself if he dies." Bertha was close to hysterics. "Call Dr. Kelly and tell him I need him now."

"Already done, Hardison. I called my son before we took him out of the cabin."

"Thanks; get Bertha and the rest of them out of here, will you."

"I send the family out, but I will not try to send Bertha anywhere; that is her husband you are working on, and well, she has every right to be here."

Dr. Kelly came in, and they got him to come around; he was weak and slightly foggy about what had happened. "Can you tell me what happened before you passed out, Tom?" Dr. Kelly asked him.

"Yes, I was trying to tell my new-found family that I was sorry for scaring them."

"Do you remember Big Girl touching your cheek?"

"No, where is Bertha?"

"I'm here, love, I'm here."

"Take me home; I'm tired, sweetheart."

"You aren't going anywhere right now, Tommy. You have had a slight heart attack, and we need to get your vitals under control. The three of them are with Thomas. He speaks their language, and he will get more information from them than we will."

Dr. Kelly gave him a shot to calm him down and told Bertha to try and talk him into staying here with Hardison for the night.

"Sure we'll stay, an ya better put up with it."

"I am only too glad to have both of you here for as long as it takes to get him back on his feet."

It took several weeks for Tommy to get back on his feet. Hardison was against him, talking to the three of them. He decided to let him speak to May-Ling.

Tommy, Faye, Thomas, and Bertha went to the cabin to speak to May-Ling and the three children. Tommy spoke to May-Ling first in Chinese, "Are they capable of handling a normal life? Can they stay with Bertha and I? The boy can play with the kids if Faye says he can."

Faye told him in Chinese, "Yes, he could. We could try. They may improve faster around all of you, and no one is trying to do anything wrong to them."

"Would you and your brother and sister like to come home with Bertha and I?"

Boy answered for them, "Yes, I want a bed of my own. She snores." He was pointing at his teen sister.

Bertha smiled at him. "Ya canna have yer own room. Ya like that idea?"

"Yes, lady." Big Girl told him in German that the lady was his new mom.

Faye said to Thomas, "How are they going to handle all of us?"

"They will do like you, Dawn and Gayle, and I have. The little one seems to handle it better."

Bertha said to the oldest, "If ya had a pick, what would yer name be?"

Faye said, "She wants to know if you had a choice, what would your name be?"

"Whatever my father gives me."

Bertha looked at Tommy and said, "Me boyo ya have ta give them names."

He knew Bertha's full name was Bertha Patrica Charlotte, and Charlotte seemed to suit the oldest.

"From now on, Big Girl, you will be called Charlotte May McCloud. Does that suit you?"

"Yes, Father, it does." She turned to her sister, "Little Girl, I'm Charlotte May McCloud." She skipped around the room, holding onto Faye's hands.

Bertha whispered to Tommy a name, and he nodded. "Little Girl, would you like to be Penelope Joan McCloud?"

"Yes, Father, yes, please. Can I be just Penny?"

"Okay, Penny, it is."

The little boy went up to his father and asked, "What is your name, Father?"

"My name is Thomas Donald James McCloud."

"Can I be James Donald McCloud, sir, please?"

"Yes, you can, James. Let's go home; family and Bertha will help me with this infernal chair." He was still in a wheelchair until Hardison said he could walk greater distances than around the house.

Hardison said, "We stop at the hut for a physical first."

Charlotte backed up against the wall and grabbed a chair. "I will not play doctor with you, nor will Penelope, so back off, you son of bitch."

Thomas spoke to her in German, explained that he was a real doctor and if she wanted, Faye or May-Ling would be with them.

She turned to Bertha, "Are you my mother too?"

"Yes, dear, I suppose I am."

"You will stay with me, watch over me, please, and my sister too."

"Yes, ya, no fear in that." Faye knew what she was afraid of.

Charlie turned his back, then went outside. Kelly followed. "What is it, Charlie?"

"Marcus raped both of them with his game of 'let's play doctor.' He killed my sister because she would not give herself to him before they married. He raped her, and she killed herself from shame. He told everyone in town she was a Chinese whore, trying to marry into a rich family. Charlotte saying that brought the image of her hanging in the tree in our family's front yard."

The new McCloud family came out of the cabin, Hardison pushing Tommy. Kelly brought the big golf cart up for the family. Charlie, Faye, and Thomas were left to walk back with Hardison. They all converged on the hut. Bertha told Hardison to make this the smallest physical ever, or he would be looking for a girl's name for himself.

After the physicals, the family came up to the chalet. Tommy had trouble getting them to enter the house. "It's just a house, guys, nothing more."

"It's a bad house for bad people. We saw the picture; it's for bad people!"

Bertha called Faye for her and Thomas to come to the front entrance. They would not go in because of some picture they were shown.

Faye opened the door. "Hi, all done at the hut. Come on in. Thomas and I were just going to have some tea and cookies. Would you like some?"

James passed between them and said, "Where do I go, Faye?"

The rest followed him in. Faye showed James the way, and Charlie made tea and coffee for the adults and orange juice and milk for those too young for tea or coffee, mainly James. He put a variety of cookies and scones with jam on the table as well.

The three of them sat in the breakfast nook, not talking at first. "Thomas, do you think they will be all right?"

"Faye, they will be as right as we let them be. We love them as you did with me. Care for them again as you did with me. They will do fine. The bad memories, well, you still have them, don't you, but you think of them less and less, right, so will they. Our father did not deserve to have his children this way, but he has accepted us, and he loves us from the second he knew we were his, in fact, with me before he knew."

"You are right. I'm whole because of him and my family. So will they."

They ate and drank and soon conversation started about what they would like to do and if they wanted special schooling.

James said, "I want to learn to speak different languages like Aunt Faye. Thomas speaks our language, and Faye tells May-Ling's. Can you speak other languages, Dad?"

It sounded strange to hear that and know that it was real. "Yes, James, I can. I speak about eight different ones."

"Would you teach me?"

"Sure, let's start with your native tongue, which is Gaelic. Thomas, Mom, and I speak it, and you can learn it too."

"Where are we from, Dad," Penny asked. "I thought we were born here?"

"You were, but you follow my line of people as well as Bertha's. We are from Scotland. I'll show you on a map I have in my office later."

"I am a Scotlander," James said.

"No, dear, yer a Scot," Bertha told him.

The twins came flying into the kitchen. "Grampa Charlie, can we have a sammach, please? Hello, my name is Mark. This is my sister Mary."

"Hello, I'm James; this is my sisters Penny and Charlotte."

"Want to come to play in our sandpit with us?"

"Sure."

Charlie asked, "Do you still want your sammach?"

"No, later. Bye, everyone." All three of them, gone.

Faye excused herself. "I need to watch them; they are my children, your niece, and nephew."

"Aunt B, they are all going to need clothes. I have some that will fit Charlotte."

Gayle came in and said, "I have some that will fit Penny. I haven't shortened them yet, and of course, they will need shoes."

"Hello, I'm Faye's sister, Gayle; here is my other sister, Dawn; we are triplets."

Charlotte and Penny stared at them. They all looked alike. "Is that normal to look like each other like that, Dad?"

"Yes, it is. I'll show you on the computer."

It took several days of shopping and hair appointments and, of course, shoes for the outfits. Liz was getting tired very quickly. She and Mitch were discussing building a chalet of their own. There were so many people now.

They were all told to be in the main dining room for breakfast. Please be on time. Tommy and Bertha were the last to arrive but still on time. The confusion was Charlie and May-Ling were there as well as June and Lois and Louise.

"Thank you for being so prompt and for coming. Let's address the elephant in the room. It is not a game table, and after breakfast, it will all be shown and explained."

Charlie was wondering what the hell they were going to eat. He hadn't cooked. Bertha rang a little bell next to her, and tea carts rolled in with platters of eggs, bacon, ham, toast, scones, four or five types of jams, three types of cereal for anyone who preferred that.

Carol and Doug showed up as the meal was winding down. Instead of sitting, they grabbed a coffee and went over to the windows just as Michael arrived.

"Good, we are all here except for Hardison, and he is always the last to arrive. I have never in my wildest dreams thought that I would have a family, let alone one this large and growing," he nodded to Carol and Michael. "So I have a plan because there are just too many for this old chalet to handle."

Carol, Michael, and Doug took the cover off the elephant in the room. Six chalets surrounded the main one—all within walking distance of each other and a park in the center, even street lights. Below a school, a therapy unit, and a hospital.

"I know all of you are feeling like we are living in each other's pockets, and frankly, we are. So here's our proposal, you each have a tag in front of you. That includes Michael, Carol, and Doug. If you choose to live in your own chalet, pick one. If you choose to stay here, put your tag on the big one."

Mitch helped Liz up, and she stood aside. Peter and Faye chose the one closest to the park. Charlie looked at his tag. It said Charlie and May-Ling. He took her hand and chose the one just off the side of the big chalet closest to his office, and she put the tag in the middle of where they both were in walking distance to work. He smiled and agreed.

Robert and Denny picked the one across from Peter and Faye. Thomas chose the one closest to the main chalet. Carol and Doug, the one nearest the mountain, lookout.

"Liz, I would have thought you would have been first to plant a flag," Tommy told her.

"I thought that is what I wanted until I looked at Mom. I want to be near her always." She put her arms around her and sat next to her.

That left the girls and his small son. "Charlotte, if you decide at a later date to move on, a place it will be there for you. Penelope,

James, you guys are stuck here until it's time for university, or marriage, or jobs wherever the world takes you. This will all be built by the fall. Whatever one you choose, Carol and Doug will be overseeing the construction. Denny will be doing interior design for each of you, and we will sit back and watch. Kelly and Louise will be moving onto one of the dorm chalets as they have announced their engagement this morning. June and you, Lois, are both old enough to be on your own, so you two get to stay where your parents are leaving. Micheal has decided to stay here; he wants to be close to his brothers and sisters."

When everyone was settled, and the room was quieter, Bertha said, "I no want any of ya ta leave me, an I knew ya felt closed in, so please our accept gift. Ya all have a copy of yer deeds and a gift we're given ya. Please stay where I canna git ta ya with oot a car or flying; Lord knows I hates flying." She started to cry.

They all hugged her and Tommy and told them they were happy, and Liz was the first one to say, "I don't want to move any farther than your front door."

Hardison came in and asked what was going on and what the hell had he missed. This earned him a slap in the back of the head. Bertha walked him over to the table and pointed to the building marked hospital. Tommy told him, "This is your new place of employment."

"What do you mean? I have to move from the hut!"

"No, it means you live in the hut, you work in the new hospital. We will be bringing more rescued kids and adults here, and they will need your help and May-Ling's help, and any other doctors you think we need."

Bertha smiled and whacked Hardison's butt. He hugged her and thanked her for it, and whacked her backside back.

The McClouds have many adventures to tell you. Michael learns the business and wants to become one of one. Thomas becomes an artist and meets a lady. The family grows, and the old ones sit back, give their help when needed; other than that, they enjoy retirement. Mitch has his import-export business up there, and it grows. They build New Town. Come visit us in their next book, *Ladies of New Town*.

More love stories, a few scary adventures, and of course, a few weddings

Lightning Source UK Ltd.
Milton Keynes UK
UKHW012151280521
384576UK00008B/525/J

9 781664 174023